BRIARDARK

BRIARDARK

BOOK ONE

S.A. HARIAN

COMPASS & FERN

This is a work of fiction. All of the characters, organizations, and events portrayed in this novel are either products of the author's imagination or are used fictitiously.

Briardark
Book One

Library of Congress Control Number: 2022918841
Hardback ISBN: 978-1-959500-02-5
Paperback ISBN: 978-1-959500-01-8
Ebook ISBN: 978-1-959500-03-2
Audiobook ISBN: 978-1-959500-03-2

Published by Compass and Fern
compassandfern.com

Cover Design by Ivan Cakamura Cakic
cakamuradesigns.com

Copy and Proof Editing by Nia Quinn
editor.niaquinn.com

2 3 4 5 6 7 8 9 10

For anyone who has ever been lost in the woods.

SEVEN YEARS AGO

After everything Avery had been through, she wasn't about to die from some damn lightning bolt. Which meant she needed to get off this wet granite. Fast.

Thunder rumbled a warning from the valley as she sprinted across the bald face of the mountain. Her feet squelched in her boots, the dangling tatters of her hiking pants slapping against her calf.

"*Naomi!*" she screamed without stopping. All Avery saw in the bouncing light of her headlamp was rain and darkness and granite stretching in every direction. She searched within her body for any sign of an imminent lightning strike, but felt no tingling, no static. The metallic taste in her mouth was from biting her tongue minutes before.

Squinting, she glimpsed the cusp of the forest and a flash of red. Naomi's rain shell. Avery was too out of breath to call out to her, not that she wanted Naomi to wait. Waiting had been a fool's game since they entered the forest.

Her worn pair of Columbia hikers—a gift from her father for her twentieth—finally lost traction on the slick granite. Avery careened forward and swore as rock tore through her palms. A violent shiver gripped her spine, her fear tossing her around like a rag doll.

Avery spit out a mouthful of blood and looked up as lightning split the sky. The rain hovered for a moment, as if the stone's throw between Naomi and herself were effervescent.

The night fell dark again, but the image was burned into Avery's retinas like she'd been staring at the sun. Naomi standing still, body drenched, dark hair plastered against her face. Behind her, a monstrous, willowy thing. Slenderman or a Dark Watcher or a Wendigo—the shape of some thin childhood evil. It had only ever appeared to them as a shadow, a shock of black against the night. Darker than *nothingness*.

It had found them. No . . . it had been with them the whole time they were running. How naïve she had been to think it had ever left.

"*Run.*" Avery's voice escaped her in a strangled yowl as she lay sprawled on the rock. The wind picked up in a *whoosh*, spraying rain against her face. She blinked the water away, her headlamp light bouncing off rock and High Sierra shrub until she found Naomi's red jacket again. The shadow behind her was gone.

But that was what this darkness did. It was cancer, leaving and returning hungrier, manifesting elsewhere, wounding deeply. Avery could feel it inside her now—the dread, the inevitability of the end. She knew Naomi felt it too.

Naomi's shoulders wilted when she finally met Avery's eyes, her body language too raw and familiar. Paige's posture had been the same. And Janet's.

Janet. Avery would die before she forgave herself for Janet. It wouldn't be long now, even after surviving this long and deep into the wilderness. She blamed herself for so much, but not for falling. Especially if it meant she was now bait and Naomi would escape one more time.

The blade at Naomi's side flashed when lightning struck again. Avery's hunting knife. She'd given it to Naomi last week. Or was it yesterday? She didn't know anymore how long she'd spent in this godforsaken place. How much time it had stolen from her.

The rain quieted, the bone-deep *hush* sudden and unsettling.

"You'll get out," Naomi cried.

Several things happened at once. A rumble within the heart of the mountain, somewhere beneath millions of years of rock and sediment. A ringing in Avery's ear that made the world spin. Her vision sharpened as the shadow reemerged, rising from the ground and curling around Naomi's feet.

Avery couldn't see much with her dim headlamp, but she knew Naomi was smiling. Naomi smiled when shit was about to take a turn for the worst. Avery had learned this about her only recently; they used to be nothing more than casual hiking partners. But trauma tended to peel away layers between those who shared it, and now Naomi meant everything. She was all Avery had left.

And yet Avery didn't fight. She took the coward's way out, like she always did, and shut her eyes.

EXCERPT FROM CHAPTER 1 OF *WITHOUT A TRACE* BY JOHN LAWSON:

Six years after the founding of Instagram, the "like" was the crux of social currency, its value an algorithmic fastpass to envy, popularity, and even fame.

This was no truer than in 2016 as vacations were planned around photo opportunities. The Digital Nomad became a coveted career. For Gen Y, the "like" and its dopamine high were as precious as oxygen. Travel without proof became meaningless, every long gaze over coastal waters, every visit to ancient ruins in impractical attire, every victory pose from alpine peaks incomplete if unaccompanied by #takemeback #wanderlust.

In the summer of 2016, five young women—one an influencer—entered the inarguably breathtaking Deadswitch Wilderness for a backpacking trip, an opportunity rich in social currency. When they failed to reemerge, Search and Rescue would begin their operation without a GPS breadcrumb.

None of the women had taken their phones.

ASCENT

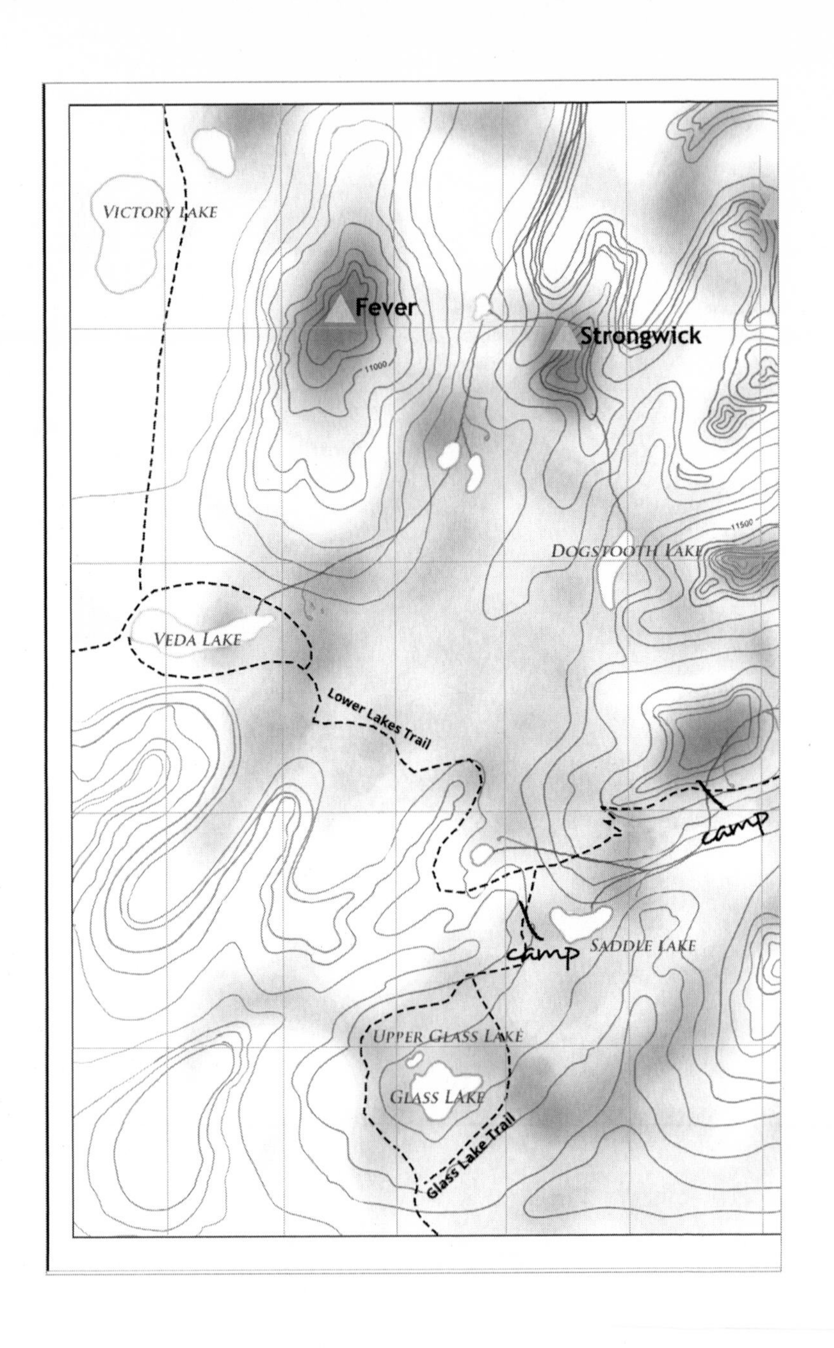

Victory Lake
Fever
11000
Strongwick
11500
Dogstooth Lake
Veda Lake
Lower Lakes Trail
camp
camp
Saddle Lake
Upper Glass Lake
Glass Lake
Glass Lake Trail

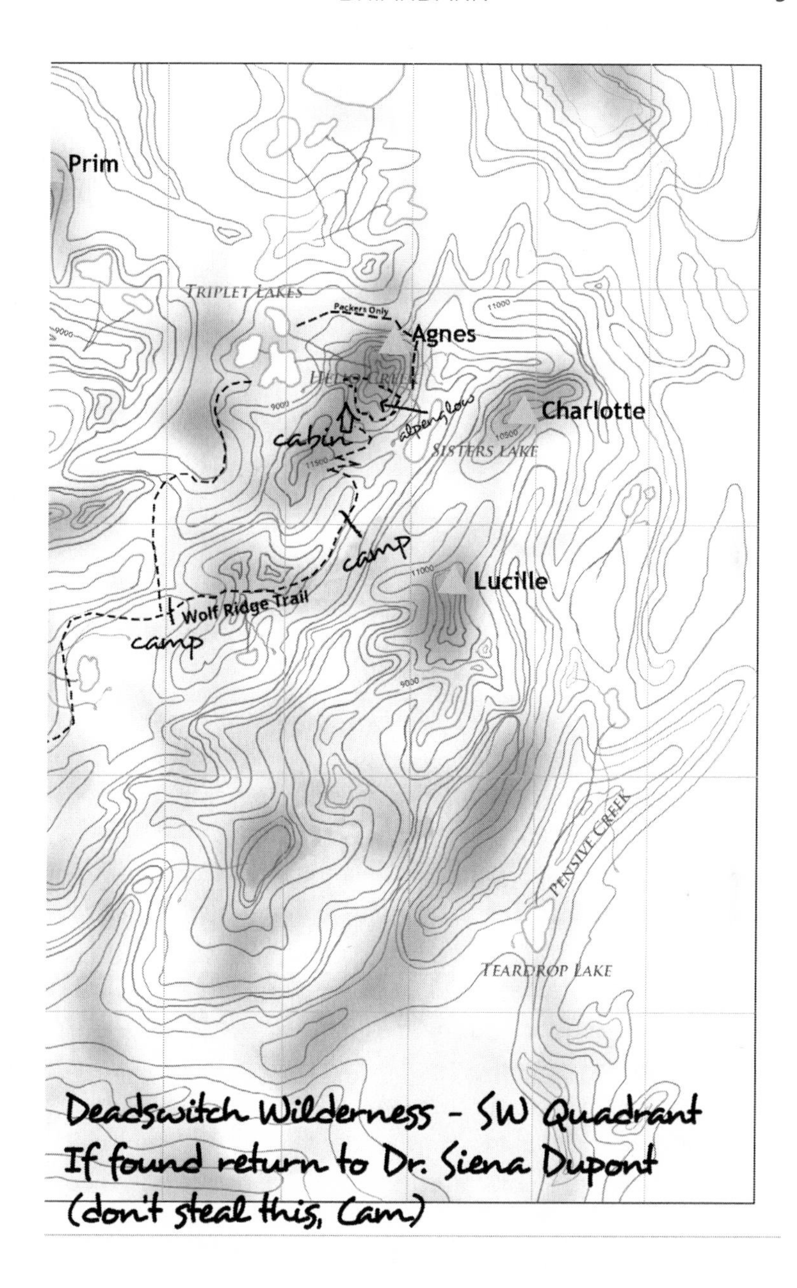
Prim
Triplet Lakes
Packers Only
Agnes
Helio Creek
alpenglow
cabin
Charlotte
Sisters Lake
camp
Lucille
Wolf Ridge Trail
camp
Pensive Creek
Teardrop Lake
Deadswitch Wilderness - SW Quadrant
If found return to Dr. Siena Dupont
(don't steal this, Cam)

SIENA

Gravel crunched beneath the tires of the SUV. In the passenger's seat, Siena looked up from her field journal as Emmett pulled into the empty trailhead lot.

Cam kicked the back of Siena's seat. "Jesus, get me out of here. My legs are about to fall off."

"Does she always complain this much?" asked Isaac.

"Yes," Emmett and Siena said in unison as Emmett parked. Siena unbuckled and hopped out before they'd even come to a complete stop, shaking out her legs as she scoped the place out. A thick grove of drooping pines lined the dirt clearing, the ground beyond the lot coated with a layer of brown needles. Unremarkable, but it sure smelled amazing.

"*Complain?*" Cam flung open her door. "I have every right to complain." She stood and rolled her neck, her short mop of ashy hair flopping to the side. "So do you, the way you were folded like a jackknife behind Emmett for four hours while he drove like a maniac."

"She's joking," Siena reassured Isaac when she caught him frowning from the back seat. Emmett drove like a grandma, and not just on mountain roads. She used to get on his case on a weekly basis. Emmett *caused* accidents with his carefulness.

But he always failed to be careful about the right things.

Dust still hung in the air from their arrival, and Siena batted it away with a cough. That was the one thing about backpacking in California in July—everything was bone dry, the wilderness a tinderbox itching for a match. At least there would be no snow. She and crampons were sworn enemies.

Isaac stood, the top of the SUV reaching his shoulders. He stretched his lanky arms before adjusting his CalTech baseball hat. He was the kind of kid who made Siena feel *old*, a baby-faced grad student without a study to his name. Siena—well, Cam, really—had taken him on as a favor for a professor, given their team was so small. A decade ago, Siena had to work much harder for her opportunities. Isaac probably didn't realize how lucky he was, but he would soon learn it.

"Can I help?" Isaac asked.

"You can help by hurrying up." Siena joined Emmett at the back of the SUV as he popped the hatch. "We're already working with a late start."

Amongst the gear, Siena spotted her stained Kelty, a High Sierra Conservationists patch from her mother slapped over a hole in the front pocket. She yanked the bag free, lowering it to the ground with a grunt. Her bathroom scale had weighed it at fifty-five-point-seven pounds, including a collection of geomorphology equipment, her laptop, sixteen pounds of freeze-dried food (in case the mules were short or late), and not nearly enough underwear. The point of the six-week trip wasn't to smell good, after all.

Cam dropped her bag next to Siena's and bent to scratch her tanned leg. Cam was lean all over, the forest her second home for as long as Siena had known her. When she stood straight, she pushed her aviators up the bridge of her nose. "Do we really need to pull everything out for an equipment check?"

Siena finished braiding her dark hair and smacked an elastic around the end. "Yes. Of course." It was Cam who'd introduced Siena to the thrill and utter anxiety of an impromptu backpacking trip, the ones slapped together day-of with all the finesse of a swamped deli clerk. And while those trips were the cornerstone of their friendship, this was different. They weren't about to head into the wilderness just to smoke a bit of weed and talk shit about their colleagues.

Cam leaned against the bumper. "Doubt anything has magically disappeared since leaving town."

"It's protocol," Siena countered with a sigh. "I swear, sometimes I do not know how you survive as a principal investigator."

Cam grinned. "Procrastination and a can-do attitude, Doc. You should try it."

Isaac sauntered toward them, smearing sunscreen on the back of his neck. "We didn't do gear checks at all during my undergrad."

"In all fairness, this isn't a field trip to a rocks and minerals museum," Siena said.

Isaac chuckled. "Got me there."

As Siena bent over to lace her boots, she felt Emmett's stare. She'd sensed his eyes on her since they left town, catching his glances through the reflection in the car window as he waited for a glimpse of her fragility. Waited for the first signs of a meltdown. She'd promised herself she'd keep him at arm's length, which was why she avoided meeting his eyes in return. They were dark and infinite and made her want to touch his tawny skin the way she used to. Either that or punch him in the throat.

"Start unpacking," said Emmett. "I've got the list."

Cam groaned. "Fine, *Dad*."

They unpacked their bags and ran over the checklist once more: pH strips, elemental analysis kits, a decent microscope, a half-decent theodolite, a less-than-decent Chittick apparatus, two laptops, field journals, extra pencils, and a sundry of extraction tools . . . everything they couldn't trust the mule packer to deliver on time.

Siena slid her recorder and phone into the outer pocket of her bag before helping her team pack everything up again. Emmett locked the SUV and tucked the spare key above the rear tire. He lifted Siena's bag onto the hitch, and Siena saddled into it, exerting far too much effort to stand up. The stark weight of her gear settled onto her hips, and she balanced herself with her trekking poles. At least she'd remembered to bring plenty of painkillers.

Emmett waved his hand toward the trail. "After you," he told Siena.

"Always a prince, certainly never an asshole," Cam muttered.

Emmett's shoulders tensed, but he said nothing, his arm remaining outstretched. It was a gesture of submission. Emmett had forgone his PhD to study carbon capture at COtwo Industries. And Emmett was the reason COtwo had awarded funding for Siena's proposal.

But Siena had helmed the fight for this study. She'd trodden the waters of bureaucratic hell, cutting years off her life from sleep deprivation alone to reopen interest in Alpenglow Glacier. And she'd put forth one hell of an argument convincing the administration to let her use the university's decommissioned cabin as a base.

Cam kicked a pinecone, which bounced off Siena's shin. "Come on, Doc. We're on COtwo's dime now," she said, her voice darkly sarcastic.

Siena's eyes flitted back to Emmett. "They should feel honored I even considered their money."

Emmett looked away. At least he knew better than to retort. She would have found extra funding without COtwo. Emmett was lucky to be here.

Siena stepped forward, pressing two fingers to her lips and touching the Glass Lake Trailhead sign as she passed. *This one's for you, old man.*

In her head, the old man responded.

Don't go.

She ignored him and entered the forest. The others followed.

Crickets droned in the foliage, and a mountain chickadee whistled from the tree boughs. Siena scoured the trail and found no footprints amongst the powdery dirt and broken needles. No one had been this way since it last rained, which was odd—Deadswitch wasn't well known by tourists and casuals, but it was a haven for nature geeks and people like her. There had to have been some activity this summer. She should've asked the ranger when they'd stopped to pick up their permit if they were likely to come across anyone.

"This isn't too bad," said Isaac, which prompted a laugh from the rest of them.

"We have a quarter mile or so more of this," Emmett said. "Then the incline hits and won't let up until we reach camp. Every day after, we'll gain about one to two K in elevation until we reach the cabin at ten and a half."

"*Thousand?*"

"You bet."

"What he's trying to say," Cam huffed, "is to not get ahead of yourself with those giant legs of yours. You get altitude sickness, and Siena will leave you behind."

"Factual," said Siena as the trees cleared. She stepped into a small meadow of alpine buttercups. A brook split the path, the air pungent with the scent of wild mint and alliums.

Decades ago, she'd held her mother's hand on a footbridge in the high meadows of Yosemite. Siena remembered little, only the smell of the air and the sparkle of clear, cold water rushing beneath their feet. She imagined her mother here, sitting near the bank, dipping her bare feet in the brook, and daydreaming away an hour.

Siena couldn't spare such a luxury this early into the hike. But a few more miles and they'd break for water and a snack with the valley beneath them, the sister peaks Agnes, Charlotte, and Lucille on full display. Agnes was their destination, and they'd camp on the mountain in the research cabin owned by CalTech, three thousand feet beneath her summit.

Reaching the brook, Siena employed a few makeshift stepping stones to get across, careful not to slip. Having a wet boot at the start of a fifty-seven-mile hike was a fate worse than death as far as she was concerned.

She hopped off the last rock and hesitated. Before her, the path curved on an incline into a set of switchbacks, and the old man's voice returned.

Don't go.

She brushed her fingers across the crescent scars on the inside of her forearm, a permanent mark left by yellowing nails.

Promise me!

"Don't tell me you're already tired, Dupont," said Cam. "I expected more from you."

Siena shook off the remnants of the memory and turned around. Emmett was right behind her, but Cam was on a stone in the middle of the brook, balancing on one foot like a total jackass.

"Just thinking about Dr. Feyrer," Siena said.

"Ah." Cam rested her foot back on the stone. "Well, he'd tell you to hurry up, wouldn't he? *Don't stray from the path, Siena.*"

Emmett shook his head. "God, Cam."

"I'm serious." Cam hopped to the next stone. "Look, we'll pour one out for him when we reach the cabin. That's what he'd want."

Siena nodded, her eyes drifting to Isaac, who awkwardly muttered "R-I-P." Even Emmett laughed then, the levity relieving the ache in Siena's chest for a moment. Then she looked at the trail along which they'd come and frowned.

There *was* no trail, only high grass and wildflowers.

She could have sworn the path had cut all the way from the woods to the brook. If she'd been paying better attention, she wouldn't have led her team tromping carelessly through a habitat.

Emmett pushed past her. "I for one don't want to be hiking in the dark. Let's go so we can make camp where we planned."

Siena gave the meadow a final fleeting glance and turned to follow Emmett.

HOLDEN

Holden was four beers deep on a Monday night, and getting too old for this shit.

That was what he kept telling himself, anyway. It didn't seem to help. He was still here, at a college bar, with Kyle and some girls Kyle met four hours ago. Holden didn't need a rebound—didn't *want* a rebound—but Kyle was convinced he did.

Going to a packed college bar, sitting in a sticky booth, and getting drunk wasn't how he wanted to get over his ex. He didn't want to get over his ex at all. And yet he continued to say yes to cheap beer and pretty girls younger than him. Women in a different phase of their life. Women he didn't connect with at all.

The girl of the night was named Chelsea—smart, pretty, driven . . . blonde. Had just graduated with her MBA. Out of his league, if she'd only realize it herself. She would, eventually—smart girls like her always did, even if it took them a minute. Holden inherited his height from his father, his olive skin and eye smile from his mother. Handsome, yet perfectly unambitious. And he wasn't about to be a mistake on Chelsea's dating curriculum vitae.

He'd never really been interested in a quick fuck. His roommate once called him a demisexual, which forced him to be introspective for once and somehow made his whole dating situation even weirder than it needed to be.

Kyle's tongue had been down Chelsea's best friend's throat for fifteen minutes, and Chelsea was leaning against Holden, her boobs pressed to his ribs. She had tanned satin skin and green fuck-me eyes, and winced every time she took a sip of her tequila soda. "So, what do you do again?"

"IT for OSU." He'd already told her this eight times.

"So, you're an engineer."

No. "Yeah, sure," he said.

"That's cool."

Girls only said his half-assed career was cool when they assumed he made a lot of money. Joke was on them. He'd graduated with his BS in Computer Science years ago, had no desire to get into software, and had been working at Oregon State University since he graduated. He could make more money bartending.

And it didn't really matter one way or another what Chelsea believed. He wasn't planning on screwing her tonight.

Holden peeled Chelsea off him and went to take a leak. When he returned, Kyle and the BFF were gone.

"Fuck that guy," he muttered.

He'd been friends with Kyle since undergrad, when they were both majoring in CompSci. Kyle used to be mildly interesting, moonlighting as a dungeon master for his D&D group but also driving a Dodge Ram. Self-identified feminist, but had a million shirtless photos on his camera roll queued up for Tinder. Then he'd graduated and let the Douche McGee part of his personality take over. Holden should have broken ties the first time Kyle tried recommending Joe Rogan.

Chelsea was the only one left waiting for Holden, glassy-eyed and extremely drunk. "I'll call you a Lyft," he said with a sigh, and pulled up the app on his phone. Chelsea was not happy to hear this, but also too drunk to protest. He guided her into the Lyft within thirty seconds of it arriving—a record for him—and then walked home.

He lived only a handful of blocks north of the bar. It was pissing rain, a normal night for Oregon in March. He preferred the years when it was pissing rain to the years when it was furiously dry in the early spring, wildfire smoke filling summer skies. Plus, the rain suited his mood as of late.

He was completely drenched by the time he made it home, tromping up the outdoor stairs and shoving the keys into 23C. When he entered, Francis waited for him.

"Hey, boy." Holden scratched behind the German shepherd's ears. Francis gave a happy whine, spun, and thwacked Holden's leg with his tail. Holden tossed his keys in the bowl on the kitchen island and read the Post-It on the counter.

Late shift. Took Francis out @ 8. -L

Holden crumpled the note and threw it in the trash. Lauren had been his roommate for two months. He knew little about her, only that she'd given up a biofuel engineering job in California, moved to Oregon, and now worked the desk at the Corvallis Marriott. She paid her rent on time and took Francis on walks. Holden didn't ask questions.

It was already well after eleven, but he could feel in his bones that he wouldn't be able to sleep. He kicked off his shoes, hung up his soaked coat, and padded across the living room to his desk, rolling out the chair until it smacked the back of the sectional. Holden plopped down and wiggled his desktop mouse. His eyes drifted to the external drive next to the keyboard.

The dweeb who manned the desk in Life Sciences had handed him a box of these things last week. They'd been sitting in lab storage, and no one had the time to check them for residual sensitive data—not even the postdocs. Which meant Holden was stuck doing the bitch work.

He untangled the drive cord and plugged the end into his desktop port. OSU didn't pay him enough to work nights, but if he got through a few of the drives now, he could dip out of the office early tomorrow.

He was halfway done with culling this drive, and all he'd

found were a bunch of corrupted files and some old effort reports he'd already forwarded along to the central admin office. He popped in his earbuds and sank deeper into the chair, scrolling through the next hundred or so temps, deleting as he went.

His finger stalled on the mouse wheel, and he inched back to a ZIP file titled **Comprehensive analysis of Alpenglow meltwater**.

Holden dragged the folder to the desktop and extracted everything. A new window expanded with 324 files.

"The fuck?" he whispered.

The files weren't just corrupted CSVs or the ghosts of old saves like everything else on the drive. They were PDFs, documents, images . . . audio files. Loads and loads of audio files.

He killed his music app and double-clicked the first WAV.

"This is Dr. Siena Dupont, and it is day thirty . . . fuck . . . thirty-two . . . I think . . . of the Alpenglow study in Deadswitch Wilderness. I . . . I . . ."

Holden sat up, amping the volume on his desktop.

"I'm so tired," she sobbed. "I'm so, so goddamn tired. His blood is all over my arm—has been since yesterday. I smelled it when I tried to sleep last night but don't have it in me to wash it off."

Dr. Dupont took a few deep breaths, and Holden shut his eyes as he tried to recall where he'd heard her voice before. A lecture? A podcast? YouTube? No . . . none of that felt right.

Dupont continued. "I scraped some of it off me and ran the cells beneath the scope. Something's not right with them . . . maybe. It's not like I'm a biologist or anything. I took a few pics with my phone. But it doesn't matter. I won't be escaping this place soon. And the others . . .

"Cam ran off yesterday without saying goodbye. Emmett's off looking for her . . . never came back last night. Which means I have to bury Isaac all by myself."

SIENA

"I miss the days of yore when any idiot could throw lighter fluid on a match." Cam tossed a stick at their lantern.

The Forest Service had banned campfires in most of the state, so the four of them sat on top of their bivy sacks around the LED. Siena scraped the gunky remains of rehydrated fettuccine Alfredo from the bottom of her bowl. "I'd prefer to live," she said, though she couldn't deny how much she missed having a campfire. The warm glow and heat were so inviting after a long day on the trail.

Siena slapped her neck and wiped away a dead bug. Campfire smoke also kept the mosquitos away.

Fortunately, there weren't too many bugs at their site, a flat spot a hundred or so yards off the trail beneath a scattering of Jeffrey pines. Saddle Lake was about a quarter mile west. They could refill on water but were far enough to not be inundated by bloodsuckers.

It was beautiful, too, of course. The stars, close enough to scrape out of the sky with her fingers. The chant of the lakeside grasshoppers. The air, so cold and dry and clean that it burned her sinuses.

She'd never backpacked into Deadswitch before, saving herself for this six-week venture. Her mother had led a conservationist group into these woods when Siena was in grade school. And Dr. Feyrer . . . he'd never shut up about how this place would change her, using the promise of Deadswitch's beauty to convince her to write the proposal in the first place.

But all wilderness had some everlasting impact on her, and it didn't matter how many times she returned. The isolation of the woods haunted and astounded her as it had the first time, distantly familiar, like she'd once been rooted in a grove in another life. Dr. Feyrer knew her weak spot after all. Leading such a study in her early thirties meant she'd be more likely to spend her career in forests like this one.

She slapped her neck again.

"*Sen . . .*" Emmett narrowed his eyes at her like she was a capricious child inflicting self-harm.

Siena made a show of presenting the mosquito to him in her outstretched palm. "Am I going to need to present evidence to you every time I smack a bug off me, Emmett?"

Cam ducked her head to hide her grin. The embers behind Emmett's eyes stirred, but before he could say anything, Isaac sliced through the tension.

"What does tomorrow look like?" The kid spun his titanium spork between his fingers, glancing at Emmett, then Cam, then Siena, who raised her eyebrows.

"I emailed you the itinerary three weeks ago," Siena said.

Isaac winced. "I forgot to download it."

"In all fairness, the document took up a gigabyte of space on my phone," Cam mumbled through a mouthful of food.

Siena rolled her eyes and then nodded at Emmett. She'd let him play the Eagle Scout dad for now.

"Same as today," said Emmett. "Another ten miles, another thousand feet of elevation gain. But it'll suck a little more because you'll be sore. We might catch a glimpse of Agnes, but we won't be close enough to gather data."

"We'll descend into a wooded area at first, before we get above the tree line." Cam dragged her fingers from the crown of her head all the way to the ends of her sideswept bangs as she spoke. "Those switchbacks are steep. Your toes'll smash into your boots, and your knees will hate you, and you'll be wishing we were going up. Then the granite starts, and we'll climb to seven thousand feet in a matter of miles."

"Sounds like you've done this before." Isaac tore off a corner of a CLIF Bar and shoved it into his mouth.

Cam and Siena shared a glance. Emmett cleared his throat.

"A long time ago." Cam gave her hair a last tug and dropped her hand. "I was a little older than you, getting my PhD and doing a lot of hiking and volunteering with the rangers. I was on the search and rescue team for a group of women who went missing up by Wolf Ridge. Five of them. Had to learn the area very well and quickly."

"No kidding," said Isaac. "Wait a sec . . . I think I heard of that. Wasn't that a famous case? They were never found."

Cam nodded. "No footprints, no tracks. No urine or buried shit. Dogs couldn't find anything. Rangers' logs showed folks going up the mountain all summer, but we couldn't find any evidence of that being true."

Siena rubbed away the goose bumps on her arms. She low-key hated when Cam told this story. Not because she feared getting lost herself, but because the story defied logic. No evidence of *anyone*? It wasn't possible, even then. Except for phone tracing, methods and technology for finding people had changed little in the past fifty years, let alone seven.

Siena thought of the trail this morning—the lack of tracks in the dirt. Maybe the soil in this part of the Sierras was too powdery to hold a print. She didn't know what kind of mineral and organic composition would cause such a thing.

As she pondered, Siena scooped up the pill waiting at the lip of her mess kit, popped it into her mouth, and swallowed some water from her Nalgene.

"So they literally found nothing?" Isaac pulled his fleece more tightly around his shoulders.

"Just a Subaru in the trailhead lot that belonged to Janet, one of the hikers."

"And the case?"

"Cold." Cam shrugged. "Not much you can do when the evidence runs dry. At the end of everything, the only bit left uninvestigated was that right before they left for their trip, one of the missing hikers had been playing a video game based on a pioneer cult from this area."

"*Pioneer cult?*" Isaac mouthed.

Cam shifted uncomfortably. She got weird every time she told this story, so for the entirety of their friendship, Siena never pressed her on the details of her time searching for the famous Deadswitch Five. But she knew when to cut in and save Cam from the obligation of divulging too much.

"There *are* rumors floating around of some freaky cultists who've lived in Deadswitch for decades," Siena said. "Probably offspring of those original pioneers. My mom used to tell me about them when I was a kid. Claim the land is divine or whatnot . . . Don't really know the details. Clearly they aren't allowed to live back here without all kinds of permits, but the rangers haven't been able to catch anyone."

"The rangers sound like boneheads." Isaac raised a hand toward Cam. "No offense."

Cam threw another stick at the lantern. "Bonehead is a term of endearment compared to what I've called some of them."

Siena could see the gears turning in Isaac's head, and Cam started tugging at her hair again.

Siena shared a glance with Cam. "We don't have to keep talking about it."

Cam quickly masked her discomfort with a wry smile. "I was just getting to the good part."

Siena nodded. "Sure you were."

"We should get to bed." Emmett grabbed the lantern, groaning as he stood. "Tomorrow's gonna hurt."

Siena tried to detach herself from the pain as her hips begged for mercy and her butt cheeks burned. The second day was always the worst. Even a liberal amount of ibuprofen and a hit off Cam's joint couldn't save her.

She led the way as they trekked up the granite, setting her eyes on a cairn and focusing all her energy on reaching it. Rounding the bend, she found the next pile of rocks as the sun beat down on the back of her neck. She could tell the others were suffering because no one spoke—not even Cam—though their labored breathing was quite the symphony.

When Siena was in her early twenties, she could have skipped up a mountainside like this and would have been at the top twenty minutes ago, double-fisting peanut butter and jelly sandwiches for an early lunch.

Damn, she was hungry.

"Did anybody bring any peanut butter?" she gasped.

"In exchange for carrying the theodolite the rest of the way, you can have my whole jar of peanut butter," Emmett yelled back.

She wasn't *that* hungry.

The ground turned to dirt and leveled out. Siena almost fell over in relief, instead peering down at the others, who were still a couple of switchbacks below her. She smiled and waved, and Cam threw her the finger.

Siena dipped into the shade of forest growth, her eyes adjusting to the change of light. She drank deeply from her CamelBak and edged forward, searching near the trail for a tall place to sit so she didn't have to take off her pack. In front of her, the trail forked, one path leading northwest up another granite face, the other northeast, dipping into a glade.

This wasn't right. There was only one trail until Wolf Ridge broke off from the main Deadswitch Trail, which wasn't until tomorrow.

Siena ungracefully floundered with her bag, tugging her map from the side pocket. She opened it, located the Glass Lake Trailhead, and followed the line with her finger. Sure enough, there was no fork, and the trail neither ascended nor descended. It was supposed to continue dead north through the forest.

She approached the fork with caution, as though it hid something insidious. Olive paint flecked an old sign in front of a fir, but as much as Siena scrutinized, she couldn't decipher what it had once read.

Siena spun toward the granite when the rest of her team reached her. Cam leaned against a tree, Emmett sat on a rock, and Isaac had freed himself from his pack, which lay sideways on the ground, abandoned.

"Something's wrong," said Siena, hating how nervous she sounded. It wasn't like anything terrible had happened. "There isn't a fork on the map."

Cam unclipped and crawled out of her pack, joining Siena by the blank trail sign. "That's not right."

"I'm sure you just missed it on the map." Emmett held his hand out toward Siena.

"Cam just said . . . You know what, forget it." She shoved the map into his hands. "I have a fucking doctorate in geomorphology, Emmett."

"I'm aware."

"Then don't patronize me."

He said nothing as he studied the map. Typical. She waited for him to magically uncover something she had missed. Instead, she was met with a frown.

"Well." He accordioned the map and gave it back to her. "The map says north, so we should go north."

"*Helpful.*" Siena yanked open the map again, almost tearing it.

"We can get there with our eyes closed, trail or no trail. You basically said so yourself."

"Hey, it's alright." Cam joined them. "Look." She pointed to a winding blue line on the map. "We'll take the right trail, and if we don't cross the creek in two miles, then we'll turn around. Easy as that."

"We'll lose time," Siena countered.

"We're up here for six weeks. We have plenty of time."

Cam was right. And panicking or being frustrated this early in the game was silly. An incorrect map didn't negate her years of wilderness training.

"The GPS is deep in the bottom of my bag somewhere." Isaac picked up his seventy-liter from the ground and smacked it a few times to dust it off. "You want me to dig for it?"

"It won't show us anything we don't already know." Siena slapped away an antlion crawling across her shoulder, checking to see where it fell and finding only the dusty trail.

It flew away. Chill out. She took a few deep breaths. "It's fine. Let's go."

Holden hurried through the dark IT-staff wing of the campus library.

All the overhead lights were off, and for once he was happy the IT staff were a bunch of goblins. His headache was killer. He'd been googling all night, trying to find out anything he could on Dr. Siena Dupont, her strangely familiar voice Holden couldn't shake, and the dead researcher named Isaac.

Uncovering the truth wasn't only to fulfill his own curiosity. He was supposed to confirm that any files on the hard drives were no longer needed before deleting them forever. It was his job, after all.

He'd found some abstracts in JSTOR written by a Dr. S. Dupont, who either was or used to be a CalTech faculty member. He'd also found a handful of social media accounts, though all of them were private. Holden had tried calling the Division of Geological and Planetary Sciences at CalTech, but he'd gone straight to voicemail, and no one had called him back yet.

The study's connection to Oregon State University still eluded him.

Holden shoved open the heavy door of his office. Office was a loose term. It was more like a Best Buy break room decorated with some cheap LED strip lighting, a bunch of monitors teetering on folding tables. Chase and Angel sat at opposite ends of the space, both drinking diet Monsters and snacking on . . .

"Are those carrots?"

Chase spun toward him, a carrot between his skinny teeth. "Doc told me to lay off the Flamin' Hot Cheetos."

Holden raised an eyebrow. "Diabetes?"

"Rectal inflammation."

"I . . . can't say I'm surprised." Other than the acne, Chase appeared healthy, with a soccer-on-weekends sort of build, but by the way he ate, he had to be rotting somewhere.

Holden kicked a chair out of the way and sat in front of a Dell. He dropped his bag, unzipped it, and pulled out the external drive. "I need you two to help me with something."

"I hate helping you." Angel tied her curly dark hair into a knot on top of her head and smeared her lips with a gooey gloss, all while her eyes remained glued to an endless video feed on her propped-up phone. Knowing her, she'd completed her daily assignments an hour ago and was sticking around because she was supposed to be on the clock.

Holden wiggled the mouse on the Dell and typed in his username and password. "What if I need help solving a mystery?"

Angel tore her attention from her phone to stare at him with skeptical brown eyes. Usually some variant of disgust filled them, but he'd caught her interest. "What kind of mystery?"

"Involves a dead guy and a creepy audio file."

Angel didn't skip a beat. "You owe me Twizzlers, two Monsters, and a burger and Cajun fries from Five Guys."

"Can't you just help me because we're coworkers?" Holden asked.

Angel threw her head back and cackled.

Holden plugged the hard drive into the Dell. "I'll get you a strawberry milkshake the next time I'm at Five Guys, but that's it.

Both of you should have dropped your bad eating habits in college, you know."

Angel clucked her tongue. "We *are* technically in college, you know. I think the term is *Lifers*."

On the monitor, the file explorer launched, and Holden navigated to Dr. Dupont's research project.

Chase sauntered over to them. "What's that? I heard something about a dead guy."

"I'm . . ." Holden hesitated and stood. "Not really sure. I think it's a collection of recent files from a study, but I can't find any info on the researcher or the project. I was wondering what hidden metadata I missed." He scratched his head. "Normally I'd just lie and write in the log that I got deletion confirmation because no one ever cares anyway, but if someone died . . ."

"Sounds like the start of a true crime podcast." Chase popped his thumbs and sat at the computer. In the file explorer, he pulled up the properties of several individual files. Every field was empty.

Holden sighed. "I already did that."

"Move." Angel took Chase's seat as he ungracefully left it. Within seconds, she had a browser open and was downloading an EXIF editor tool. "This only works on images, but it's a start."

Holden was more interested in Dr. Dupont's audio files than her image data, but it ended up not mattering. After Angel launched the tool and spent several minutes searching the code within the dialog box, she shook her head. "I can't find anything."

"No time stamp?" asked Holden.

"No, it's so weird." Angel slid a Twizzler from the package and chewed on it thoughtfully. "The fields where the dates should be are nonsense. Random numbers and symbols."

"A cipher?"

Angel slowly turned toward Holden, her eyes narrowing. "Calm down, DaVinci Code."

"What?"

Angel waved a hand in front of her face. "I see you are as versed in pop culture as you are in women."

"That's . . . not nice."

"No, not a cipher. More like some weird corruption. Though I've never seen a corrupted file like this. Why do you need to know the dates of these files, anyway? Shouldn't you turn this over to the right department, mention the dead guy, and let them deal with it? I don't think we get paid enough for this shit."

"It belongs to CalTech, and I'm working to get ahold of someone there. Just thought I'd see what I could figure out in the meantime."

Angel stood from the chair and stretched her arms, stepping aside for Holden. "I'd be careful with nosing around in research projects. You don't know how much of this is confidential."

Holden sat. "It's not exactly like they are being diligent in securing their data." *They.* Holden only knew the full name of one woman. Maybe he could find the last names of the others she'd mentioned, specifically Isaac. There had to be an obituary listed somewhere.

There were 324 files on the drive. There was no rhyme or reason to their names, and most were gibberish, but some referenced funding and permits. He clicked on a file labeled KEY CONTACTS. The date on the form was blank, go figure. He scanned through a bunch of bureaucratic crap until he found a typeset list.

Lead Principal Investigator: Dr. Cameron Yarrow, Dept. of Geomorphology, California Institute of Technology
Co-Principal Investigator: Dr. Siena Dupont, Dept. of Geomorphology, California Institute of Technology
Researcher: Emmett Ghosh, COtwo Industries, California Institute of Technology MS graduate
Graduate Student: Isaac Perez, Dept. of Geology, California Institute of Technology

Dr. Dupont had mentioned all of her team in the recording:

Emmett, Cam—who must have been Cameron—and Isaac . . . the dead guy. Holden scrolled past the study sponsors to the list of other contacts until one of them caught his eye.

Contact: Dr. Maidei Chari, Dept. of Forestry, Oregon State University

Dr. Chari was the only contact on the form from OSU, which meant the drive had belonged to her at some point. Maybe she had forgotten to erase the data before returning it.

If this were any other case, Holden would take the drive to the College of Life Sciences and drop it off at the front desk with a sticky note. He didn't know Siena Dupont, and the data was so corrupt that the study was clearly years old, if not decades.

But her voice . . . her fear on the recording struck some deeply personal chord in his chest. He wanted to know why.

Holden pulled up the roster of faculty at OSU on his computer and clicked on the Department of Forestry. A list of names populated. Dr. Maidei Chari was still faculty on campus. Even better, her office hours were right now, and she had enabled direct messaging. He could contact her through the student and faculty portal.

Holden logged on, searched for Maidei Chari in the chat app, and started typing.

SHARPE: Hi, Dr. Chari. My name is Holden Sharpe, and I'm with campus IT. I found an external drive with some of your data and was wondering if I could drop it by your office.

CHARI: ?

CHARI: What data?

SHARPE: A study you were involved in? I can't find the study name or date, but the PIs were Dr. Cameron Yarrow and Dr. Siena Dupont.

CHARI: I don't recognize either of those names. Can you give me more info?

SHARPE: They're from the Dept. of Geomorphology @ CalTech. I can walk the drive over to you to see if anything is relevant? If you don't need the data, I'll wipe it for someone else.

CHARI: I suppose that's fine. Where was the lab location? Perhaps that will spark my memory. When you've been in the field as much as I have, everything blurs together :)

SHARPE: I don't know a lot about the study, but I listened to one of Dr. Dupont's audio files, and she mentioned Deadswitch Wilderness. Ring any bells?

Holden sat back and waited for a response, disappointment weighing in his gut. If Dr. Chari couldn't remember the study, finding out what happened to Dr. Dupont was going to be difficult, especially if CalTech didn't get back in touch with him.

Holden checked his phone. He swiped away a text from Kyle and opened one from Lauren to a photo of Francis on the couch, belly up and out cold, tongue flopping out of his mouth.

Wish I were doing the same, Holden texted back.

He stole one of Angel's Twizzlers before she slapped his hand away, and was almost finished eating it when Dr. Chari began typing again.

CHARI: Is this a joke?

SHARPE: ???

SHARPE: I don't understand.

CHARI: Wipe the drive. Don't come to my office.

MAIDEI CHARI HAS BLOCKED YOU. IF YOU THINK THIS IS A MISTAKE, PLEASE CONTACT OSU IT.

SIENA

They passed the creek right when they were supposed to.

Cam had been right, but Siena didn't care. Her insides felt uncalibrated, like she'd left a part of herself back at the fork, still obsessing over the blank sign. She should have studied it more closely . . . done a pencil impression. She could have taken a picture to send to the damn map company so they could fix their faulty merchandise.

All she had now was a memory.

At least her team had picked up speed, clearing eleven miles by late afternoon the next day. They found a camping spot on the ridge near snowmelt and a killer view of the sister peaks.

Siena sat on a small boulder, studying Agnes through her binoculars as Emmett and Isaac left for water and Cam set up the kitchen.

Agnes outshone her sisters—a gorgeous alpine peak as visually intimidating as Whitney or Rainier. Siena had always dreamt of summiting, though she doubted that would happen this trip, given the sad state of their technical gear. It didn't matter—she was certain she'd return to Deadswitch Wilderness sooner rather than later. It was still on her list to hike the path her mother used to take all those years ago with the High Sierra Conservationists, a pilgrimage to the habitats they once protected. One day, she'd have the time.

Siena dropped her binoculars and scribbled a note in her field journal: *Alpenglow not visible from Wolf Ridge. Significant melt projected.*

Alpenglow Glacier was somewhere in the middle of the cirque pack—not the smallest, but certainly not the most impressive. But the meltwater was unique, teeming with mineral and biological components absent from the rest of the Sierras. CalTech's cabin right beneath the tree line of Agnes was a relic from a twenty-something-year-old study led by Dr. Wilder Feyrer, Siena's mentor. The geomorphology department had abandoned Alpenglow soon after, along with the cabin. Satellites were all that watched the glacier now.

Dr. Feyrer had wanted to change that. He'd put his faith in Siena to ignite a new study.

Don't go.

"What if it's gone?" Siena asked Cam, who sat on the ground next to the prepped camp kitchen while shoving a Snickers into her mouth.

"If the satellites could talk, they'd tell you to quit the hand-wringing," said Cam as she picked some peanut out of her teeth. "I checked the images before we left. There's *something*, just not a lot of something. Doubt there will be anything in five years, but at least we'll have significant meltwater to analyze now. That's all we need anyway, right? To publish the research and move on with our long and lucrative careers?"

Siena slid from the rock and took a seat next to Cam, grabbing her mess kit, meds, and a bag of freeze-dried beef Stroganoff. "And care about climate change?"

"Caring won't convince corporations to do anything. We're fucked either way." Cam crumpled the candy bar wrapper in her hands. "We know that, Feyrer knew that. He wanted both of us here because it's an easy and impressive PI credit. That's it."

Siena wished she could channel Cam's practicality. Yes, Feyrer had wanted Siena and Cam on this study because he had cared about them, and leading potentially groundbreaking research was an opportunity of a lifetime. But that wasn't the only reason. He'd been obsessed with this place long before Siena came along, claiming to know Deadswitch's secrets.

The research stays in the woods.

Cam's lip twitched as she watched Siena. "Don't overthink it."

"You know that's impossible." Siena disassembled her mess kit, tucked a pill in the lip of her plate, and tore open the bag of food with her teeth. "Mmm . . . delicious."

Cam gave a faux gag. "Fuck astronaut food."

"Pedigree Country Stew for canines tastes just as good. Don't ask me how I know that."

"Now I *have* to know."

"Emmett was dog sitting for his brother when the shrink prescribed me new sleep meds."

Now Cam really gagged. "I hope you fired that shrink."

Siena laughed. She pushed away her mess kit and looked over her shoulder to see if she could spot Emmett and Isaac coming back from the snowmelt.

"Is it weird with him here?" Cam asked.

"Emmett?" Siena shook her head. "Nah, we've been working on this project for four years, haven't we? Even after . . . you know. Things between us won't suddenly become *weird* just because we're out here."

"Spending every waking moment with him is a little different from showing up to a lab for a few hours."

Siena couldn't argue with that. "It doesn't really matter, though, does it? Both of us have to see this project through to the end because we're equally stubborn. That would have been the case even if he'd done something worse. Tried to murder me, or whatever."

"Or you him."

They shared a smile, and Cam's vanished as her eyes flickered to the woods. "They're coming back."

Siena returned her attention to the powder in her bowl. "I'm more worried about *you* and him."

"I'll play nice," said Cam, but Siena knew it wasn't a promise.

Siena shot up from her sleeping bag.

Her sweat-drenched bottom layer cooled in a matter of seconds, and she shivered. She patted the surrounding space, searching for her headlamp while clinging to the phantom noise.

That *noise*. Had it been real, or a remnant of a dream?

She found her headlamp and wrapped it around her wrist, clicking it on. Her breath left her in a cloud until she held it, listening, but even the grasshoppers were quiet.

Siena unzipped her bivy and crawled out, stepping into her loosened and waiting boots. Holding up her wrist, she slowly scanned the perimeter of camp opposite the ridge. Nothing but evergreens. Someone shuffled around in their bivy sack, and she tuned them out to try and remember the noise. A rumble? A growl? The more Siena fought to recall it, the faster it slipped away.

She turned and yelped when her headlamp beam caught Emmett's face.

He grabbed her arm and hushed her. "You'll wake the others. What the hell are you doing up?"

She yanked free of him. "Get off me."

"Sorry," he hissed through his teeth, though his expression told her otherwise. He always looked the same when he was pissed at her, like an overprotective dad with a rare hangover. Authoritative and grumpy, with a hint of guilt.

"Did you hear that noise?" she asked.

"What noise?"

"Out in the woods."

"Which direction?"

"I don't . . ." She scanned the forest again. It responded with silence. "I don't know. I was asleep."

"An animal?"

She shook her head. "Not an animal. I can't describe it. It sounded familiar, but I'd just woken up, so maybe . . ." God, she sounded stupid. She turned back to Emmett, expecting his quintessential stinkface, but much to her dismay, he looked worried.

He didn't have the right to be worried about her, and she wasn't obligated to explain herself to him. And yet . . .

"In case you forgot, I don't suffer from auditory hallucinations."

"I know you don't."

"And I've been taking my meds."

"So it was probably just a dream, Sen."

"Then why are you up, if you didn't hear it too?"

Emmett opened his mouth and shut it again. Siena knew the answer. He was hypertuned to every one of her movements, every shift she made in her sleep. He woke when she woke. It had been that way for years.

"Go back to bed," he finally said. "We have a long hike tomorrow."

"I know that," she snapped.

"What is this, a communal midnight piss?" Cam mumbled from inside her bivy. "Shut the hell up."

Emmett threw a dirty look over his shoulder before returning his attention to Siena. "Night, Sen." With that he headed back to his bivy.

He doesn't believe me.

She opened her mouth, words bubbling to fruition on her tongue. "You're not my fucking caretaker," she muttered beneath her breath. Never had been, never would be.

A cry echoed across the mountainside. Siena's jaw snapped shut, and Emmett jumped back up.

"The fuck was that?" Cam thrashed against her bivy, tearing open the zipper.

Mountain lion. Wait, no . . .

Not an animal. The sound was distinctly human.

Siena directed her light toward Isaac's open and empty bivy.

"Shit," she hissed, and glanced up to catch Emmett disappearing into the woods.

Siena sprinted after him. Within moments, the forest was thick around her, and she had little time to react to the sudden decline. She slipped and caught herself on a pine branch, the bark skinning her palm. Her headlamp bounced around until she spotted Emmett again. Siena wove through the trees, tripping over brush and her own shoelaces until she joined him in a small clearing.

He'd found Isaac.

In the center of the clearing, Isaac was stone-still, head tilted back and mouth agape. He must have been taking a leak, before . . .

Siena looked up.

A dead body—a woman—draped over a tree bough like a discarded piece of clothing. Hanging from the waist, she faced the ground, eyes open and flooded with burst blood vessels. Something twitched within her open mouth.

No. Siena's light wavered as she trembled. *No, no, no . . .*

A beetle crawled from the dead woman's blue lips, skittering over a bloated cheek before disappearing behind her ear.

AUDIO_39232001.WAV

"Umm . . . hi.

"This is Dr. Siena Dupont, and it's around 8 a.m. on day four of the expedition to Mount Agnes. I . . ."

[Siena laughs. It isn't happy.]

"It's funny. Feyrer almost predicted the amount of misfortune I'd run into on this trip. He always said nothing in Deadswitch was easy. Called it a curse. I used to give him shit for it. Researchers aren't supposed to even entertain the thought of curses, especially when it comes to their magnum opus.

"Are curses passed on when the bearer dies? I know magnum opuses are.

"I shouldn't digress. I'm recording this on the ridge while the others are by the body, and I don't have a lot of time.

"Oh yeah . . . we found a body. Way to bury the lede, Sen.

"The woman's in her twenties, Asian, designer gear . . . hanging over a tree limb like she'd been thrown up there. There are no other signs of violence and little decomposition. She must have died recently . . . maybe fell from something, though I don't know where from other than the freaking sky.

"We booted up the satellite phone but haven't been able to reach anyone, not even 911. It's . . . strange. I finally gave up when the sun rose, but Cam says I shouldn't have hung up.

"She's acting weird. I mean, all of us are messed up from this, but Cam . . . she's quiet. Retreating inward and tuning the rest of us out. Since I've known her, I've only seen her do that once or twice. I wonder if it has something to do with her time in Search and Rescue. I'll ask later.

"Before we left, I taped a list of emergency numbers to the back of the satellite phone. The school office, the ranger station, the local sheriff . . . I've spent the entire morning dialing out without luck. I keep getting a single tone, like a landline off the hook. Phone's busted.

“I’m starting to believe in this curse.

“I really wish Feyrer was here for guidance. I’m feeling . . . I don’t know . . . shook. Wondering if we should just pack up and head home once we get hold of the police and they question us.

“I’m trying to search for a good memory of him to keep me going . . . maybe inspire me to continue on despite, you know, finding a dead body. He spoke so fondly of this place. But every time I think of him, trying to find a reason to continue, all I can picture is the hospital.

“Shit, gotta run. Emmett’s coming.”

A body.

Holden pulled his headphones from his ears and leaned back in his chair. Francis snored at his feet, and the living room clock ticked above his head, the time wildly inaccurate.

A playlist of all the audio files he had found from Dr. Dupont's project filled the folder on his desktop screen. Other than this file and the first WAV he'd played a couple of days ago, they were corrupted and unplayable.

Holden opened a browser and typed *Deadswitch Wilderness body found* into the search bar, the search engine returning thousands of results. He sifted through the first four pages and a couple dozen news articles, but none of the bodies matched the description of the woman Dupont had found.

He could call the Deadswitch Ranger Station in the morning and ask if they knew anything, but they'd been worthless yesterday when Holden inquired about Dupont's permit. Apparently they kept no records dated before the current year. The ranger had blamed the state of their data on their office potato, which still ran Windows 95.

Page five proved less helpful, the results peppered with info sites about an application that would automatically send out a text or an email to a person if the app thought you were incapacitated.

"Deadman's switch," Holden muttered, and kept scrolling. More missing persons never to be found again, something about the Deadswitch Five . . . It was all too much to read through. He'd be here all night. At least he was actually doing something productive instead of lying in bed and staring at the ceiling.

This newfound motivation bordered on obsessiveness. Holden wasn't ignorant of this. His dopamine-starved brain lapped up every new clue about the study and only craved more. He'd felt less depressed over the last few days than he had in months.

Sure, finding the origin of the files was his job. But Holden couldn't deny that his heart raced every time he heard Dupont's voice.

He wanted to learn everything he could. And his only lead was Dr. Chari.

CAMERON

The woman's open eyes were so blood-drenched, Cam couldn't even see what color they were.

She stood directly beneath the body, a little surprised something viscous hadn't splattered on her yet. The corpse dangled motionless from the branch, petrified like a bug trapped in amber.

Thirty-four years old, and this was the first dead body she'd ever seen. Search and Rescue was supposed to have prepared her for this.

"You're freaking me out."

Cam dropped her eyes to Emmett, who stood at the edge of the clearing, watching her like a chaperone during a violent game of kickball. *She* was freaking *him* out? Her instinct was to laugh at him and tell him to go annoy someone else, but she didn't have it in her.

She'd been here since the middle of the night, since she stumbled blindly through the woods after the rest of her team. The last one to see the body, and also the only one who hadn't left the scene yet. Had she even spoken a word since she entered the clearing? She couldn't remember.

Cam peeled her tongue from the roof of her mouth and ran it over her dry bottom lip. "Where's Isaac?"

"I don't know."

"You should find him. I don't think he's taking this well."

There was no one taking this worse than her, but Emmett didn't need to know that.

"What about Siena?" asked Emmett. "Aren't you worried?"

God, how had Siena been with this guy for half her adult life? He still didn't know how she operated. "Siena isn't fragile. She can handle herself. Go find Isaac."

Cam knew he wanted to argue. She could feel his brewing rebuttal vibrating through the entire clearing, and was genuinely surprised when he eventually left her alone.

But she wasn't alone, was she?

Cam glanced up, meeting bloody, shock-filled eyes. The woman's dull hair hung past her face in curtains. The longer Cam studied her, the more delusional she felt.

"Not possible," she said aloud to the body. "Stop trying to trick me."

Cam finally tore herself away from the dead woman and headed back to the ridge. Emmett had yet to return with Isaac, and Siena was alone, perched on the boulder she'd sat on last night while viewing Mount Agnes. Agnes was still there. It looked even sharper in the day-blue sky, like a thousand broken blades tilted together to form a point.

Siena ignored the mountain, her eyes pinched shut as she spoke into the phone.

"This is Dr. Siena Dupont. I'm about thirty-two miles north of Glass Lake Trailhead in the Deadswitch Wilderness area with Dr. Cameron Yarrow and researchers Emmett Ghosh and Isaac Perez. We are on an expedition and have come across . . . a body. Two days old at most, and no sign of what she died from. Please call me back as soon as you can. We have enough supplies on us to wait here for law enforcement . . . if it remains safe for us to stay."

Siena jammed her finger down on the END button, dropped the phone in her lap, and buried her face in her hands.

"You got through?" asked Cam.

"Sheriff's office. Had to leave a message on the voicemail. Unbelievable."

"At least you left a message."

Siena let her hands fall and stared at Cam. She looked as bad as Cam felt—dark bags beneath her blue eyes, her hair having freed itself from her braid to create a halo of chaos. "Maybe I did, but who knows? The signal could have died in the middle of the message, and I wouldn't have known."

"Any luck calling home?"

Siena wilted even more and shook her head. "I'll try 911 again."

Cam stooped to enter her bivy. "I need to lie down."

"You okay?" Siena asked softly.

"Why?" Cam winced at her own defensive tone.

"You've been . . . I don't know." Siena shrugged. "Quiet."

Cam pushed her hair back. "Just caught off guard. I'll be okay." She tried to smile and grimaced instead before ducking into her bivy.

Cam zipped up both the screen and the privacy shade, and felt around in her sleeping bag. Her fingers skimmed the worn copy of the book she carried with her on every backcountry trip she'd taken in the last five years. She tugged it free from the nylon folds.

A crease split the cover, an artsy shot of Janet Warren and Avery Mathis. The design focused on the point between them—the woods. *Without a Trace* by John Lawson. The title was so lame. Hell, the whole book was lame—over-the-top sensational and dramatic. And yet Cam had pored through it countless times as a punishment. She had been on the Search and Rescue team. *She* had failed to find them.

Cam opened the paperback to the ten glossy flyleaves filled with photos. One of the pages had a picture of all five of the women with their packs on the ground in front of them. It was the only photo Janet had taken of them before leaving her phone in the car at the trailhead.

From left to right: Tasha Gonzalez, Paige Reeves, Janet Warren, Avery Mathis, Naomi Vo.

Cam brushed her thumb across Naomi Vo—a tall athletic young woman with a smile full of white teeth. She wore her dark hair in braids, bright pink Wayfarer sunglasses perched on top. An effortlessly cool girl. A smart girl, just a term away from wrapping up her undergrad at Stanford. A girl Cam was supposed to find all those years ago.

She'd seen dozens of photos of Naomi during the search and rescue response. Naomi in a purple bikini on the California coast, holding a Corona. Naomi and Avery in front of a snow-white background before the two summited Mount Hood.

She'd seen Naomi enough times. Studied Naomi. Imagined stumbling upon Naomi dead at the bottom of a cliff, a probable fate for a missing hiker.

Cam slammed her eyes shut and swore, dropping the book and pulling at her hair with her fist. But it didn't help. Burned into the back of her eyelids was Naomi, bloody-eyed and blue-lipped, hanging from a tree. Naomi, who looked like she had died yesterday but had disappeared seven years ago. Naomi, who hadn't aged at all.

"It's not Naomi," Cam muttered to herself. "Because that would be impossible."

This conspiracy needed to die while it was only a spark in her brain. She'd make a sick joke of it, casually letting Siena know she thought the woman looked like Naomi Vo. Siena would groan and tell her to go to therapy already, and Cam would shoot some smartass comment back. Then they'd walk back to the clearing together, and Cam would see the dead woman clearly—*clearly*—wasn't Naomi.

When Cam emerged from her bivy, Siena was staring stone-faced at the woods. The blood had drained from her face. "What are we gonna do, Cam? What if someone killed her and they're still out there? What if no one gets the message and we can't get through again? We can't just leave her here. And we can't get ahold of anyone."

"I . . ." *Goddammit*. She hid the book behind her back and tugged at her hair with her free hand. There was no point in overwhelming Siena more.

"We'll have to head down the mountain," Cam said. "Cut our losses and replan the expedition." To her own surprise, relief flooded Cam's chest. They'd tripped right out the gate; Feyrer wasn't here, Siena wasn't lead PI, and Cam . . . Deadswitch still haunted Cam.

"Is it bad that I'm angry at the dead woman?" Siena gave a sad laugh and wiped her nose with her shirt. "We can't delay this much longer or we're going to lose our funding. Cam . . ." Siena shook her head. "You know this is all I want."

Guilt doused the rest of Cam's relief. She'd let fear cloud her judgment. Circumstances would never be perfect. So what if Feyrer wasn't here and Siena wasn't lead PI? They'd found a body, not a ghost. Time to follow protocol and move on.

Cam stepped forward and grabbed the phone from Siena's lap. "We won't stop trying, okay? We'll get through, eventually. Get some rest, and I'll try calling out for a bit."

Siena nodded, left her boulder, and retreated to her bivy.

As Cam left camp, she ran her thumb over the Post-It note taped to the phone's battery case. *Call 911, Dingus,* it read. Listed beneath were three numbers: Deadswitch Ranger Station, the local sheriff's office, and the main line for CalTech.

Cam tried the sheriff's number, halting in the woods when it rang.

She'd gotten through on the first try.

"This is Sheriff Ainsley's Office. No one can come to the phone right now . . ."

She knew Sheriff Ainsley. *Had* known. Robert Ainsley had been the county sheriff of the nearby town when Cam was volunteering seven years ago, and had been assigned to the case of the missing hikers. He died of cancer two years back. There was a new sheriff. It seemed more than strange that they wouldn't have changed the voicemail on his phone by now.

"Hi, this is Dr. Cameron Yarrow. My colleague tried calling a few minutes ago. Listen, we aren't able to get through to anyone, but we've found a body in Deadswitch Wilderness, and we need an emergency team up here immediately. We're starting our research project, and we need to continue . . . You know what, never mind. A woman is dead, call me back." She rattled off the number for the satellite phone and hung up. Then she dialed the university and didn't get through.

Siena was right. They really were screwed.

She tried the ranger station for the hell of it.

It rang once before someone picked up. "Yello!"

Cam's heart leapt into her throat. "Is this the ranger station for the Deadswitch Wilderness area?"

"This is the southern Ansel Adams Wilderness station, sweetheart."

Ansel Adams was close to Deadswitch. "We found a dead hiker, and I need—"

"Now hold on. You say someone's dead?"

Oh, for fuck's sakes. "Yes! I need an emergency team in Deadswitch Wilderness immediately. We're about thirty-two miles from the Glass Lake Trailhead."

"I think you're confused, sweetheart."

She bit back her growl, prepped to verbally tear this guy a new asshole if he called her sweetheart one more time.

"Perhaps you got the number for a different state. There's no Deadswitch Wilderness in California."

"I *am* in California!" Cam pinched the bridge of her nose. "Listen, it doesn't matter. We're in the vicinity of Ansel Adams Wilderness, so I know you'll be able to help. I'm calling you from a satellite phone. You'll be able to track its location and get a team to us. There's a dead woman . . . looks like she died yesterday. We're going to stay with her until . . . Hello?"

Dial tone.

"*Fucker!*" she screamed at the phone. The connection hadn't dropped. The twat of a ranger had *hung up on her*.

Oh, she couldn't wait to get down the mountain and sic law enforcement on his ass. How dare he not take her seriously?

She realized she hadn't gotten his name.

Cam tried calling back and got a dead line. She took a deep breath and attempted to reorganize her brain to pinpoint the things she could control. Naomi. She still had the book in her hand. The photo would prove the woman in the tree wasn't her. She just had to compare them.

Cam retraced her steps to the clearing. She looked up and frowned. Then she looked down at the footprints all over the dirt —her own, Isaac's big ones, Siena's small ones . . . She looked up again.

Where the hell—

Cam was in the right place. She'd suffered through committing the damn clearing to memory when she'd been here early this morning. The body had been hanging from the tree with the roots that spidered out above the ground. From the bough right above Cam's head. Cam had stared into her bloody eyes for *hours*.

She was gone. Naomi . . . Naomi was gone.

EXCERPT FROM CHAPTER 3 OF *WITHOUT A TRACE* BY JOHN LAWSON:

To this day, Naomi Vo's participation in the hike remains a mystery. She didn't know most of the women, and had only met Avery Mathis on a Mount Hood group summit.

Naomi hadn't told her parents about the trip, both of whom were in denial when Sheriff Ainsley called to let them know their daughter was missing in Deadswitch. She was supposed to be in Palm Springs with her boyfriend, who hadn't been in Palm Springs at all, but was visiting family in New Hampshire.

So why did she go? And even more importantly, why did she lie?

SIENA

The team spread out, Cam and Emmett searching the woods. Isaac climbed a nearby tree for a better view, and Siena scoured beneath for tracks or blood.

Nothing. It was like the body was never there. Like they all had imagined it.

"Had to have been an animal," Isaac yelled down at her before quietly uttering, "R-Right?"

Siena shook her head. "No drag marks," she hollered back, and winced. It was dumb to be yelling. If the woman had been murdered, the killer could have returned for her body. But there would still be a trail if that were true.

They'd failed to report the body to anyone except for the ranger in the Ansel Adams station who had hung up on Cam. It was like the whole thing had never happened.

"We have a duty to notify authorities even now." Emmett stomped around camp, packing up the kitchen and his bivy, as though the brash movements would make him seem more commanding. "We need to turn around."

Siena hated the idea of turning around, and hated even more that she agreed with him. A woman was dead, whatever had killed her still out there. Her loved ones could already be looking for her. Even if they'd lost the body, they had to notify the police so a larger search could begin.

Siena took her cowboy coffee into her bivy to think. Cam joined her, and they crouched together while sipping from their mugs in silence. Filling the quiet void never felt necessary with Cam, one reason Siena loved her so much.

"You're the PI," Siena finally said. "You should decide."

Cam shook her head, running her index finger absently around the rim of her cup. "You know that's bullshit. I'm a stand-in PI."

Siena bit back her frustration. "Do I need to remind you why I'm not the lead PI?"

"I only stepped up because you asked me to, but I never believed at any point you were incapable of leading this team. Not even at your worst. Feyrer thought the same. This is your project, Siena."

It was the first time Cam had brought up Feyrer on her own in a while. Cam didn't enjoy talking about death, something Siena began noticing when Cam first told Siena about her Search and Rescue stint. Cam always referred to the missing hikers as *gone*, not dead. She used that word a lot.

Siena finally responded. "Feyrer told me not to go . . ."

"In the hospital, you told me. You know he wasn't in his right mind toward the end." Cam elbowed her. "Listen . . . I thought Feyrer was a conspiratorial nut . . . you know that. But he was right to put his faith in you. What he told you on his deathbed doesn't change that."

Siena stared down at her oily coffee. "It never felt real, what he said." The cancer had returned with a vengeance. Siena had planned this expedition with him until his hospitalization. His daughter had called Siena only a few weeks later for her to say her goodbyes.

Emmett had met Siena at the hospital. She'd wished she were

alone but refused to waste her last moments with her mentor frustrated with Emmett.

Wilder had looked dead already. Siena had almost wished he *were* dead with the unnatural way he blinked and breathed—like an animatronic in some fucked-up haunted house.

As she'd held his icy hand, he hadn't recognized her right away, his eyes struggling to match a name to her face. And when he finally did, he'd wept.

"Don't go. Don't go, don't go, don't go . . ." Each plea had been louder than the last, his yellowed fingernails breaking the flesh of her arm. Siena's own grip on him had tightened, and she hadn't let go until Emmett pulled her away.

Emmett—always pushing and pulling her. He'd pull her back down the mountain if he could. She wasn't about to give him the opportunity.

"We keep going," Siena said. "We're about thirty miles deep. It's quicker to reach the cabin than it would be to turn around. There's radio equipment there. Maybe we can finally contact someone, or get a better signal on the phone."

Cam finished the dregs of her coffee with an unreadable expression, but swallowed with a nod. "Sounds good, Doc."

"But only if you're okay to keep going. I know finding the body upset you." Siena touched Cam's arm. "You don't have to hide things from me."

Cam smiled crookedly. "I'm okay. But I'll be even better if I get to tell Emmett the plan."

Siena shook her head in disbelief. "You live to cause trouble."

"Only with him, promise." Cam lifted her pinkie.

Siena hooked her finger with Cam's. "Don't piss him off too much. We need him to carry gear up the mountain."

Cam ducked out of the bivy. "I'll do my best, boss."

Siena packed up to the sound of them arguing. Cam eventually played her *I'm the PI* card, and Siena vacated the area before witnessing any carnage. She scoured the campground for Isaac before finding him along the ridge, his lanky legs crossed beneath him as he scratched at his field journal with a pencil. He looked haggard even from a distance.

Siena approached him, peering over his shoulder to glimpse an impressive sketch of the sister peaks.

She caught his attention, and he flipped the book shut.

"Sorry," she said. "I didn't mean to intrude. Your drawing is beautiful. Can I see?"

He flashed a hesitant smile, opening the field book and passing it to her. "It's just this one so far. I haven't had much time. I usually sketch when I want to learn an area. Or . . . umm . . . when I'm feeling anxious."

"I'm not feeling too great myself," said Siena as she studied the sketch of the range. "You have genuine talent." Everything—the shading, scale, realism—was perfect, with one exception.

"You drew four peaks." Siena looked up, shielding her eyes to double-check there were only three mountains: Agnes in front of them, and Charlotte and Lucille to the east. "I can only see the sisters from here."

Isaac frowned and scrutinized the sketch when Siena handed it back. His eyes flickered to the mountain range. "That's weird. I thought I'd drawn it exactly as I saw it."

"Maybe you can see a fourth peak from a different angle," Siena suggested, though she knew this wasn't true. She'd been glued to the view of the valley since the start of the trip and would have seen a fourth peak if there was one.

Isaac heaved a dejected sigh and rubbed at his eyes. "Dammit."

From the look on his face, Siena wished she had said nothing at all.

They gained thirteen miles that day with no further deviations from the map, and Siena soon forgot about the strange fork in the path. After making camp near an alpine pond, the group woke before sunrise for the last stretch to the cabin.

No one mentioned the body. In fact, no one said much of anything, granting Siena the opportunity to listen for signs of predators. Or people.

But the trip remained uneventful, and on the bare granite face of the final incline, she stopped and turned to gaze over the wilderness and the valley's carpet of evergreens. The rosy beacons of Mount Charlotte and Lucille glowed against the lilac sky.

Worth it. Even without Feyrer. Even after finding the body. Few people in the world got to experience this much natural beauty in their lives, and publishing her findings bettered her chances of researching places like this for the rest of her life.

Siena looked down, squinting when she couldn't find the trail or the cairns they'd spent the last hour following.

"Come on." Cam slapped Siena's shoulder as she passed her. "I'm starving."

Siena followed, trailing the others until the mountain leveled out, granite giving way to a thick grove of foxtail pines. The twilight air felt cool and moist—strange, given how dry the rest of the hike had been.

Deep into the grove, the log-linked cabin sat on a slab of stone. Some windows were boarded over, the sun-bleached roof covered in a layer of dead needles. Ugly, run-down, and patiently waiting all these years for the next generation. For them.

"*You'll never want to leave,*" Feyrer had told her.

Siena's throat tightened as she followed the others to the cabin porch.

Emmett sauntered forward, slapping the crates stacked in front of a boarded window. "Looks like the mules made it."

Siena fished for the cabin keys in her belt pocket, unclipped her pack, and shimmied free. "Thank god." She'd heard too many horror stories of packers screwing up orders or not showing up at all, which was why they'd suffered with fifty-five-pound packs all this way.

Cam kicked away a clump of dried dung. "They left a while ago. They're actually on schedule for once."

"Maybe they found the body on their way back down?" Isaac asked hopefully.

"What, and the packers took it?" Cam shook her head. "We would have run into them or their donkey shit. Plus, they take the east trail off the mountain to drop stuff off at the station by Triplet Lakes."

"Someone will find her," Siena assured Isaac as he frowned, though the statement was more a wish than anything else. She tugged her phone from her pocket and located the padlock on the first crate, swiping through her photos until she found one of the packer's code scribbled hastily on a Post-It note. She entered the code and yanked open the crate, sliding the lid off. It landed on the ground with a satisfying *thunk*.

Siena peered inside and sighed in relief. Hundreds of food packs filled the crate. The others contained supplies for their studies and pleasantries—a few bottles of whiskey, biodegradable soap, tampons, and extra clothes.

"Good." Cam sniffed her shirt. "God, I need to burn this."

Siena frowned at the cabin, creeping across the porch for a closer look.

The plaque near the door should have read *Property of CalTech*, like it had in the dozens of photos she'd seen from previous expeditions. But it didn't. It was blank and flecked with olive paint.

Just like the sign at the fork.

Siena ran the tips of her fingers over the sign, searching for an imprint—any lettering at all—but the surface was as smooth as driftwood.

The Forest Service made do with a tight budget. Perhaps the upkeep of signs wasn't their top priority. This place needed a little

TLC anyway—maybe she'd get around to repainting it one of these evenings.

She reached down for the doorknob and halted, her eyes resting on a splintered frame, cracked door, and the sliver of darkness beyond.

The door was open.

Holden logged out of his work computer and slid his phone from his pocket, checking the screen.

Becca: Hey, just checking in. Haven't talked in a while. Hope you're well.

Hope you're *well.*

Holden's anger morphed to shame in a matter of seconds. The emotion was crisp and buzzed much like panic did. Shame and panic had always felt the same to him—a loss of control, an inability to process thought. He stared dumbly at the message until the sensation fizzled out.

His fingers itched to fly across the keyboard.

IstillmissyouIloveyouInevercheatedonyou—-

Stop. He locked his phone and shoved it back into his pocket. Any response to Becca needed to be well marinated; he couldn't let his guard down with her, not when she dissected his every word.

Holden packed up his stuff and left the library, heading down Jefferson toward the Forestry building. In his hands were the external drive and a folder of key PDFs from Dr. Dupont's project.

He was just past Sackett Place when he heard his name. He shielded his eyes as Chelsea hurried toward him from the quad, flipping back her hair.

Today was cursed. Had to be. Then again, he hadn't received this much unexpected attention from a sober woman in months.

He forced a grin. "What's up? What are you doing on campus?" From his fragmented conversations with Chelsea the other night, he remembered her saying she'd just graduated with her MBA.

"I had some B.S. parking tickets from the campus police that I still had to take care of. Thought I'd say hi to a professor while I was at it." Her teeth sunk into her perfectly glossed lower lip, green eyes popping against her dark makeup. She looked great for an outing to pay off a ticket.

"Wanted to apologize for the other night," she said. "I got out of a shitty relationship a couple of months ago and haven't been coping well. I shouldn't have drunk that much . . . especially on a date."

Holden hadn't considered it a *date*; even so, she seemed sincere enough. "It's not a big deal, really."

"I appreciate you not taking advantage of the situation."

"You really don't have to thank me for doing the bare minimum to not be a shithead."

She smiled. "Can I make it up to you? Dinner, on me?" His surprise must have shown on his face, because Chelsea flushed and added, "You don't have to say yes."

"No," he said. "I mean, yes. I'd like that."

"Awesome. I'll text you the place and time. I . . . uhh . . . don't think I have your number. But Emma has Kyle's."

". . . Emma?"

"My BFF. You met her! Anyway, I'll get it, don't worry."

"I can just give—"

"Looking forward to it." Chelsea waved. "See ya."

Holden scratched his head as Chelsea crossed the street and disappeared down 30th. Maybe hanging out with Kyle wasn't a total waste of his time, after all.

Despite everything that had happened in the last twenty minutes, Holden was certain Becca and Chelsea weren't the strangest interactions he'd have today. He passed the Forest Science Complex, a modern beast of a building paneled with alder and glass, and entered Richardson Hall.

According to the directory, Chari's office was on the second floor. An adjunct waved at him in passing, and Holden lifted a hand in response. He visited the faculty offices a lot, given the adjuncts shared crusty desktops and there was no accountability. Hell, he understood. None of them were paid enough to be accountable.

He took the stairs and traveled the length of the hall. Across from the water fountain, Dr. Chari's door waited for him. She had no cute or quirky posters on her door like the surrounding professors—no ironic *Hang in there!* kitty signs like he'd seen a dozen times across campus. And her mailbox was empty.

Maybe she wasn't even here. There was only one way to find out.

Holden rapped his knuckles against the door.

The response was faint. "It's open."

He turned the knob and entered. The lamp on the desk glowed dimly in front of closed horizontal blinds. A scattering of house plants topped mismatched file cabinets, but other than that, the room was sterile.

Dr. Chari sat at her desk, her dark braids piled atop her head. She didn't bother to look up, but paused in feverishly typing out an email to point in his direction. "Tip's on the table."

Holden cast a glance at a crumpled ten-dollar bill atop the table near the door. "Excuse me?"

Chari finally turned her attention toward him and frowned. "Ah. I thought you were my Thai."

"Sorry to disappoint."

Her eyes dipped to the drive he held, and her face hardened. "I thought I told you not to come here," she said. He suspected she had been thinking about their chat encounter as much as he had.

"Just hear me out," Holden pled. "I need your help—I don't know who else to contact. CalTech hasn't called me back, and my only other option is to take this drive to the university police. Or the real police."

Dr. Chari didn't so much as twitch her lip, but still managed to project blistering irritation toward him. "The police? What makes you think I want anything to do with the trouble you've gotten yourself into?"

"Not legal trouble." Holden raised the drive. "Life-threatening trouble, for a woman named Dr. Siena Dupont."

"I told you already that I don't know her. Who is she to you?"

"I . . ."

When Holden hesitated, Dr. Chari raised her eyebrows.

"A stranger, but it doesn't matter. It's my job to make sure I delete nothing important off this drive. Most of Dupont's audio files are corrupted, but the ones I could listen to were pretty—I don't know—distressing, I guess. She found a body in the woods. And then one of her team members died. I just want to report this if need be— Hey, are you okay?"

Dr. Chari looked like she'd swallowed a live roach. "Did . . . did she make it out?"

"I mean, someone did if I have the recording, unless she had service—"

"There is no service in Deadswitch."

"I—I don't know, then. Can you at least look at the key contacts sheet for this study? Maybe it'll spark something." Holden shuffled the drive into his other hand and passed Dr. Chari the folder, surprised when she grasped it from him and flipped it open. She licked her thumb and sifted through the pages, and after a few moments, nodded. "I know a few of the folks on this list, not from this study, but another on Deadswitch. My department pulled me off the project prematurely."

"Why?"

"My institution at the time thought it was a hoax. We were studying lodgepole pine seedlings that matured more quickly than any other species in the world."

She said this with a gravity that surely was supposed to mean something to Holden. He stared at her blankly. "How quickly?" he finally asked.

Dr. Chari closed the folder and rested her hands on top. "Two days."

He didn't understand. "I'm sorry. When you said matured, I thought you meant matured into . . . uhh . . . trees."

"That *is* what I meant."

Maybe this was Dr. Chari's way of fucking with Holden to get him the hell out of her office. "So, you're saying you planted seedlings, and they fully matured into pine trees in two days."

Chari swiveled toward her file cabinet, unhooking a set of keys from her belt and unlocking the bottom drawer. She dug through files until she slid one free, handing it to him.

The file was clearly old, cardstock so thin it felt like the whole thing was going to disintegrate in his hands. He carefully opened it and found faded photos inside, almost sepia tone, as though Chari had taken them forty years ago. Which was strange, considering Dr. Chari didn't look a day over forty-five.

Orange time stamps in the corner of each print spanned the period of a week, the first photo of a forest edge. The one underneath, taken six hours later, was of the same forest edge with several saplings that weren't there before. He flipped it over to a photo of the same area twenty-four hours later, the saplings over thirty feet tall, new saplings scattered in front of them.

"We did not plant these seedlings," said Dr. Chari. "They propagated themselves."

The other photos captured different groves—bird's-eye images showing a cluster of trees multiplying by the hundreds and crowding an empty field in a matter of days. Holden finally understood why the institution had thought this was a hoax. It *looked* like a hoax.

"You don't believe me," said Dr. Chari.

Holden shut the folder. No, he didn't believe her. He couldn't. A forest growing at this speed would have overrun more than just a field, but roads and towns, too. He would have heard about something like this happening. The entire world would have.

But Dr. Chari seemed so sincere. So *convinced*. And that was the most fascinating part of it all.

"I *will* believe you," said Holden. "If you help me."

SIENA

If Siena brought Emmett's attention to the busted doorframe now, he'd make a deal of it. He'd insist on entering the cabin first in order to protect her, as he always did, like he possessed some sort of power that made this situation less dangerous for him than it was for her.

His only power was brawn. She preferred stealth, instead.

She rested her hand on the doorknob. If someone had broken in, they likely weren't here anymore. Thru-hikers and weekend backpackers didn't often travel Wolf Ridge Trail. It was too long, difficult, and didn't have a discernible exit other than hiking back out.

Siena stole a quick glance over her shoulder. Emmett and Isaac continued to sort through the goods left by the mule packer. Cam stood behind them, shielding her eyes and gazing up at the top of Mount Agnes, distracted.

Siena pushed open the door and slipped into the dark cabin. A wood plank creaked beneath her foot. She froze and listened, but heard nothing other than Emmett giving Isaac a lesson in gear.

Avocado-colored curtains hung over the windows in the empty common room and in the kitchen, the space cast in dim green light. The dust covering the floor was free of footprints, and when she inhaled, she caught no hint of food or body odor. In fact, the place smelled spectacularly stale, untouched since the '90s. Alpine storms were intense, after all. It was possible that one had blown open the door.

In the kitchen, a utility sink stood between a wood stove and pine-paneled counter, a pair of rickety cabinets anchored to the wall. Benches flanked a slab table that comfortably seated four. There was nothing else—no clutter or anything—just a shotgun hallway in front of her with two branching rooms.

Siena crept deeper down the hall to investigate. Four compact bunk beds with vinyl pads filled the room on the left. The right door was shut. She turned the knob and pushed, wincing as the rusty hinge screamed.

A big dirty window broadcasted the dense forest. Two adjacent plywood desks took up most of the room, their surfaces covered in dust and old equipment, a ham radio, notebooks, and loose yellowed papers. Papers, *everywhere.* The desk, the chair, the floor. It was like someone had opened a window during a storm and hadn't bothered cleaning up, or the previous team had left in a whirlwind of chaos. Feyrer had never mentioned that.

Siena plucked the papers from the floor and stacked them on the desk, and coaxed a toppled chair back to its feet. A stain on the doorframe caught her attention, and she crouched for a closer look.

Only rust. The hinges had gotten wet, perhaps in the storm that had busted the front door and blown the papers all over this room.

No . . . evidence of such a scenario was too tenuous. The stain was darker than rust. Fingers had clearly dragged the smear of color across the wood.

Backpackers cut their palms on rocks, sticks, and pocket knives all the time, didn't they? The researchers before her had trudged up and down Agnes during their projects, just like she would. It was nothing. It *had* to be nothing.

"What happened to the door?" Emmett boomed from the common room.

"Broken," Siena yelled. "No one's here, though. And nothing's stolen . . . I don't think."

The ham radio was all that mattered, anyway. She needed to get a message out so she could stop thinking about the body, and start on the glacier.

After they tucked away the gear in various corners of the cabin, and Siena had scrubbed herself raw with a bar of degradable soap and a bucket of water from the storage barrels, she sat down in front of the ham radio as Emmett boiled water for dinner. The transceiver and tuner were both the size of small bricks and easily thirty years old. She replaced the corroded external battery pack with a rechargeable lithium from the packer supply.

She knew little about radios, but more than the rest of her team combined thanks to a technical course she'd taken in college. Luckily, she found a list of repeaters and the last user's call sign in a small notebook next to the radio.

Cam joined her at the table, a hydrating dinner in one hand and whiskey in the other. "This'll be exciting."

Siena flipped the power switch, set the frequency and offset of the first repeater in the notebook, and picked up the mic.

"This is Whiskey Six Lima Delta, does anyone copy? Over."

Nothing.

She tried the next repeater in the book.

"Whiskey Six Lima Delta, is anyone there? I need help. Over."

Siena waited. No tone and no response, just like the last. Either the repeater list was bad, or the radio was busted.

"You probably just need a larger antenna." Isaac sat across from her with a deck of cards he'd found in a kitchen cabinet.

Siena bit back her irritation. "And where do you propose I find one of those?"

Isaac shrugged and began shuffling the cards. "You can make one out of anything, really. An empty paper towel roll and some paper clips, a hanger . . . Learned all about it in fifth grade."

"Fifth grade?" Cam popped open the whiskey. "I can't remember anything from fifth grade."

"I figured out I wanted to be a scientist in fifth grade," Isaac responded proudly.

Cam and Siena shared an entertained look.

"What made you decide that?" Siena asked.

"Parents are Messianic Jews." Isaac grinned.

Cam sighed. "I love me a good ol' fashioned act of rebellion."

Isaac pulled his field journal toward him. "I've been obsessed with geologic formations since I was a little kid." He flipped through the pages of his sketches. "I wanted to know why they were there. The real reason, not the Genesis 1:1 reason. But I didn't just want to be some douchey, selfish bro either, figuring stuff out just to satisfy myself. I want to help people, too. And glacial research is climate research."

"Douchey, selfish bro." Cam nodded, though it was clear she was trying not to laugh. "That's . . . admirable of you."

"I think it is," Siena said with a bit more sincerity. "It's important to find that intersection of something you love and something meaningful. My mom was a conservationist. It's the reason I became a scientist."

Isaac shut his book. "She must be proud of you."

Siena's throat tightened for the second time that day. "She's . . ."

"Very proud," Cam finished, raising the bottle. "Cheers to that."

Siena smiled at her in thanks, and Cam winked at her.

"My brother Levi's proud of me . . . I think he's the only one," Isaac said with a shrug. "I still question my decision every day."

"We *all* question it every day," Siena said. She remembered what it was like at his age, educated enough for a career but so young that everything seemed daunting as hell. She was lucky enough to have had a true mentor in Dr. Feyrer. Despite the trip's early setbacks, Agnes Cabin was exactly where she belonged, and she wouldn't be here if it weren't for him.

She just wished he were here, too.

Emmett plopped a bowl of rehydrated chili slop in front of her.

"Gross. I mean thank you, but gross."

"Eat," he replied. "Where are your meds?"

"The pouch near my bed. I'll grab them when I'm done."

"I'll get them for you."

"Thanks, Dad," Siena muttered when Emmett left for the bedroom. Isaac snorted, and Cam smirked around the whiskey.

Siena choked down her dinner before returning to the radio, trying every receiver on the list. When she restarted from the top, the novelty of the radio evaporated, and the others drifted into the bunk room one by one until only Siena remained at the table with the camp lantern.

She'd read through the reports of previous studies that had taken place at Agnes Cabin. Too many studies. If the researchers had experienced trouble using the radio, they would have made a note. Then again, the radio *was* old, and twenty-something years had passed since the last expedition. Maybe the repeaters had changed.

Calling out of these woods was becoming harder than getting ahold of her absent father on a good day. And that was saying something.

With the defunct phone and radio, hiking out of Deadswitch was the only way they could report the body. And then what? All they had were coordinates to the location of the dead hiker, who was no longer there.

"Come on," Siena muttered, rolling the dial on the radio until the speaker popped with static. She paused and listened, and then carefully rolled the dial back and forth until a tune broke through the noise.

The song was a little flat, almost as though it was playing off a warped record. It sounded like something from an oldies station. She couldn't tell the exact era, but the tune reminded her of "Dream a Little Dream of Me." Soft and melancholy.

She wasn't even on the FM broadcast band. Why would someone be transmitting music on a shortwave frequency?

"*Meet me in the briardark, beneath a moon we will embark, deeper till we've lost our way, until the sky turns bright as day. And then I'll follow you way down, the moment we're about to drown, we'll meet a mother pure and gold, she'll know our will and save our souls.*"

Siena dropped her mic and flipped the radio's power switch.

Blood pulsed through her ears, and she couldn't think around the sound. She could only *feel*—the sweat prickling the back of her neck, the inexplicable dread building inside her like an approaching train horn.

The radio mic hung off the side of the table. Siena focused on the way it bobbed at the end of its coiled cord, trying to dull the primal, bone-deep fear the song had stirred within her.

EXCERPT FROM CHAPTER 5 OF *WITHOUT A TRACE* BY JOHN LAWSON:

Journalists, true crime obsessors, and Twitter hot take aficionados alike have wondered whether the story of the five missing hikers would have gained media traction without Avery Mathis, a starlet in the throes of launching her career, and one of the most prolific female gamers on YouTube. Avery's channel had just crossed three million subscribers the summer she entered Deadswitch Wilderness. She mostly played indie horror games.

Many of her fans were so distraught at the news of her disappearance that they created conspiracy theories of their own, claiming they'd seen her incognito at gas stations and seedy hotels across the US. To them, the trip to Deadswitch was simply a ruse for Avery to disappear forever.

Rumors had been circulating that Avery's sudden internet popularity had been affecting her mental health, something her father confirmed during several interviews with various detectives. Maybe she couldn't handle the pressure, the exposure, and the invasive nature of fame. Maybe she had tried to make it all go away.

Of course, these conspiracy theories completely disregarded the four other young women who had disappeared as well.

CAMERON

Cam jerked awake, a decaying Naomi burned into her brain, as if she'd been beneath the tree on Wolf Ridge seconds before.

Dawn leached into the cold blue morning; it couldn't have been later than five. She sat up in her bottom bunk and caught her breath quietly, wiping a bead of sweat from the back of her neck and hoping she had woken no one else.

She grabbed her headlamp and *Without a Trace* from beneath her sleeping bag and snuck from the bunks to the common room. On the lumpy couch, Cam stretched out and opened the book to the flyleaves. She flipped to the collage on the last page and peeled away the Post-It note atop the last photo.

In her dorm room at San José State, Avery Mathis sat cross-legged in her computer chair, her messy blonde hair falling past her shoulders. She wore star-spangled boxers and a *Dead Space* tank top. Makeupless. Midlaugh. Happy.

Cam knew she'd been happy, because Cam had taken that photo.

She'd spent so long building a wall around those memories, until she'd convinced herself that Avery Mathis was just another pretty face, a tragedy fit for an HBO docuseries. Cam never knew her, not really. Avery was an acquaintance, the kind you forgot about until you stumbled across their social media profile five years later, half-drunk and lonely.

Cam had actually tricked herself into believing this. And for what? To soften the pain of knowing Avery was deader than that corpse on Wolf Ridge?

"*Don't,*" Cam hissed at herself with a wince. "Don't go there."

She had told no one she'd known Avery. Not Frank the ranger when he listed off the names of the missing women to the Search and Rescue team and Cam's heart had dropped to the pit of her stomach. Not Siena, though there was a lot Cam needed to tell Siena.

Not John Lawson when she anonymously mailed him the photo of Avery. Lawson had hungered for Cam's identity more than once.

Cam shut the book and lifted it so her eyes were level with John Lawson's name. She sneered.

"It was yogurt-covered *raisins*, dumbass."

Early morning sun grazed the mountain ridge across the valley. The four of them stood on the south-facing ridge, the jagged slope of the mountain stretching another few miles to the top of the peak. But they didn't have to summit the mountain to reach the cirque a couple hundred feet above them. They were still too far away to see the glacier.

"If there's a tarn, maybe we'll get to go swimming," said Isaac.

Cam dragged her aviators from the top of her head to her face. "Thirty new viruses were discovered in a Tibetan tarn just last week, but go for it."

"You're no fun," he muttered back, sounding genuinely disappointed as he continued hiking upward.

Cam fell back, hoping for a private moment with Siena. But just like at the Wolf Ridge camp, Siena looked like she hadn't slept at all.

"Something obviously kept you up last night," Cam said.

The corners of Siena's mouth perked up. "Emmett told me I looked ill and tossed me a bottle of vitamin C."

"That's because he has the intuition of a dead raccoon." Cam elbowed her.

"It's dumb."

"Try me."

"The radio picked up a broadcast last night. A weird song . . ." Siena tugged on the straps of her pack. "Have you ever woken up in the middle of the night and had this terrible feeling someone was in the room with you? And then you're like, knocking things over trying to find the lamp switch and are positive your throat is going to get slit, or a demon is going to possess you at any second?"

Cam failed at suppressing her laugh. "Sure."

"That's how it felt when I heard that song. It was wrong in the way that nightmares feel wrong. And now that I'm saying this out loud, I can't believe I let it upset me so much. God, I feel like I'm already losing my mind." Siena rubbed one of her temples. "I thought I had at least two weeks until the isolated wilderness got to me," she joked.

"Look, we've already been through a lot on this trip, and all of us are a little sleep deprived. Don't be hard on yourself." Cam hesitated, but it was time to spill the beans to Siena. "I mean, when I saw that dead woman in the tree, I was convinced up and down that she was Naomi Vo." She laughed. "So if you're losing your mind, then so am I."

Cam turned to face Siena, who'd stopped.

Siena stared up at her with a look of shock. "Why didn't you tell me?"

"Because I was clearly having a moment. The woman couldn't have been Naomi."

The surprise on Siena's face didn't dissipate.

"Right?" Cam pressed, her pulse quickening.

"No." Siena shook her head, almost as though she were leaving a trance. "Of course it wasn't Naomi. It's just . . ."

Emmett yelled something unintelligible at them, his tone urgent.

"Come on," said Cam, turning back toward the incline and wishing she'd kept her mouth shut. The exchange hadn't played out how she had hoped. Siena wasn't supposed to take Cam's admission seriously. She was supposed to laugh. Cam *needed* her to laugh.

And if Siena couldn't laugh it off, then Cam needed to do it herself. She needed to forget about Naomi Vo, and stop dreaming about her, for fuck's sakes.

"Hey!" Siena called. Cam stopped and waited for her to catch up, and when she did, Siena breathlessly held out her pinkie finger.

"Let's not forget to check in on each other, okay? Mental health and whatnot. Sometimes I forget talking to someone helps . . . and I'd rather not go to Emmett."

Cam's shoulders wilted. It was a mistake, keeping secrets from Siena. Maybe with enough "check-ins," Cam could finally tell her about Avery.

Cam hooked her pinkie with Siena's. "Deal." She nodded uphill. "Let's go."

They hurried to catch up with Isaac and Emmett, who'd both already reached the cirque. As Emmett looked back at them, Cam caught his bewildered expression.

"Something's wrong," Siena gasped.

As the ground leveled out and Cam gazed upon the cirque's headwall, she almost fell over.

Siena threw her bag to the ground. "What . . . the *fuck*?"

Cam steadied herself, peeling off her sunglasses and dropping her bag.

The glacier was gone.

In its place, beneath the mountain's shadow, a tarn glowed ice blue. Water trickled musically from the cliffside into the glacial lake.

Feyrer always used a nauseating amount of hyperbole when talking of Deadswitch, but maybe he hadn't always been exaggerating. This was the most beautiful thing Cam had ever seen.

"Looks like copper," said Emmett, gesturing to the colors of the headwall.

Cam stupidly nodded.

It *was* copper. A gorgeous amalgamation of teal, sea green, and umber painted the headwall. The tarn—a glacial lake filled with sediment—nestled at the headwall's base. Normally the sediment transformed glacial waters into a shock of turquoise on its own, but against the copper—even with the entire lake in the mountain's shadow—the water seemed to glow.

"It's melted." Siena wiped the hair from her face. "All of it. I thought you said you saw it!"

"I *did*." Cam gaped at the water. It must have been two or three weeks ago that she had checked the satellite images and the acres of Alpenglow ice still left on this rock. For all of it to melt since then was impossible. Either that, or a discovery larger than she'd ever expected.

As if she could read Cam's mind, Siena uttered, "This is going to be bigger for us than a little bit of PI credit."

Cam's ear rang at the same time something shifted beneath the water near the cliff's base. Not an animal—the lake's surface was far too placid.

Something else.

A shadow drew toward the surface, bleeding out darkness, pluming like ink. It infectiously leached into the aqua blue water, rumbling a question to her.

It could *speak*.

But Cam couldn't understand its language, nor interpret its urgency. The darkness pled with her, as though Cam's answer was the only thing that mattered. The only thing that had *ever* mattered.

"*Cam!*"

Cam blinked. The shadow was gone, and her legs . . . her legs were cold.

She tried to move and didn't expect the resistance around her feet, almost falling over in thigh-high turquoise water.

"What the hell are you doing?" said Emmett.

She glanced behind her. The others were still on the shore.

What the hell *was* she doing?

Cam trudged from the water as if she'd planned on entering it. "We need to get the soil cored and enough sediment for an analysis with the Chittick. Collect some water samples, but check the pH of the lake itself before we leave. And I want some of that copper . . . I don't know how we'll get it, but we will need to figure it out. Lake measurements, too."

Siena got to work right away, dropping her pack and digging through it for the right gear. But Emmett hesitated, his distrusting eyes still on Cam.

"Did I stutter?"

Emmett frowned and dropped his pack.

"And you . . ." She turned to Isaac, pushed back her hair, and frowned.

Sweat dotted his forehead, his complexion pale. He looked sick.

"That was close," he said.

"Close? To what, puking? You gonna puke?"

Isaac shook his head.

"Good. Go get me a coffee or something."

He mopped his forehead with the back of his hand. "I'm not an intern. I want to do something helpful. That's why I'm here, right?"

Cam dismissed him with a wave of her hand. "Don't be so sensitive. I need you to take a video of the lake. Hike up the ridge for a top-down view. Don't forget photos. And don't drop your phone in the water."

Isaac seemed satisfied enough with the task. As soon as he got busy, Cam returned to her bag and grabbed her field notebook and a pencil. She flipped the book open and pressed the tip of the lead to the page, but couldn't write anything.

Her hand was trembling too much.

HOLDEN

It was the first time in over a month where Holden and his roommate were both home for dinner. They made an evening of it, going to the *market* (another name for a grocery store with a hot bar and nine-dollar cartons of eggs), buying vegetables and fresh chicken neither of them could afford, and cooking all of it over their cheap electric stove. But it was worth it; Francis appreciated the meal scraps, and Holden enjoyed spending time with Lauren. And since he had nothing else exciting to talk about, he told her about the drive.

"Here's what I don't understand," said Lauren as she dried a plate. "Why do you care so much?"

Holden rinsed off a handful of forks and passed them to her. "What do you mean?"

Lauren wiped off the forks and tossed them in their unorganized utensil drawer. "I mean, yeah, those files are spooky. But what are you hoping to find?"

"I just need to figure out who the files belong to and get permission to wipe the drive. It's protocol."

"No, Holden. What are you *hoping* to find?"

Holden turned off the water, grabbed a towel from the

counter, and clinically wiped his hands as he dissected her question. "I'm hoping to find that Dupont is okay, I guess."

Lauren sat at the kitchen island and gestured to the clamshell of organic brownies they'd purchased with their dinner ingredients. "Help me eat these."

Holden sat. "I want to know what happened to all of them. Wouldn't you be curious?"

Lauren cracked open the clamshell. "I don't know. I'd be too afraid of a bad ending. Have you thought of that?"

"Well . . . yeah." Holden stole a brownie. "I guess it would suck to find out she was dead or something."

The thought made his heart sink more than he cared to admit, and it was like Lauren could tell. She smiled sadly at him. "I hope by the end of your quest, you find out she's alright."

Quest. The word was far too grandiose a description for his pathetic gumshoeing, and even though he'd only known Lauren for a couple of months, she was the type of person who cycled through the same worn shirts and two pairs of jeans every week and thought *Jeopardy!* was too dramatic. Quest was quite a theatrical word for her to use, unless she was making fun of him. Holden hoped that wasn't the case.

"Maybe it's good for you," she continued, picking at a brownie. "The distraction you need after what's-her-face."

"Becca," Holden corrected.

"Sorry. Meant nothing by it."

"It's fine." He was less irritated by her bringing up Becca than the fact she was right. He *did* need a distraction from his ex. Maybe that was all this hard drive obsession was. "It was a tough breakup. I still love her."

Holden winced after he said it. No one had asked him how he'd been since Becca broke up with him. No one cared. He had no family close by, and all his relationships in Corvallis were superficial. How pathetic of him to blurt his feelings to the first person who actually listened. Lauren of all people, his quick-fix roommate after Becca moved out. The two hadn't even met.

"What happened?" Lauren asked casually.

"She thought I was cheating on her."

Lauren's eyes flicked from her brownie to his face. "Were you?"

"I'd kill myself first."

She held up her free hand in defense. "Just asking."

An awkward silence lingered. Holden grabbed a brownie.

"I know you probably don't want to hear this," Lauren began. "But if she couldn't trust you, she isn't someone you want to spend your life with."

Holden knew that. But he also couldn't blame Becca for wanting to leave him.

"What?" Lauren asked, almost like she could tell he wanted to say something else. The whole truth. But he couldn't. He couldn't tell anyone.

"Nothing," Holden said, and shoved the brownie in his mouth.

On nights like this, when he couldn't sleep, Holden replayed a memory in his head.

A couple of months into their relationship, he and Becca had rented a vacation cottage in the middle of nowhere, eastern Oregon. They'd attempted to defy the weather forecast and go hiking—even though neither of them were hikers—and scrambled back to base when the sky started dumping rain.

They'd forfeited the cottage's wood stove for the floral sheets and worn quilt. After stripping each other, Holden had licked the rain from Becca's skin. They'd had sex. The kind of sex in poetry, the romance novel bullshit that wasn't supposed to exist in the real world. The sex you thought about later to feel a dam of heat break in your stomach and rush through every one of your nerve endings. A fucking divine, hormone-drenched high, not from the thought of her body, but from the thought of *her*.

They'd talked until the sun went down. About their childhoods, their careers, their fears of the future. About mustard being the superior condiment and how belly buttons were weird. How old music actually sucked even though people pretended to like it to seem cultured. They had talked until she fell asleep midsentence.

It was his favorite memory. And it wasn't real.

He'd believed it had been real. He'd argued with Becca until he lost his voice, not just over the memory of the cabin, but many perfect nights and conversations that had never happened. But he'd been so certain, he'd convinced Becca that his memories *had* happened. Just with another woman.

They hadn't happened with another woman. If Becca hadn't experienced those moments with Holden, then he had made all those memories up.

He needed a shrink. Too bad his health insurance sucked dick.

Holden sat up and rubbed his eyes. If sleep was going to be impossible, he'd rather not torture himself. He rolled Francis over so he could get out of bed and left his room, sitting at his computer behind the couch. On his desktop, he'd organized the files of Dr. Dupont's Deadswitch Wilderness study into stuff he'd gone through and stuff he hadn't.

He exited out of a pile of these folders, stalling on the close button of the last one. Dupont's audio files. The last time he tried listening to them, only two would play, the others sporting red exclamation marks next to the filenames to indicate corruption. But now three didn't have an exclamation mark next to them. The last recording on the list, about Isaac's burial, the first recording about the body, and the second recording, which Holden had yet to listen to.

He pored over the metadata enough times to barf, but nothing stood out as to how or why the audio was suddenly accessible. Then again, there was a reason he was the IT guy at OSU and not making a quarter of a million at some tech firm.

Holden picked up his earbuds, and double-clicked on the file.

AUDIO_99284002.WAV

"Things have been different since we visited the glacier.

"I hesitate to say bad, because they aren't bad. The loss of Alpenglow is rough, but to be honest, I feel more guilty than anything. I should mourn another melted glacier. Instead, I'm even more excited for the study.

"Just as Feyrer promised, the meltwater makeup is fascinating. There's a massive array of minerals here: calcium, magnesium, and potassium, zinc and copper from the deposits, and many more I've yet to identify. The microbial community of the sample is more diverse than one from a lower lake. There's a bacteria block party beneath the microscope right now. I won't know more until I resample at the end of our trip and submit for DNA sequencing, then compare the findings to that of Feyrer's original study. But I think we've found more than what he did all those years ago. I only wish he were with us to confirm it.

"The entire team's feeding off the energy. Isaac has spent most of his time at the cirque, sketching it for hours. But I'm wondering if we're too distracted by it. It's like we're using the glacier to forget about the body . . . especially Cam.

"If the woman we found really looked like Naomi Vo, at least now I know why she's been acting so strange. But I've brought up the body to Cam twice since the glacier, and she's changed the subject both times. We can't just pretend it never happened.

"I'm concerned we aren't doing enough . . . and that I made the wrong decision by not turning around for help back at Wolf Ridge. I've been trying the radio the past couple of nights, manually scanning for repeaters. Nothing. Not even the oldies station I picked up the first time. Though maybe that's for the better.

"Even Emmett is trying to get me off the radio and to come to bed early. I don't know what it's going to take for him to realize he no longer has power over me. Probably a freaking miracle."

SIENA

Siena clicked the stop button on the recorder, set it on the desk, and typed up a few notes on her laptop before closing out the word processor. Filling the desktop wallpaper, dressed in knee-high rubber boots and the dorkiest sun hat Siena had ever seen, Crystal Dupont candidly collected water samples from a marshy pond.

Like mother, like daughter.

Siena smiled before gazing upon the organized clutter atop the table. She'd taken over the lab room opposite the bunks. After returning the ham radio to its spot near the bay window, she'd rearranged some of the older equipment to free up space on the dual desks. Her phone, connected to its solar charger, rested in a beam of light at the table's far end.

Dr. Feyrer's original research team had been twice as large as hers. Siena couldn't imagine this tiny cabin buzzing with so much energy. Cam and Emmett were distracting enough as they ran in and out, organizing collected samples and analyzing data. Despite their constant presence, the space felt like hers. She even considered a wildflower hunt to fill an old liquor bottle she'd found in a kitchen cupboard. Maybe she'd scrub the handprint from the doorframe.

Siena shut her laptop lid and found behind it the deck of cards Isaac had been shuffling on their first night. He must have gotten distracted and forgotten them there.

She picked them up. The texture of the pack felt like parchment. Sketched on the front were songbirds perched on the antlers of a buck's skull, stylized like a tarot card.

She slid the crescent of her fingernail into the flap to open it.

Something crashed against the window.

Siena screamed, clutching her chest when Cam started laughing from the other side of the window, hand still in a fist from banging on the glass.

"Bitch," Siena yelled.

"Watch your mouth," Cam yelled back.

"You're not my mom."

"But I'm the PI."

Siena crossed her arms. "Is this my punishment for handing over my lead principal investigator title to you?"

Cam rolled her eyes. "Get your ass out here. You need to see this."

"Why?"

"Because I'm the PI," Cam and Siena said at the same time. Cam added, "And I said so."

"Now you sound like Emmett."

Cam pressed her hand to her chest and stumbled back in mock offense. "Harsh."

Siena sighed. "Fine." Dropping the deck of cards on the desk, she left the cabin and headed around back. When she arrived, she nodded at the dinged-up shovel Cam held. "Where'd you get that?"

"I have my sources." Cam pointed the shovel head to a hatchway next to the cabin. "Look what I found."

It was the first time Siena had noticed the entrance. Then again, she'd been distracted since they arrived. She approached the door and squatted, jangling the rusted chain wrapped around the handles. An equally ancient combination lock held the chain in place.

Siena brushed her thumb against one of the four dials. With a click, the number changed from 9 to 0; at least the whole thing wasn't rusted together. She rotated each dial until the visible sequence read *0824* and yanked on the lock. It didn't budge.

"Damn, I was sure that was going to work."

"What was it?" Cam asked.

"Tiffany's birthday."

"Tiffany?"

"Feyrer's daughter. He used it for everything, literally. Computers, file cabinets . . . I could have stolen everything he owned if I wanted to."

"But not the items in his secret, spooky cellar."

"He had seven other researchers with him. This isn't *his* cellar."

Cam tapped Siena's hip with the shovel. "Let me try."

Siena moved out of the way, and Cam brought the shovel down on the lock. It shattered on the fourth attempt.

"Is that how *you* steal things?" Siena asked.

Cam popped her hip and blew the bangs from her eyes. "It's how I steal hearts."

Siena snorted. "Yeah, sure. I've seen you with women."

"Hey, fuck off."

Siena shook her head and stooped to shake the rusty chain from the handles, and then she and Cam each hauled open one door.

A rickety staircase disappeared into the shadows. The entrance smelled earthy and rotten. Something chittered at them from the darkness. A bug, probably. A *big* bug. Siena rubbed the goose bumps on her arms.

"You got a flashlight?" Cam asked.

Cam nudged a moldering box with her foot. "It's all junk."

Siena held up their camp lantern, illuminating the cellar. All that kept the space from collapsing inward was cement, stacks of river rocks, and several persistent tree roots that had slithered through the cracks in the walls. It was no wonder the mountain of discolored boxes in the center of the room was about to disintegrate into mulch.

"Who hikes in a bunch of cardboard file boxes?" Siena squatted, lifting the top off the nearest one. Yellowing papers filled the box to the brim, similar to the papers she had found upstairs when they had first arrived. She picked up the top page and scrutinized it, but it was blank, just like all the others in the box.

"*The research stays in the woods,*" Cam said, repeating words Feyrer once uttered to them.

Unease filled Siena's chest. "The papers are all blank."

"Unfortunate. Hey, check it out." Cam hopped over some boxes to a rusted safe as tall as she was. "Who hikes in one of *these*?" The door squealed open as she pulled on the handle.

Siena clambered over boxes to reach Cam. Something skittered across her bicep, and she slapped it away, wincing when her arm smarted.

Cam shoved open the door the rest of the way. Three rifles and a shotgun sat on their butts inside the safe, two pistols hanging from the safe door. A nasty-looking spiderweb covered a few stacks of ammo and a case of cigarettes on the top shelf.

"I can't tell you how many times I've read through the original study and its proposal." Siena poked one of the pistols. "I saw none of this in the equipment lists. What were they planning on shooting? Bears?" Dr. Feyrer had been a soft-spoken vegetarian, and she couldn't imagine him loading up this gun safe. Then again, she'd never met the other researchers. They'd all left academia after the study.

Siena should have sought them out after Feyrer had died. Asked if they knew of a good reason he would have suddenly wanted her to cancel the expedition. Perhaps then she would have been able to write off his dying wish.

Don't go.

Cam pulled out the shotgun and flipped it around. "Safety's off." She checked the chamber. "Not loaded."

"How do you know how to do that?" Siena asked with a flinch. She hated guns.

"The same way I know how to smoke those." Cam nodded toward the carton of cigarettes. "Finest woman I ever knew taught me both."

"A girlfriend?"

"My grandma. Wanna have a go?"

Siena made a face. "I'm sure your grandma was great and all, but hell no."

Fifteen minutes later, Cam had fetched whiskey from upstairs and returned, and they sat against the wall near the stairs with a wayward root and the bottle between them. Siena sucked on the worst thing she'd ever put in her mouth.

"This is terrible," she coughed.

"They're stale, darling." Cam inhaled, the cherry of her cigarette burning red. "Not too bad if you can get over the rotten aftertaste." She lifted her head and blew out smoke.

Siena dry heaved and stubbed out her cigarette on the cellar floor. She uncorked the bottle and drank, sloshing the whiskey around her mouth. She swallowed and cleared her throat. "So . . ."

"So," Cam repeated, resting the back of her head against the wall.

"You still seeing that chick . . . what's her name? Linda?"

Cam scoffed. "Linda? I'm not dating a fifty-year-old. Lauren."

"Lauren, right."

"And no, I stopped seeing her months ago. Jesus, you're my best friend."

"Don't blame me," Siena said with another cough. "The only way I can pry details of your love life from you is when you're drunk."

"Ah, well . . ." Cam shrugged. "I guess I need to work on my divulging skills."

"Sure do." Siena took a second swig of whiskey and winced. "What happened?"

"Your average dating bullshit. Stopped texting, and things fizzled out. Probably my fault . . . been feeling listless for a while."

They settled into an awkward silence. Cam scuffed her foot against the ground. It was time to follow through with their pinkie promise.

"Checking in. Are you okay?" Siena asked.

"Dandy. Time heals all casual-relationship wounds."

"I mean, are you okay, *now*? You know, with the glacier . . . and the Naomi thing."

"There is no Naomi thing." Cam stubbed her cigarette out next to Siena's. "The dead woman wasn't Naomi. My brain was trying to force closure on something that happened seven years ago."

"And yet every time I bring up the body, you change the subject." Siena rolled her head toward Cam. The camp lantern cast shadows across Cam's face, but didn't hide her hard expression. Cam was shutting her out—*again*—and Siena didn't know why.

"Don't you think we have a moral obligation to do something about it?" Siena asked.

"We *are* doing something about it," Cam snapped. "We both left the sheriff messages, and I reported the body to that dumbfuck ranger. You've been on the radio every damn night. I don't know what else we're supposed to do other than end the trip. I mean, we got our samples, so maybe that would be best at this point. Is that what you want?"

Siena didn't understand why she was getting so upset. "Are you mad at me?"

Cam rubbed her face and sighed. "I'm . . . No. I'm not. I just don't get why this is happening to us. Our map is wrong, we find a dead girl, we have shit luck calling out for help, and then she disappears, and then we have more shit luck with the radio. And now thirty-five acres of glacier has melted in the time it took us to hike this mountain. We're dealing with a bizarre string of events, or . . ." Cam hesitated.

Siena *hated* the way she hesitated, and hated even more that the same connections had been threading themselves together in her own brain. Everything they'd done so far on this trip had an asterisk next to it, but none of the annotations made any sense when pieced together.

"Or what?" Siena asked.

Cam turned toward Siena. "The universe is telling us to hike the hell off this mountain."

So that was it . . . Cam feared their misfortune. But she wasn't superstitious. "You don't believe in signs from the universe."

"I know." The corners of Cam's lips perked up. "And that's why I keep convincing myself we need to stay."

Something crawled up Siena's wrist, and she smacked at it.

Cam's smile vanished, her eyes widening.

Siena rubbed her wrist. "Don't look at me like that."

"Now it's my turn. Are *you* okay?" Cam asked.

"It was a spider or something. Stop acting like Emmett."

"Stop telling me I'm acting like Emmett, because you know very well that bastard and I are completely different."

Siena didn't want to admit she was only trying to deflect. Luckily, she didn't have to.

Siena pointed at the ground. A hairy spider skittered between the camp lantern and the whiskey.

Cam's shoulders sagged.

"I'm fine," said Siena. "I'd tell you if I wasn't."

Cam nodded, but she didn't look convinced.

Meet me in the briardark beneath the moon we will embark—

DON'T. GO.

Siena lifted her foot and brought it down again, smashing the spider with the heel of her boot.

EMMETT

"What's up with you and Siena?" asked Isaac as he and Emmett hiked back to the cabin from Alpenglow.

It was late. Emmett was tired and regretting not taking the whiskey with them. He hated answering questions about Siena when he was sober.

He kicked a loose rock. It bounced down the rest of the granite slope and disappeared into the forest. "What do you mean?"

"I don't know. You're weird together."

Emmett almost laughed. Luckily, Isaac was behind him and couldn't see his face. "Is that so?"

"She your ex?"

"You could say that."

"I mean, either she is, or she isn't."

This little shit.

The shock of orange across the western range was tenuous, and Emmett slowed, fishing his headlamp out of his daypack to avoid answering a question far more complicated than *is* or *isn't*. There were high school sweethearts. A college girlfriend who lasted a handful of months before growing bored with him. There was the Greek girl he had followed around Europe after his undergrad. Those were the exes Isaac meant, not an ex like Siena.

"Do *you* have exes?" Emmett asked.

"I have mistakes," Isaac said.

Emmett had guessed as much. Isaac was old enough to have mistakes, but not old enough to have fucked up a seasoned relationship as deeply as Emmett had.

Emmett pushed a branch out of the way as they dipped into the grove of pines between the incline and the cabin. "Want advice?"

"Uhh, sure?"

"Don't get engaged until you've gotten all those *mistakes* out of your system."

Emmett could sense a thousand questions boiling up inside the kid, and braced for something else related to Siena.

"Why'd you go corporate?"

Somehow, this was worse. But at least Emmett could answer honestly. "Money."

"That's . . . that's it?" Isaac's voice brimmed with disappointment.

I'm not a role model, kid, Emmett wanted to say, but bit his tongue and thought up a more gracious answer. "I get that you're aspirational. And I think it's great . . . really. Being a scientist is hard. But sometimes, work is just work. It's how you afford the things you really care about."

Or how you lose the things you care about. But Emmett would leave that part out.

He looked up and stopped short. Isaac ran into him.

The mountains swallowed the last dregs of sunlight, and all Emmett could see were shadows. But one stood out to the left of the path, just beyond the range of his light—a dark, nebulous patch between the trees.

"Do you see that?" asked Emmett.

Isaac stepped around him and craned his neck. "See what?"

Emmett blinked several times, but the shadow was still there, stone-still and hovering five or so feet off the ground. As he stepped off the trail, his pant leg caught on underbrush. He startled before kicking it away and creeping deeper.

A trick of the light. The tension eased in his chest. He just needed to confirm nothing was really there.

"Where are you going?"

Emmett held his hand out, motioning Isaac to stay. He carefully maneuvered over tree roots and chokecherry. The shadow retreated just beyond his light. His vision wasn't playing tricks on him; the shape was far too dark—onyx against the night—like someone had thrown a bucket of black paint against an invisible wall.

Emmett took another step, and then another, quickening his pace until he was jogging through the woods. He tripped over young growth and punched the taller shrubs out of his way. He'd reach the damn thing if it was the last thing he did.

And then the shadow stopped. Emmett didn't.

A blinding mist washed over his face and arms. Emmett stumbled to a halt as his headlamp flickered out. His inner ear sang, the mist hitting the back of his throat when he tried to breathe. His cough was silent; he could hear nothing but the dizzying shriek that grew until he thought his head was going to split open.

A strange sensation filled his abdomen. It felt like an emotion, like guilt—a deeply rooted guilt he had only experienced once before, right after Siena left him. That guilt had almost killed him then, and now . . .

The shriek died. Emmett choked down air, coughing and sputtering. With his hands on his knees, he caught his breath and shivered. The light from his headlamp wavered against the bare dirt.

He touched his face. His skin was cold, but dry. Whatever he had charged into had evaporated.

What a trip. Something this weird hadn't happened to him since he was young and stupid and thought experimenting with salvia was a good idea. And even then . . .

He moved his head upward, following the light as it cascaded over a gnarled tree trunk. The bark was smoother than the scaly foxtail pines surrounding the cabin, the tree itself as massive as a cypress. But giants didn't survive at this altitude, not with the wind as it was.

Something crashed through the woods behind him. "Dude, what the hell?" Isaac called.

What the hell was right.

Emmett caught a flicker of movement near his feet. He dragged his eyes down the trunk, just as the shadow disappeared into a hollow.

HOLDEN

"Where you going?" Angel asked as Holden packed up his stuff. She leaned back in her broken chair, chewing on a Twizzler as she tied up her dark ringlets in a bun. She'd finished her work hours ago, but had stuck around the office. Holden had assumed it was because she didn't want to clock out early, but at some point, fifteen bucks an hour wasn't worth sticking around for.

Holden slung his backpack over his arm. "I have a meeting with Dr. Chari."

Angel nodded as she chewed.

". . . Why are you staring at me?" asked Holden.

She shrugged. "Want company?"

He raised an eyebrow, threading his arm through the other strap of his bag. "I thought you hated being around me."

Angel waved her hand in dismissal. "Hate is a strong word."

"You've literally told me, '*I can't stand you, go jump off a bridge.*'"

"Humor is a fine art, Holden. I wouldn't expect you to appreciate my wit and charm."

"I don't know how exciting this is going to be," Holden admitted. "I think Dr. Chari just likes the fact I'm listening to her."

"I thought she said she never wanted to meet your ugly face. Why does she suddenly want you to listen to her?"

"She didn't . . . That's not . . ." Holden sighed. "Don't you have better things to do than follow me around campus and insult me?"

"Not today. I'm getting a divorce, and my ex is cleaning his stuff out of the apartment. I'm trying to avoid the place."

Holden frowned. "You're too young for a divorce."

Angel stood and dropped her phone in her purse. "Hate to break it to you, but you're not the only loser in their thirties stuck in this crummy job. I just have better skin than you." She sauntered past him, opening the door of the office. "So tell me more about this sciencey mystery of yours."

Holden caught Angel up on the Dupont saga as they walked to the Forest Science Complex. He even mentioned Dupont's last recording.

"Other than the trees and their superspawn, the creepiest thing is the whole bit about the dead hiker." Angel shuddered. "This is why I don't camp."

"I googled Naomi Vo." Holden held the door open for Angel. "She'd be our age if she were still alive. The study isn't as old as I thought."

"The plot thickens." Angel rubbed her hands together. "This is much more exciting than arguing with my ex over who keeps the Egyptian cotton bedsheets."

The inside of the Forest Science Complex smelled like the woods, which felt eerie, given why they were here. Holden pulled up the email from Dr. Chari on his phone. "Four-B. Is that the basement level?"

Angel pointed to a door marked *Stairs*. "Are you sure she isn't planning on killing you?"

Holden *wasn't* sure; he didn't really know her, after all. Angel had been right back in the office—his brief interactions with Chari didn't add up. She'd been near-threatening at first. Maybe it was a defense mechanism, since her old institution hadn't taken her work seriously.

But she was his only lead. CalTech still hadn't called him back, which likely meant they didn't need Dr. Dupont's data. And the closer Holden got to this thing, the more he felt like an outsider.

The other night, Lauren had asked him why he cared so much, and he'd given her a half answer because he didn't have a good one. The mystery of the drive distracted him from the pathetic fact he needed to get his life together, and he didn't think he'd feel otherwise after today.

Maybe it was time to hand the drive over to his boss. This was all above his pay grade, anyway.

They descended into the basement. The door to 4B was cracked open, and the lights were off when Holden and Angel entered. Stacked desks and chairs lined the walls. In the center, on a cart, a projector hummed—an ancient one with the carousel wheel and photo slides the size of a thumb. It was on and warmed up, shining an empty square against the front wall.

Dressed in slacks and a button-up shirt, Dr. Chari casually sat on top of a desk with her laptop, typing away.

She glanced up and nodded toward Angel. "Who's she?"

"A coworker following me around to avoid her ex-husband," said Holden.

"Way to air my dirty laundry," Angel muttered.

Chari frowned. "I wasn't expecting guests."

"I . . . uhh . . . was with Holden when he brought the drive into IT." Angel jutted her chin. "You can say I'm helping him."

Holden rolled his eyes.

Chari looked unimpressed, but didn't tell Angel to leave. Instead, she slid off the desk and handed Holden her open laptop. "Found your girl."

Holden dropped his bag and took the laptop from her, setting it on a nearby desk. He sat and read the article title.

Caltech Researchers Awarded Funding to Return to Alpenglow Glacier.

The caption of the first photo read: *From left to right: Emmett Ghosh, Dr. Cameron Yarrow, Dr. Siena Dupont, Dr. Wilder Feyrer.*

It was a casual photo from the field. The four of them stood crowded together, backdropped by a mountain vista. The older man, Dr. Feyrer, was the one taking the selfie, looking sharp in a Sierra Club hat and neon Croakies. He seemed happy.

They all seemed *so* happy. And the other three—they were nothing like Holden had imagined.

What *had* he imagined? Withered dorks in khakis and tucked-in t-shirts, sort of like Dr. Feyrer? Holden had even heard Dupont speak, but he hadn't expected a bright-eyed woman with a gap between her front teeth and her hair in two braids. He hadn't expected someone his age. And Cameron and Emmett—they couldn't have been much older, if older at all. Cameron was thin, boyish and tan. She looked like she'd been laughing. She and Siena were both white. Emmett was Indian and Abercrombie-handsome, the type of guy you'd find on a football field, not in a lab.

Holden skimmed the article. There was no mention of an Isaac Perez. The article dated from four years ago, which meant the study wasn't old at all. Between then and now, Isaac had joined the team and died during the expedition.

Angel slid behind Holden. "Ohhh, I get why you care about all this, now. That Dr. Dupont is cute."

Holden regretted letting Angel tag along, even though she was onto something. In a strange way, Siena reminded him of Becca. Same eyes, he concluded. Maybe their face shape. But it didn't matter—Holden wasn't here to pine after Dr. Dupont. "This is the first time I've ever seen her."

"Cute girls have cute voices."

He ignored her and looked up at Dr. Chari. "You're sure you don't know them?"

"I knew Wilder, the older gentleman. Just learned he passed away from cancer, sadly. He contacted me several years ago, after I was pulled off my Deadswitch study. Wanted to compare my cell samples to his own findings a couple of decades prior."

"I thought they were geologists, or something." Holden stood from the desk. "They were studying a glacier. Why would they care about your cell samples?"

"Geo*morpho*logists." Dr. Chari approached the projector and began fiddling with it. "They study the topography of the earth, but also the processes that affect it, including the biological ones. Wilder had taken an interest in some of the old growth on Mount Agnes—trees with root systems uncommon for the area. He found cellular anomalies—as did I."

Dr. Chari advanced the slides until the microscopic image of a cell cluster projected onto the wall. Even given the old analog machine, the image was sharp and detailed, the cells the size of basketballs.

"These cells are from my samples of the lodgepole xylem tissue—the wood that matured in forty-eight hours. Notice anything?"

Holden studied the cells, wondering if his brain could dredge up something that would make him seem smarter than he was. "I barely passed biology," he finally admitted.

"I thought plant cells were supposed to look different," Angel said. "More like bricks, or something."

"Perhaps leaf or vegetable skin patterns," Chari said. "But xylem has a structure made up of mostly long, dead cells that transport minerals and water to the rest of the tree."

"I take it these aren't those cells," said Holden.

"No. Instead, these cells have a similar structure to live plant cells: cell walls, cytoplasm, nuclei, et cetera. But if you look here—come closer. Do you see that fine fuzz around the cell?"

Holden could see it, but just barely. The fuzz reminded him of eyelashes or feathers.

"Those are cilia," she said. "Plant cells don't have cilia."

"What kind of cells have cilia?"

"Animal."

Holden tore his eyes from the screen to stare at her. Dr. Chari stared back.

"What the hell does *that* mean?" asked Holden.

"I don't know what it means, but I'm certain of its connection to Dr. Feyrer's research. We were on the brink of a discovery that would have changed our rudimentary understanding of life. Then I was pulled, and the project lost its funding," Chari bitterly concluded.

Holden recalled the last recording in the file list—the one he'd listened to first.

I scraped some of it off me and ran the cells beneath the scope. Something's not right with them.

SIENA

A few years before Deadswitch, Siena, Cam, Emmett, and Dr. Feyrer were on an expedition to collect samples at Garnet Lake in Ansel Adams. Siena busied herself with prepping equipment when they arrived, like she always did, but Dr. Feyrer stole the test tube from her hand.

"Stop acting like you shouldn't have earned your PhD." He pointed to the stump near the water. "Sit."

Feyrer didn't so much as give Cam and Emmett a second glance as they checked the barologger left by a previous group. He held Siena to a higher standard than the rest of his mentees, but he had never blatantly insulted her before.

Siena crossed her arms and glared at him. "Good thing my PhD isn't something you can take away."

"What are you doing wrong?" he asked.

She refused to answer. "I'm not your student anymore."

He smiled. "You will always be a student, as will I."

Siena took a deep breath and focused on not rolling her eyes.

Feyrer gestured to the stump again. "Sit."

Siena sat. He plopped on the ground next to her, groaning as he did so. Feyrer was in his midsixties and could charge up a mountain as easily as the rest of them, but hinted at his aches and pains from minor tasks.

"How many times have you been to this lake?" he asked.

Siena shrugged. "Five, six."

"And what is it trying to tell you this time?"

"Well, I was prepping for samples until you—"

"Don't poke and prod it, Siena. *Look* at it."

She sighed and gazed out at the lake.

The first time she'd ever visited Garnet Lake, she was seventeen.

Her mother had died a few months before.

Siena had signed up for the Young Environmentalists program, her last-ditch attempt at capturing what was left of her mother in this world and clinging to it. She'd never been allowed on Crystal Dupont's conservationist outings. The Young Environmentalists trip was all Siena had.

She'd spent most of the trip by herself, sitting in wildflower banks, swimming in the clearest waters she'd ever seen in her life, and crying. Cradled between jutting alpine ridges, the lake was surreal in its beauty—as though enchanted—and she'd tapped into grief in a way she hadn't been able to back home.

But sitting with Feyrer, she no longer felt so enamored of it. The water was cloudier. Algae bloom covered the far shore, where the wildflowers had grown all those years ago.

"The lake is sick," she stated. It was a fundamentally unscientific statement, but a true one.

Feyrer was right. She'd been so focused on the samples that she hadn't noticed something growing where it hadn't before.

"I want you to know Emmett told me about your recent struggles."

Surprised, Siena turned to Feyrer. Her cheeks flushed with embarrassment.

"It was wrong of him to tell me," Feyrer continued. "Your illness is a part of *your* story, not his. He'll learn eventually."

Siena's eyes burned. "Please don't pity me."

"I don't," he said with a smile. "You're undeserving of pity, Siena, which is how I know you're strong enough for Deadswitch. Just promise me you'll let me know what you need, and I'll be there."

Emmett woke the entire team at the crack of dawn. With a duffel of scaling gear hanging from his shoulder, he summoned them outside and through the woods to present to Siena and Cam what he and Isaac had found last night.

What would Wilder Feyrer think of you? Siena gazed up at the primeval giant.

An ashen trunk stretched between the waxy needle crown and the tapered base of knobby fingers. Siena counted thirty paces around its perimeter, almost running into Emmett.

"It looks like a swamp cypress," he said. "Maybe someone planted it here as an experiment and it took root."

"But that's impossible, right?" Siena approached the tree and rested her hand against the peeling bark. "If any environment is the complete opposite of a South Carolina marsh, it's here."

"Well, it's definitely not a sequoia. I brought some gear to scale the thing for canopy samples, but looking at it now, I don't think we can safely climb it." Emmett shielded his eyes and craned his neck upward. "It's too tall."

"Weird how nothing's growing around it." Cam circled the tree from a distance as she sipped at the mug in her hand. "No undergrowth beneath the canopy. The pines aren't crowding it, either."

"How did you find it?" Siena asked Emmett.

Emmett didn't answer right away, and Siena turned to Isaac, who sat at the edge of the clearing with his sketchbook open.

Isaac shrugged. "Dude took off after something in the woods. I didn't see what it was."

Siena returned her attention to Emmett. "Are you the *dude* in this scenario?"

"It was an animal," said Emmett.

It was unlike Emmett to act so impulsively. "What kind of animal? And why would you take off after it?"

"I don't know," he snapped at her, and threw his hand in the tree's direction. "All I know is it disappeared into that hole before I could see what it was."

Siena followed his extended finger to a fissure in the tree's knobby base. She left Emmett's side and squatted near his duffel, rifling through climbing equipment until she found a flashlight.

When she approached the tree, he said her name in a familiar warning. Cam had aptly titled this tone "Emmett's Dad Call," in which *Siena* actually meant *Siena Ivy Dupont, don't you even think about it.*

"Oh, relax." Siena lowered herself to her knees next to the hollow.

"If anything, she'll discover the Lost City of Marmots," Cam drawled. Siena snorted.

Emmett huffed as he joined them. "It wasn't a marmot."

"You aren't giving us a lot of clues to work with," Cam shot back.

"Children," Siena muttered, clicking on her light and shining it into the hollow.

Emmett Dad-called her again. To spite him, she sat on the ground and stuck her head into the hole, propping the light beneath her chin.

She blinked a few times to filter through the darkness, but there was nothing. The entire inside of the tree was cavernous, the inner walls onyx and smooth like petrified wood. At the back of the cavity, tucked between a few exposed roots, was an entrance to a burrow. If Emmett had seen an animal, then this was likely its home, though the start of the channel was bizarrely smooth and straight. She felt like she was shining a light down someone's esophagus.

Siena pulled her head out of the tree's innards. Cam and Emmett stood next to her, both with their arms crossed. Neither looked pleased with the other.

"There's a burrow," Siena said. "Probably big enough for me to crawl through. I want to see if it's a habitat."

Emmett shook his head. "Absolutely not."

"I could get a xylem and root sample while I'm in there, since we don't have a borer. We need to bring something back to a dendrologist."

"We can take pictures, instead. Bark and needle samples."

Siena shrugged dramatically. "Sure, we can do that too. Let's do all of it. There's a slim chance this growth is at all related to the Alpenglow melt, but the more data we have, the more we'll know."

"And what if the tunnel collapses on you?"

"You'll dig me out."

"And if we can't reach you?"

"Then I guess I'll die, Emmett."

Cam covered her mouth with her hand to block her smile.

Emmett turned on Cam. "You think this is funny?"

Cam dropped her hand. "I think you have a stick up your ass. Siena is an intelligent and capable adult who can make her own decisions."

Emmett sneered at her. Siena knew he was mere seconds from losing his cool, but too smart to do so. Devolving into anger wouldn't win him any points.

"Then I'll do it. I'll go in and get the samples," he said.

Siena cocked her head at him. She wasn't naïve. Emmett was only saying this to maintain control over the situation, but she also knew he was trying to compromise because he still cared about her.

"You won't fit," she said.

He released a grunt of frustration and stomped away from them, scratching the back of his head. "I don't like this."

"Of course you don't." Cam retreated to the duffel bag,

digging through it until she procured a climbing harness, a couple of carabiners, and a long coil of rope. She brought the gear over to Siena. "So Emmett can keep track of you." She winked.

Siena stood and climbed into the harness. "Do you think I'm being an idiot?"

"I think you're being stubborn." Cam clipped a carabiner to the back of the harness. "Which I fully support. Do I think you're going to find anything more than a few nasty bugs? Probably not." She circled back to Siena's front and adjusted the harness buckles. "But it's worth exploring. That's why we're up here, after all."

"We're here for the glacier," Siena said, almost as a reflex.

Cam met her eyes. "The glacier. Right."

Cautious intrigue swept over Siena, tethered to a memory—a warm, quiet bar on a rare rainy evening in wine country. The old man muttering stories over too many pints of English ale.

"Feyrer was drunk that night," Siena said.

"I'm not arguing that." Cam released Siena's harness and lifted her pinkie. "Don't get bitten by a marmot, okay? Those things carry rabies, and I don't want to hike your ass out."

Siena glanced back at Emmett, who stood near Isaac and watched her from the back of the clearing. He frowned, keeping his eyes on her like he used to. When he loved her.

He still loved her, but that didn't mean she had to tend to his every concern.

Siena hooked her pinkie with Cam's and then fixed her headlamp in place. She checked her pockets for her knife, recorder, and the sample tubes. Kneeling to meet the hollow, Siena tilted sideways and wriggled through the opening.

Once in the tree, she pressed her palms to the earth, inching forward until her hips were through the fissure. The damp ground smelled of decay and lichen, not the dust and pine she'd grown accustomed to over the past week. She took a sample and pocketed the vial, then squeezed between the thick roots into the burrow. Her pocket chirped as she wriggled around and set off every button on her recorder. She'd worry about that later.

"You okay, Doc?" Cam called, shining her own light into the entrance.

"I'd tell you if I wasn't," Siena sang.

The passage sloped downward, and once she passed the initial cluster of roots, she could push up to her hands and knees as the tunnel fanned wider. She couldn't imagine any marmot large or meticulous enough to create such an artery.

"What do you see?" This time it was Emmett. He had ceased his pouting to rejoin Cam near the hollow's entrance.

Siena squinted down the tunnel's throat. "Nothing, yet. Give me some slack so I can push forward a little."

"Be careful!"

"Yeah, yeah," Siena whispered. The tension on her belt lessened as Cam fed her more rope.

As she crawled deeper, blood pulsed in her ears. She felt no different—no dizziness or change in pressure. No fear. But her heartbeat grew louder until it echoed through her skull.

She held two fingers to her neck. Her own heartbeat carried a separate rhythm, its thrum divorced from the thudding she heard. As the beat thundered, Siena sat up to orient herself, reaching upward for balance. No sooner had she pressed her hand against the passage than she jerked it back.

An icy chill washed through her blood, and the ghost of a heartbeat lingered against her palm.

The noise wasn't coming from her. It was coming from the earth.

SIENA

"There are many things I haven't told you about the Deadswitch expeditions." Wilder Feyrer's finger circled the rim of his half-empty pint. "We spent so little time at the actual glacier. The study . . . well, the study was a ruse." He laughed at this declaration. "I can't believe we were never found out."

Siena had stayed distracted through the conversation's devolution. Emmett's hand had inched higher on her thigh. Beautiful raindrops streaked the dark window near their booth, toying with the pub's dim light. They'd just finished up a conference and had gone somewhere to let loose and celebrate their funding. Now she was drunk, far too drunk for stories or science, but the old man opened like a faucet every time he had a couple of beers in him.

Wilder's confession caught her attention. Emmett's hand froze on her thigh. Even Cam glanced up from her phone.

"What does that even mean?" Siena asked.

The reflection of the table's candle flickered on Wilder's glasses. "There were anomalies on Mount Agnes far more important than Alpenglow. But we had to keep the research a secret, or the university would have pulled our funding."

"Okay." Cam began stacking the empty pint glasses. "I'm cutting you off."

Wilder placed a hand on her arm, stopping her. "This is important."

Cam sat back and cast a look of reluctance at Siena.

"I told you Deadswitch will change your lives, but I don't think you understand how much."

"You said the prestige of a *study* will change our lives," Cam said.

"I—I don't get it." Siena leaned forward. "What exactly are you getting us into?"

Wilder shook his head. "The research stays in the woods. We don't discuss it unless we're there. I made the mistake of divulging once. Never again."

Don't go.

The tunnel vibrated beneath Siena as she crawled deeper into the darkness and the endless dirt throat of the tunnel, the heartbeat thudding in her ears. She pled with herself to turn around, but the second she lifted her hand, the tunnel summoned her forward once more.

"What did you get us into, Wilder?" she whispered.

She was close. Close to something. A secret, just out of reach. She couldn't have been less than a hundred feet deep, but she hadn't run out of rope. It wasn't possible. Cam would have stopped her at the end of the line.

"How deep am I?" she yelled over her shoulder.

Thuthump . . . thuthump . . . thuthump . . . thuthump . . .

"Cam!"

Thuthump . . . thuthump . . . thuthump . . . thuthump . . .

"CAM!"

Fear ate at the edges of her nerves. Sweat dripped past her temples, and she shut her eyes to clear her head and think.

Just turn around. Turn around, you idiot.

Siena opened her eyes.

A dirt-clotted root dangled in front of her. Beyond, the tunnel's ceiling swept upward into a wall of river rock and cement. About five feet up the rocks had crumbled, leaving an opening.

Grit dug into her knees and the flesh of her palms, the ground no longer smooth. The air reeked of mildew and rot, but the smell was familiar. It reminded her of the cellar.

It can't be.

She crawled to the tunnel's end and grabbed on to the bottom of the hole in the wall, lifting herself until she was eye level with the cellar's floor. She and Cam must have missed this opening in the wall when they were here yesterday.

"I've reached the cabin!" Siena yelled, listening for a response. None came, but the heartbeat was gone. The muscles in her chest relaxed.

She couldn't hear Cam, but maybe Cam could hear her.

"I'm gonna unclip!" she yelled. "I'll meet you back at the tree!"

She unfastened the carabiner from her harness, clipped it to a rebar jutting from the concrete, and found a leg up into the cellar. Crawling through the hole in the wall, Siena shimmied on her belly across the floor until she was out of the tunnel. She stood, brushing herself off.

She needed to hurry back to the tree, in case Cam and Emmett hadn't heard her. If they pulled back a loose rope, Emmett would flip his shit, and neither of them would forgive her —or let her do anything like this again.

Siena jogged up the stairs and punched open the cellar doors. A spray of mist coated her face, the sky the color of waning twilight. Strange—it had been a sunny morning. A cap cloud must have settled on the mountain in the past fifteen minutes.

She started heading toward the tree, and then stopped and spun, her eyes flicking across the trees in the surrounding forest. Panic burned in her fingertips.

Something was wrong. No . . . not just one thing. *Everything* was wrong.

The trees were much older than she remembered, moss dripping from gnarled limbs. Between the elders, the forest was utterly dense with young pine, spruce, maple, and hemlock. Dozens of saplings burst from the decay of fallen trees, the air rich with rot and soil and life.

And the sun—the sun was *setting*.

Where the hell was she?

Beads of mist dripped down her face as she ran to the other side of the cabin and along the porch. She grasped on to the doorknob and froze. Scrawling olive text covered the plaque on the wall.

THE WAY BACK

Siena reached out and touched it, then rubbed her fingers together. The paint was wet.

Every cell inside her screamed to return to the tunnel, but how could she leave amid this phenomenon? She was a scientist because she searched relentlessly for answers. Here, she was on the brink of discovery, and nothing made sense. She needed to understand what the hell was going on.

She pushed open the door.

Wood creaked beneath her feet as her eyes darted around the front room and the kitchen. Avocado-green curtains covered the windows. The utility sink stood between the stove and the counter. A few things were scattered atop the slab table's surface.

As she drew closer, she identified an unfurled map, its corners pinned down by a collection of items—a pair of old binoculars with a leather strap, a jar of water, the deck of cards with the songbirds on the buck's skull, and a tarnished lighter.

Siena ran her fingers over the map's illustration of a forested valley and surrounding range. The paper was worn and weathered. Old water stains blurred once-meticulous sketches of trees, structures, and peaks. Someone had drawn the entire map by hand.

She glanced up at the map's title.

The Briardark

She yanked her hand from the map and clenched her fingers to keep them from trembling. The mist, the trees, the paint. The Briardark, just like the song from the radio. She was incapable of comprehending whatever this was, like an infant desperately trying to understand language.

Siena left the kitchen and crept down the hall, pushing open the lab door.

The window was boarded up so tightly that no light penetrated the space. Siena's headlamp beam floated across the wall as she turned toward the back of the room.

A strangled cry escaped her throat. She grasped blindly for the doorknob, clutching on to it before her knees gave out.

Hunting knives pinned a severed mule head to the wall, its eyes and tongue carved out. Blood ran from its mouth, dripping into a metal bucket on the floor.

Someone else was in the cabin, someone with enough depravity inside them to mutilate an animal and paint a message across the wall in its blood.

THE MOTHER REIGNS

GetoutgetoutgetoutgetoutGETOUTGETOUT—

It felt like decades before her body registered the message from her brain. Siena coaxed herself backward, out of the room, and into the hallway.

"*You shouldn't be here.*"

She whipped her head toward the deep, muffled voice. A tall figure stood between her and the back of the cabin, their hulking form wrapped in a hooded coat. A Soviet-era gas mask covered their face. She saw nothing behind the clouded lenses and snout-like filter.

GETOUTGETOUTGETOUT—

But she couldn't. She couldn't so much as lift a foot, her petrified body betraying her. The figure took a step toward her, and then another, lifting a glove-covered finger to touch her cheek.

"*You aren't strong enough.*"

She tried to say something, but her voice died beneath a wave of tremors.

"*It will fight to keep you here. Drag you deeper. You can't let it.*"

He dropped his hand.

"PROMISE ME."

The spell broke. Siena stumbled back and spun, nearly tripping as she bolted through the hall and out of the cabin. She halted, heart thundering, headlamp beam wildly bouncing between the darkness and the trees.

Siena held her breath as a visceral rumble stirred from deep within the woods, vibrating the ground beneath her. *Hunger*. It sounded like hunger. And the hunger wanted *her*.

She sprinted around the cabin to the open cellar door, taking the steps two at a time until she fell down the rest of the staircase and skidded across the floor. She crawled to the hole and swung her feet around, dropping into the tunnel.

The rope and carabiner were where she'd left them. She willed her panicked fingers to work the latch, snapped the rope to her harness, and crawled as fast as she could through the passage.

Thuthump . . . thuthump . . . thuthump . . . thuthump . . .

As the passage narrowed, her light flashed across an insect skittering along the tunnel floor as a second darted between her fingers. She ripped her hand from the ground with a cry.

Thuthump . . . thuthump . . . thuthump . . . thuthump . . .

A beetle fluttered into her face. As she stopped to slap it away, a chittering whir crescendoed above the heartbeat.

Bugs. Thoraxes and spines popping and snapping. The hiss of intimidation of the glistening roil of insects in front of her.

THUTHUMP.

The beetles scattered, surrounding her in a black-shelled swarm. Buzzing wings and crunching exoskeletons clouded the air, sheathed the ground, dripped in strings from the tunnel ceiling.

Siena opened her mouth to scream. A beetle landed on her lower lip, and she smacked it off her face, yanking her fingers through her hair and ripping another from her braid.

It didn't matter—there were more. Thousands more, their legs twitching against her skull, wings beating in the tangles of her hair. They crawled down her shirt and under the hem of her pants. They clogged the artery before her, roiling waves of screeching insects building a living wall to block her way out.

It will fight to keep you here. Drag you deeper.

Her brain. Her *delusional* brain was fighting to keep her here. Trap her. Just like it had before. And these delusions . . . they'd taken everything from her once. This manifestation of paranoia. These bugs. They'd stolen her sanity. Her job. Her fucking fiancé.

Never again.

A scream tore from Siena's mouth as she launched herself forward and through the beetles.

CAMERON

Cam shone the flashlight into the tree hollow. Other than Siena's rope disappearing into darkness, she saw nothing else.

Emmett must have decided angsting next to Isaac wasn't everything he'd hoped for, and came hulking back. It wasn't worth the elbow fight needed to keep her spot near the tree, so Cam stepped back and let Emmett crowd the space—his version of manspreading.

"What do you see?" he shouted into the hole. So subtle.

"Nothing, yet," Siena called back. "Give me some slack so I can push forward a little."

Emmett turned toward Cam. "Don't—"

She let out the rope. "You need to relax."

"Be careful!" Emmett shouted.

Cam sighed and turned toward Isaac at the edge of the clearing. The kid's mouth hung open as he gaped upward at the tree, but Cam couldn't tell if it was because he was surprised, about to say something, or totally spaced out.

Isaac finally snapped out of it and returned to his sketchbook, scribbling intently.

"Shit," Emmett hissed, sticking his head into the hole. "I can't see her. She's too deep."

Cam held up the rope as it slowly slid through her hand. "At least we know she's alive."

"That means nothing."

"For fuck's sakes, Emmett. Go take a soil sample, will you?"

"Someone has to watch her, and you're distracted."

"By *what*?"

"You're always goofing off, Cameron."

She tilted her head back and laughed at him. "Is it cathartic for you to control everything all the time? Is that why you're not sitting pretty at your cushy corporate job right now?"

"COtwo sponsored half this trip. Don't forget it."

She hated the way he said *coh-two* like a tech bro, and she hated even more that he made four times the amount of money she did—though she'd never sell out to a bunch of carbon capture goons in Silicon Valley. Emmett didn't even have the decency to finish his PhD.

"We shouldn't have applied for that funding." Cam sat back against the tree. This conversation was tiring her. "Not worth managing the conflict of interest."

"Didn't think you'd be one to put your ego above the environment."

She shook her head. "God, you're such a shill."

"*Excuse* me?"

"Your bosses are trying to monetize carbon—they're just lucky they found an efficient way to suck it out of the air before anyone else did. Do you honestly think they give two shits about climate collapse?"

Emmett said nothing, staring at the fissure in the tree as though he were trying to melt it with his eyes. Cam took pleasure in the vein popping from his forehead.

"Just admit the only reason you haven't resigned from this project is because you want Siena back."

"Fuck you, Cam."

She knew it. "You're wasting your time. Let her move on."

Emmett finally tore his eyes away from the hollow and glared at her as she sat defenseless beneath him. Would he throw a punch if she were a man?

"And you think I'm controlling?" Emmett said.

"There's a difference between control and my fury with you on her behalf."

"Sure, Cam. You're the one who's always pretending you know what's best for her."

"I am very cognizant of the fact I don't know what's best for anyone, including myself. But what I do know is what you did to her was unforgivable. Jesus, if you wanted to hurt her so badly, you should have just slept with another woman. At least you'd have a better chance of getting her back."

His expression told her one thing: he hated her. For a moment she was worried—not for her own safety, but about making things unbearable for the rest of the trip, especially for Siena. This trip was all Siena had been looking forward to after the wedding had been called off, and too much shit going sideways had already marred her experience.

Cam pushed her luck. "You don't deserve her forgiveness, you know. If it were me, you'd no longer have testicles. Or a job, for that matter."

Emmett bared his teeth, but before he could utter another word, Siena released a bloodcurdling scream.

Emmett was quicker to react than Cam was, ripping the coil of rope from her hands. "*SIENA!*" He wrapped the rope around his ungloved hand and yanked.

Cam jumped to her feet, her pulse thundering in her ears. "Let me climb in after her!"

As she leaned in toward the hollow to climb through, Emmett shoved her away.

"She's my best friend, you *fuck*! Move out of the way and let me find her!"

"I'll knock you unconscious, Cam. I swear to god." Emmett yanked on the rope once more and swore as it slipped through his hand. Cam geared up to shove him out of the way again, but on his third try, Emmett gained ground.

Siena was crawling back toward them.

Isaac rushed over. "What's going on? Is she okay? Why is she screaming?"

"I don't know!" Emmett and Cam yelled at the same time.

Isaac tore his fingers through his hair. "Let me help! How do I help?!"

"She's here. I got her." Emmett reached both his arms into the hollow, groaning as he hauled Siena out by her armpits.

Siena fell onto her back in the dirt, gasping for breath.

Emmett crawled over her and cupped her face. "Are you hurt? Did you get bitten? What happened?"

"Back up and let her breathe!" Cam yelled, but Emmett didn't listen.

Siena lay on the ground, shivering. She blinked a few times, her eyes darting around at the three of them. "I'm—I'm f-fine. I just . . ."

"What?" Emmett brushed the hair from her eyes. "What did you see?"

Cam suppressed the urge to kick him over.

"Nothing." Siena lifted a dirty hand, wiping away a tear forming at the corner of her eye. "Nothing real. I had an episode. That's all."

Emmett craned his neck to stare at Cam, and Cam knew exactly what he was trying to communicate.

I told you so.

"Goddammit," Cam muttered.

FIVE YEARS AGO

Emmett gripped Siena's waist as he stood by her side at the front of the wine bar, whispering embarrassing things about their audience in her ear.

"Uncle Naman's fly is down."

"I wish I were as drunk as your grandma."

"Cam looks bored enough to blow her brains out."

Siena covered her mouth to hide her laughter. He always did this before she spoke at conferences, when she was nervous enough to throw up. She was just as nervous now, mostly because she hated being a spectacle for something as pedestrian as getting engaged. But also, she knew how much these events meant to Emmett and his family. She'd negotiated for days with his mother about her request for a multiday wedding, which sounded like a pure unadulterated nightmare to Siena. If it were up to her, she'd elope to Denali.

The stress of the engagement party also sucked. The entire week had been stressful. She was getting married, and yet she couldn't stop thinking about the massive pile of late reports sitting on her desk back at the lab. She had already caught herself multiple times ordering and reordering her to-do list in her head.

If she could just get through this night with grace, she

wouldn't have to worry about another wedding event until the shower.

"I want to make a toast to my bride-to-be." Emmett raised his glass, and the room fell quiet.

Sweat prickled across Siena's hairline. She held her oversized wineglass in front of her like a bouquet, trying not to clutch it too tightly in case it shattered. Looking like a cabernet-flavored murder scene would be a *great* way to make a first impression on Emmett's family and friends.

"Siena intimidated the hell out of me when I first met her, and it's only gotten worse over the four years we've been together."

The room gave a polite chuckle. Siena could see Cam's eye roll all the way at the back table.

"I think about the last twenty-five years of my life, and I've had incredible mentors. My family, my teachers, my friends—who've mostly taught me how to get out of trouble."

Another polite chuckle.

"But no person on this earth has taught me as much as Siena has."

"*Awww.*"

He turned toward her, and Siena locked eyes with him and grinned.

"That was unbearably cheesy," she whispered.

"You love it," he said, before returning to their audience. "I didn't prepare a huge speech because I don't want to spoil my vows, but I love you, Siena. And I can't wait to spend the rest of my life with you."

She smiled sincerely then, because she loved him back. He'd been her rock since they worked as grunts in the lab all those years ago, two kids just trying to get through school. Life lost its sharp edges when he smiled at her. When he encouraged her. And yeah, maybe it was a little cheesy, but that was okay. Cam could roll her eyes all she wanted.

Emmett kissed Siena, and she leaned into it. When they parted, they raised their wineglasses higher.

"To Siena," said Emmett.

Siena interjected. "And to my mother, who would have loved you, Emmett."

The crowd cooed, and Emmett kissed Siena once more. "I would have loved her, too," he whispered against her lips.

Siena pressed her palms to the sides of Emmett's face. "This was perfect. Thank you."

Emmett nodded toward the tables. "Go find your dad. I think he's in the back, with Cam. You should tell him we saved him a seat up front."

Siena sighed. "He doesn't like crowds. People, really. I'll go find him."

She left the stage and cut between groups until she reached the back table, sitting between Cam and her father and stretching her arms out to either side.

"What are you doing?" asked Cam, eyeing Siena suspiciously while swirling her old-fashioned.

"Airing out my pits," said Siena.

Her father's blue eyes crinkled as he chuckled, and he grabbed Siena's hand as soon as she set it on the table.

She squeezed his fingers. "You hanging in there?"

"Haven't seen this many people at once since your mother's funeral. But I'll manage."

"Your pops was telling me many stories about the Yukon," Cam said. "Invited me to come check out his cabin."

"It's a ten-hour drive," Siena said.

Cam waved her hand. "That's nothing."

"From the nearest airport. After a fifteen-hundred-dollar plane ticket," Siena finished.

Cam blanched. "Jesus, Dave, you didn't mention that part."

He beamed. "Told you I was off-grid."

Siena's heart clenched. He was so proud of his distance—his

isolation. The last time she saw him was three years ago, and that was only because *she* had made the trek to the Yukon.

But he was here now, and she couldn't be angry with him. People dealt with grief in their own ways, and her father was taking exceptionally long getting over her mother's death.

She missed him was all. And even now—even as he laughed and smiled—he felt a million miles away from her.

"Wilder incoming," Cam said, and polished off her drink.

Siena stood as Feyrer approached the table.

"Well, you look mighty dapper," she said, nodding toward his bright yellow bowtie.

"Tiffany picked it out," Feyrer said with a sigh.

Siena grinned. "She has good taste." Turning, she gestured toward her dad. "This is my dad. Dad, this is Dr. Feyrer, my mentor."

"Your daughter is brilliant," Feyrer said. "I'm honored to work with her."

Her father nodded, taking a long sip of his water.

Say something, Dad.

He rested his glass back on the table and wiped his chin with his sleeve. Behind them, a server dropped a tray, and someone yelled "*Opa!*"

Siena spun back to Dr. Feyrer with an apologetic smile. "Thank you for coming. I'm glad you're here."

He nodded, lifting his hand to squeeze her shoulder. "I'm proud of you."

Siena chuckled. "For what? Bagging Emmett?"

Feyrer's eyes twinkled. "Sure."

Siena glanced at Emmett, who stood near the front of the room with his family. As she caught his eye, he winked at her, and she feigned a swoon.

She returned her attention to the space before her, but Feyrer was gone. She spotted him as he slid out the venue exit and into the night, his jacket tossed over his shoulder.

Siena woke to screaming.

She was standing for some reason, the surrounding space too dark for her to see. But she could feel, her flesh crawling with a life of its own. Twitching legs scurried over her body, digging into her skin.

She gasped, and the screaming ceased. The noise had come from her own mouth.

Siena smacked at her arms until they were numb, flipping her hair upside down and shaking it out. She scraped her fingers through her locks, hands closing around twitching beetles. Their shells crunched as she crushed them.

Her vision flooded with light, and she stumbled into the wall.

"Sen! What the hell is going on?"

She recognized her room. Emmett, jumping from the bed. Rushing toward her.

"Get them off me!" she screamed.

"*What?*"

"Spiders, bugs, I don't know!"

"*Where?*"

"ALL FUCKING OVER ME, EMMETT. GET THEM OFF!"

"Sen . . . *Sen!*" Emmett grabbed her arms. "You're having a dream!"

She shoved him away and grasped at the hem of her shirt. She tore the garment from her body as bugs skittered over her breasts and stomach.

"Check the bed!"

"What are you—"

"JUST CHECK THE FUCKING BED."

She felt a beetle burrowing into her belly button and clawed it out, but when she lifted her hand, it had somehow escaped her grasp.

Emmett stomped over to the bedroom door and flipped on the harsh overhead light. He returned to the bed and ripped the covers back.

Siena scoured the sheets, smacking a bug from her arm. "They're hiding. They probably went into the mattress. We can't sleep here."

"I'm losing my patience," said Emmett. It was the dark tone he reserved for his deadbeat sister and no one else. Certainly not Siena. "I told you, you had a dream."

"I'm not a child, Emmett!" How *dare* he take that tone with her? Why didn't he believe her?

Emmett's shoulders sagged as he sighed. "Okay, okay. Sit down, and I'll check you for bites."

Siena crossed her arms over her bare chest. "I'm not sitting on that bed. No way."

"Then I'll check you in the living room."

"Fine," she conceded, following him from the bedroom. She sat before Emmett on the living room's modern couch, and he stood over her, dragging his fingers across her skin as he searched her.

They lived in a one-bedroom in South Arroyo, one of the nicest neighborhoods in the city, thanks to Emmett's salary. If there were bugs here on the third floor, then they infested the entire building. She'd need to notify the apartment manager. It would be a whole *thing*.

Emmett dropped his hands. "I can't find anything, Sen."

She smacked at something skittering from her shoulder to her arm, her eyes welling with tears. "You're not looking hard enough."

He sat next to her on the couch and wrapped his arms around her. For a moment she wanted to shove him away, but she was too exhausted to do anything but wilt into him.

He kissed her forehead. "I believe you. I'll call the apartment manager in the morning."

"Delusional disorder," Dr. Reyes said. "It is a soft diagnosis, so I want us to continue meeting regularly."

Siena's throat constricted as she sat on the couch in the psychiatrist's office. "You don't believe me?"

Dr. Reyes leaned toward Siena and folded her hands. "You and I have a strong doctor-patient relationship, Siena. You are an intelligent and very self-aware individual. It is often difficult to broach such diagnoses with patients, but I feel like we've built up enough trust between each other."

It had been eight months since her engagement to Emmett, and since then, the infestation within their apartment had grown unbearable. No one believed her: not Emmett, not his parents—not even Cam, who had told her she needed to go to therapy to manage her stress. Except therapy was expensive; she had a fifty-thousand-dollar salary and no mental health insurance. Emmett was paying the bill right now, and Siena was certainly racking one up: a handful of clinical therapists, an MRI, and now months of sessions with a psychiatrist. She hated the idea of relying on him for medication costs as well.

But she had no other option. Not even a parent to confide in.

"So I'm imagining things. I'm paranoid."

Dr. Reyes shook her head. "It isn't so simple," she said gently. "Delusional disorder is very rare and hard to diagnose because patients are often in good health." She nodded. "As you are. Delusions are also based in reality. It's completely feasible for your house to be infested with bugs."

Because it is! Siena had felt them crawling all over her for months, infesting her very skin. Wasn't that enough?

Of course it wasn't. She was a scientist and knew the rules of reality didn't bend for her. She hadn't seen the bugs. Emmett hadn't. Pest control hadn't.

Her eyes welled up, and she quickly blinked. "Why?"

"There isn't enough known about the disease to be sure." Dr. Reyes gave her a sympathetic smile. "Stress, most likely. You've just finished eight years of school, you have loans, you're getting married . . ."

"But that's just life. That doesn't make me unique."

"You published six papers last year, Siena. And now you're vying for senior research positions while you're still in your twenties. That is an extreme amount of pressure you're putting on yourself."

Siena wiped a tear from her cheek and looked away. "It's all I've ever wanted."

"And you'll get it. But maybe it's okay to lay off the gas a little. Give yourself another year to plan the wedding—I'm sure your fiancé will understand. You can even aim for fewer papers, and you'll still be prolific."

A long stretch of silence passed. Dr. Reyes was right. The real trick was convincing herself.

"I'm going to prescribe a minor antipsychotic. We'll continue psychotherapy for the time being and monitor your progress. How does that sound?"

Siena shook her head. This wasn't right. She'd struggled with generalized anxiety her entire life. She'd taken medication and gone to therapy after her mother died. Mental health was as important as her physical well-being.

But something felt off about this diagnosis, and even worse, she couldn't argue with it. Denial was a core symptom of delusional disorder.

If she didn't accept the reality of this disease, she'd never recover.

Siena wiped her nose with the back of her hand, sheepishly pulling a tissue from the box Dr. Reyes offered.

"I just want my life back," Siena said.

Dr. Reyes nodded. "And you'll get it. We'll work together to make sure that happens."

I expect you to take me out to the nicest place in town after what you put me through. (Message Sent)

Chelsea: There are no nice places in town. I'd have to drive us up to Portland. Which I would . . . if that's what you really want.

Holden grinned at his phone.

What about a burger, beer, and good conversation? (Message Sent)

Chelsea: Good conversation with . . . ?

A pretty girl. (Message Sent)

Chelsea: Block 15?

I'll pick you up at 7 (Message Sent)

Chelsea: I'll pick YOU up at 7

Holden sent Chelsea his address, and then leaned back in his work chair, stretching out his arms. It was only four, and all he had to work on were a handful of emails from old professors who had forgotten how to reset their passwords. Chase played some uninteresting MMO that ran like shit on the school desktop, so Holden stole one of Angel's Twizzlers from behind her back and watched over her shoulder as she dug into Dr. Dupont's files.

He'd let her copy the contents of the hard drive after she wouldn't stop begging. Given she always completed her work within the first couple hours of her shift, she'd spent the bulk of the week reading through files and narrating to Holden what she'd found.

Dr. Dupont had run lots of analyses on chemical components of melting glacier ice. There were many big words like *ablation* and *parametrization* and *perfluoroalkyl*. One of her studies was literally about dust accumulating on ice and was about as boring as *watching* dust accumulate on ice. But Angel found it all interesting and had been glued to one of Dupont's analyses since ten o'clock this morning.

Angel suddenly jerked her head up, tapping her chin in thought. "You know what we should do?"

"I'm afraid to ask," Holden said.

"Hack Dupont's socials." Angel snatched her phone from the table, her thumbs flying across the keyboard.

"Whoa whoa whoa. Hack her? Like her Instagram?"

"Yes, Holden. Like her Instagram."

"*Why?*"

"So we can see if she's okay, duh."

Holden rubbed his forehead. "I know I'm not a genius—"

"Understatement."

"—but you can't just *hack* someone. Dr. Dupont is smart. I'm sure she didn't set her password as *Iheartgeomorphologylol*."

"We'll just buy her leaked passwords from a data broker. Easy peasy!"

"Angel, *no*."

Angel huffed. "You know, Holden, real detectives think outside the box. You disappoint me."

"Why don't you just . . . I don't know . . . try friending her like a normal person?"

Angel glanced up at him. Holden stared at her.

"Fine-uh," she finally said, resting her elbow on a book left on the table. The spine read *Without a Trace: The Story of the Deadswitch Five.*

Holden tapped her arm and pointed to the book. "Can I see that?"

Angel pushed the book toward him and continued staring at her screen.

Holden read the inside flap; the book was about the group of hikers that had gone missing, including Naomi Vo, the woman resembling the dead body Dr. Dupont had found. "Where did you get this?" Holden asked.

"I bought it from this place called a bookstore. Fascinating concept."

Holden flipped through the pages. "Did you read it?"

"Twice."

"Can I borrow it?"

"For a week, then I'm charging interest."

Holden reached the glossy pages at the back and paused, studying photos of the hikers in their early twenties. He tapped his finger on a photo of two women in front of a snowcapped peak.

Avery Mathis and Naomi Vo summiting Mount Hood, the caption read.

He remembered Avery Mathis from his early college years, but back then she was *Avablade*, the hot gamer and YouTuber who all the neckbeards wanted to hate-fuck. He'd known she had disappeared, but it hadn't clicked in his head that she and Naomi were a part of the same group until now.

Holden had watched some of Avablade's videos back in the day. She was gorgeous, but she also played extremely dark, difficult games. She was funny too and had a habit of falling out of her chair during jump scares.

Holden's college roommate used to have Avablade playing on the monitor in their apartment several hours a day, so Holden was familiar with many of her VODs by proxy.

She had disappeared during the summer. His roommate had been backpacking Europe, so Holden had missed all his lamentations. But he'd seen one of her gameplays that summer, hadn't he? He only remembered because the game had been so weird.

Holden pulled the browser up on his desktop and started typing in the search.

avablade last game

He found the answer after skimming through a handful of gaming articles and returned to the search.

avablade out of the woods

The first result was the original video from her channel. He popped in his earbuds and clicked on it.

In the small box at the top of the screen, Avablade sat in her gaming chair. The room behind her was dark, as she usually had it, with pockets of violet ambient lighting. The lighting matched her signature oversized headphones. Her blonde hair fell perfectly straight over her shoulders.

The larger screen was the main menu of the game. In front of a black background, the branches of pixelated trees slowly wavered back and forth. There were no settings or options, only a start button at the very center of the screen.

"Hey, wildcats, this is Avablade, and you and I are gonna try and get *Out of the Woods.*"

Holden turned up the volume and leaned forward.

"Now, this is an early alpha edition. The game isn't on Steam yet, so I'm super lucky to be a part of a small group of early players."

That was weird. The whole point of a developer giving streamers an early version of a game was so their subscribers would go purchase it or put it on their wishlist.

"There are only three things I know about this game." Avablade held up a finger. "One, it's super scary. Two, it's difficult enough to make *Dark Souls* players weep. And three, the dev let me know there's a massive twist at the end, so if you're not into spoilers, go watch Kaxsonate or something. I think he's playing through *Skyrim* for the millionth time.

"But if you're in it for the long haul, buckle up. I will fall off my chair at least a few times this run."

Avablade clicked Start, and Holden stole another one of Angel's Twizzlers while she wasn't looking.

The game began in a small village in the middle of the woods. Avablade played the main character of the butcher's daughter. As she went about the village making sales to the other villagers and tending to the slaughterhouse, the tutorial taught actions like how to talk to NPCs and use a weapon. The game was clearly indie, but the rendering proved beautiful and a little disturbing. Meat in the slaughterhouse swung on hooks and dripped crimson pixels. Forest shading cast a creepy perma-twilight over every individual structure. The subtle and eerie soundtrack mixed well with the ambient sounds of footsteps, door creaks, and wind through the trees.

As the tutorial and first in-game day ended, Avablade summarized the story so far for her fans.

"So every villager I've talked to is clearly freaked out by the surrounding woods for undisclosed reasons. I mean, they're freaked about everything—winter, getting sick, their dumbass village children. Maybe parasites from these tasty meat slabs I'm selling have wormed into their brains and are making them paranoid.

"I'm digging the vibe so far. Super spooky. And I definitely want to know what is in the woods. My interest is hooked."

Holden paused the video, opened another tab, and searched:

out of the woods game twist ending

He dug unsuccessfully through the first page before coming across an ancient Reddit post:

Obviously it sucks about Avablade going missing, but man I really want to know what the twist ending was. Anyone have more info?

The replies were unhelpful.

Holden tried searching just **out of the woods game** and clicked on the Wikipedia link.

Out of the Woods *is a survival horror video game developed by Cold Alpine Studio. The game was never released in full, the alpha version only sent to six influencers. The story takes place in a village within a mysterious forest, where the main character is chosen by the townspeople to escape through the woods and discover what is beyond the forest.*

The status of the game is currently unknown, as are the whereabouts of the developers.

Holden scanned the page for more details. The plot summary was taken from Avery's VOD. According to the article, she was the first to record gameplay and didn't make it through the entire game. By the time it gained traction with the other players—after her disappearance—the game threw errors as they tried to install it, crashing their expensive rigs repeatedly. From the sound of it, none of them ever succeeded in getting the game to run.

Holden scrolled to the bottom. John Lawson's book, the very book that sat in his lap, was one of the article's references. But before he could pick it up and flip through the pages again, his phone buzzed.

He checked the caller ID.

California Institute of Technology

He hit accept and pressed the phone to his ear.

"Hello?"

"Hi, Holden?"

"Yeah?"

"This is Callie Eisenberg from Geo and Planetary Sciences at CalTech. I'm calling you back. Sorry for the late response."

"It's been like three weeks."

"Four, actually. Again, super sorry. Our admin is on maternity leave, and you know how things get. Anyway, I wanted to let you know we don't need the data on the drive."

Holden reeled. "You . . . you don't?"

"Oh, no, central admin has all the study files they need, and Dr. Dupont and Dr. Yarrow have their own separate databases."

"So Dr. Dupont's okay?"

"Okay? I mean, yeah, she's fine given the circumstances. Our department is closely knit, and we weren't expecting to lose one of our own. It's definitely a hard thing to go through. Such a tragedy."

Isaac.

"Do you know her personally?" Callie asked.

"I—uhh—no. I'm IT at OSU and cleaning out some of our hard drives. Found her notes from a study."

"Gotcha," Callie said. "She's been out in the field, which is why she personally couldn't take this call."

"I understand."

"If you could destroy the files for security purposes, that would be great. Otherwise, we need nothing else at the moment."

When Holden ended the call with Callie, he tried not to feel deflated. Of course Dr. Dupont was fine, and of course CalTech already had all the study files. This wasn't some mystery to be solved. He wasn't a "DaVinci Code," or whatever the hell Angel had called him.

Angel . . . Maybe she was onto something.

Holden scrolled through his apps and opened Instagram. He didn't need to hack Dupont or even friend her to find the last picture she was publicly tagged in.

A handful of accounts popped up when Holden typed in Dupont's name. The most promising handle, **DrDee411**, had a squashed CLIF Bar with a thumbs-up next to it as the profile pic.

Holden searched "DrDee411." Only a few rows of photos popped up, the newest one time-stamped a couple of months ago.

Dupont stood on a stage in front of a PowerPoint presentation with her hands on her hips and a cheesy grin on her face. The slide behind her had a picture of an erupting volcano, *Mountain Fountain* in meme text beneath it.

@DrDee411 coming at us with all the important scientific terms. #lectureseries #caltechlectureseries #scienceishot

Two months ago, Dr. Dupont presented at a seminar. She made puns about volcanoes and grinned like a dork.

Lauren had asked Holden what he was hoping to find, and this was it. The good ending at the end of his quest. Siena Dupont was fine. She really was completely, perfectly fine.

So why did he feel disappointed?

SIENA

She'd thought she was better.

She took her meds on time and slept through the night and hadn't felt a single bug in two years.

And seen the bugs? Never.

But she hadn't only seen beetles in the tunnel beneath the tree. She'd hallucinated an entire reality. The heartbeat in the roots, the cabin in the woods. The man with the mask.

Terrified by the song on the radio, she'd let it ferment in her brain long enough to cause a psychotic break. Was she truly so fragile?

Siena sat hunched in the desk chair, hugging her torso, and tried calming herself with a few deep breaths. Her whole body vibrated as she shivered. Cam and Emmett stood on the porch, arguing loud enough for her to hear all the way from the closed lab.

"I told you she shouldn't be alone," Emmett said. "Not in that tunnel, and not right now."

It didn't matter what the situation was . . . he still managed to be a prick.

"And you're the one walking meat sack here who's a trigger for her," Cam said. "Or are you too arrogant to realize that?"

"She needs a companion."

"You should have thought about that before—"

"Fuck, Cam! I don't care if it isn't me! She just needs someone watching her!"

"Well, it's a good thing you didn't knock me unconscious, isn't it?"

"I . . . didn't mean that."

"Don't worry, Emmett. I know stress brings out the worst in you."

Siena rubbed her forehead. God, their fighting was getting out of control.

Something knocked against the window, and she jerked her head up. Isaac stood on the other side of the glass in his backward CalTech baseball hat, bashfully holding up a bottle of whiskey and a Twix.

She rolled her eyes, but got up anyway, rounding the desk and shoving open the grimy window.

Isaac pushed the bottle and the candy into Siena's hands. "Cam told me to bring you these."

Siena rested the items on the desk. "And you complied?"

"No, I told her I wasn't her intern and to get lost."

Siena burst out laughing, clapping a hand over her mouth in surprise.

Isaac grinned. "But I like you, so I brought them anyway. I'm sorry that, uhh . . ." His expression sobered, and he scratched the back of his neck. "I'm sorry that happened to you. Freaked me out, T-B-H. Freaked everyone out."

"Thanks," she said. "I'll be okay."

He nodded. "Cool."

Desperate to change the subject, Siena asked, "You get a good sketch of the tree?"

"*Oh*, yeah." Isaac flipped his hat around. "Way sick. Trying to figure it out, though, you know? Soil nutrients, genetic mutation, fluke . . ."

"Don't forget to journal your hypotheses. You should do that while today is still fresh." It was something Feyrer would have told her to do when she was his age.

Isaac tapped his forehead. "Smart."

"And we probably need a few more soil samples." She thought of the body. "Just be careful, okay? Maybe ask Emmett to go with you."

"Oh, don't worry about me. I can watch my back. Got a blue belt in karate."

Siena pressed her lips together to hide another wave of laughter, unsure if Isaac was being serious this time. She gave him a thumbs-up, and he shot one right back, darting around to the front of the cabin and taking off.

Siena returned to her seat at the desk and tuned back in to Emmett and Cam, but their argument had devolved into whispers. Distracting herself, she cleaned out her pockets, lining up her soil and bark samples next to her knife and recorder.

The front door slammed a few minutes later, and someone approached the lab with a quiet knock.

"I know you don't want to talk—" Cam began.

"It's fine," Siena said. "I heard Emmett."

The door creaked open, and Cam slipped in. She gave an awkward smile before sliding down the wall and sitting on the ground. She said nothing at first, which Siena appreciated, but soon the silence became uncomfortable.

Dr. Reyes had told her she shouldn't keep mental health stuff to herself, but confide in someone she trusted. Even when she was engaged, that person had never been Emmett. But Cam hadn't treated Siena any differently after her diagnosis. Maybe she could help drag Siena back to reality.

"I saw shit, Cam," Siena said. "I hallucinated. That's never happened before. Not visually." She hated how scared she sounded—how out of control she felt.

Cam watched her, but didn't react right away. Finally, she asked, "Hallucinated what? The bugs?"

"And other things." Siena's eyes burned, and she looked out

the window. "I . . . I thought I'd found a passage back to the cellar. I thought I was at the cabin, but things didn't look right. The trees were different. There was a man inside, and . . ." She trailed off, deciding to skip the part about the mule head. Dr. Reyes was right, but Siena wasn't yet ready to describe some of the horrible things her brain had conjured up.

"Hey . . . *hey*," Cam said.

Siena looked at her.

"You are *not* schizophrenic." Cam was calm. Serious, too. There was something comforting about the way she acted when she threw all jokes aside. "I don't know what happened to you in there, but there could be a bunch of reasons you saw what you did. A lack of oxygen in the tunnel. Maybe the air was toxic."

Siena wanted to believe her, but she couldn't blame what had happened on a lack of oxygen. "I don't know, Cam. What I saw was—"

"Don't move."

Cam's eyes had widened, her expression fixed and cautious. She pushed herself from the wall and crawled forward, sitting up on her knees when she was in front of Siena. Reaching forward behind Siena's ear, she pulled something from Siena's hair and opened her hand between them.

Shock pulsed through Siena's body.

An injured beetle twitched in Cam's palm. "These your bugs?" she asked.

Siena opened her mouth to say something—anything—but any coherent string of thought inside the chaos of her brain proved impossible to locate.

"But . . . they're not real," she finally stammered.

"Feels pretty real to me," Cam said. "Maybe they have some sort of self-defense biotoxin that makes you see things." Cam set the beetle belly-up on the ground and wiped her hands on her pants.

"I didn't *eat* one." Siena rubbed her eyes, anger burning

through her fog of confusion. "The bugs aren't real, Cam. Everyone told me. *You* told me!"

"Because they *weren't* real."

Siena pointed at the now-dead beetle. "Then what is that? A figment of my fucking imagination? What about everything else I saw?" Cold sweat prickled the back of her neck. *No*. There was no way. No way in hell.

"Okay, okay." Cam pressed her fingers to her temples. "Let's just think about this for a sec."

A blinking light on the desk caught Siena's eye. Her recorder.

She picked it up and read the screen, the newest recording time-stamped an hour ago. "How long was I in the tunnel?"

Cam shrugged. "Five, ten minutes."

"I mashed the buttons on my recorder while I was crawling." Siena's thumb hovered over the play button, but she couldn't push down, unsure she was ready to confront whatever she was about to learn.

Cam grabbed the recorder from her and hit play.

They listened. Nothing.

Cam fast-forwarded a bit and hit play again.

"*Give me some slack so I can push forward a little!*" Recorder Siena yelled. A few seconds later, she muttered to herself, but it was unintelligible.

There was some feedback—the rustle of fabric scraping against the microphone. Just noise, until amid it all, Siena made out a pattern. A beat.

Cam leaned closer to the recorder. "What is that?"

Siena's blood ran cold, just as it had in the tunnel when she had realized the pulse of blood wasn't coming from her own ears.

"*How deep am I?*" Recorder Siena yelled. "*Cam . . . CAM!*"

"I didn't hear you," said Cam. "I'm sorry. I . . . I was arguing with Emmett. Is that . . . is that noise your heart? Did you have the recorder in a shirt pocket?"

"No," Siena whispered. She ducked her head and listened,

biting down hard on her lower lip until she tasted a small burst of blood.

"*I've reached the cabin! . . . I'm gonna unclip. I'll meet you back at the tree!*"

"Siena . . ." Cam began.

"I was seeing things," Siena said. "Imagining them." *Please,* she begged silently. *Let this prove it.*

The recording fell quiet. Siena shut her eyes and began counting. Every now and again, the fabric of her pants shifted against the mic.

"We would have pulled you out by this point," Cam said.

"Then why haven't I screamed yet?" Siena tilted her head, as if it would somehow help her hear better. Nothing on the recording changed.

"Maybe that's the end," Cam said.

Siena shook her head, her eyes still shut. "Play it until the recording stops."

She kept listening through the rustle of Recorder Siena's clothes, past the noise of muffled movement in the background.

Eight-hundred and six. Eight hundred and seven. Eight hundred and—

"You shouldn't be here."

Siena's eyes snapped open. She slapped a hand over her own mouth as Cam stared in horror at the recorder.

On the recording, Siena softly whimpered as the other voice spoke.

"***You aren't strong enough . . . It will fight to keep you here. Drag you deeper. You can't let it. PROMISE ME.***"

Siena grabbed the recorder from Cam, turned it off, and threw it across the room. It crashed into the wall and clattered against the ground. She slid from her chair onto the floor next to Cam, her hands pressed to her mouth so she wouldn't scream.

Even if she could make her voice sound as deep as this one, she'd heard herself whimpering as it spoke. She hadn't pulled some *Exorcism* shit. She'd been with someone else. The man in the mask.

All of it had been real.

Cam took Siena's face in her hands. "Siena, what the hell happened to you in there?"

Siena shook her head. How was she supposed to explain? She couldn't, not yet.

Not here.

She'd wanted to complete the study so badly that she'd ignored all the signs. Even science couldn't dissuade her from believing Dr. Feyrer had been right. This place was cursed.

"We're not safe here," Siena said. "We need to get off this mountain, Cam. *Now.*"

HOLDEN

Holden's dreams of Becca were as vivid as his false memories.

The storm, the cabin, the quilt atop the bed. The smell of her deodorant and shampoo. The way they kissed in the middle of the room, her hands trailing beneath his soaking shirt and up his stomach. Rain splattered against the window as the wind gusted through the trees just outside, rushing as fast as the blood through his body. He shut his eyes and opened his mouth to feel Becca's tongue flick against his. As it would. As it had always done.

"*Holden.*"

His eyes snapped open.

Becca was no longer kissing him. She was gone, as was the storm and the rest of the afternoon light. In the darkness, two lit candles sat atop crooked end tables on either side of the cabin's small room. The only other light streamed from the cracked bathroom door, shining across watered-down puddles of blood.

"*Holden, help.*"

The voice came from the bathroom—feminine, but not Becca's. But he *knew* the voice. He'd heard it on one too many audio files.

The shower turned on. Holden stepped forward, roaches scurrying across the floor and hiding in the cracks between the boards. He pushed open the bathroom door as a woman peeled off her blood-soaked shirt. Crimson smeared her pale skin and stained her bra. Even her dark hair was drenched, pink water streaming in rivulets from the ends of her locks.

Dr. Siena Dupont.

"Clean everything up. *Everything*." She started unbuttoning her pants. "Start a fire. We'll need to burn our clothes." She looked at him, her expression morphing into anger. "She's going to find us! *Why are you just standing there?*"

He felt it then. No, smelled it. A thick iron tang threaded a cloying stench.

He looked down at himself. At the blood.

Holden woke to a gorgeous naked woman sleeping on top of him.

It wasn't a terrible way to come to, minus the awful juxtaposition between his hard-on and his heart still pounding in terror. He supposed he'd take what he could get.

Carefully, he rolled to the side until Chelsea slid off him and onto her pillow. She murmured something in her sleep, and he tucked the covers around her and sat up, pushing the hair from his eyes and checking his phone on the nightstand.

Angel: my dude. dr Duponts next recording just unlocked

Holden texted back: **Unlocked?**

Angel: Yeah. like I cab listen to it now

Angel: can*

Angel: freaky af

Angel: when u coming in

Holden got out of bed, typing as he padded to the bathroom. **It's 730. I just woke up. Why are you at work so early?**

Angel: ex being royal pita. no sleep. Figured id come in early.

sorry (Message Sent)

Angel: don't need ur pity just get ur ass over here

He wouldn't be caught dead at work before nine, especially because it was the middle of finals and the ticket queue was high. He wasn't about to answer panicked professor emails off the clock.

He messaged back: **let me shower**

When he was in the bathroom, he turned on the shower and brushed his teeth as the water heated up. He and Chelsea had been dating for a month now, way too early for him to have a spare toothbrush at her place, but by the eighth time spending the night, Holden figured formalities were out the door and quickly got used to the casual nature of it all. She was great. So was the sex. Maybe it would turn into more than that, but for now, Chelsea was a palate cleanser. Normally he'd feel like an asshole for thinking such a thing, but she'd essentially told him the same after the first time they'd slept together.

Disappointments stung less when Chelsea distracted him, like the email he'd received from Dr. Chari a few weeks ago.

I've discovered I don't do well with dusting off old skeletons. Now that we know Dr. Dupont is okay, I will no longer be sharing the details of my Deadswitch studies with you or your friend. I appreciate you understanding, Holden.

Returning to these memories is placing too much of an emotional burden on me at this point in my life.

I wish you well,
Maidei

Between the email and CalTech contacting him about Dr. Dupont, his interest in the mystery had dwindled to almost nothing. Angel had begged him to let her keep the files, even though CalTech had requested their deletion.

Holden didn't know why he'd let her have them; maybe because the files were a good distraction from her divorce, and he felt sorry for her.

He hadn't thought about Dr. Dupont and her research trip for a couple of weeks. It was quite the coincidence that her next audio file had *unlocked* right after he dreamt of her.

And that dream . . . What the fuck was that all about?

He didn't leave himself time to ponder as he showered and changed. Chelsea was awake when he reentered her bedroom, wrapped in a white sheet as she lounged in the morning light.

She smiled languidly at him. "Early day?"

"Finals week," he said. "A few more days of this and summer will be dead." He leaned forward to kiss her and grabbed his backpack from the side of the bed.

"Don't work too hard, Holden Sharpe," she called after him as he left her room. "I need a destressor tonight."

"Listen to this," Angel said as Holden walked into the office. She stood by the desktop, holding out a pair of headphones like she'd been anticipating him walking through the door ever since she texted him.

He scoffed, walking toward her and dropping his bag. "I told you, I'm no longer invested in this."

"Listen, you little hipster bitch, I'll tell you when something is no longer cool."

Holden barked a laugh. "Do you need me to go get you a coffee?"

Angel wilted and rubbed her eyes. "Sorry, rough night. My cranky threshold is thin."

He took the headphones from her. "If I listen, will that placate you enough to make it through your shift without another outburst?"

She smiled and started the recording. "No promises."

Holden waited. "It's not playing."

"Patience," Angel said.

The recording was a half hour, and for the first part, it was like he was listening in on a painfully boring butt-dial with a weird thudding in the background until Dr. Dupont started calling for Dr. Yarrow. Holden leaned forward and began to actually pay attention. "What the hell is going on?"

"Keep listening," Angel said.

Holden did. He listened to the noise of almost nothing for minutes until a strange voice broke the silence.

"You shouldn't be here."

Holden pressed his fingers against the right headphone.

"You aren't strong enough . . . It will fight to keep you here. Drag you deeper. You can't let it. PROMISE ME."

"Who is that?" Holden asked. "Isaac? Or that other guy who's with them?"

"Emmett. And I don't know." Angel bounced on her toes as she hovered over him. This was exciting for her. "Do you hear her whimpering, though? She's freaked out."

And running. Dr. Dupont's footsteps thundered as she crashed into things. At the end, the recording filled with chittering before Dupont screamed. Holden ripped the headphones from his ears.

"Wild, right?" Angel grinned like a maniac.

"What happened to her?"

She shrugged. "Your guess is as good as mine. But whoever it was who spoke, he definitely scared her." She tilted her head as she thought. "Actually, his voice sort of sounded like it belonged to your distant possessed cousin, or something."

Holden raised his eyebrows. "My distant possessed cousin?"

"Same deep baritone."

"So, I sound possessed."

Angel rolled her eyes. "Oh my god, why do I always have to spell things out for you? When I say you have a *deep baritone* voice, I'm using romance novel words, Holden. It's sexy. And no, that is not an invitation to hit on me."

Holden deadpanned.

Angel nodded toward the computer monitor. "But that guy? Creepy, not sexy. If it was Emmett or Isaac, I don't know why they'd try to scare her, or why she'd be so afraid of them."

Or why she screamed. He shook his head. "It doesn't matter. CalTech already has these files. They know what happened to Isaac. And Dr. Dupont . . . she's fine."

Angel groaned. "But aren't you dying to know what happened on their trip? Don't *you* care?"

Did he care enough to keep digging? There was something about these uncorrupting recordings that made him feel like he was on some hidden-camera reality show meant to scare him. And now, Dr. Dupont had invaded a false memory that had been vividly seared into his brain for almost a year. The night in the cabin with Becca had always played in his head like an uncut film. Now, a woman he didn't even know had sullied it.

He hated that this bothered him. He and Becca were over. And Dr. Dupont was unaware of Holden's existence. There was no reason for that ever to change.

"I guess I don't really care," Holden said. "Not anymore."

Without a Trace: The Story of the Deadswitch Five
By John Lawson (Goodreads Author)

Coffee, Crime, and CRPGs rated it ★☆☆☆☆ · review of another edition
Jan 21, 2019
Shelves: nonfiction, garbage-author, fact-check-on-aisle-nine, profiting-from-pain, dnf
Actual Rating: 0/5 stars

If John Lawson spent as much time researching as he did with his head up his ass, he'd know Avery Mathis didn't give two flying fucks about "social currency." Avablade never had a Facebook or Twitter account. Her Instagram activity consisted of three posts about her geriatric cat. All she cared about was hiking, games, and her community.

Lawson thinks "Gen Y," his old-person term for millenials, is full of vapid bimbos who care only about their fifteen minutes of fame. Makes you wonder what else he generalized.

I'm sick and tired of old white men's obsession with writing about dead young women. Leave it to the authors who won't misrepresent them.

EDIT: The irony of this review getting over 400 likes is not lost on me, but thank you for your concern. (less)

462 likes · Like · see review

CAMERON

We need to get off this mountain. Now.

Siena's trembling voice took up residence in Cam's head as she stealthed through the grove east of the cabin.

Leaving now wasn't an option; they couldn't hike off Agnes before nightfall. But they could prepare for the morning.

Siena kept trying to contact repeaters on the radio while Isaac packed up their communal belongings. This left Emmett and Cam searching their side of the mountain for any other sign that what she'd seen in the tree tunnel had been real, and in order for them to be effective, Siena had needed to tell them everything she remembered.

The risk of capture by a masked man and Cam's own head pinned to the wall by knives was far more desirable than alone time with Emmett, so they split up, leaving her ample time with her own thoughts.

Deadswitch was all Siena had to look forward to for over a year. Completing the study was all she'd wanted. Even if they found no other evidence in these woods, Siena's fear alone was enough to convince Cam they needed to call it.

But they had more evidence, didn't they? They'd found a dead woman, for crying out loud.

Stupid. They'd been acting stupid since the body. For all they knew, they were dicking around while sharing some prime mountain real estate with a serial killer.

Maybe waiting until morning to leave wasn't the best idea.

Isaac joined Emmett and Cam as they reconvened on the porch, both returning empty-handed.

"So we're just gonna go?" Emmett gave Cam one of those shitty patronizing smiles he always gave when he was frustrated. "Because Siena had a meltdown?"

As much as Cam deeply desired to tear Emmett a new asshole, the stakes were too high to fight again. Clearly, he felt differently.

"You know her, Emmett. She wanted to be here more than she wanted to marry you."

Okay, so maybe the no-fighting thing was a little too aspirational. Luckily he only rolled his eyes at her.

"She'd live up here if she could," Cam said. "We wouldn't be able to drag her off this mountain after only a week if she didn't think we were in danger."

"She has delusional disorder!"

"That doesn't make her inept! You heard the recording for yourself. We all did. If that audio is the product of Siena's delusional disorder, then we all have it."

Emmett crossed his arms. "The recording isn't proof of anything."

Jesus, was he trying to gaslight her now? Cam took a deep breath, but it didn't douse the heat in her chest. "I don't get why you're suddenly so averse to leaving. You're the one who wanted to hike back when we were at Wolf Ridge."

"And now we're here," said Emmett.

"And now we have more to worry about than Naomi."

Emmett frowned. "Naomi?"

Shit. "Nothing. Freudian slip."

"The reason I wanted to turn back before is because we were only a couple of days in. It would have been a lot easier to cover our losses then than it is now, after we've already started our work."

Cam barked a frustrated laugh. "So this is about money?"

Emmett sucked on his bottom lip, shaking his head. "Don't you dare."

"It's always about money with you, isn't it? And always at Siena's expense."

Emmett sneered, opening his mouth to cut into her before Isaac spoke up.

"I think we should go, too."

His voice was quiet, boyish in a way that caught Cam's attention. He stared vacantly at the forest, clutching his field journal in front of him as he ran his thumb along the page edges. The cardboard covers of the notebook were frayed all over.

"Why?" Cam asked.

"The omens. Every day there's another."

Omens. The word sent a shiver up her spine. She combed her fingers through her hair, following Isaac's eyes when they left her again for the forest beyond the porch. "I'm not superstitious, but you're not wrong. I said it from the very beginning . . . it feels like the universe doesn't want us here."

Not the universe, she corrected herself. *Deadswitch.* She thought of the night in the pub after they'd won funding, and Dr. Feyrer's glassy eyes as he talked about his research.

There were anomalies on Mount Agnes far more important than Alpenglow . . .

Cam wasn't like Siena. Siena had trusted the old man like a father, but Wilder was always a little too woo-woo for Cam. His field journals—the ones she'd gotten her hands on—were all about *following his senses* and *feeling out the energy of a place.*

Cam fucking *hated* that.

He had an obsession with trails, too. Or was it paths? He'd remind himself at the end of every entry: stay on the trail or follow the path or . . .

Don't stray from the path. That was it. *Don't stray from the path, Wilder,* he'd write to himself in third person. She fucking hated that too. Unfairly hated, perhaps. She was critical of him because her entire professional career had been an addendum to his research. She hadn't brought up that night in the pub to Siena after, not because she'd forgotten, but because it had made her angry. How dare he keep research from them? This was her and Siena's livelihood—especially Siena's. Feyrer had wanted so badly for Siena to be his acolyte; Siena had been too enamored of the idea of this study to realize she didn't need him.

But now . . . now, Wilder Feyrer made a little more sense to her. Because how the hell *did* you explain what had happened to Siena? The body hanging in the tree? The mysteriously melted glacier?

Were the anomalies found by Dr. Feyrer's research team similar to their own? Maybe they'd know if he hadn't hidden the bulk of his findings.

The research stays in the woods.

"It's like God isn't here."

Cam's attention snapped back to Isaac. "What the hell did you just say?"

"I . . ." He shook his head, his thought remaining unfinished.

"Why would you say something like that?" Emmett asked before sharing a look with Cam. For the first time this trip—maybe the first time ever—she and Emmett were on the same bewildered wavelength.

"I thought you didn't believe in that shit," Cam said.

"It's . . . not so simple," Isaac stammered.

Cam raised her eyebrows. "Is that so? Care to explain?"

Cam waited, but Isaac didn't elaborate. Even in the dark, she could see the flush of his cheeks.

"God isn't anywhere, kid. You better get used to it." Cam had learned that lesson the hard way.

She headed for the door. "Get some sleep. We have a long day tomorrow."

They left their equipment tucked away behind the broken door of the cabin. If Cam could find any leftover funds in their budget, she would hire a packer to come fetch what they abandoned. But she was too tired to think about that now.

Dawn warmed the trail as they left Agnes Cabin. Emmett fell to the back of the group with Siena as Cam took the lead. She couldn't make out any of what they muttered back and forth to each other, only Emmett's persistence. Siena didn't sound as annoyed as she usually did, which meant she was exhausted. Cam could convince Siena to do anything when she was exhausted, like going to the pub with Feyrer after the conference. That had been Cam's doing.

A part of her wished they'd never gone and heard Feyrer whisper about anomalies on Agnes. He'd died before telling them the truth. Cam had thought she'd uncover his secrets on this trip. Perhaps she had been on the brink.

She always entered these woods looking for something and always left empty-handed.

"Cam!"

Cam turned around.

Siena had stopped. "This doesn't look right."

Cam glanced back at the trail and frowned. She'd been so caught up in her head that she hadn't even noticed the trail thinning to the size of a rabbit run.

"Maybe we took a wrong turn," Emmett said. "Let's double back."

"There's only one path off the southern face, and we're headed in the right direction," Cam said, and inhaled. The air smelled different here, too. Muted and damp. Foliage ran thick along the path's edge. She couldn't recall such density when they'd hiked up.

"We're obviously not going the right way," Emmett insisted.

Isaac unclipped his pack and slid it from his shoulders. "I'll run back and see if we missed a fork."

"Isaac, no!" Cam barked. "We need to stick together."

"You all are worse than my mom. I'll be back in like thirty seconds, tops."

Before Cam could argue any further, Isaac's giraffe legs had already carried him back up the trail and out of sight.

Cam threw her hands up. "Dude . . ."

"Don't worry," said Siena. "He has a blue belt in karate."

She would have laughed if any of this were funny.

Siena unclipped her chest strap. "I can run and get him."

"No," Cam and Emmett said at once.

Cam sighed. "Just . . . stay here and wait for him to come back. I'm going to see if I can reach the descent from this trail. I should be able to spot the cairns once the trees are out of the way."

"You just said—"

"I'll literally be right there." Cam pointed to the thicket ahead. "You can throw a rock and hit me."

"Plan on it!" Siena called after her as Cam pushed forward, branches catching on her backpack as she shoved herself through the thick growth. The trail only thinned, but there was no other way. This path had to lead them down the mountain.

The granite was farther away than she thought, which made no sense. But she'd be hypocritical if she didn't turn back now.

Her stubbornness won out, and after a couple hundred paces, the trees cleared, and Cam approached the ledge, shielding her eyes from the sun.

The valley was big. It had always been big, something that travel journalists dubbed *breathtaking* in their columns for local papers and *Backpacker* magazine. But it looked different, now—more grandiose—as though the divide and the peaks beyond covered the entire state of California.

Three peaks jutted boldly from the horizon. Charlotte, Lucille, and . . .

She'd never seen this other mountain before, not in person, and not on a map. The peak's skirt was sharper and more chiseled than the sisters, the summit uncapped by snow, like a diamond resting on its face. A black forest flanked its base, but she couldn't tell if a fire had swept through the area. A dark shadow cast over that part of the valley.

Panic fluttered through her chest, the same emotion she always had the first few nights on the trail when she woke up in her bivy thinking she was still at home. The longer she stared at the mountain, the harder she fought to figure out why she couldn't remember ever seeing it before, and the more lost she felt.

She needed to find something familiar, and quickly, but when she turned back to the forest to locate the rest of her team, the forest wasn't there.

Cam stood face-to-face with a cliffside. Water dripped from its moss-laden surface. She took a step back, eyes following a switchback trail as it wound up the side of the mountain, stretching onward and onward until it disappeared between jutting crags.

She wasn't at the top of Mount Agnes. She didn't know *where* she was.

And the sun was setting.

SIENA

"*CAM!*"

Siena's shout echoed through the forest. She dropped her cupped hands. How long had it been—fifteen, twenty minutes? Too long. And neither Cam nor Isaac had returned.

"I need to go find her," Siena said, sick with panic.

"Just give her another five minutes, okay?" Emmett's voice was frustratingly calm as he scanned the upper part of the trail for Isaac. "I'm sure she'll be back."

Siena grimaced, abandoning her backpack near a rock by the trail. She paced the dirt, following her own path of footprints until it looked like hundreds of people had walked by.

"What's that?" Emmett asked.

Siena jerked her head up. He was watching her.

"Your arms. Where'd you get those scars?"

She crossed her arms to hide the marks, her reaction to protect not herself, but Wilder. Emmett had been at the hospital. Surely he remembered. "Dr. Feyrer."

Emmett raised his eyebrows. "He grabbed you that hard?"

"Yes, Emmett. That hard."

"Guess he really didn't want you coming on this trip. Maybe you should have listened."

She opened her mouth to defend herself, but was it really worth it? Emmett knew how sick Feyrer had been, and how his dying words contradicted everything he'd ever told Siena. And yet Emmett still used one of the worst moments of her life against her.

It didn't matter what the truth was. Emmett would manipulate it regardless. He hadn't changed, and he never would.

"You know . . ." She gave a hollow laugh. "He told me it was cursed. This trip. Or this place. I'm not sure what he meant, exactly. He said it one evening last year when we were working late and planning out the budget. I'd forgotten about that conversation until we found the body.

"I guess I should have asked for clarification, huh?" She looked up in mock thought. "But I suppose if I had taken him seriously that night and again while he was on his deathbed, then blamed my decision on some curse, you would have called me hysterical. Am I right, Emmett?"

His shoulders sagged. "Sen . . ."

"I'm gonna go find Cam, because she's the only one I have left who doesn't hurt me." She wiped her cheek and turned on her heel, following the path south, where Cam was.

"Sen, wait. I didn't mean . . . You don't have to be so sensitive."

Siena stopped, and then smiled a gracious, patient smile to herself. She'd fallen for this act of his too many times, but she was smarter now. Wiser.

When she glanced back at him, it was clear Emmett knew he'd fucked up.

"I'm not your wife," she said. "I'm not your girlfriend, or some kid in college you got stuck doing a group project with. I'm your boss."

"I didn't mean—"

"I'm going to go find our lead PI. Stay here."

This time, he didn't follow her, at least not right away. And

Siena would have felt somewhat vindicated if she'd been able to hike farther than fifty feet ahead.

The thread of a trail ended in a lush tangle of branches and underbrush higher than her waist. She couldn't get through even if she had a machete. This was the wrong way, and the forest told her as much. Tufts of moss and lichen clung to the evergreens, the air earthier, the soil yielding to her weight. This neck of the woods teemed with moisture, but not from the weather. Siena sensed it beneath her. A spill bleeding upward.

Ever since they entered Deadswitch, nothing had made sense. She'd brushed it all off, hadn't she? Made excuses for every aberration, even going so far as to believe she'd had a psychotic episode. But she couldn't anymore.

No more excuses.

"Cam!" she screamed. "*Cam! CAM!*"

"What the hell is going on?" Emmett had followed her after all.

"It's a dead end. She isn't here." Siena sounded as helpless as she had years ago, on bad nights when the bugs wouldn't leave her alone.

Emmett must have recognized her tone, because he softened his voice. "She said she was trying to get to the granite. Maybe she went another way."

"Which way, Emmett? There is no other way." Tremors shook her voice. "I can't even tell what's on the other side of this. Arewene-uh . . . Are we in a ravine?" She was tripping over her words now, her brain unable to keep up with her fear. "I . . . I don't . . . I don't know how we could have gotten so turned around."

For once, he didn't have an answer for her. No *We probably just did X* or *I'm sure Cam is Y.* Siena saw the shift behind his eyes, a vulnerability he never displayed when he was desperate to control a situation.

It terrified her.

Emmett took a deep breath. "Cam!" he yelled. "CAM!"

Siena listened, but only the wind from the valley responded.

"What do we do?" God, when was the last time she'd asked him this question? Long before they'd broken up, when she felt like the only way they could stay together—the only way she could live with herself—was if she lessened her reliance on him.

Again, he didn't have a good answer. Not even an answer to fake confidence. That was how she knew they were really in trouble.

"Let's just think for a second." Emmett glanced back the way they'd come. "I could run back and try to find Isaac."

"No. I . . . I don't have a good feeling about us separating."

"Yeah . . . you're probably right."

"Let's both go. We're not even a half mile from the cabin. Cam will think to circle around eventually." *Please let that be true.*

As unsettled as Emmett appeared, he nodded, and she followed him back up the trail, rubbing the small risen scars left on her arms by Wilder Feyrer. Feyrer, who'd drunkenly spouted about anomalies years ago. Everything that had happened to them so far had been a damn anomaly—an entropic nightmare. But was it her luck, or this place?

They passed Isaac's bag, and Siena looked down, the path beneath her feet smooth and dusty, even though she'd spent the past quarter of an hour pacing right here.

She thought of the pristine trail back at the Glass Lake Trailhead—the lack of footprints.

A ringing in her right ear crescendoed into a shriek, and Siena stumbled and slowed. Beneath the ringing, a wet, visceral rumble echoed somewhere beneath her, deep within the mountain.

She'd heard this before, not once but twice. When she escaped the masked man in the cabin, in the woods on her way to the cellar. And at Wolf Ridge, right before they found the body in the tree. The noise that had woken her that night—she finally remembered.

Her eyes watered as a potent dread rose in her chest, like her brain had lost control of its ability to regulate her fear. She tried focusing on Emmett hiking in front of her, but when she caught sight of the state of the trail before them, her stomach lurched.

He wasn't paying attention.

She screamed his name until she tasted blood, but it was too late. By the time Emmett skidded to a halt, he was too close, pinwheeling his arms to push himself backward.

As he lost his balance, Siena launched forward and grabbed on to his pack, yanking as hard as she could. Emmett fell backward into the dirt.

Her breath left her in a hiss. Before them, the edge of the trail disappeared into a sinkhole the size of a car. She inched close enough to watch the dirt crumble from an exposed weave of thick roots and trickle into the pit.

Emmett lay dazed on top of his pack. He blinked and shook his head.

"Are you okay?" she asked.

He unclipped his chest and waist straps. "What . . . what happened?"

Siena prodded her pockets, finding her flashlight and clicking it on. She inched forward again, shining her light into the hole. But the beam couldn't pierce the bottomless dark.

Siena stared into the mouth of a void.

HOLDEN

Holden grabbed his sweatshirt off his bed and tugged it over his head.

He couldn't remember the last time he went to a party. Not an all-nighter with beer, half-finished bags of chips, and *Call of Duty*. An actual party, with kegs and girls and regrets.

He wasn't looking forward to this.

But he was being a sport. Because that was what boyfriends did, right? They were sports. And Chelsea wanted to go to a party. A *party* party. Even though Holden wasn't her *boyfriend* boyfriend.

Well, maybe he was. They hadn't actually established their relationship status, and he didn't want to bring it up only to scare her away. He'd never had such a casual relationship before and didn't quite understand the rules.

"I guess I was wrong about you being a demi," Lauren said as she laced up her work shoes in the living room. "I haven't even met this fling of yours yet. Why haven't you brought her over?"

Holden stepped from his room. "She's afraid of dogs."

Lauren scoffed. "Francis isn't a dog. He's a teddy bear."

Francis lay panting contentedly on the couch. Holden had

just taken him for a run in the park, and the dog was about five-point-three seconds away from conking out.

Lauren grabbed her backpack off the kitchen island stool. "Where are you going, again?"

Holden shrugged. "Some party in the woods."

"The woods, eh? Make sure you have a Mike's Hard Lemonade for me. They're usually in the cooler by the cheerleaders."

"Oh, fuck off."

"Though they may just be chasing Pinnacle with Diet Coke." Lauren deadpanned. "And don't forget to wear a condom. I don't like kids."

Holden sighed when Lauren opened the door to leave, but then seized up when he saw who was waiting outside.

He'd never mistake that shiny dark hair and those icy eyes.

"Ummm, hi?" Lauren glanced back at Holden in confusion.

"It's fine, I got it," Holden said.

Recognition crossed Lauren's face. She gave him a *sorry, dude* look, and then bolted out the door. Apparently, she didn't want to stay for the show.

Becca watched Lauren leave and then turned back to Holden. "Replaced me quickly, I see."

Seriously? He hadn't seen her for months, and jealousy was still her first instinct.

"Are you here for a reason?" he asked. "I'm about to leave."

"She's cute."

"She's also gay," Holden said without missing a beat. "I needed someone to pay the other half of the rent, not like it's any of your business."

Before she could retort, Francis zoomed past Holden to greet Becca, breaking the tension between them.

Becca bent over and scratched Francis between the ears. "Oh, hello, my sweet boy. I've missed you so much!"

"Seriously, Becca. I really have plans."

She stood straight with an injured expression, almost like

she'd expected him to beg for her back. Was he so predictably pathetic?

"I needed one of my things and realized I left it here," she said. "I was hoping to pick up the rest of my stuff."

Holden nodded, vaguely recalling the box of items he had collected from around the apartment prior to Lauren moving in. He retreated to his room to grab the box.

"Umm, can I come in?" she yelled.

"I guess, but I'm *really* on my way out." He entered his room and opened his closet, scrounging around the bottom for the unlabeled box. When he returned to the living room with the box in tow, Becca was flipping through *Without a Trace*, which Holden had left on the coffee table.

"Never mind, this is what I needed. I'm re-reading it for book club. Thought you would have put it away by now."

"That's not . . ." Holden flipped open the box lid, and the girls on the cover of a beat-up copy of *Without a Trace* stared back at him. He fished the book out of the box and handed it to Becca. "I don't remember you ever reading this."

Becca reluctantly placed Angel's pristine hardback copy of *Without a Trace* back on the coffee table. "I don't remember you ever reading."

"I read," he said, though it was a flat-out lie Becca definitely wouldn't fall for.

She gave him a soft smile, the kind of sympathetic smile reserved for kids who have just fallen off the monkey bars. Becca smiled that way when she was flirting.

"Well, did you like it, then?" she asked. "*Without a Trace*?"

Word vomit bubbled up from Holden's stomach into his esophagus. It had always been so easy to talk to her. His instinct was to tell her everything—the recordings of Dr. Dupont, Maidei Chari's research, how it tied in to the Deadswitch Five, and the spooky oddities surrounding all he'd uncovered.

It played out perfectly in his head: he'd speak, and Becca would slowly lower herself onto the couch, hanging on to his every word. Hours would pass, and he'd miss every single text from Chelsea, and when he finally realized the time, it would be too late. He'd make Becca tea, or something. He didn't have wine. She'd be as fascinated with the case as he used to be, picking apart all the details and clues he and Angel had missed.

She'd stay late. And then what? What would happen next in this imaginary scenario?

For the first time, the thought of getting back with Becca revolted him. Not because he no longer loved her, but because time had finally given him a fresh perspective.

She even looked different. Not completely, of course, just a little less beautiful. Like his loneliness had rendered his memory of her more perfect.

"You're right," Holden said. "I didn't read it." He checked his phone. "I really do need to go. I'll walk you out."

Holden pulled his beat-up Camry to the side of the dirt road, at the end of a long line of cars. "What did you say this place was called?"

"The Playground." Chelsea flipped down the visor mirror and applied lip gloss. "That's what the kids call it."

"The kids?"

"Oh, you know, the local Newport high schoolers who want to party."

"The coast is an hour from here."

From beyond the windshield, people-silhouettes with flashlights veered from the road into the woods.

Chelsea shrugged. "Some kids really need to get away from their parents."

"There are no high schoolers at *this* party, though, right?" He despised the idea of being the older leering creep in the woods.

"Ugh, god, no." She dropped her lip gloss in her purse and kicked open the car door. "Just undergrads."

Not much better, but at least there were no minors.

"Hurry up. I think Emma is already here."

Emma . . . Emma . . .

Oh right. The friend Chelsea was with all those months ago back at Clodfelter's. God, he hoped Kyle wasn't here. He'd been dodging every one of that guy's texts since March.

Holden got out of his car and locked it. Chelsea pulled a flashlight from her purse, clicked it on, and held his hand. He tugged his flimsy sweatshirt tighter around him, feeling woefully unprepared for this. He'd been hoping to get back home before midnight, snuggle with Francis, and watch some stupid videos on his phone—definitely the thought process of a tired almost-middle-aged person.

Chelsea dragged him off the road into the woods. A bright orange flame about a quarter mile away illuminated the forest. Shrieks and laughter filled the night.

"Is that a bonfire?" he asked.

"Looks like."

"You can't have bonfires out here. It's *July*."

"Okay, Daddy," she said in a faux-sexy tone that just pissed him off.

"I'm serious. You could burn half the state down."

"*Me?* I didn't start it! God, let me have my fun."

He *had* been letting her have her fun. Every time she asked, he came to her place. He didn't fall asleep until she'd gotten off at least twice. He paid for her dinners, her movie tickets, her tampons from restroom dispensers when she didn't want to "lug her purse all over town." Fun was all Chelsea had been having with him lately. It was exhausting.

As they neared the fire, he took stock of the area. There were about fifty people, all about a decade younger than he was. A few coolers, a keg, and crumpled red cups littered the clearing. Someone had driven a pickup truck all the way from the road.

Obnoxious music pulsed from the stereo as girls drunkenly danced in the truck bed.

Chelsea screamed gleefully and darted from his side to hug Emma, like she hadn't seen her in years. A couple of guys Holden didn't know flanked Emma. One of them hugged Chelsea for ten seconds too long. When they separated, Chelsea glanced at Holden before turning her attention back to Emma and giggling.

Well, this was dredging up all his worst undergrad memories.

Holden shoved his hands in his pockets, plotting a way to escape back to his car for the rest of the night and not piss off Chelsea, though she seemed perfectly distracted. He jumped as some jackass poured lighter fluid on the bonfire. As the flame plumed, Holden caught sight of a scrawny guy on the other side of the fire, smoking a cigarette and staring at him.

The guy dropped his cigarette and stomped it out, then walked the edge of the clearing around the fire. As he approached, he nodded. "You Holden?"

Holden took a step back on instinct, out of shanking distance. "Who's asking?"

The scrawny guy extended his arm, pointing into the woods behind him. "There's a chick out there looking for you."

"A . . . chick?"

"I was trying to find a spot to take a leak. She's got a whole setup out there for the party, reading those weird fortune cards the way goth chicks do. I asked to bum a cigarette, and she told me she'd give me one if I found you."

A goth chick giving fortunes? No one in Holden's life fit that description. "Do you know her name?"

The kid shrugged. "You gonna go, or not?"

"Uhh . . ." Holden glanced back at Chelsea, but she and her group of friends were gone. He quickly scanned the crowd around the fire and failed to find her.

"Listen," the kid said, picking his tooth with his thumbnail. "I already got my smoke, so I'm gonna get out of here. This party is lame."

He passed Holden and took off toward the road. Bewildered, Holden watched him disappear between the trees, and then returned his attention to the *goth chick* part of the woods. A trail led to a soft glow about fifty yards into the forest.

Holden walked toward the trail, ignoring the warning sirens going off in his brain. This scenario was too weird to not end with him getting jumped, but absolutely anything was better than being the old guy standing alone at a college party. He couldn't believe he'd gotten suckered into driving all the way out here only to be ditched.

He passed a group of young women in sweatshirts and jeans whispering back and forth to each other about *tarot*. The soft glow came from a pair of oil lamps—*actual* oil lamps—arranged on a wooden table about to collapse from dry rot.

A woman sat on the other side of the table. She wore her long hair in two braids beneath a wide-brimmed black hat, her vest patterned with gold leaves. The choker around her neck was also gold, a replica of stag's antlers resting just above her collarbone. A hand-rolled cigarette hung from her lips as she shuffled a deck of cards. But the smoke didn't smell of cigarettes. It didn't smell of marijuana or some shitty vape pen flavor either. It reminded Holden of burning citrus rind.

The woman rested the cards on the table, plucked the cigarette from her mouth with slender brown fingers, and blew smoke from her lips. Her enormous eyes squinted as she smiled at him. She looked vaguely familiar, but for the life of him, Holden couldn't remember where he'd seen her before.

"You've finally arrived," she announced, her voice sultry.

"Do I know you?" he asked.

"I suppose you do." She took a final drag from her smoke and stubbed it out amid a graveyard of burn marks on the table. "Though you won't remember my name if you try recalling it." She gestured to the folding chair next to him. "Please sit."

Holden was no longer afraid of getting jumped. Still, he was nervous. And confused. He wouldn't be able to recall her name? What the hell did that mean?

Just like the warning siren screaming in his brain, he ignored every jolty nerve ending in his body and sat, nodding toward the deck of cards. "Are you giving tarot readings to partiers?"

"Not tarot." She slid the deck of cards to the center of the table. "This is a different type of reading." Drawing two cards, she placed them next to each other, facedown. "Less about what has and will happen to you, and more about who you are."

Holden scratched his head, studying the backs of the cards and the hand-drawn sketch of birds perched on the skull of a dead stag. "Shouldn't I know who I am?"

The woman cocked her head. "That depends. You tell me."

He sank a little deeper into his thin sweatshirt.

She flipped over the card on his right. The words **THE RANGER** topped a drawing of a cloaked and faceless figure in the middle of a forest.

"The Ranger," said the woman. "Faced with peril, you are reactive. You do not make decisions, but support the ones of those you protect. And those you protect—they are your identity, Holden. You are their hand, not their hero."

She spoke as though her message was grave, but it was all gibberish to him. A hokey fortune reading at an equally hokey party. He could still hear the drunken hollers and shitty music playing from the truck.

Only one thing nagged him.

"How do you know my name?" Suspicion crawled up his spine, the way it had when he listened to the last *unlocked* recording of Dr. Dupont. Like he was the butt of a joke far more elaborate than his puny brain could comprehend.

The woman didn't answer him, flipping over the card on her left.

THE MOTHER

Beneath the title was an illustration of a woman in a dark green gown, backdropped once again by a forest. She wore a majestic pair of antlers as a headdress, with more prongs than Holden could count before the woman across from him sighed and touched her fingers to her own antler choker. Her shoulders sagged, like she was relieved.

"What does this card mean?" he asked, returning his attention to the sketch of the antlered *Mother*. He was wrong; the antlers weren't a headdress. Blood seeped from The Mother's temples, where the antlers had sprouted. They were a part of her.

"It means we are on the same side," the woman said.

Holden tore his eyes away from the card to her. "The same side of what?"

The woman blinked her big glassy eyes, and stared at Holden like he was a thing of wonder. Like he was an *answer* to something.

She smiled. "The apocalypse."

EXCERPT FROM CHAPTER 7 OF *WITHOUT A TRACE* BY JOHN LAWSON:

The Deadswitch Trip wasn't the first Avery Mathis and Janet Warren had planned together. The two had a brief history of group wilderness expeditions between their sophomore year of college and when they went missing. Most women I interviewed who went on these trips said the same thing: Janet always planned, but people went because of Avery.

Avery was magnetic—funny, charming, and flirtatious. She refused to talk about her own successful starlet career on these trips, instead showering the other women with compliments and praise. In fact, the only one ever at odds with Avery was Janet.

"Janet chastised Avery for everything she did," one of the previous hikers told me. "Avery was always being too loud, risky, lazy, or a kiss-ass. Sure, they were best friends, but Janet was obviously jealous of her."

Janet had a reason for jealousy. By the time she was twenty-five, she'd cultivated a middling career as a folk singer and guitarist. Her local shows were never more than half-full. Avery had everything Janet didn't—beauty, personality, and fans.

I asked if things ever became uncomfortably contentious, or even violent, between them.

"Only once," said the hiker.

CAMERON

Had she blacked out? Why else would Cam be at the bottom of the mountain, alone, with no recollection of the descent?

She'd promised the others she'd be right back. Siena had to be freaking out.

Her pack . . . Cam patted her shoulders and spun around.

It was gone.

She took a lot of precautions to never freak out in the woods; certifications up the ass—everything from Wilderness First Responder to Bushcraft 101 to a Navigation Intensive. She was even certified to be an instructor, not that she ever wanted to go that route. In grad school, she'd realized she lacked the patience to teach.

Cam couldn't take the time to worry about where the last twelve hours had gone. Water was more important, and she was thirsty. The only safe water was back at the cabin, at least a thousand feet above her.

The sun was setting at her back, which meant she stood on the western slope of the mountain—not the south—on a trail between the summit and Triplet Lakes. At least she didn't have to scramble up.

Dusk had fallen by the time Cam ascended, her mouth so dry

she couldn't even swallow. She tugged a flashlight from her pocket and clicked it on.

Before her, the trail thinned to nothing, but water babbled a couple dozen yards ahead. Helio Creek was the major artery of snowmelt from the glacier to the lakes below. She'd collected water from it only yesterday, which meant she just needed to follow it upstream to reach the cabin.

Cam stumbled through the brush to the creek, the air dense with moisture. She muttered curses at herself for not having a Nalgene and a damn filter on her. But it wouldn't matter, not for much longer. The cabin was just ahead. Then she'd be able to figure this whole mess out, and whether the others had left the mountain without her. Siena wouldn't dare. Emmett on the other hand . . .

Her light caught on a pile of junk near a tree to the right. It looked like someone had made an impromptu camp and then left all their stuff. Weird—she, Emmett, and Isaac had scoured the area yesterday. No one had mentioned anything about finding an abandoned site.

Cam stopped, kicking the end of a degrading sleeping bag half-buried by needles and brush. Stepping over tufts of down and ripped nylon, she stooped near the abandoned backpack and shone her light on the faded pink fabric, and the Mount Whitney patch sewn to its belly.

A soft "oh" escaped Cam's mouth. She pressed her fingers to her lips.

Time had plucked away half the stitches of the patch, stitches Avery had meticulously sewn by hand as she sat sprawled out on the floor of her dorm.

"*Dad took me up a couple weeks ago. Right before term started. He doesn't know how to spend time with me, you know? Thought I'd like the summit, but I was miserable the whole hike. I was sure my heart was gonna stop and my ass was gonna fall off, and I kinda hated him for it. And then we got to the top, and it was like, oh my god. The pain was worth the pure rush. You can see everything. I swear, you can see the curvature of the earth."*

Back then, the pack was a shade of plum wine so deep you could get drunk off the color alone. Avery's father had given it to her after Whitney, hoping she'd caught a bug for the great outdoors.

Cam sank to her knees in front of the bag. It was the first time in a while that she wanted to cry, if only for the surprise of it all. The *possibility* of what it meant.

She held her breath and tilted her light upward, expecting Avery in the boughs above her, eyes filled with blood. But Avery wasn't there, and she exhaled, the relief too familiar.

Seven years ago she'd scoured these woods for Avery in a search that lasted weeks. No one in SAR ever enjoyed a mission's transition from rescue to recovery.

But Cam . . . She'd flat out denied it. She'd begun requesting more paperwork, more supply-run shifts. Finding Avery dead was worse than never finding her at all.

The ranger she'd shadowed had caught on. He'd given her more paperwork. More supply-run shifts. She'd never even told him she knew Avery. It was one of the kindest things anyone had ever done for her.

But no ranger had her back now, and Cam returned her attention to the bag, grabbing its top and popping the end of the flashlight into her mouth. She pulled the flap back and looked inside, but there was only darkness. Even her light illuminated nothing more than a pit inside a moldering sack.

Cam reached inside.

A strange sensation flowed through the tips of her fingers, up her arm, and into her heart, where it weighed like guilt. Guilt paired with these mountains perfectly in her memory, days spent searching the woods, empty-handed nights with her team around a fire, staring at the texts on her phone until it finally died.

Avery: Janet told me you're volunteering in deadswitch this

summer. im taking a group next week. Camping at would ridge

Avery: would*

Avery: wolf* fuck

Avery: could I see you at the ranger station?

Avery: maybe?

Avery: i miss you

Avery: a lot

Avery: shit its late. Just got done with a con and got to the hotel. drunk. lonely. just ignore me.

Avery: sorry for blowing up your phone. and making you mad at some point bc i must have. I dont know what I did Cameron. But im real sorry.

Avery had done nothing. Cam was just an idiot. A jealous, sensitive idiot who never responded to those texts.

And even worse—the person who'd put it all into perspective for her was John Fucking Lawson.

Cam's fingers wrapped around something soft, and she tugged it free. Her eyes burned as she held the hat up to the light, a worn mauve beanie.

She'd brought it with her.

Full circle. The color looked terrible on Cam, but it had made the browns in Avery's eyes pop in a way that warmed the pit of Cam's stomach.

Cam pressed the hat to her nose and inhaled, but the smell was stale. She tucked it into her pocket before searching the rest of the bag, almost missing the only other item: a map hidden away in the water bladder pouch. Cam owned the same edition. It was filthy, the paper worn to almost nothing at the creases. She could tear it in half if she sneezed wrong, but Cam unfolded it anyway, laying the map flat on the dirt near the deflated Osprey.

She stared at the topography, and frowned.

Avery had taken a Sharpie to the whole thing. Inky trails connected chevron peaks, ridges scribbled out and new bodies of water scribbled in. It was like a child had gotten hold of it and changed around the landmarks a bit.

A hundred or so miles north of Agnes, within the inaccessible northern stretch of Deadswitch, Avery had drawn an upside-down V and circled it. Beneath, a hastily scrawled message read:

Find the butcher's daughter.

So I just finished Without a Trace . . .
r/avablade · Posted by u/shitsgettingweird 5 years ago

. . . and like everyone else still lurking on this sub, feeling let down and a little pissed off.
JL spent so much time explaining the relationship between the hikers. Sure, fine, that's important for context or whatever. But all the clues as to what actually happened to them felt so incredibly glossed over. Out of the Woods was only mentioned in 1 CHAPTER IN PASSING. Why didn't JL spend more time on the game Avery was playing right before she died, especially given that it's about a girl who can't escape the woods, and THE DEVELOPERS DISAPPEARED OUT OF THIN AIR AT THE SAME TIME AVERY DID????

u/tdub_chronic · 5y
Bc ootw literally has nothing to do with avablades disappearance. stop spreading conspiracy theories

|

u/rememberthe7 · 5y
I strongly disagree with this.
Without a Trace sucks, and John Lawson is a hack. I think everyone on this sub can agree with this. Too many of us have done our own investigating because we actually care about what happened to ALL those hikers and aren't writing a book for the cash grab. Anyone capitalizing on this story for their own monetary gain without actually helping to solve the case is gross.
We don't know if Out of the Woods has anything to do with the disappearance of Avery or the others because neither the game nor Cold Alpine Studio were fully investigated by the police. The police came across too many dead ends, like the fact no tax or business information could be found for CAS and their devs

couldn't be contacted. They chalked it up to a prank because they were too stupid to dig for clues within the game itself.
There are a few aspects of the game I want to highlight here:

1. This game was clearly made for Avery. She liked indie games, cosmic horror, rich stories, female protagonists, and had told her fans she'd recently taken up the hobbies of backpacking and mountaineering. She began her playthrough the day after CAS sent it to her. We don't even know when the files that the other streamers had became corrupted because none of the streamers were interested in the game until after Avery's disappearance.

2. The storyline of OOTW: In Chapter 1, we learn no one in the village has ever made it all the way through the woods to the outside. The villagers worship a harvest goddess they call The Mother. As part of a ritual, the villagers choose one of their own to sacrifice to the forest every year, and the butcher's daughter is selected. But The Mother doesn't kill her right away; instead, as the butcher's daughter tries to escape to the outside, she meets a cast of characters living in the woods who assist her in one way or another, including the archgod The Shadow, Mother's nemesis. Obviously we don't know how the story ends because Avery never finished playing and the police couldn't find the game files.

3. HERE'S THE THING: historians and archaeologists who've studied Deadswitch Wilderness have found evidence of cults in the area that began during the pioneer era. Journal entries and religious documents of these supposed cult members mention not only The Mother and The Shadow, but other prophet or saintlike characters too who also appear in the game to help the butcher's daughter, such as The Ranger, The Lover, The Warden, etc.

The connection between Avery, Out of the Woods, and the

pioneer cult WAS NEVER FULLY INVESTIGATED BY THE POLICE.

|

u/tdub_chronic · 5y
that still doesnt mean anything. ootw could have been inspired by the pioneer cult, and avablade could have found that out and then decided to go backpacking in deadswitch after because of the game.

|

u/rememberthe7 · 5y
Yes, you are absolutely right. But we will never know because that connection wasn't ruled out. It's not a conspiracy. It's a legitimate lead.

|

u/shitsgettingweird OP · 5y
I know you just said you're against capitalizing on this story, but you should really start a podcast.

|

u/rememberthe7 · 5y
Don't tempt me.

EMMETT

Emmett stared at the sinkhole, fighting against the fog clouding his head.

Fog that had almost killed him.

Not that he hadn't registered the pit on the trail. He'd been compelled forward by a sick curiosity that had overridden all his other senses, like someone—something—had hijacked him. *Hypnotized* him.

Still on the ground, he wriggled from his pack, propping himself up on his elbows and failing to catch his breath. His heart pounded so violently that his whole chest hurt.

If Siena had reacted a second slower, he'd be dead.

She dropped her pack and knelt next to him, his fear ebbing as she rested a palm on his chest.

"Are you okay?" she asked.

A voice in the back of his head screamed to get the hell up and pull Siena away from the pit.

Keep her safe. He couldn't. He couldn't lie, either. Not this time.

"No."

He was angry with himself. Scared. Confused. And he wished

more than anything Siena would hold him in her arms like she used to.

"I thought you . . . I thought I wasn't going to be able to . . ." She drifted off and turned back to the pit. "Oh, god. Isaac . . ."

Fuck. Isaac had run off in this direction. The thought of him plummeting into the dark shook Emmett from his stupor. He scrambled to his feet, and inched as close to the edge as he dared. "Isaac. *ISAAC!*"

Siena dragged her pack toward her and tore into it, throwing clothing and food to the side until she tugged her emergency kit free. She dug through the contents until she found a flare, holding the thing away from her as she stood and uncapped it. An orange flame erupted from the tip with a loud *rip*, molten liquid dripping into the dirt. Siena flung it into the hole. It twirled deeper into the darkness before hitting the bottom with a scatter of sparks.

"What is that?" she asked. "Fifty, sixty feet?"

"About." The flare hardly illuminated anything around it. He shouted Isaac's name again to no response.

"There isn't a cavern system this high, is there?" Her voice wavered, but she was doing a better job of holding it together than he was.

Emmett didn't know if there were systems in these mountains. Hell, he couldn't even remember if caverns this high in the Sierras were a normal thing. He remembered jack shit from school. The only science he needed to remember was what COtwo Industries wanted him to know.

He and Siena stared in silence at the flare before Emmett finally bested his fear. "I have to go down there."

"Emmett, no."

"And if Isaac's hurt . . ."

"We don't even know if he fell. And we don't know where Cam is. She could be hurt, too."

"I can't do it alone, Sen. I need your help."

Hesitation flickered behind her eyes as she retreated into her own thoughts. She was trying to find another solution, but unless Isaac was waiting for them back at the cabin, there was none.

"Let's get the gear from the cabin. I'll only rappel until I can see the bottom," he promised.

Her lower lip trembled. "I hate this."

Emmett tried to swallow, but his throat was too dry. "I know. So do I."

Neither Cam nor Isaac was waiting for them when Emmett and Siena returned to the cabin for the climbing gear, and when the reality that they were alone settled in, Emmett grabbed Siena's elbows, pulled her toward him, and wrapped his arms around her.

He knew it was wrong of him the moment he did it. He should have asked her first. Everything felt so fragmented—what was happening to them, his emotions, his and Siena's relationship . . . He wanted to give half-baked answers for all of it, like he'd been doing for this entire trip. But he couldn't.

She wrapped her arms around his torso and buried her face in his t-shirt, her body shaking as she cried. He pressed his lips to the top of her head and inhaled the scent of her sweat.

Fuck, he missed her.

"I don't even know why I'm afraid, and that's the worst part." She sniffed. "Nothing makes sense, and nothing is logical, and I just feel like anything could happen to us at any moment and I wouldn't see it coming. I'm scared . . . about Cam, and Isaac, and you."

He pushed her away and gathered her face in his hands. "I'm going to be okay."

"I said the same thing to you yesterday," she said. "And I know you don't believe what happened to me, even with the recording—"

"I do believe you." *I just don't want to.* He'd never be able to tell her that last part, because she wouldn't understand his denial was how he protected himself. The vulnerability he felt facing the unknown was worse than the unknown itself.

Her eyes searched his, a plea for elaboration. He wanted to kiss her instead. But her fear left her unguarded, and it wouldn't be right.

Dropping his hands, he stepped away from Siena to resist temptation. "You said there were guns in the cellar?"

She cast a suspicious glance at him. "Why?"

"I want you to hold on to one for now." He headed toward the front door. "Like you said, we don't know what's going to happen."

"I don't know how to shoot a gun, Emmett!" she shouted.

"It's not hard. I'll be right back." Emmett punched open the door and headed around the cabin, spotting the cellar doors. He lugged one open and hurried down the steps. A ringing grew in his right ear, and he unhinged his jaw to pop it. The weird pressure at this altitude was driving him crazy.

Emmett pulled his flashlight from his pocket and clicked it on, skidding to a halt when a beetle fluttered across the beam of light.

Behind a few scattered stacks of boxes, a hole in the back cellar wall yawned open. A dozen black beetles skittered from its mouth, roots dangling from the top like skinny teeth.

Just like the hole in the cabin Siena had found.

Emmett spotted the gun safe, carefully climbing over boxes and removing a rifle when he reached it. He took an ammo box off the shelf and clumsily reloaded the gun, returning his attention to the hole.

Whatever was happening to them, the answer was close. He could feel it.

The sooner he could figure out what the hell was going on, the sooner he could get them off this mountain.

SIENA

"It's not hard. I'll be right back," Emmett shouted, the cabin door slamming shut behind him.

"Great," Siena hissed between her teeth. The last thing she wanted amid all this was to be responsible for a gun.

She spun on her heel and hurried down the hall and into the lab. Before they'd tried leaving the first time, she'd stacked the climbing gear in the corner. Rifling through it, she found a harness and yanked it free. But the heaping mess of rope didn't play along so nicely, and the more she worked at the knots, the more tangled it became.

She slammed her fist into the ground. "*FUCK!*"

Burying her face in her hands, Siena took a few deep breaths. Her time was better spent detangling the heaping mass of anxiety in her brain. But every time she attempted to tease apart a problem she could solve, a wave of nausea swelled in her stomach. Her shoulders itched with stress in the way they used to long before the bugs, when her good ol' panic attacks manifested in a perfectly acceptable textbook fashion.

She dropped her hands and opened her eyes to darkness, a hazier, twilight-tinged world like the one she'd emerged into yesterday. The world with the map and the masked stranger and the beheaded animal. The world where The Mother reigned, whatever the hell that meant.

The stress in her neck tightened into a hook that tried to drag her to her feet until she saw a beat-up field journal lying on the floor of the lab. Isaac's. He'd carried that damn thing with him everywhere, yet left it at the cabin? It made no sense.

Unless he had come back here after he left them on the trail. Maybe he hadn't fallen into the pit after all.

Siena scrambled to the journal and flipped it open to the sketch of the valley he'd shown her two weeks prior: three sister peaks and an imposter. The jagged, unnatural thing reminded her of a fantasy-novel mountain. Mount Doom or something.

She turned the page to a sketch of the melted glacier. Just like the valley, the detail of the copper cliffside was incredible. But the water . . . he'd scribbled it in. The entire tarn was a smeared mess of graphite. He'd even pressed hard enough with the pencil to rip the page in a few spots.

So destructive for someone so meticulous.

Siena flipped the page again.

The next sketch was of the tree they'd found. The tree she'd entered. It was as grandiose as she remembered, except another smeared dark scribble within the branches had ripped open the page.

She swiped the sketch away to the next. A cry escaped her throat, and she pressed her fingers to her lips.

In a meadow, a mule lay dead. The contents of its slashed pack—rope, a canteen, a first aid tin—rested in the grass. The animal was decapitated, its spine falling limply from its neck like wet rope. Fungus sprouted from the gaping hole where its head once was.

Had he found this? Had he found this and never told them—the body of the mutilated trophy she'd discovered?

No. Isaac would have told them. He hadn't acted disturbed enough to keep it to himself.

But maybe she hadn't been paying close enough attention to him.

Siena wiped her hand across her face and pulled away, rubbing tears between her fingers as the front door slammed. She hopped up and hurried toward the living room, expecting Emmett with a rifle.

But it wasn't Emmett.

Cam stood at the entrance to the cabin. She was as filthy and haggard as the unfamiliar backpack over her shoulder, which she dropped on the floor in front of her.

Siena ran to her and threw her arms around Cam's neck, sobbing in a way Cam usually made fun of her for. But Siena didn't care. "Where the hell have you been?"

Cam's body trembled as she hugged Siena back. "I—I don't know. But I'm being punished. Punished for lying to everyone. For lying to you."

EMMETT

Emmett always wanted to have and eat his cake. The prestige of academia *and* the corporate salary. His freedom *and* his parents' approval.

His secrets *and* the girl.

Sometimes he got everything he wanted, but when it really mattered, he always lost the thing he cared about most. A hundred paces into the rock-crusted tunnel, his only guidance the weak beam of his flashlight, he knew the same thing could happen now.

If answers were at the end of this tunnel—if he could lay whatever was going on to rest—then maybe he could find Isaac and Cam, and all of them could stay and finish their work. For once on this trip, he'd be respected.

The other side of the coin? Safety. His life. The tunnel was only getting narrower, and he had no evidence that whatever lay at its end could be handled with a rifle.

And if the worst happened to him and the other two never returned, then Siena would be all alone. He couldn't let that happen. Protecting her was the only way he could make up for the pain he'd caused her.

Before he could second-guess himself, the tunnel walls

bloomed wider. Behind the stalactites, a faint light reflected against the artery wall until it shimmered. He reached to the side, the hand that held his light grazing jagged rock, moisture, and the slime of algae. The mist from the air clung to his body and beaded down his face and neck.

He tilted the light upward. A dense weave of roots covered the tunnel's ceiling, and he followed it forward to the protrusions.

Not stalactites. Spruce.

Right in the middle of the path, tiny saplings stretched from the ceiling toward the ground, shimmering water collecting in their needles. They grew upside down, defying biology like it was nothing.

His eyes flickered down to the largest of the evergreen cave teeth, a spruce more disfigured than the others. Emmett swallowed back bile when he saw why.

One of the sapling's branches threaded right through the cracked eye socket of a jawless human skull. It hung there like a Christmas ornament.

He reached out to touch it and then stopped himself. The skull could belong to anyone. One of the missing hikers from seven years ago. He could stumble upon their bodies right beneath the research cabin.

The air smelled of rot. There had to be more.

Leaving the skull, he ducked through the upside-down spruce. A few more steps and the tunnel fanned out into a large chamber. More than five bodies' worth of bones lay strewn across the ground. It was like he'd entered the lair of a human-hungry monster, the stagnant air so dense with the stench of death that he could taste it in the back of his throat.

Emmett gagged, pulling the neck of his t-shirt up over his mouth. It hardly helped. Desperate for a palate cleanser, he focused on the light above that permeated the foggy space. It came from an opening at the very top of the cavern.

The sinkhole. It looked so small from all the way down here.

He followed the soft beam of light to a grotto in the cavern wall. A stone statue of a woman stood at three times his height, her head adorned with a massive rack of antlers dripping with lichen. One arm stretched upward, and she held a skull that looked as real as those littering the ground. A thick tendril of carved obsidian began at the statue's sandaled feet and twisted up around her torso once, ending at her raised hand, where it also cradled the skull.

Atop the bones, a man lay prostrate at the statue's feet, recently dead. The body hadn't decomposed at all.

The man's back rose and fell.

Emmett's gut clenched. "Hey," he called hoarsely, but the man didn't move.

The pulse beating in his ear was surreally loud as he stepped over bones, creeping closer to the man. He'd never passed out from fear before, but if ever there were a time for him to faint, it would be now. He raised his rifle but kept the safety on, aiming it at the man, who was too low to the ground for Emmett to see his face, or anything other than his long filthy hair and the patchwork of furs and fabric he wore.

"*Hey,*" Emmett said again. He lifted his foot and nudged the man with his boot.

The man stiffened and then shuddered an exhale, long and pained, like a dying breath. "Is it time?" he asked the ground.

"Time?" Emmett repeated.

The man slowly sat and stretched, his spine popping. He craned his neck to look at Emmett.

Shock stole the warmth from Emmett's body.

The gun slipped from his fingers, the surrounding bones clattering as it hit the ground.

A scar cut clean across the man's weathered face. He was sallow. Starving. A set of haunted eyes stared at Emmett without a single spark of recognition, even though they'd last seen each other only hours ago.

Isaac.

HOLDEN

"She told me I was a catalyst for the apocalypse," Holden said.

He was lying on the grimy floor of the air-conditioned IT office with his backpack under his head, he and Angel taking turns playing patient–therapist to pass the dead hours of summer. He'd just listened to her unload about her ex wanting to take her to court over their junky Nissan. Now it was his turn, Saturday night's party still fresh in his head.

"Those were her exact words?" Angel sat in a plastic chair near one of the monitors, painting her nails as she half listened. "'Holden Sharpe, the world is going to end because of you'?"

"She might as well have said that. Seriously, I was having a perfectly horrible night without some fortune-teller calling me the harbinger of doom. Chelsea didn't even want to go home with me. She probably hooked up with that other guy who hugged her all creepy."

"Oh yes, poor you." Angel splayed her fingers to scrutinize her nails. "You got to fuck a cute blonde for a couple of months, knowing full well that was the extent of the relationship, and then some manic pixie dream girl reads your cards in the woods and calls you special. You have a cool roommate who takes time out of her life to listen to your sad boy problems, and then there is me, the hot piece of ass who *also* listens to your sad boy problems." She pointed a glistening nail at him. "Don't get any ideas. I may go for the tall, dark, ethnically ambiguous type, but you are far too pathetic for me."

He glared at her from the ground. "You're a terrible therapist."

"And *you* are choosing to be miserable."

He propped himself up on his elbows. "I'm not *choosing* anything. I'm depressed."

"Then get on antidepressants."

"I can't afford them."

"Then get a second job. Or move back in with your parents."

"We're not on good terms. And I hardly have time as it is."

Angel groaned. "Are you even listening to yourself right now? Does it feel good to make excuses for every shitty thing that comes your way? I swear to god, Holden. You're good-looking and smart and not a raging dickhole. Find something that tickles your pickle and do something meaningful with your life for once."

"Wow, you should be a motivational speaker," he said dryly.

"You better be glad I'm not, or else I'd be charging you for this, and you'd have to pay me with your antidepressant money."

Holden fell back onto his backpack. The worst thing about all this was that Angel was right. After graduating, he never tried leaving Corvallis. He never tried searching for a career he loved, settling because he was happy with Becca. But settling meant never taking risks and never disappointing himself. In theory, at least. But now he was in his thirties and still disappointed. He'd blown the past decade of his life with nothing to show for it.

Great, now he was feeling even *sorrier* for himself.

"This was a bad idea," said Holden.

"Welp." Angel blew on her nails. "We can always listen to Dr. Dupont's next recording."

Holden sat up. "It unlocked?"

"Yesterday."

"And you haven't listened to it yet?"

"No, darling." She curled her fingers and studied her nails from a different angle. "I was waiting for you."

That was bullshit, because she had never waited for him before, but he didn't pry. Instead, he stood with a grunt and joined her by the monitor. The screen brightened as Angel wiggled the mouse, and she dug into her Dropbox, pulling up the recordings. There was only one item left with a red exclamation. All the others had uncorrupted themselves, including the third to last file, which they hadn't listened to yet. It was less than a minute long.

Angel yanked her earbuds out of the computer's headphone jack and double-clicked the file.

"*Day eighteen of the Alpenglow study. Thought I broke the recorder when I threw it against the wall this morning, but alas, dumb thing is still working. I guess I can count that as a win . . . not that I'll be needing it much longer.*

"*It's late. I should be asleep right now given we're leaving tomorrow, but every time I close my eyes, all I see is the mule.*

"*We should have left today. This place—it's scaring the shit out of me. That doesn't mean I don't hate myself a little for giving up. After all the work we've done, I don't think I can bring myself to ever come back here.*

"*I know I need to document my recollection of what has happened so far, but I won't have the bandwidth until we're back down the mountain. Shouldn't be more than a five-day trip. So I guess you'll hear from me again after eight-four-twenty-three.*"

"Don't have the bandwidth until we're back down the mountain? Girl!" Angel clicked out of the audio player. "You're killing me. Just tell me what happened to you."

Eight, four, twenty-three.

"Holden? Bud? Can you give me back my arm?"

Holden blinked at the monitor and glanced down at the desk, where he clutched Angel's wrist in a death grip. He quickly relaxed his hand, and she stole her arm back. "Eight, four, twenty-three. What is that?"

Angel shrugged. "I don't know. A date?"

They stared at each other.

"A date," Holden repeated. "A date as in, August 4th, 2023?"

Angel opened her mouth, shut it, and shook her head. "No, wait. That makes no sense."

"Dupont said, 'You'll hear from me again after eight, four, twenty-three.'"

"I know what she said."

"They left in July. Eighteen days had passed, so it would be August. It's a date."

"Then she misspoke." Angel's words were hesitant. She stared at Holden as hard as he stared at her, the tension between them tight enough to snap. "I mean . . ." She pulled at her lower lip with her teeth. "You heard from CalTech months ago. They said Dupont was back in the field, and the department was still trying to cope with a death. If the Deadswitch Expedition took place in 2022, then that timeline adds up."

"Unless it wasn't Isaac's death they were talking about." Sweat prickled the back of Holden's neck, like how it always did right before he threw up.

"Whose death would it be, then?" Angel asked.

"Wilder Feyrer. Dupont's mentor. Chari said he just died of cancer. I assumed from the other recordings that he wasn't on the expedition because he was sick, not because he was dead."

Silence lapsed between them until Angel laughed uncomfortably. "I don't really know what you're getting at, here. You found those files back in March. We're not in a sci-fi movie, Holden. The rules of space and time don't bend when they feel like it."

Holden swallowed and nodded, picking up his phone. "It doesn't have to stay a mystery, right? We can find out when they left right now."

"How?"

"If they went this summer, there will be a record." Holden swiped his thumb across the screen of his phone to unlock it. The date and time glared back at him.

2:17 p.m.
July 31st, 2023

Angel was right. He was being absurd.

He searched through his call history and in seconds found the number for the Deadswitch Ranger Station. He double-tapped the string of digits and turned on speaker mode as it dialed out.

Someone picked up on the third ring. "This is Frank."

"Uhh, hi. Is this the Deadswitch Wilderness Ranger Station?"

"You bet. What can I do for you?"

"I, uhh . . ." Holden cleared his throat. "I'm from CalTech and need to check on the permit of some of our researchers."

"Oh yeah, I remember them."

Holden clenched his phone. "You do?"

"Picked up their permit a couple weeks ago. Four of them. A young group."

Holden locked eyes with Angel. She looked as nervous and confused as he felt. "Can you do me a favor and read me their names and the entrance and exit dates?"

Frank grunted. "I guess. You're lucky we aren't busy or I'd tell you you're SOL. One sec here, gotta find where Carol put the binder. We're not digital yet—that'll probably come back to bite us in the ass one day. Ah, here it is. Right where it's supposed to be. Let's see . . . July, July. Here we go. Siena Dupont, party of four. Other names listed are Cameron Yarrow, Emmett Ghosh, and Isaac Perez. Entrance date . . . looks like seven-thirteen-twenty-three. They got an extended permit for the old cabin on Agnes, exit date set for the week of eight-twenty-eight-twenty-three. So, they'll be out by the end of the month."

Blood rushed through Holden's ears. He gripped the side of the desk. "Are you sure?"

"That's what the permit says. Anything else I can do you for?"

July 13th, 2023. The day Siena Dupont entered Deadswitch Wilderness was eighteen days ago. Which was impossible. It meant he and Angel had listened to her recordings days, weeks, *months* before she ever recorded them. Before she'd even stepped foot into Deadswitch.

And if Dupont had made the recording about Isaac's death on day thirty-two of the expedition, it meant he was supposed to die within two weeks.

"Sir? Can I help you with anything else?"

Impossible.

Holden had made the acquaintance of the impossible months ago. His favorite memories, a string of impossibilities with a partner who couldn't remember. But they were real. Deep down, he *knew* they were real, regardless of what Becca believed.

Just like this. The recordings were real, too. He couldn't explain how, but it didn't matter. He was out of time.

Because if the recordings were real, then something was going to stop Siena Dupont and her team from hiking back home. They were still going to be in Deadswitch in two weeks, burying Isaac in the ground.

"She's in trouble," he finally said. "Siena Dupont—all of them. They're in trouble, and we need to find them. Now."

TWO HOURS AGO

Isaac jogged back toward the cabin, keeping his eyes peeled for a fork in the path, and the right way down Mount Agnes.

The generous man will be prosperous, And he who waters will himself be watered.

Proverbs 11:25—Levi's favorite. It was one of the few verses Isaac remembered after five years of religious neglect. He'd stopped going to church when his parents divorced. He'd quit caring long before that.

Isaac's pot-smoking, unkempt older brother kept nuggets of biblical wisdom in his back pocket for when he was feeling philosophical. Levi was a walking contradiction, one reason Isaac loved him so unequivocally.

Even with Levi's sage and often stoned advice, helpfulness eluded Isaac in his teens. He hadn't been helpful all those years when his parents were fighting, too obsessed with music and parties and the girl down the street. His consequence was their divorce.

The bad luck that followed his team around Deadswitch—maybe it was all because he hadn't really been helping. He spent too many hours in his sketchbook, a distraction as he decided if he even wanted to be a scientist. He'd thought he knew at twelve, when Levi took him to the waterfall behind their house. Isaac couldn't fathom the creation of such a beautiful place.

He loved land—loved sketching it, loved the sheer expanse of it. How and why it formed. How many millions and millions of years it took. Maybe his obsession stemmed from the need to rebel against his creationist parents, to find God in an ancient world long before Christians believed the world existed.

And he couldn't find anything else careerworthy that he cared enough about. Being a poor artist wasn't an option. So after a BS in geology from the University of Tennessee, he applied to CalTech's grad program and got in. His mother called it a miracle. Isaac hated that she was probably right.

And finding the trail that led off the mountain would be another miracle, because nothing surrounding him looked familiar.

Isaac slowed and spun around. How long had he been jogging —ten minutes? The trees differed from the ones near the cabin, the sky darker and the air thicker. It smelled like home. Like Memphis in the fall.

The others—Emmett and Siena and Cam—kept trying to use capital-R Reason to explain the scenery shifts. But Isaac's body wasn't void of all spiritual bones. Deadswitch was haunted. Something had been given free rein to roam and manipulate this place, just like the devil over Earth.

The devil didn't care for logic. And here, he could manifest. Isaac had seen it. He'd drawn it.

Cam had gotten angry with him when he said God wasn't here, but that was exactly how he felt. This place—this mountain —was unprotected, which meant they were unprotected. Just like the victims in all those exorcism movies he'd inhaled as a teenager.

In front of him, the path ended in a mess of weeds and shrubs. His eyes drifted to a scraggly opening that looked less like a trail for people and more for animals, and he followed the path down a damp embankment. Water gushed in the distance, and Isaac batted branches from his eyes until the trees cleared. A waterfall spilled over a ledge across from him.

He scuffed his boot at the edge of the water. The pool before him was deep, but so clear, he could see the fuzzy green rocks all the way at the bottom. It was like the one Levi had shown him all those years ago, miles behind their house, on a bad day between Mom and Dad. This pool wasn't a replica, but it had the same ingredients. The mist that clung to the air. The waterfall. Everything so green that even the air was green. Isaac breathed in green, exhaled green, and extended his hand in front of him. He half expected to find moss sprouting between his fingers, but only mist beaded around his nails and rolled down his hands.

He dropped his hand, squinting at the water. He wasn't alone.

He'd expected this. It was only a matter of time before The Shadow appeared, coiled at the bottom of the pool as it had been in the melted glacier. Yes, he'd seen it there. He'd seen it just like Cam, though Cam pretended she hadn't.

Familiar rebellion flared up in him again.

If you are the devil, I'm going to find out what you want.

This was how he could finally be helpful. And as long as he was helpful—really helpful—everything would work itself out. Just like Levi used to tell him. He missed Levi. He wished he were here.

Isaac's ear rang as he waded into the water. The Shadow unraveled and opened. He knew deep in his warm bones that it had something very important to say. It just needed someone to listen.

Isaac pushed his hiking boots off the silky green rocks and swam closer.

DESCENT

EXCERPT FROM CHAPTER 10 OF *WITHOUT A TRACE* BY JOHN LAWSON:

Avablade's YouTube channel, now a shrine for the lost creator, was once a home to her three million wildcats—Avery's pet name for her fans. By the time this book is published, the channel's subscriber count will have grown to over seven million.

Many new subscribers are wildcat cubs who stumbled over Avablade's trove of over fifteen hundred videos too late. Others are true crime fanatics, the channel's sub count spiking when the popular podcast *Wilderness Realm* featured the Deadswitch Five.

And, of course, the late streamer's account isn't immune to trolls.

"It's hard sometimes," Lewis Mathis says. He's taken over moderation of his daughter's channel since late 2016. "I have to go through everything, you know? All the comments, even the ones that are crude or sexual. Sometimes they're violent. Sometimes they speculate on all the horrible ways she could have died. Sometimes I think about deleting all of it, but I just can't bring myself to hurt her fans.

"They need the memory of Avery as much as I do."

CAMERON

For seven years, Cam pretended she hardly knew Avery Mathis.

It was a pretty good lie, palatable solely because of the period they'd lived near each other. Cam interacted with many acquaintances—classmates, research assistants, rangers—for a year before promptly forgetting they ever existed.

Avery was just another passerby in the current of Cam's life. A pretty face. A hot-minute crush. Someone who would have been fodder for bar conversations if the circumstances had played out differently. *"Hey, you know that famous YouTuber, Avablade? I had the dorm next to her in college. Wild, right? Yeah, I know . . .* so *hot."*

But Cam hadn't bothered fine-tuning these would-have moments. She'd be dead before she casually said that someone was *so hot*. And to boil Avery down to her physical parts meant Cam wasn't better than any other fuckboy fan. Maybe she wasn't.

The start of the 2010 fall term settled over San José State like a sweaty towel. It was 102 degrees the day Cam moved back into her dorm, and according to the listserv, the air-conditioning in the wing remained in a semipermanent state of *technicians are investigating*.

Her roommate, Brittani-with-an-I, was best friends with the

girl in the room across the hall, Lyndsey-with-two-Ys. Brittani liked to escape the heat at night by going to parties on the lawns of fraternity houses. Cam didn't blame her, though she'd rather lie on the pavement in the middle of the day than attend a frat party.

Plus, Cam was older than the other sophomores thanks to month-long backpacking trips and the corresponding ton of weed. She was old enough to buy alcohol, which Brittani knew. And if Brittani knew something, then the entire school did.

So in the evenings, Cam stayed back in her roasting dorm and studied.

During the second week of the semester, she discovered a crisp airflow in the hall, and kept the door to the room propped open until Brittani stumbled back at midnight. The night after, as Cam sat on her bed with her computer and a bag of pretzels, she asked Brittani to leave the door open as she left.

"Just ooonnnneee time, Avery. That's all I'm asking. It'll be fun! I'll stay with you the whole time, *promise*."

Cam looked up from her online calculus homework. Lyndsey stood in the hall sporting platform sandals and a kimono jacket. She held a half-finished iced Starbucks Something in her hand as she talked to someone through her open dorm door, though Cam was at the wrong angle to see what this Avery person looked like.

"I'm behind on work," said Avery. "Maybe if I catch up—"

Lyndsey gave an exasperated sigh. "That's what you said last night."

As Brittani and Lyndsey left, Avery yelled after them, "Well, if you keep going to these parties at the rate you are now, I'll have plenty of chances, won't I?"

She sounded like the droll and sexy Mary Elizabeth Winstead in *Scott Pilgrim vs. the World*, a movie Cam had caught the week before school started. Avery surpassed even those high expectations when she swung into Cam's doorway minutes later.

Her blonde hair was twisted into a knot on the top of her head. She wore a loose tank top—on it a bloody, gross-looking man with a sword, and a diamond for a head—and a pink sports bra beneath.

She pointed a hitchhiker's thumb down the hall. "You mind if I crank up the AC?"

Cam tried to never stare at pretty girls for more than a couple of seconds. Her androgyny was hard enough to navigate without someone accusing her of being a leering butch. Going to college—a California college at that—hadn't shielded her from the stereotype. At least things were going better than they had in high school.

But Avery's question caught her off guard, and Cam blankly stared at her. "Up?"

"Umm, yes, I believe the word 'up' came out of my mouth, though I can repeat myself if that would be best." Avery's expression was frustratingly vacant. Cam couldn't tell if she was irritated or trying to be funny.

"I thought it was broken," Cam said.

"Oh," Avery chuckled. "Oh, no. They just tell us that because the budget got cut again and the admins are finding sneaky ways to save money."

Cam raised her eyebrows. This was news. "Are you serious? I'm taking out a shit-ton of loans. I'm going to have to sell a kidney to recover from debt. The least they could give me is air-conditioning until October."

Avery grinned and then wrinkled her nose. "Tuition here isn't that bad."

"It is when I'm going to be in school for the next seven years."

This seemed to pique her interest. "PhD?"

"If I'm motivated enough."

"Seven years is a long time. You're gonna need to learn all the tricks to be that committed." She waved her hand. "I'll show you."

Cam hesitated for a second before shutting her laptop and sliding from the bed. She followed Avery down a hall that smelled like old Chinese food and BO.

"What's your last name?" Avery asked.

Cam thought it was a weird question, but responded anyway. "Yarrow."

"Dr. Yarrow . . . very nice ring to it. And your first?"

"Cam."

Avery tossed a look over her shoulder. "Short for something?"

Cam suppressed the urge to smile, hyperaware of how much she was enjoying Avery's prying. "Cameron."

"Cameron." Avery hummed. "That's pretty. Can I call you Cameron?"

Pretty. No one ever said *pretty* as a gut reaction to her first name. They said *like a boy* or *like Cameron Diaz.*

Cam scratched the back of her head and tugged her hair. "Uhh, sure."

"Great." Avery stopped in front of a dusty vent at the end and carefully lifted the lip, cringing as the hinges squeaked. "Just gotta make sure we set it back before the dorm super clocks in tomorrow morning. He's supposed to get in at eight thirty, but he's always late." She reached into the vent. Cam ducked her head beneath the cover to watch Avery fiddle with a small wiry thermostat, its face reading 87 degrees.

Avery jammed her thumb on the down button until the number 72 blinked back. A cold gust of wind hit Cam's face, and her knees almost gave out from sheer relief.

"There." Avery lowered the cover and turned toward Cam. "Now you know my most valuable secret, and you don't even know my name." She winked.

"Or do I, Avery?" *Dumb joke,* Cam immediately thought as she leaned against the wall. "I heard Lyndsey say it."

Avery smiled at her.

Cam cleared her throat and nodded at Avery's tank top. "Who's that?"

Avery pulled out the bottom of her shirt and glanced down at the silk screen print. "Pyramid Head." She dropped her shirt. "He's my boyfriend."

"He's ugly."

Avery laughed in surprise. "He's misunderstood is all."

Cam waited for clarification, but Avery didn't offer it.

"It's nice meeting you, Dr. Cameron Yarrow."

Cam flushed. "You're gonna jinx it."

Avery waved in dismissal and placed her hand on her hip, leaning against the wall to mirror Cam. She offered a delicate shrug. "Why believe in jinxes when you can believe in manifestation instead?"

Cam paced the floor of the cabin kitchen as she clutched Siena's near-empty Nalgene. Even as the exhaustion settled in, her body refused to sit still.

Siena watched her from the dining table. "Why didn't you tell anyone you knew her?"

"Because." Cam combed her fingers through her hair and tugged. "I'm an asshole who is terrible with that kind of grief stuff. Admitting we were close meant I'd have to mourn her. And now . . ." She cast a glance at Avery's destroyed bag lying in front of the door.

Avery had wanted Cam's attention, and Cam had kept pushing her away.

"This is karma. I fucked up, and now she's haunting us. Or *something* is."

"You don't believe in karma," Siena gently said. "Or ghosts. And telling someone you knew her after she disappeared wouldn't have changed the outcome."

Cam shook her head. "You don't know that."

"I *do* know you aren't being punished." When Cam didn't agree with her, Siena continued. "Were you close enough to her to know something the police didn't? Were you withholding information?"

"No," Cam replied. "I wanted her found as much as anyone."

"Did you sleep with her?"

Cam barked a bitter laugh to hide her discomfort. "Why the interrogation?"

"I'm your best friend," Siena said, lifting her pinkie. "It's just a question."

Cam sighed, releasing her hair and dropping her hand. "Sorry. No, I never slept with her. She kissed me, once. It's . . ." Cam quickly knocked the thought of that night out of her brain. "Not a good memory."

Siena didn't press further, which Cam appreciated as she leaned against the counter and rubbed the bridge of her nose. She despised how vulnerable the past few hours made her feel, and not just because she couldn't remember half of it. There were too many reasons she never wanted to think about Avery Mathis again. Hell, she'd almost backed out of the Alpenglow project when they got funded. Even years later, the thought of reentering Deadswitch made her stomach churn.

But the biggest reason she never wanted to think about Avery was that the past didn't care about Cam's guilt. She'd searched these woods for Avery once before. It had been seven years. She was gone. "I'm not expecting to find her alive, for the record."

"But some closure would be nice. I know it doesn't feel like it, but finding her bag is a good sign, even if it makes little sense. Nothing makes sense right now." Siena pushed her chair back and stood. "Something's wrong with this forest. I found a cabin at the end of a tunnel. You were transported down the mountain and don't remember it. Who's to say Avery and those other hikers didn't experience something similar?"

"Siena . . ." False hope ached worse than grief. "Hundreds of bodies have never been recovered from public land. *Hundreds.*"

"I'm not saying she's alive," Siena argued. "All I'm saying is maybe her disappearance is more complicated than anyone thought."

Before Cam could respond, something thudded across the

porch. Cam jumped as the door flew open and Emmett stumbled into the cabin. Another person clung to his neck, and Emmett held them up while their feet dragged across the floor.

Siena shouted Emmett's name and hurried toward him, but hesitated when Emmett lowered the person to the floor. Cam spotted a mess of facial hair beneath a mop of matted graying locks. The man wore an ensemble of animal skins and filth, and she could smell his fecal, salty stench all the way from where she stood.

He finally looked up. Cam dropped the Nalgene. It hit the ground and rolled toward Isaac.

"Holy shit," she whispered.

"Are you sure?" Dr. Maidei Chari asked. She sat opposite Holden and Angel in the coffee shop, clutching a macchiato in a worn porcelain cup. Concern lined her face, like she was on the brink of believing them, or already did.

"Of course I'm not sure," Holden responded in an injured hiss. Her *concern* was betrayal.

"Holden wants you to knock some sense into him," Angel interjected. "Explain all this so we can both move on with our mediocre lives."

Dr. Chari's dark eyes flitted back and forth between the two of them before she took a sip of coffee and stared out the window. It was a blistering day, the café lobby bright and full of weeping plants. The atmosphere oddly coincided with Holden's anxiety.

Chari returned her attention to them. "I can't give you a reasonable explanation. The ranger wouldn't tell you an incorrect date on purpose unless he was mistaken."

Holden loosened his grip on his coffee glass before he broke it. "That doesn't explain the audio files."

"I suppose you're right," Chari conceded, as though Holden was pointing out that the sky was blue. "What did you say to the ranger, exactly?"

"I didn't tell him I received a *message from the future*, if that's what you're asking."

"Holden told him our team intercepted a distress signal." Angel slurped her iced drink. "Which sounds about as believable as a message from the future."

"They said they'd look into it," Holden finished.

Chari frowned. "That's not promising. I know how bureaucracy operates."

"Yeah, so do I. We both work at a university, remember?" Every bit of evidence Holden had to convince authorities that Dupont's team actually needed rescuing would only spark more questions. More questions meant more time, and they had none to spare. "What can we do?"

"You already did it. You reported what you knew." Maidei raised her mug to her lips in such apathy that Holden repressed the urge to flip the table.

"It isn't enough if nothing is done. This is someone's life!"

"Lives, plural. Four, to be exact," Angel said. "According to Siena's files, Isaac died—or he dies, whatever—but we have no evidence the other three make it out."

Angel may have invited herself into this mess, but Holden felt less delirious with her here. He couldn't remember the last time anyone took him so seriously. And that was saying a lot, because she was, well, *Angel*.

"Then you need to convince the ranger that they truly are in danger," Maidei said. "He needs to hear the files himself. I just don't know how you're going to get them to him. I'd be surprised if the stations in those mountains have internet."

Holden pushed his coffee away, his anxiety morphing into jitters. "You worked in Deadswitch for years. Are you sure you don't know anyone who can help us?"

A pained expression crossed Maidei's face. She opened her mouth like she was going to speak, but then shut it, shaking her head.

"Please," Holden begged.

"I already told you, I can't get involved."

"*Why not?*"

"Trauma," she stated simply, and stood. "I need to go."

"Wait, hold on. I didn't mean—I didn't know." Holden fumbled over his words, racking his brain for anything he could say to keep her here. "I've never been to Deadswitch before. I didn't mean to be ignorant or upset you."

"You didn't upset me. It's complicated." Dr. Chari dragged the strap of her purse over her shoulder. "I think you're doing the right thing, pursuing this. I hope you find help for them."

"Dammit," he muttered as she hurried out of the coffee shop. He clenched his hands into fists and shoved them into his lap. "What the hell do we do now?"

"Oh, come on." Angel got up and slid into Dr. Chari's old seat. "You know exactly what we need to do." She pulled out her phone, her thumbs flying across the surface. "I'm calling us both out of work for the next two weeks."

"Stop it." He made a swipe at her phone, which Angel gracefully dodged. "You're going to get us fired."

She dodged Holden a second time, not missing a beat with her typing. "No, we're not. We possess way too much domain knowledge, and the school can't afford to replace us. Plus, it's summer, and all Chase does is play games. Working for once won't kill him."

Holden pressed his palms to the top of the table. "What exactly are you suggesting? That we fly the files there ourselves?"

"*Fly?*" She laughed. "Do I look like I'm made of money? No, honey. We're taking your Camry."

"That piece of junk will fall apart before we get to Ashland."

"It's a Toyota. It will last another hundred thousand miles, easy." Angel tapped the screen of her phone with her index finger. "There. All sent."

"I have obligations here."

Angel raised her eyebrows. "You can go without screwing Chelsea for a couple of weeks."

"Not Chelsea. A dog. A roommate."

"Bring the dog. Have a chat with your roommate. She'll understand."

"I can't just—"

"Holden." Angel leaned forward and placed her hands flat next to his. "Like you said, people's lives are at stake. You were practically yelling at Dr. Chari."

"I was *not*."

"You care about this, so why are you hesitating? Neither of us have anything to lose." Angel bit her lip, watching him for a moment before continuing. "I welcome an escape from the shit-show that is my divorce right now. I know you and I aren't close or whatever, but if anything, do this to humor me."

Holden gritted his teeth and shook his head, reminding himself Angel didn't understand because he had never told her about the last time this happened, when he'd been so damn sure of something that hadn't been real.

He peeled through his false memories like a flip book. Holding Becca, screwing Becca, dragging Becca through the rain and laughing until his stomach hurt. When he'd thought these moments were real, they'd served not only as a desperately needed dose of serotonin—they'd also split open the patina of heavy fog around his heart and made him fucking *feel* something for once, just like he *felt* something now. This was different, of course—a sundry of fear-related emotions instead of love—but it rushed through his body and lit up his nerve endings all the same.

How could he explain to Angel that the only time he had ever cared about anything so deeply had ended with him realizing he was delusional?

"This is some conspiracy-level shit. If we're wrong about this, it means . . ." He drifted off.

"It means what? That we're crazy?" Angel scoffed, but then her face fell. "I hope we're crazy, Holden. I don't think you yet realize what the alternative means."

The cut was clean. Bloody, but clean.

He'd only ever sutured himself, though he'd made plenty of thread thanks to the intestines of the buck he'd killed some time ago. The needle, however, was crudely bent and looked like a death sentence in itself.

"You've been through worse," he told her, pouring water from his canteen over the wound in her calf. It spilled in pink rivulets over her flesh before splattering on the rotted pine planks.

She groaned against the rope between her teeth and fell back against the wall.

He slammed his canteen on the floor, crushing a skittering beetle. His only tool to push the needle through was his fingers. He'd have to be more careful with her than he had been with himself, not because she couldn't handle it, but because he still had to prove himself to her.

He cupped his free hand around her leg to steady her, or maybe just to feel her realness, her warmth, her muscles hardened from exhaustion and malnourishment and the wild.

The needle almost broke when she jerked and shrieked into her bite. Pinning her down, he coaxed the thread through the wound. She whimpered and writhed, and he was sorry. He knew this pain. He wouldn't wish it on anyone.

After he tied the first successful stitch, she pulled the rope from her mouth. "Wait." Her chest heaved. A bead of sweat rolled across her forehead, straight between her distrusting, frightened eyes.

"Who are you?"

Holden woke as Francis licked the cold sweat from his face. Pushing the dog away, he sat and swung his legs over the side of the bed, hunching to catch his breath. He rubbed his hands, half expecting to find blood caked to his fingers.

He could still hear her voice, worn and husky from the elements. Recognizable. And those eyes . . . Becca? No.

Siena.

Holden still smelled her sweat, blood, and fear as though she'd been in his bed. He could sense her will to survive like it was his own, more tenuous than the gut he had threaded through her injured leg.

Only a dream, but dreams had merit, didn't they? Dreams had messages.

I need you, he imagined her saying. No one else knew she was in danger.

No one else was coming for her.

Holden flipped on his bedside lamp, stood, and began to pack.

SIENA

Isaac sat on the front-room couch cross-legged, scraping the bottom of his second bowl of rehydrated rice and chicken. Siena knelt in the center of the floor and stared at him as Cam returned from the water barrels and Emmett scoured the cabin for extra clothes.

Rags, hides, and a mat of graying hair covered most of him. Blood blisters lived beneath his nails, the joints in his fingers swollen with arthritis. Scars covered so much of his hands, it was like he'd shoved them in a blender.

He held his fork strangely as he ate, like he'd forgotten how to use it. She fought the urge to reach out and help him, something she'd done often with her mother right before she died. And if she couldn't help her mother eat, she'd cast about the hospital room folding garments and stacking empty take-out tins and boxes for the janitor. And then she'd wait in a stupor for her brain to latch on to another task, if only to distract herself.

He met her eyes a few times as he ate, his own wary, but it was clear he recognized her. His teeth weren't in the worst condition —surprising, given how awful he smelled—and his mouth had been spared from the diagonal gash running from his brow to his jaw. His nose hadn't been so lucky.

"What happened to your face?" It was an easier question than *what the hell happened to you*, which he had yet to answer. He had said nothing yet.

Isaac set the empty bowl next to him. When he looked at her again, his eyes were glassy and injured, like a child who'd done something wrong.

He didn't answer her.

"We lost you two hours ago. You were twenty-three. How old are you now?"

Cam brought the Nalgene over and set it on the ground next to Isaac. "Maybe he doesn't remember."

"Do you remember Emmett finding you?"

Isaac lifted his chin and brought it back down again. A nod.

"And before that?"

He stared at her again, his attention flicking back and forth between her left and right eye, like he was searching for something.

"Do you remember what happened before that?" Siena asked again. She couldn't even bring him back to the place Emmett found him. The tunnel entrance in the cellar was gone, as if it had never been there. But she had no reason to disbelieve Emmett's story. Weirder shit had happened to her.

Isaac dropped his chin. Another nod.

"Will you tell me?"

"Not with the deck so stacked," he said. His weathered, unrecognizable voice threw Siena off guard.

"Stacked? Against *what*?"

Isaac closed his eyes and licked his chapped bottom lip. His shoulders heaved as he took a breath, like he was readying himself to relay something monumental. But then his body relaxed, his next words leaving him in a long groan. "I'm . . . tired."

His eyes stayed shut.

Emmett entered from the hallway. "Here's a t-shirt, and he can borrow my sweats." He glanced up and scowled. "Hey, wake him up."

Siena stood. "He's delirious, and useless to us until he gets some rest."

"We need to know what the *fuck* is going on," Emmett growled.

"If you'd aged half your life in a couple of hours, you'd also be too exhausted to talk." Cam picked up Isaac's abandoned bowl from the couch and walked it to the kitchen.

"It's not like we have to sit here and wait." Siena hurried across the room, down the hall, and into the lab. She flipped on the camp lantern on the desk and pulled the phone out of her pocket, booting it up. 1:03 p.m.—way too early to be so dark.

Emmett pulled out his own phone when he entered, tapping his thumb across the surface a few times. "Just because we can't get back to the sinkhole doesn't mean you need to rely on your imagination." He passed the phone to her. "I took these before we left. They don't do the place justice, but they're something."

Cam joined them as Siena swiped through photos of inverted saplings. Surreal. Unexplainable. Had Feyrer discovered something similar? Had he drafted hypotheses? Theories?

Her stomach rolled as she flicked through photos of the bone piles, her thumb freezing atop the statue of the antlered woman.

"A shrine," she mused.

Cam stole the phone from her.

"I've never come across any record of shrines or memorials," Siena said. "Not in this area."

Cam pinched the screen, zooming in and out on different parts of the photo. "Remember that cult?"

"The pioneer cult?" Siena asked.

"Before she disappeared, Avery was in the middle of this weird game. A bunch of her fans thought she'd chosen Deadswitch for the backpacking trip because that game clearly drew its inspiration from this area's history, specifically the cult shit. Damn." She handed the phone back to Emmett. "I wish I could remember more about that game, but a woman with antlers is ringing some bells."

Emmett pocketed his phone. "Who's Avery?"

"Deadswitch Five woman. Went missing," Siena said, and Cam flashed her a soft smile of appreciation for not divulging any further.

"So it might be related, might not." Emmett blew out a breath of frustration. "Where the hell does that get us?"

Siena pressed her fingers to her temples to think. *Anomalies.* There were too many anomalies and not enough connections. "We need to see everything at once." She swiped a once-abandoned Sharpie from the desk's surface, uncapping it and stepping toward an empty wall. With her free hand, she reached out and slid her fingers across the wood paneling.

Yesterday, she had crawled through a tunnel and entered a cabin, stepping into a room just like this one, the head of a mule nailed to the wall.

This wall.

The cabin she'd entered had been this cabin, not an identical one on the mountain. And Isaac . . . he hadn't aged twenty years in the past few hours. He'd lived those twenty years. She didn't know how or why it was true, just that it was. Call it intuition, something she'd been ignoring for years for the sake of science.

Dr. Feyrer hadn't. He'd always followed his intuition. And maybe there was a reason he had.

Siena pressed the Sharpie to the wall and wrote *Time Discrepancy.*

"So we're just writing on walls, now, Doc?" Cam drawled.

"I'm out of whiteboards and patience." Beneath *Time Discrepancy*, Siena wrote: *Isaac, Cam losing half a day, strange twilight, cabin through the tunnel.* She made another column header: *Landscape.* Beneath, she wrote: *weird cypress, sinkhole, glacier melt.* She thought back to when they'd entered Deadswitch and added: *fork in the path.*

Cam took the Sharpie when Siena was done, adding a new column. *Communication*: *no cell reception, no receivers, idiotic ranger?*

"Why the question mark?" Siena asked.

"Because he was certain Deadswitch Wilderness didn't exist. I thought he was just a moron, but now . . ." Cam shook her head and ran her fingers through her hair. "Fuck, I don't know. We're just listing weird shit, right? Well, that was weird."

Siena pushed her hand against her stomach, attempting to knock loose the growing sense of dread. She turned back to Emmett, surprised to find him captivated by their brainstorming session. His arms were crossed, but his shoulders were hunched like he was trying to make himself smaller. Like this was scaring him.

"Anything to add?" she asked.

To her surprise, he stepped forward. Cam gave him the pen, and he started a new column.

Cult Shit.

He wrote *antlered woman statue* beneath. *Computer game.*

Siena took the pen from him, adding: *beheaded mule, The Mother Reigns.* She stepped back, rubbing her thumb along her chin as she thought. "Do you think The Mother is the antlered woman? Does that ring any bells, Cam?"

Cam clenched the hair at the nape of her neck in her fist. "Maybe . . . I don't remember. I watched too many of her videos to keep them all straight." She dropped her hand and took the pen from Siena once more, moving back to the *Time Discrepancies* column.

Avery's bag. Naomi.

Cam returned the pen to Siena with a sigh. "I should go check on the kid . . . errr, Isaac."

"Naomi?" Emmett asked when Cam was gone.

"The dead woman on Wolf Ridge," Siena explained. "Cam thought it looked like Naomi Vo, another one of the missing hikers. Which would have been impossible, of course. But now . . ."

"Now anything is possible," Emmett finished, glaring at the wall. "If Dr. Feyrer somehow knew any of this would happen to us, he's a bastard for not saying anything." He scoffed. "*The research stays in the woods*, my ass."

"The last thing he told me was not to go. And I shrugged it off to him losing his mind."

"It shouldn't have taken him losing his mind to tell you the truth, Sen."

"Do you really think he'd put us in danger on purpose?" Her body leadened at the thought.

"Hey." Emmett lifted his fingers to the base of her chin, tilting her head back until their eyes met. The back of her knees used to weaken when he did this, in the days when the power moves turned her on. And as much as she knew she should push him away, she took comfort in the familiarity of his hands and his eyes. His body had been a harbor for her anxiety, a vessel that calmed her pulse in the middle of the night when her adrenaline yanked her awake. She needed him now more than ever.

But the safety she felt was a lie. One selfish mistake and he had ruined everything.

"Can you try the satellite phone again?" she asked.

Disappointment crossed his face before he dropped his hand. "Yeah . . . sure."

"Don't get lost." The last part was supposed to be a joke, a cheeky comment meant to break the tension and elicit an eye roll. They exchanged an unsettled glance, and he left saying nothing.

She was about to leave herself—let the wall behind her marinate for a bit as she checked on Isaac and Cam—when she spotted the deck of cards on the desk next to the radio.

The cards had appeared in the cabin through the tunnel, next to the map of *The Briardark*. She had thought it a residual memory from her subconscious.

Not with the deck so stacked—Isaac's response when she had asked if he could tell her what had happened to him. It could have been figurative, but even figuratively, it made no sense.

Siena sat and picked up the deck, running her thumb over the buck's skull on the pack. She lifted the box flap to a message written on the inside:

Play two.

Rules to some game? Seemed uncomplicated. She wiggled the cards out, the deck the size of a standard fifty-two. The stock was thick but unlaminated. The back of each card had the same skull and bird print as the box, but when she turned the deck over, a solid olive tone greeted her. Blank. She shuffled through them, but they were all the same. Blank, blank, blank. Not even playable as regular cards.

Siena grabbed the box to shove them back in, lifting the flap again.

Play two, it taunted.

"Screw it," she whispered, dropping the box and shuffling the deck twice. She peeled off the top card and flipped it over, yanking her hand back in surprise.

On the face of the card, a painted woman dressed in an open hunter's coat knelt in the forest. She was filthy and emaciated, her face twisted in anguish as she attempted to rip an arrow from the flesh between her collarbone and shoulder. On the ground next to her, almost buried in the grass, rested a bloodied knife. *The Butcher's Daughter* was scrawled above the illustration.

Siena touched the space beneath her own collarbone, increasing the pressure until she dug her fingers into her taut muscle just to feel an ounce of the pain this poor woman felt. She winced and pulled the second card.

An upside-down evergreen, like the photos Emmett had shown her, hovered in midair, its tangled root system filling an empty and enigmatic sky. *The Verdantry*, the card read. It was beautiful and odd, and left her head empty, like she was trying to recall something that had slipped her mind.

Siena pulled another card that showed nothing, and flipped over the deck, fanning the rest across the surface.

They were all as they'd been before: blank. Like a magic trick.

EMMETT

Emmett lacked all desire to walk any further from the cabin than he had to. From the closest clearing, the sun-bleached roof peeked between the trees. Emmett glanced up from the phone's screen every couple of seconds to make sure he didn't lose sight of it. Even staying in line of sight was still too far away for his liking, especially given one of them had just disappeared in the woods and reemerged decades older.

He hated the idea of aging. His twenties and thirties had been a chaotic cycle of gain and loss. If he suddenly turned sixty today, he would be in the negative. If he was killed here, he would die on this mountain in the negative. His lack of legacy had haunted him ever since he stumbled upon the bones around the shrine. His mortality—something he'd never denied, but never expected to face so soon—lurked behind trees, hovering just above the ground like a mist.

Not knowing the source of the danger was the worst part.

Emmett extended the antenna and booted the phone. It locked onto GPS, and two signal bars blinked back at him, which wasn't worth getting his hopes up. Both Siena and Cam had called out, too. It hadn't gotten them anywhere.

Emmett could count the phone numbers he knew by heart on

his hand. Nine-one-one had proven useless to them over and over, as had all the numbers listed on the back of the phone. He'd already tried his parents several times to no avail.

There was one more number he hadn't tried yet. He'd memorized the digits last year, when he'd made the call from lab landlines and other places in the maze of university offices with poor service. And he was supposed to check in halfway through the trip anyway, he just hated calling when he didn't need to. The residual guilt always left him sick.

Emmett dialed a double-zero, the country code, and the number. He held the phone to his ear and shut his eyes, blocking his view of the cabin.

The phone connected and rang.

"This is Cora for Mr. Belmont, how can I help you?"

Emmett's eyes popped open. "Cora?"

"Emmett? You aren't supposed to check in for another week."

"Cora, listen to me. I'm stranded on Mount Agnes. It's a long story but someone is really hurt. I need you to call 911 and get a helicopter out to us."

There was a long pause. He checked the screen of the phone to make sure the call was still connected.

"Cora?"

"I . . . I don't think I can do that. It isn't protocol."

Anger and panic flared in his chest. "What the hell do you mean, it isn't protocol?"

"All emergency plans must be set by the board for these types of things, and Mr. Belmont didn't approve one for this expedition."

"Well, that was fucking stupid, wasn't it?" Emmett said through gritted teeth. His jaw was clenched tight enough to crack a molar.

Cora's voice dropped. "You can't say stuff like that on this line!"

"Did you not just hear what I said? I'm stranded. Someone's hurt. This is the first time we've been able to reach anyone who can help!" Emmett took a breath, remembering the man this assistant worked for, and tried again. "We already have data, which will be lost if we don't get out of here."

"Alright, alright," said Cora. "Let's see . . . looks like his two o'clock ended early. I'll try putting you through, but no promises."

Emmett released his breath. "Thank you."

The line fell quiet. He checked the face of the phone again to make sure the connection didn't drop.

"Emmett," came a sultry, delighted voice. It wouldn't matter if you told him the apocalypse was nigh; Emmett's boss always sounded delighted.

"Hi, Brock." Belmont insisted Emmett call him by his first name, perhaps a way to establish trust. He was about to see how far that trust could get him.

"Cora relayed your predicament."

"The summarized version. Something is wrong with our phone, and I don't want to waste time explaining everything, but one of our team is injured, and we need to get airlifted out."

"Who is injured?"

Why does it matter? Emmett wanted to ask, but Belmont valued patience from his reports above all else. "Isaac Perez."

Belmont hummed. "I can imagine how dangerous this must feel."

"No offense, sir, but I don't think you can. There is something wrong with—"

He cut Emmett off. "You'd be surprised. Unfortunately, I need you to stay on the mountain."

Emmett stopped short in his pacing. "I'm sorry, what?"

"It is vital you stay on Agnes, for now. We will reevaluate after three more weeks. I understand that with an injured researcher, the morale of the team must be low. I hope I can trust you to keep them in high spirits and keep them put, Ms. Dupont specifically."

"Dr. Dupont," Emmett corrected.

"My apologies."

"Why?" Emmett's voice trembled. "Why do we need to stay? Our research is at a standstill. Everyone's *life* is at risk. This isn't worth some glacier data!"

"You're right. You are a smart man, Emmett. You've made a lot of sacrifices for COtwo Industries, even your relationship."

A metal bat to his stomach would have hurt less. He struggled for air like the wind had been knocked from him. "I would have done things differently if I knew—"

"I would not be asking you to continue the expedition if all I cared about was glacial carbon emissions."

Emmett's head swam. Glacial carbon emissions had always been the one reason COtwo was involved in this project. He'd even helped draft the paperwork and put forth the grueling amount of effort to convince Cam to take the grant.

"You need to convince Ms. Dupont to stay on the mountain. Know that I hate informing you your tenure at COtwo is at stake. More than that, I suppose, if you really can't escape Deadswitch Wilderness without my help. You are a valuable asset, Emmett. It would be a shame to lose you."

There was another pause, and Emmett thought the connection dropped before he added, "Consider your midpoint check-in complete. Do not call back."

Mr. Belmont hung up.

MAIDEI

Maidei sat in her favorite chair in the corner of the living room, nursing a cup of chamomile that Huang had made her. It was her comfort place—her only comfort place, as of late. Her nightmares had been keeping her from sinking into the bed she shared with her husband.

"I will be okay here on my own," Huang said softly. He sat across from her on the sofa, reading one of those trashy men's adventure novels he loved so much. He'd been on the same page since she told him she was considering a trip south.

"I know you will, but it's still unfair to you."

He glanced up at her over his reading glasses, smiling. "You will simply owe me one."

She sipped her tea. "I never paid you back for the last time I owed you one."

The last time felt like another life, Maidei a fresh postdoc and the mother of a young child. Huang had taken care of their three-year-old son during her Deadswitch Wilderness project, which had kept her on site in a trailer for eight weeks.

Huang pretended to return to his book. "I consider your success a repayment."

He was too nice to her. He'd always been too nice to her, and she wondered if his attitude would be different if he knew she'd been keeping secrets all these years.

Her eyes flitted to a photo of their son's graduation that she'd placed in a kitschy frame on the side table. "You'll need to help Bobby move into his dorm."

"I can handle it, Mai. Promise."

Maidei heaved a sigh, something she did when her chest tightened with anxiety. It was a way to tell her body it was fine, all the oxygen she needed was right here, in this room. There was no use worrying, yet.

She had told herself many lies over the years.

Maidei stood. "I'll be in my office. Come get me when you head to bed."

He nodded absently, and she left for the basement office, sitting in the dark amid bookcases and boxes of files.

The paperwork was all from the closed Deadswitch project—the stuff she didn't keep on campus. Stuff she hadn't shown Holden yet. Just because he seemed sincere didn't mean she trusted him, yet. Much like with Huang, she wasn't sure how he would react if she told him the whole of the truth.

The project had shut down shortly after the discovery of the flourishing lodgepole pines, the final absurdity of that summer. Three weeks before, Maidei took a walk to the ranger station to make a call.

The researchers had taken up residence in a few trailers near the border of Deadswitch Wilderness, the ranger station only a two-mile walk away. The familiar trail was worn and well traveled, and Maidei walked it often to get exercise. But that morning, consumed by her thoughts on how to get the study schedule back on track, Maidei halted in front of a fork in the path she didn't remember.

Not turning around was one of the worst mistakes of her life, but then she thought nothing of it. She was walking west. With the station south of her, she followed the left fork. A couple hundred feet later, unfamiliar lichen hung from tree boughs, the air dense with mist. The spruce looked more like Sitka than Douglas, which made no sense. Sitka spruce only thrived in the wettest parts of the Pacific Northwest.

It was too late to turn around. She'd wandered from the path, and no matter the direction she went, the thicket never eased up.

Four frightful nights passed in those woods. She thought she had died and hell was this forest, shifting beneath her feet and holding her hostage. She slept in spurts beneath layers of branches, needles, and lichen, surviving off a creek and spruce tips, and took a chance on ruffled fungi sprouting from dead trunks.

In the early morning after the third night, when she woke to pee, a shadow man waited for her in the thicket near her shelter. She couldn't recall his words, only that they were nonsense, and she swore off the fungi as she continued south, following the creek. The man followed a few paces behind wordlessly, as though she was his subject and he was merely observing her.

Trauma had smothered those memories, and Maidei remembered little more about this hallucination. The fourth night she never left her shelter, and woke in the morning on the dusty ground beneath a sugar pine to a ranger shaking her. He escorted her back to the research camp after feeding her tomato soup from his thermos.

She'd never told Huang. Getting lost a few miles from camp didn't happen to trained professionals, and that level of sheer terror was something unfelt at any point in her life prior. Her research group was just happy she was alive, except for Zaid, her field partner.

Despite Maidei's protests of not wanting to relive the horror of the past four days, Zaid begged for a rehash of every moment she'd been alone in those woods. Weeks later when they found those monstrous pines that grew and stretched into the sky right before their eyes, Zaid was not awestruck like the others. He'd been afraid. What had he said? That her disappearance wasn't a fluke. And the pines weren't an isolated phenomenon.

Something is wrong with these woods.

Maidei pulled her phone from her pocket and scrolled to the very bottom of her contacts, tapping his name and pressing the phone to her ear.

"Hello, old friend," Zaid said when he picked up. "It's late."

"I know, but this is important," she told him. "It's about Deadswitch. Something else has happened."

SIENA

Siena jerked awake, her stomach clenched, nerve endings on fire. She sat up and blinked the sleep from her eyes.

The twilight that had permeated her entire restless night was gone, replaced by moss green light, like the cabin had been dropped into the middle of a pond.

Cam and Emmett were still asleep, Cam muttering something fierce and unintelligible in her dreams. Isaac remained on the couch in the main room; Siena had checked on him twice last night and was due for another.

Siena hurried out of bed and into a hallway drenched in the same scummy light. She entered the dark main room to an empty couch and yanked back the curtain, a startled feline cry escaping her throat.

A scream brewed at the bottom of her rib cage.

Trees. Not the drought-tolerant pines, nor the scraggly high Sierra shrubs that signified normalcy. Before her, an array of rain-forest evergreens dripped with moss. Mist collected on the window and trailed down the glass.

Siena stumbled across the room and flung open the front door. The moisture in the air fed the panic in her chest, almost suffocating her. Heavy fog carried the green tinge, like the top of the mountain was caught in the opening breath of a thunderstorm. But the air was still, the forest silent. Thick fern growth covered the trail leading from the cabin. Either that, or the path had vanished.

Delirious laughter bubbled up in Siena's throat. Where were the Munchkins? The Yellow Brick Road? Glinda the Good Witch, so she could get the hell out of here? She wiped the tears from beneath her eyes and thought again of releasing the scream in her chest, like her voice alone could shatter this mirage.

But it wasn't fake. She wasn't in Deadswitch anymore, though that made no sense. Their cabin hadn't been swept up by a tornado in the middle of the night; she instinctively knew they were still on a mountain. They'd run into pockets of these evergreens and this moisture for the past few days. Whatever this was—it was growing. They'd been swallowed by it.

A visceral rumble in the mountain sounded beneath her. Just like at Wolf Ridge, and the parallel cabin, and again when they were trying to leave. Siena finally realized it wasn't a sound. She wasn't *hearing* the noise, but processed it through her gut the same as an emotion or intuition, a voiceless language that wanted her to listen closely.

Fear got the best of her, and she stumbled back inside and slammed the door behind her, swearing when it popped right back open thanks to the broken latch. She pressed her back against it and spread her arms wide across the frame, as if that would help.

Nothing protected her from that hunger—whatever it was. Not even a functioning door.

Maybe she was losing it. Maybe this was just her disorder slamming into her at full force. The thought eased her stomach. Never in her life had she hoped for sickness, but circumstances had changed.

Isaac stared at her from the end of the hallway, where he stood with a mess kit full of oatmeal, eating it spoonful by hefty spoonful. He wore Emmett's sweats, his hair somehow more of a tangle than yesterday. Wiping his chin with the back of his hand, he turned his attention toward the lab's open doorway and shoveled another spoonful of oatmeal into his mouth.

Unlike his outfit of animal skin, the sweats didn't hide the definition of his body. She swore Emmett had lugged an emaciated Isaac into the cabin, but maybe she'd been fooled by the hollows of his face. Muscle padded his frame, more muscle than when he'd entered Deadswitch as a scrawny kid. Regardless of where Emmett had found him, he couldn't have been without ample food for more than a couple of weeks. And not just nuts and berries, either.

Isaac muttered something beneath his breath. She caught the phrases "glacier melt" and "fork in the path" as he read from the list they'd written on the wall.

"I've tried to lay it all out too," he told her, his voice as gravelly as last night.

Lay it out—he meant their clues. "When?" she asked. "When did you try to lay it all out? Last night?"

He flashed her an expression that looked like a mix of curiosity and pity, like he found her endearing. She'd looked at him the same way countless times this trip when he'd said something naïve.

"You were gone for two hours, Isaac," she said defensively. "Do you want to tell me what happened to you, or do you want me to keep making assumptions?"

Isaac walked into the main room, setting his bowl on the end table near the couch. "Weird being back."

The statement sounded more like the old Isaac—simple and obvious. But Siena knew the words held multitudes.

She tried taming her frustration. "Back from *where*?"

Isaac stepped up onto the couch so he stood on the cushions. He ran his hands along the rustic wallpaper and began scraping at the center with his thumbnail.

Siena pushed herself from the door. "What are you doing?"

He ignored her and dug the rest of his fingers into the hole he'd worn through, ripping off a strip and tossing it to the ground. He did it again, clawing away paper to reveal a mountain.

No, not just one. A whole range, cradling a long valley. Isaac tore off another strip. Landmarks dotted a thick forest: cabins, lakes, a swirling pit of some sort to the south. A town or a village north of a bog. Vast expanses of woodland inked with the occasional skull. All of it was painted in the same olive tone that flecked and smeared the signs throughout Deadswitch.

But the map itself wasn't of Deadswitch.

Isaac didn't stop until all the brown paper littered the floor and the entire map was visible. It had been hiding in the cabin this whole time.

How old was it? Had Feyrer and his team known it was here?

"I've seen this before," Siena said. "When I went through the tunnel beneath the tree. The other cabin had a map just like this one. *The Briardark.*"

Isaac stepped off the couch. "I made a few of these while I was gone."

"*You?* You drew this? No, that can't . . . that's . . ." *Impossible*, she wanted to say, until she remembered one column on the wall in the lab: *Time Discrepancies*. The rules of physics didn't apply here for whatever reason. As far as she knew, nothing was impossible.

She glanced at the cedar branch pressed up to the window, and the pattern of green mildew on the glass. "Are we in the Briardark now?"

His response was instant. "No. You'd know if we were."

She didn't know what the hell that meant, but she wasn't sure that mattered at this point. "But you've been there. How long?"

He opened his arms, as if inviting Siena to look at him. "I lost track."

"Well, you look like you're fifty."

He thought for a moment. "I'm probably less old than I look."

Siena scoffed. "So what, two decades?"

"That sounds about right."

She pushed back her hair, dizzy at the thought. "Unbelievable. And how'd you get back?"

"I returned to Agnes. I chose to come back."

"What? Why didn't you—"

He cut her off. "Remember that story I told you about why I became a scientist?" He pointed at the kitchen table and then let his hand fall, his shoulders slumping. "We were sitting over there, and you were trying to call out on the radio."

Siena nodded. It had only been a couple of weeks ago, the conversation mostly small talk. Yet Isaac's expression twisted in pain as he recalled it.

"The choice I made to study how the world was really formed changed my entire perspective of reality and God. It seems . . . trivial, I guess, but it scared me."

"Yeah, I get it," she said. "It takes a lot of courage to change your worldviews."

"Worldviews . . ." He turned his attention to the window and the teeming life beyond the walls of the cabin. "It was like that. Every day since I . . . since I left. But the fear was constant. Every time I remembered what had happened to me. Every time I remembered where I was. It doesn't matter if it was two decades or three. Everything I knew about space and time and life . . . love . . . it was wrong. And I never learned to cope with that. I still . . ."

He drifted off, and Siena stood frozen, unable to form any response amid her shock. She understood nothing of what Isaac was saying, yet the gravity of his words terrified her.

He blinked, a tear falling into his facial hair, and turned back to her. "I want to tell you everything, but it would take too much time. I shouldn't have slept last night. I should have fought my exhaustion to prepare you to leave."

"Leave?" Siena shook her head, trying to reorient herself. "You don't need to prepare me to leave—I'm ready. We tried getting out of here yesterday, and I plan on trying again."

Isaac took another step toward her and grabbed her arms. Siena tensed up, but she was too surprised to yank away from him.

"Emmett is going to try and keep you here," he whispered. "Cam . . . Cam will run the other direction, and you'll waste too much time trying to find her."

"No," she hissed. "That's not true. Cam wants to go home. And Emmett . . ."

His grip on her tightened, his tear-filled eyes now wild. "What you think they'll do doesn't matter. All that matters is that *you* get out of here, Siena. Just you."

She didn't understand. "Why just me? Why don't you care about the others?"

"Something is after you. Not Emmett. Not Cam. *You*. And when it—when he finds you, he will hurt you and force you to do things more horrible than you could dream.

"And then after all that, Siena . . . after everything, he will kill you."

HOLDEN

Angel grabbed Holden's phone from the car's magnetic dock. "New music. I'm tired of your indie shit. Francis is tired of it, too."

"Fine," Holden yielded. In all fairness to Angel, they had been listening to *his indie shit* for almost twelve hours after leaving Oregon before dawn. It was a little after 6 p.m. in the Sierra Nevadas, evergreen giants casting gloomy shadows along the serpentine road.

"Ah, crap. Accidentally exited out of it. Spotify, Spotify . . . jeez, you have a million apps. Do you even use all these?"

"Does anyone use all the apps on their phone?" The pavement ended, and his Camry hit the dirt with a small groan, the road narrowing as it curved around the foothills.

"Maybe not, but you have to housekeep every once in a while. You still have your ex as your wallpaper, for crying out loud."

"Are you going to change the music, or pry into my phone and judge me for the next thirty minutes?"

"She *is* a babe. What's her name again?"

Holden wondered how long he could go without responding, but it was Angel . . . with *his phone*. If he wasn't careful, she'd start digging into his texts. "Becca."

"You know who she kind of looks like?"

"I'm afraid to ask," he said.

"Dr. Dupont."

Holden quickly scoffed. "Yeah, okay, sure."

"You can't look me in the eyes and tell me your ex-girlfriend doesn't look a little bit like Dr. Dupont. Both white girls, long brown hair, blue eyes, that cutie-next-door look . . ."

"I don't even remember what Dr. Dupont looks like," Holden argued, which was a flat-out lie. He remembered exactly what she looked like, and even worse, had made the Becca-Siena connection himself.

"You just clearly have a type is all."

Holden groaned along with the car as it teetered over the uneven road. "I don't know how many times I need to tell you I'm not doing this because Dupont is an attractive woman. How shallow do you think I am?"

"Chiiilllll. I'm just joking." Angel changed the music to Halsey and set the phone on the dock.

Francis released a louder whine. Holden reached back and scratched his ears. "I know, boy. I feel your pain." His own body hurt from driving, a cruel reminder that being in his thirties meant he was no longer the spry kid who used to be totally cool with impromptu road trips. The forest development roads were particularly terrible, but at least they were almost to the station.

Even with the whining, Francis was taking the drive better than Holden, his head hanging out the back window for most of the trip, happily peeing alongside the road every time they stopped.

Be more like the dog. Holden touched the outside of his pocket and the lump of a thumb drive. He and Angel didn't exactly have a Plan B if the ranger at the station turned them away with or without listening to Dupont's recordings. Drive back into town and get a hotel? Try again the next day? It was that or search for Dupont's team themselves, and the latter was completely out of the question. They had no gear, Holden knew nothing about backpacking, and he didn't really feel like ending his summer dead in the bottom of a canyon.

Angel screamed his name.

From out of nowhere, something dark and large leapt from the brush into the middle of the road. Holden slammed on the brakes, tires scraping against the gravel as the car drifted. He shot his right hand out and caught Francis as the dog lurched forward.

Angel swore when the car stopped. Before Holden could ask if she was okay, Francis released a deafening string of barks, scrambling to the open back window.

"Shit." Holden lunged backward, fighting against the seat belt as he grabbed the dog's hind leg. Francis kicked against him as the barking and snapping continued, and Holden unbuckled, wormed over the divider and into the back seat, and wrestled Francis back into the car.

Angel mashed the button to roll up the window. "Are you okay?"

Holden released Francis, though the dog's attention remained fixed on the window as he growled beneath his breath, his hackles raised.

"Yeah. What the hell was that?"

Angel shook her head. "I—I don't know. It happened so fast and—"

Holden kicked open the back door and got out of the car, making sure Francis didn't wiggle out before shutting it. He circled his car to check for any damage. Luckily, the dirt road had kept him below 25 mph, or they would have slid off the road and down the embankment to their right.

The road . . .

Holden lifted his gaze to the empty road as Angel climbed out of the car. A plume of dust dispersed around them. The forest was quiet, the shadows cold and deep despite the dry summer day. Holden shivered and replayed the moment before he had braked, the animal leaping from the woods, large and black and amorphous.

"A deer?" Holden asked.

"Had to be." Angel wrapped her arms around her torso and rocked back on her heels. "It was too big to be anything else."

Unsatisfied with the answer, Holden walked out to the middle of the road, right where the animal had landed before diving into the brush again. Though, had he actually seen it disappear? He'd been too distracted with the car and the dog, the three or four seconds nothing more than a blur in his head. His right ear rang, and he jammed his finger into it and walked back toward the car.

"Let's get the hell out of here," he called to Angel as he slid into the driver's seat. "We're almost there, anyway."

And they were. Fifteen minutes later he spotted the sign for the ranger station, quaint and freshly painted, a reprieve from the forest shadows and his jittery fingers. The dog had calmed down, and Angel released an audible breath. "Thank God," she muttered. "I'm still shook. And I need to pee."

The stretch of gravel to the parking lot was wider than the road had been. The actual station was a cabin painted green and yellow, its aging roof coated in dead needles. Several emergency vehicles filled the lot, along with the local sheriff's SUV. Behind the chain-link fence near the station, a small group in orange jackets circled up. A German shepherd and a Lab flanked one of them.

Holden parked in the lot's corner and shook out his hands, tremors still crawling through his body from the animal incident.

Angel threw off her seat belt. "You think they actually listened to you?"

"Either that or someone else went missing." It would be quite the coincidence.

Holden let Francis run around for a few minutes away from the other dogs and then rounded him up into the cool car with a treat and a promise to be back soon. He and Angel made their way to the front of the ranger station, Holden failing to catch bits of the team's conversation. He held the door open for Angel, who stopped right in the middle of the entryway. Holden ran into her.

In the cramped office, Dr. Maidei Chari sat on top of a scuffed-up desk, much like Holden had found her in the basement of the Forestry building. Her braids were tied back, and she'd swapped her flats for hiking boots and her white button-down for a flannel one. She nodded at them politely.

Seated at the desk was the ranger, a Native American man in his early fifties with a round face and a streak of white through his cropped hair.

"So you just show up places and sit on people's desks now?" Angel asked.

"You could say I do it when I've had a change of heart." Maidei's eyes flickered to Holden.

Hope and relief swelled inside him. "You're the reason Search and Rescue's here? Were you able to convince, well . . ." Holden nodded at the ranger. "Hi."

The ranger nodded back. "Frank. We talked on the phone. And no, Search and Rescue isn't here because of Maidei, though when she showed up, I knew I did the right thing listening to you."

"We go back," Maidei added when Holden frowned. "Frank's been around for a while."

Holden approached the desk. "What happened? Did you find anything else?"

Frank and Maidei shared a look. "I wasn't going to follow up," Frank said. "But I recognized one of the scientists when they got their permit. Cameron Yarrow. Interned for me, well, feels like a million years ago. We put her through the wringer when those girls disappeared back in '16. She took it hard, too, especially when the mission switched from rescue to recovery. She did a lot for me in those weeks, though. Figured I owed her the same amount of attention." Frank sat straighter in his chair and rested his elbows on the desk. "So I called CalTech and got the number for their satellite phone. Couldn't get through, but there's a ranger out at Triplet Lakes a few miles from the base of Agnes. He's required to have his phone on. Tried calling him to see if he could hike up and figure out what was going on. Thing is, I can't get ahold of him, either. I can't even get ahold of the ranger at the base of Charlotte."

"How likely is it that their phones can't reach a satellite?" Angel asked.

Frank shook his head. "Not likely. I don't know what's going on, but I don't like it. I figure we know where these folks are supposed to be, so we might as well send a team in."

"Are you sure you want to send a team in?" Holden asked against his better judgment. This was exactly what he wanted, wasn't it? A rescue team?

So why did he feel so uneasy?

Frank smiled and then looked at Maidei. "You been telling the kid stories?"

Maidei's somber expression didn't evoke the same untroubled attitude. "Not many. Holden has been telling *me* stories, though."

Holden rifled through his pocket for the flash drive. He set it on Frank's desk. "You need to listen to these. I found them on a drive in storage at Oregon State back in March. I don't know how . . . I can't explain . . . umm . . ."

"Frank." Maidei slid off the desk. "You've been watching over these woods for long enough. You understand. Those files? They won't make sense. Just like . . . just like everything else. But they are real, I promise you."

Holden hadn't expected this from her. Hell, the fact Maidei was here at all was nothing short of a miracle. He wished he knew what had changed her mind.

"Alright, alright. I'll sift through them," said Frank. "Still sending in that SAR team, though."

Maidei pulled out her phone. "Zaid should be here by now. He's just coming up from the valley."

"Zaid? You dragged him into this mess, too?" Frank chuckled.

"Who's Zaid?" Holden and Angel asked at the same time.

"My old research partner," Maidei murmured.

"He probably went straight up to the Fort," Frank said.

A blank look passed over Maidei's face.

"He didn't tell you?" Frank stood. "Not surprising. Even all those years ago, I could tell he was always extra careful to not hurt your feelings."

"What are you saying?" Maidei asked.

Frank grabbed a set of keys off the wall. "He didn't stop your research, Maidei. Hasn't stopped for fifteen years." He started toward the door. "Hope you're all ready for a bumpy ride."

EXCERPT FROM CHAPTER 13 OF *WITHOUT A TRACE* BY JOHN LAWSON:

On the eve of Ranger Frank Soledad's twenty-year anniversary stewarding the Deadswitch area, he drives me to the Glass Lake Trailhead parking lot in his four-door Wrangler. For the locals, this place is unremarkable. Every trailhead in the area is the same —a dirt clearing with a few logs to serve as parking barriers, and a map in a pine frame that has seen better days. Also near the map is a lockbox where day hikers are supposed to drop a five-dollar fee, but Frank says he gave up stocking the envelopes years ago. No one ever paid.

The only car in the lot is a Subaru Forester. Frank says it belongs to a pair of regulars who spend a few weeks near Triplet Lakes every summer.

"Found Janet's car right over there." Frank points to a spot to the left of the trail map. "Only sign of them we ever found."

I ask him about the cellphones and the possible naïveté of leaving them at home, to which he shakes his head.

"Listen, I can't speak for why they wouldn't want to take photos of their hike. But I spent a lot of time talking with the parents of all the women. These young ladies spent more time in national forests and wilderness areas than most of our visitors. They knew their stuff." He shrugs. "Maybe they didn't take their phones because of the extra weight, or because they were afraid they'd lose them. Janet's dad said she always rented a satellite phone anyway. That phone we tried tracing, but the device hadn't been turned on since it left the rental office. Again, that's typical of backpackers. Satellite phones stay off unless there's reason to call out."

And there it is, the second half of the communication mystery. The scenarios where all five women wouldn't think to call out for help are limited. Either they lost the phone, or the elements, such as a lightning bolt on granite, killed them all at once.

"Trust me, I've speculated long and hard on this." Frank scratches his chin with a solemn glance toward the trailhead. "But it's useless with no other evidence. All I know is this isn't some kind of Chris McCandless tragedy," he says, referring to the famous case of the unprepared young man who lost his life in the Alaska wilderness. "These women weren't known for recklessness. That to me is the most frightening part of this whole thing."

CAMERON

Cam handled death poorly from the moment Grandma June died. Her overbearing mother made sure she would never forget how old she'd been.

Twelve-year-olds cry quietly. Twelve-year-olds don't throw fits at funerals.

June Hayworth owned a dilapidated sheet metal barn and a big house on fifty-three acres in Raymond, California. She lived alone except for every birthday and holiday and family barbeque, when her three children, their spouses, and their children came over, leaving the foyer in a stinky disarray of tennis shoes and covering all kitchen surfaces with casseroles and wilted salads. Everything always had too much mayonnaise. Cam had spent a lot of time picking at the leftover food as a form of entertainment.

Out of the eight grandkids, Cam was the only girl. She was also the youngest, and had never been close with her brother, Coulter, who was five years older and five times stupider than she was, nor any of her other meathead cousins. They'd take off in a raucous pack at these gatherings, leaving an invisible cloud of fart smell in their wake.

They were never mean to Cam . . . not even Coulter. They were indifferent toward her, which was worse.

It didn't take long for Grandma June to catch on when Cam was old enough to be miserable. After dinner, when the adults were drinking wine on the deck and the teenagers were playing football by the horse corral, June would whisk Cam away from the mayonnaise to help with chores. Not cleaning up dinner or sweeping up the dirt the boys tracked in—the other adults would take care of that. But real chores, collecting eggs and feeding the goats and hauling hay with the tractor. She taught Cam how to mend chicken wire fences and fill the horse troughs and clean a rifle. Out in the unkempt field behind the house, she showed Cam which wild weeds you could eat, and which ones would leave you swollen and itchy for weeks.

June did it all with a limp and a Camel cigarette hanging from her lips. She wore a silver revolver in a leather holster on her good hip—to scare the coyotes, she claimed, though Cam never saw her use it. Her jeans were dingy from the red clay, her skin leathered from the sun and the smokes. Her gray hair never left the braid that hung past her shoulders.

June was the only person who Cam loved unconditionally before she even understood what unconditional love meant. And then she was gone, just like that. Heart attack. *It was her time to go. She's in the arms of Jesus, now,* her mother told her, which was a load of shit because they never went to church and neither did Grandma June. Jesus was an excuse her mother used to avoid explaining death to Cam, but it was too late. June was gone, and Cam was unprepared to deal with the grief on her own, something she never grew out of.

Cam stood on the porch in the mist, leaning against the cabin wall as she smoked one of the horrendously stale cigarettes from the cellar. A rifle rested on the cement in front of her.

Cam was beyond writing lists on walls or trying to figure out what the hell was happening. Even if they knew what was happening, would it matter? They would still need to escape this forest in the end.

They had only tried leaving once. Losing the path and her

sense of time felt like a warning. The next attempt wouldn't be so easy. Worse things could happen to her than whatever Isaac had endured. Death . . . death was always the worst thing.

And even worse than her death was the death of someone she loved.

In a flurry of hushed whispers over breakfast, Siena had relayed to Cam and Emmett the warning she'd received from Isaac. To Cam, it sounded like the fever dream of someone who'd taken way too many mushrooms. Something from the mythical place of the Briardark wanted to hurt Siena, and Isaac knew this for fuck knows what reason. He wouldn't even tell them why Siena was the only target. And Cam would be quick to brush Isaac off if it weren't for the morphing forest and Isaac's age and Siena's recorder and Avery's bag magically appearing like a goddamn omen. But she couldn't. The thought of Siena dying filled Cam with an incapacitating dread.

Cam caught a flicker of movement in the woods. She dropped her cigarette, smashed it with her boot, and slowly bent to pick up the rifle. She double-checked the chamber for ammo, and when she looked up, she caught the wavering again, like a lick of black flame.

Her chest tightened, every vein in her body constricting until blood thudded through her painfully. She spotted it once more, a finger of darkness beckoning her closer.

She could run in and tell the others. Stay on the porch until whatever was out there came to her.

She could meet it in the woods. Keep it away from the others.

The thought enticed her, hooking her by her navel and tugging her forward. She didn't want to go, but she had to, didn't she? She could almost hear it threatening the safety of those inside, holding them hostage until Cam was brave enough to meet it face-to-face. Whatever *it* was.

"Cam."

Cam released a breath and turned around. Emmett hung out

the door of the cabin. She flipped on the safety of the gun, not remembering when she took it off.

"I need your help."

That's rich, she wanted to say. Yesterday's Cam would have said that.

"Doing what?" She scanned the forest for the black flicker, but it was gone.

"Siena wants to *leave*," he told her, like it was the most absurd thing in the entire world.

No shit, yesterday's Cam would have said. *And you're going to let her.*

She lowered the barrel of the rifle and pushed past Emmett into the cabin. In the kitchen, Isaac used the help of the window's reflection to cut his hair with medical scissors over the sink. He looked much better, his beard only an inch or so from his face. But without all the hair, Cam could see how old he truly was. She preferred the tangled mop instead.

Siena's gear lay sprawled across the kitchen table as she repacked her bag.

"When are you leaving?" Cam asked.

Siena shot an irritated glare at Emmett. "The question is, when are *we* leaving? All of us. And I propose as soon as possible."

"We can't, Siena." Emmett paced from window to window in the main room. Only the dense new forest greeted him back. "Whatever the hell this is, we can't navigate it. It could be dangerous."

"So you want to wait here until what?" Siena leaned against the counter and waved her hand. "It all just goes away? Until the phone magically works? Until someone back home realizes we've been gone longer than we should and sends in a team to get us? That's weeks from now."

"They won't find you," Isaac muttered.

Every muscle in Emmett's body tensed, just like when Cam fought with him back at the tunnel tree.

"So you're going to listen to this lunatic?" Emmett seethed. "Are you out of your mind?"

"I'm not talking about this with you anymore. Not when you're angry." Siena clipped her Nalgene to the outside of her pack and left the kitchen, hurrying down the hall. The lab door slammed shut.

"Fuck," Emmett hissed. The map Isaac had unearthed loomed behind him in all its inky majesty. Not Deadswitch, but somewhere with similar topography. She thought of the map in Avery's bag.

Emmett spun toward Cam. "You need to convince her."

"Who said I agreed with you?"

Emmett threw his hands in the air. "Oh, I don't know, Cam. I thought the fact you got lost the last time we tried leaving spoke for itself. Aren't you search and rescue trained? Isn't the first rule of Safety 101 to stay where you are?"

"I must have skipped the chapter on what to do if the mountain on which our designated shelter is constructed is overrun with masked killers and tunnels to corpse piles and tears in the fabric of space and time."

Emmett pointed to the door. "Who says that shit isn't out there? Who says it's safe once we're off the mountain? We found a dead woman on Wolf Ridge. That's thirty miles from here!"

Cam gritted her teeth, acknowledging and hating his logic. They simultaneously turned toward Isaac, who shook out his hair in the center of the kitchen.

"You want my answer? You already know it, but you won't listen," Isaac said.

"How are you sure we'll make it if we leave now?" Cam asked.

"You misunderstand." Isaac gently set the scissors on the table.

"We *misunderstand*?" Emmett growled.

"I never said you'd make it. But what happens if you stay here is worse than anything you'd find out there."

Cam tightened her grip on the rifle, imagining Emmett

yanking it from her hands and shooting Isaac with it. "And you know how? Your crystal ball?"

To Cam's surprise, Isaac smiled at her, extending his arms to either side. "Look at me. There's a reason I'm old, and it isn't because I drank from the wrong Holy Grail."

Cam cracked a smirk. "If that's true, I'm surprised you remember movies."

"It was a couple of decades, not eternity."

"Fair." As much trepidation as she felt, Cam couldn't be mad at Isaac. He'd clearly suffered more than any of them.

"No. No, no, no. No way." Emmett waved his arms back and forth. "This isn't up for debate."

"And you aren't God," Cam said. "Look, I'll talk with Siena, but I can't promise I'll sway her one way or the other." She nodded toward Isaac. "Be easy on him. I mean it."

Cam took the rifle with her to the lab, the tension behind her palpable. She forgot about it as soon as she saw Siena messing with the radio at the desk.

"Whiskey Six Lima Delta, does anyone copy? Over. Whiskey Six Lima Delta . . . we are a party of four in danger on Mount Agnes. In need of evacuation. Do you copy? Over."

Cam propped the rifle against the wall. "Hey."

Siena looked up at Cam, her shoulders wilting. "I don't want to fight about this anymore."

"Why the hell would you think I'm not on your side? I've stood my ground through all Emmett's fits, Siena. This one isn't different." She ignored the sting in her chest. It wasn't the time to feel betrayed.

"I . . . I know." Siena rubbed her forehead. "I'm sorry. It's just Isaac—"

"Fuck what Isaac said. He's obviously traumatized, and we can't take his word as the end-all be-all. What do *you* think is best? Because I can tell you from my experience—not Isaac's, not Emmett's, *mine*—it's a crapshoot. Unless Isaac quits being so damn enigmatic, we don't know what we don't know. But if you believe him, I'll go with you." She held her pinkie up. "I trust you. You should know that by now."

Siena smiled, but before she could respond, static crackled through the radio speakers.

Beneath the noise, a song faintly played. Siena reeled back from the radio and held her hands in the air like she was in the middle of a stickup. "This is it! The station I found the other day."

Cam knelt next to Siena at the desk. "Tune it, will you?"

"I'm gonna lose the transmission if I touch the dial. This is only the second time I've found it."

"Just don't fat-finger it. Here." Cam reached out, carefully nudging the dial to one side. The static cleared to a melancholy pick of the guitar strings, and a feminine voice singing about rain and heartbreak.

No way. No way in hell.

"This isn't the same song I—"

"I know it," Cam interrupted.

Siena turned toward her. "You know the song?"

"The song. The singer." Cam had watched countless online videos in the wake of Avery's disappearance, and again after *Without a Trace* was published, trying to understand parts of Avery's life Cam hadn't known intimately. Trying to understand who she'd spent her time with. So many of those videos had been from Twitch streams of one of the disappeared, a desperate folk singer trying to make a name for herself—wild auburn hair, a cheap guitar, and playlists of sad, haunting lullabies.

First Naomi, and now . . .

"Janet," Cam whispered.

HOLDEN

As Frank's Jeep crawled up the washed-out clay road, Holden held on to the ceiling handlebar with a white-knuckled grip, his other arm wrapped around Francis. The dog sat between him and Angel in the back.

Maidei sat in front with her hands in her lap, relaxed as she stared out her window, even as they hit a rock and the entire Jeep bounced.

"Hey, Frank," Angel said as she stroked Francis's head. "Is your name short for Franklin or Francis?"

"Francis. Who's asking?"

"Oh, just thought you'd be delighted to know you share a name with Holden's dog."

Frank chuckled. "You know, I always got along with dogs better than I did people." He nodded at the German shepherd through the rearview mirror. "He can keep the name. Never fit me, personally."

"Frank suits you much better," Maidei said.

Old friends, thought Holden. If Frank was a Deadswitch ranger back when Cameron Yarrow was interning, then he must have been the ranger during Maidei's project. He took comfort in the connection. Maidei vouching for Holden meant Frank was more likely to believe him. If there was any hope of finding the research team, they'd need to have the ranger on board . . . whatever that ended up meaning.

The incline steepened even further. The Jeep rocked on the uneven clay, and Holden held his breath until they'd made it over the hump into a dirt clearing.

Hidden behind a cluster of pines was a vacation house down on its luck, aged and gray, with a crumbling stone chimney. He counted three stories, the windows grimier the higher they were, and imagined the rental listing: *Entire residential home - Great location, charmingly rustic, probably haunted. $190/night.*

They parked, and the five of them climbed out, Francis circling Holden's legs before finding a tree to pee on.

Angel held up her phone, wiggling it in her hand as Maidei and Frank headed toward the porch. "You let your sidepiece know where you were going?"

"Chelsea? I doubt she cares. Why?"

"Doesn't look like we have service." She studied the screen of her phone. "Mine isn't even telling me *Emergency Calls Only* near the signal icon. It's just blank." She shuddered. "Sort of creepy, right? I'd prefer a *Fuck you, I'm out* message to nothing at all."

"Do you think we'll be actually staying here?" Holden asked.

"Not like we have options. Neither of us can afford a hotel."

Angel was right; they hadn't exactly thought that part through. And Holden wouldn't have guessed their only realistic option would end up being the setting of a horror movie.

They joined Maidei and Frank, and Frank knocked on the door, his hand still raised when the door swung inward. A skinny man stood in the entryway, scruffy beard covering his jaw, his salt-and-pepper hair pulled back into a ponytail. His eyes were dark and beady, but kind, and when he saw Maidei, he grinned wide enough to show off a pair of silver caps.

Maidei embraced him, and they hugged long enough for

Holden to realize the reunion was significant. Zaid—Maidei's old research partner. She probably hadn't seen him in years.

As soon as they parted, Zaid waved an arm to all of them. "Come in, come in. These are the folks you were telling me about, yeah, Mai?" Zaid patted Holden on the back as the group funneled into the house. "Can't believe you kept 'em a secret for so long."

"You understand my hesitation." Silent words brewed beneath Maidei's statement. Holden wished she would say the quiet part out loud, but settled on patience.

The dark foyer smelled of woodsmoke and breakfast. With the others behind him, Holden followed Zaid to a big open space that served as both the living and dining room. Old topographic maps and framed yellowing articles decorated the walls around a pair of large bay windows. A mounted buck glared down at them from above the dirty fireplace, and a slab table extended from the kitchen tile through the living room. A laptop sat in the center of a mess of papers, wires, textbooks, and stained coffee mugs. Zaid hurried to it and sat.

"You *own* this place, Zaid?" Maidei asked, her voice a mix of awe and horror.

"Yes, yes. Bought it a few years back as a stakeout fort, furniture and everything."

Holden glanced at Angel, who mouthed, *Stakeout?* Holden shrugged.

"I'll give you the full tour later," Zaid said. "But there is something I need all of you to see now. Even you, Frank."

Frank huffed. "If you caught something on fire, again—"

"Such little faith in me." Zaid waved his hand with more urgency. "Come, come."

Francis took off into the kitchen, his nose glued to the ground as he swept back and forth across the floor. Holden and the rest of the humans crowded behind Zaid.

"I haven't been up here for quite some time," Zaid said. "Life gets in the way, you know? It especially gets in the way of things that don't pay me."

"So your grant money ran out?" Maidei asked.

Zaid laughed. "Grant money? No, I haven't seen grant money since they pulled the last of ours all those years ago. I paid for this in cash."

"Cash," Maidei repeated.

"Teaching summer classes, liquidating assets, stealing from dead parents. The usual. Anyway, I was letting things just run on their own, like I often do. But when you called me last night, Maidei, and I came back this morning, well . . ."

Zaid pulled up a new window on his screen, some kind of surveillance application with four black video feeds, all with the same text in the center: **Lost Connection**.

"I don't get it," Frank said.

"They're the feeds from four cameras I placed in parts of Deadswitch years ago."

"I don't believe we have a permit on file for that."

"Frank. *Frank*. You know how I work. That doesn't matter right now, anyway." Zaid held one finger in the air as he dragged back the toggle on all four feeds to two weeks prior, and then sped up the video to 228X.

"Glass Lake Trailhead, Triplet Lakes, Mount Charlotte, and Ranger Station 5E. Just watch."

The cameras were placed in trees and trained on one forest trail or another. Other than the position of the sun, nothing in the videos changed until all four of them went out at once. The **Lost Connection** message displayed again.

"Whoa," Angel whispered, elbowing Holden like he hadn't seen the feed for himself.

"Exact same time," Zaid said. "Down to the millisecond."

Everyone looked to Frank, who shook his head. "Downed satellite."

"I did some digging. No outages reported," Zaid countered.

Frank seemed more irritated by this than anything. “Did you contact the maker of the cameras?”

“I did everything, Frank. There were no issues with the network, and no problems with the hardware that could explain this.”

An awkward silence fell over the group. The malfunctioning equipment was clearly causing Maidei distress, but Holden couldn’t tease apart why.

“So what does this have to do with Dr. Dupont?” Holden asked.

“I have a feeling we all own pieces to a larger puzzle,” Zaid said. “Fitting them together may take a while.”

“A while?” Angel rubbed her chin with her thumb. “We talking a couple hours here, or . . .”

Maidei sighed. “I don’t think we know the answer to that. Might as well get your things from the Jeep and settle in.” She turned to Zaid. “I’m guessing you haven’t made up the rooms yet?”

“Shouldn’t take too long.” Zaid stood. “Just strip the beds when you go up, yeah? We’ll toss everything in the wash. Frank, stay as long as you want. I’ll get some coffee going.”

Holden and Angel headed back out to the Jeep alone. As they grabbed their bags from the back, Angel asked, “Why do I feel like we’ve gotten ourselves into something even freakier than we first thought?” The excitement once in her eyes had darkened into something warier.

He shut the back of the Jeep. “You don’t have to stay here, you know that, right? I’m sure we can scrape together enough for a one-way ticket back home. I’ll drive you to the Fresno airport and everything.”

“Me, alone? And you, stay? I don’t think so, Holden. I can’t leave you to your own devices. Who knows what you’ll try to do? Probably hike into the Forbidden Forest to find the research team yourself.” She lugged her backpack over her shoulder. “Plus, I have nothing to go back to. We already talked about this. Come on, let's go see our rooms. I'm sure I'll have to thoroughly disinfect wherever I sleep."

Holden followed Angel back up the steps to the house as she lamented about needing to locate the cleaning supplies. He'd spent a lot of time with her the past few months, and even though she talked a lot about herself, he still hadn't figured her out completely. But he knew one thing: she rambled when she was nervous.

"Room on the first floor is off-limits, but everything else is up for grabs," Zaid called from the kitchen. "The higher up, the more privacy you get. Just don't complain about the cold."

The untreated wood stairs creaked beneath Holden's feet as they ascended. The upstairs hall was stuffier, the sconces near each room layered with cobwebs. Angel made a dissatisfied noise as they passed each open door, the small spaces crammed with '90s log cabin decor that looked undusted since purchase.

"This one has the least crap in it." Angel tossed her bag inside the room at the end.

Holden headed back toward the staircase. "I sleep hot. I'll see what's upstairs."

He climbed to the third floor, where the rooms were sparser and somehow dustier. A mildewy stench permeated from the bathroom—he'd clean that later.

An extended pull-down staircase at the end of the hall caught his attention. The trapdoor was open. Holden's curiosity got the best of him, and he carefully climbed the rickety steps, expecting an attic crammed with all sorts of abandoned, moldering furniture and boxes.

Instead, he found a spacious loft beneath an A-frame, a double tucked under the dormer window, and a nightstand with a desk lamp. The air smelled less bad, too.

As Holden neared, he noticed the bedspread and stopped.

The quilt was thin, its yellow patches faded with wear. Alarm flushed his body. His hand shook as he touched the blanket, the fabric as supple as he remembered . . . when he and Becca lay wrapped in it during their mountain getaway in the Cascades. The taste of salt and sweat, the glide of cotton against his skin . . . The memory wasn't real, and yet the quilt and all its familiarity was.

Right here, of all places, waiting for him.

ISAAC

Isaac was tired.

He'd been tired most of his life. Fatigue that had leached into his bones over the course of his later life never left, and now everything felt like a dream. He'd lost track of time a while back. Maybe he had been gone two decades, but it could have easily been four. Not that it mattered. His age meant little to him anymore.

This morning, the fatigue was no different, his trauma feeding from him like a parasite as he sat alone, palms flat and rigid against the kitchen table. He had woken too early. In the dark, the flames of adrenaline licked his blood as he stared out the black window and waited for the sun.

Every time he inhaled, he smelled the Briardark. The rain. The decaying, broken beams of the final outpost, the fungus crawling across the floor before his eyes. Waking to mushrooms burrowing into his hands, the crack of branches, the bottomless growl of a night pregnant with hunters.

The Briardark smelled of rot and iron. It tasted like the salt caked to his face. All the sweat and sobbing. His body leaked sweat and tears and piss when he was afraid, and that fear . . . that fear was always the worst part, as he wondered if he'd be better off walking into the dark night to end his life than living through another.

Through the window, he deciphered the silhouette of branches. Mossy light streamed into the cabin soon after, and Isaac eased the tension in his hands.

He had survived, again.

Down the hall, a door shut. Siena stumbled into the living room, rubbing her eye with a knuckle. It was clear she hadn't slept. She yawned and wrapped her teal fleece tighter around her body. Isaac was unused to seeing colors so bright.

"You want breakfast?" she asked. "No one else is awake. Cam fell asleep at the radio last night. She won't be up for a while."

"That's alright," he said. "You should save your packaged meals for your hike out. I've already eaten too much of your food."

She furrowed her brow as she poured filtered water into the cooking pot. "It's your food too, technically. You need to eat something."

"I know how to go without eating. I'll forage later."

"*Forage*," she repeated with a snort. "Sure."

He said nothing, and an awkward silence lingered between them as the water boiled. Siena crossed her arms and paced in front of the table. "I have a theory, if you'll humor me."

Isaac shrugged. "Alright."

"It kills me to even entertain the thought, but this place—this wilderness—is *multiversal*. Is that a word?" She scratched her head. "What I mean is this Briardark place is a parallel dimension, and for some reason, parts of it are . . . umm . . . bleeding into Deadswitch. Time has to move differently there, which is why you're so old." She glared at the floor as her pacing slowed. "I'm not a physicist. I don't even know if theoretical science supports this. And I don't know why a man from that world would know who I am, much less want me dead."

She looked at him now, as though expecting an answer on her accuracy.

He isn't a man, Isaac thought of saying, but that would spark more questions. Curiosity was Siena's weakness, not her strength. It was why he'd been so careful not to relay much to her.

He couldn't give her reasons to stay.

"You won't be able to use science to explain everything the Briardark is," he said. When she frowned, he added, "I know that's hard for you. It was hard for me too."

She grimaced. "That's a load of horseshit."

He took a deep breath. *Patience*. "You won't be able to use *current* scientific theories to explain the Briardark. Better?"

She seemed less averse to this idea, but irritated nonetheless. "So who is this asshole who wants me dead?"

Isaac hesitated, remembering the moment he discovered the cards in the kitchen cabinet of this very cabin. He'd been young, bored, and attempting to mitigate the anxiety of finding a body in the woods. The cards would have been a perfect distraction had he been able to play solitaire. But they were trick cards, the kind you'd get at a magic shop, or so he'd thought. No matter how many times he shuffled the deck, the top two in the pile would always be the same, the rest of the deck blank.

The first card, the huntsman with two faces: **The Defector**.

The second card, nothing but a pitch-black stain: **The Shadow**.

As a child, his mother warned him of tarot, Ouija, and other sins of the occult. Playing those games was an invitation for the devil. And when Isaac saw amorphous dark shapes looming in the woods, he'd thought the cards were one of those games. That he'd invited the devil to play.

What had happened to him was much worse. He never wanted to think about it again and wished Siena would do the impossible and just listen to him instead of asking questions.

"Who he is doesn't matter," he finally said. "As long as you escape, he'll never bother you."

Siena sneered. "Emmett's right. Maybe you are just crazy." She turned back to her oatmeal, poured the boiling water, and hopped back when it almost splashed on her. Grumbling, she mashed the glutinous mixture with a spoon.

Isaac's shoulders sank. This was what he was trying to avoid—the tipping point between having her attention and her disregard. "Doesn't matter whether I'm crazy, which you know. Because you want to leave, too."

Siena crossed her arms and stared hard at the window, and Isaac wondered if she was deciding whether she was going to trust him. He walked around the table, catching sight of the map on the wall. His map.

Mount Agnes was The Way Back, this cabin its safety box. He'd deposited many secrets here over the years, all to prepare for returning to Siena. He just needed to remember where they were hidden.

He began toeing the kitchen floor planks until a board squealed with his weight. Kneeling, he wiggled his fingers around the edges, prying the board upward after a few attempts and reaching into the cavity beneath.

Siena knelt next to Isaac as he carefully lifted the bow from its hiding spot, running his fingers along the sanded wood he'd cured himself. He plucked the string of dried gut he'd harvested. It was brittler than it had been all those years ago.

"Is . . . is this yours?" Siena reached out hesitantly, caressing the wood as he'd done. "Did you make this?"

"A long time ago," he responded. From beneath the floor, he fished for the arrows—ten in all, hand-carved dowels topped with earth glass and balanced with raven feathers.

"I'll teach you," he said.

She looked at him in surprise.

"The basics. You'll need something to protect yourself out there. Something quieter than a gun."

Her face was enigmatic, but she nodded.

In return, all he could do was teach her to survive, and pray she'd leave soon after.

SIENA

Siena used to take solace in the wilderness. The sharp, verdant air. The bright sorbet mountains in the early morning. The quiet. Even during storms, silence somehow permeated the bad weather and difficult experiments and constant threat of wildfire. Her mother had taught her how to love the quiet, and so she came to the woods when her mother passed. When she left Emmett. When Feyrer died. She came to the woods to search for silence, and when it met her, it sank into her bones, hushing wayward thoughts, dousing moments of despair.

But now, the distance of that silence was galactic.

In the clearing outside the cabin, a darkness settled beneath the boughs of the surrounding damp evergreens. Whatever that darkness was, she could hear it as an unrelenting ring in her inner ear. She didn't know if the sound was real or in her head. It reminded her she was lost.

Siena bared her teeth at the forest and nocked an arrow. She turned back toward the side of the cabin, where she had set up a target using the boxes of blank paper in the cellar.

"Lift the bow first," Isaac said when she began pulling back the string. He'd taken up residence on a nearby stump to watch her. “Up. There you go. Now draw back . . . closer to your face. Closer. Don’t be afraid of it.”

“I’m not,” Siena growled. The feathers of the arrow brushed her cheek.

“Elbow back. Alright.”

Siena released the arrow. It smacked against the cabin roof and rolled off the eaves.

She stretched out her sore fingers. “I suck at this.”

“Everyone sucks at the beginning.”

She tried again, nocking an arrow and raising Isaac’s handmade bow. The grain on the grip was worn, as though the bow had been shot thousands of times.

Had Isaac been hunter, or prey?

She pulled back and released. The arrow flew over the mark, not sparing her the courtesy of sinking into the cabin wall as it bounced and toppled to the ground.

“I can’t nail the basics down before I leave. I don’t have enough time.” She wiped away the hair clinging to her face. “Fuck this.”

Isaac smiled at her. She saw how old he truly was, the way his scars and pocked skin stretched and wrinkled. The way he looked like he had a million secret lifetimes brewing behind his eyes.

She quickly glanced away and caught sight of Emmett through the bedroom window.

Maybe he wanted her to stay so she could never get away from him.

She nocked another arrow and aimed lower. It sailed over the mark and sank into the cabin’s exterior.

“Good,” Isaac said.

The praise only grated against her. She swung toward him and waved the bow. “Why the fuck did you need to make this? What the fuck happened to you? Where the fuck have you been?”

Her shoulders heaved amid their staring contest. She felt like she couldn’t take in enough air, and he didn’t even look like he was breathing.

"Why won't you say anything more? Why won't you tell me who's trying to kill me?" She threw the bow down. "I don't understand why you're holding all this information hostage. It's like you don't want me to trust you—"

"Not everything is about you, Siena." His eyes had lost their depth, closing her off. "Maybe I'm not ready to relive what has happened to me. Maybe I don't want to place that burden on you."

"It isn't a—"

"You already know what you need to know. Getting out of here is all that matters. It may not look like we're in Deadswitch, but it is . . . for now. You reach the border, and you're home."

"What do you mean, *for now*?"

"There's a reason this place looks different than it did two days ago, and it isn't going to change back."

She clenched her teeth. Maybe he was right. Maybe she needed to stop asking questions and get the hell out of here, because whatever had happened to Isaac she didn't want happening to her. Isaac wanted the same for her, and she should have been grateful. Instead, she was angry. Angry with Isaac. With Feyrer, who was dead and didn't even know what he'd put them through.

She picked up an arrow for another shot. It tumbled from her fingers onto the ground.

Anger at Emmett for trying to trap her. At her father, for not coming to visit since she broke up with Emmett. For not seeing her one last time, before she disappeared into this forest forever.

She shot again. The arrow scraped the top of the stack of boxes.

"Good," Isaac said again, as though she hadn't yelled at him.

She picked up another arrow, her rage now much louder than the steady ringing in her ear.

Emmett sat in the kitchen eating a late lunch by himself when Isaac and Siena reentered the cabin. "You spent all day out there."

"Isaac was teaching me a few things." She gently set the bow on the kitchen table like she hadn't thrown it to the ground earlier that day.

He sneered at it. "You need to eat. And we need to discuss our strategy for dealing with . . ." His eyes shot to Isaac and then back at her. "Everything."

They'd already discussed the strategy last night. Emmett's strategy was to wait at the cabin. For what, she didn't know. Rescue wasn't coming. They weren't going to be able to suddenly call out or pick up a receiver. And yet he wanted to continue to discuss staying until she agreed with him. It wouldn't happen.

She suddenly craved someone who thought the way she did, someone who would anchor her sanity and fight alongside her.

"Where's Cam?"

Emmett glanced down at his food. He stabbed at the mush in his bowl with a fork. "The glacier."

Siena's heart jolted. "That isn't funny."

"I'm not joking." He continued to avoid her eyes.

The glacier?

Rage screamed through her like a train horn. "What the *fuck* were you thinking, letting her go alone?"

Emmett jumped from his chair. "So when I care what happens to people, I'm controlling, but I let her do what she wants, and suddenly it's *what the fuck were you thinking*?"

"That is different!" Siena swiped a full Nalgene from the kitchen table and charged toward the door. She tried flinging it open, but the lock was, magically, no longer broken.

It didn't matter. All that mattered was Cam.

"Siena, wait," Emmett ordered.

Siena turned the knob and yanked open the door. She hurried off the porch and veered toward the peak. The cabin door slammed behind her, and Emmett called her name again. She picked up her pace and jogged into the dark undergrowth.

The path up the mountain no longer existed, the ground beneath her covered in rot and moss as thick as carpet. She maneuvered through ferns as high as her waist, resting her palm against an old tree for support. Its trunk was just like that of the giant they'd found back in Deadswitch—tapered, like a cypress.

She pushed deeper, until the ferns were to her chest and her clothes were soaked, and stopped to catch her breath. In front of her, the ground slanted upward and continued beyond the tree canopy, hopefully the way to the mountain summit. She could no longer hear Emmett behind her, but the ringing in her ear had returned.

She shut her eyes. Water dripped from her hair and trailed along her cheek in a rivulet. Her heart thundered an angry warning of panic.

She reminded herself she wouldn't be out here if it weren't for Emmett, and opened her eyes. A stone's throw away stood a silhouette.

It hovered above the ground amid the evergreen branches, impossibly onyx, sucking the light from the very sky like a cosmic gash. She blinked, and it was still there, waiting right before the mountain ascent. Waiting for her.

The ringing in her ear morphed into vowels and consonants that composed her name. He called her closer.

EXCERPT FROM CHAPTER 14 OF *WITHOUT A TRACE* BY JOHN LAWSON:

The hiker who hinted at tension between Avery and Janet prefers to remain anonymous, so I will refer to her as Leslie.

Leslie went on a Kings Canyon hiking trip Avery and Janet had led in late spring, about three months before the fateful Deadswitch trip. Backpacking in the spring in California can be tricky because of the elevation. When most of the state feels like summer, the Sierra Nevadas may still be inundated with snow. The year 2016 was no different.

"We hit snow on the first day," Leslie says. "Most of us were comfortable with winter hiking, but we didn't have the right gear. Avery was supposed to do the research on the trail and had told Janet everything would be clear. The sun was setting, and we were still a couple of miles away from where we were supposed to make camp. Janet laid into Avery in front of everyone, and Avery . . . she just *slapped* her. Right across the face. And then she turned around and kept trying to find her way through the snow like it was nothing. Janet was still holding her cheek in shock. None of us knew what to say. I had never seen Avery act that way toward anyone."

After the premature ending to the trip, Avery apologized to Leslie over text for causing a scene. She explained she hadn't been herself lately and had been losing sleep over an online stalker.

"I didn't question it," Leslie tells me. "She had the type of life that made her vulnerable to creeps. It's difficult being a woman on the internet."

Leslie isn't wrong, and one quick glance beneath any comment thread on an Avablade video proves it. But when mentioning my conversation with Leslie to the detective, he tells me they uncovered no evidence she was being stalked.

This is also new information to her father.

CAMERON

Above the tree line, Cam could see the world for miles. If she let her eyes relax a bit, it all looked just like the forest she'd entered. But she was trained to notice the detail—every ridge and valley, every seismic altering of the landscape.

It was wrong.

First was the extra mountain—the stepsister of the triplet peaks. That was the obvious difference. But the valley was deeper, the carpet of trees thicker. She saw nothing beyond other than more wilderness—no haze from the city or hints of civilization.

The melted glacier still rested in the cirque beneath the summit. Against the murky green light that patinated the very air, the tarn no longer looked like blue Gatorade—something she'd written on a geology report when she was in seventh grade. Now it was dull and dark, like a pond in some backwater dale.

Cam hardly remembered the reckless walk up here. Hell, she'd summited without a weapon, only a half-full Nalgene. She didn't even know why she'd made the climb other than to see the whole of this world beneath her, like she'd be able to pinpoint its exit. Either that, or find where in this hinterland the radio transmission was coming from.

She'd never met Janet Warren. Avery had invited Cam to one

of Janet's shows about a month after they'd first met, since Brittani thought folk music was lame and Avery had no one else to go with. But Cam had been too afraid to be alone with her. At the time she didn't know Avery was a hiker, and didn't know what they'd talk about. Awkward silence was the worst form of slow torture. She needed that on a mug, or something. Maybe she'd get it on a mug if she ever escaped this place, though that was looking less likely by the second.

Cam set the water bottle at the lip of the shore and followed the still surface right to the wall of rock and oxidized copper. The water there was as dark as night, but as she stared at it, the tension in her chest uncoiled.

The water looked *warm*. Everything seemed sort of hazy out there, muddled in a steam that rose off the surface. Was that why the glacier had melted? New geothermal activity? It didn't seem plausible, but it would explain everything.

Cam stepped past the shoreline. Cold bled through the leather of her boot.

The heat wasn't here, but out there. If she could just swim out, the heart of the tarn would wrap around her like a blanket and infuse her with warmth. She would relax and clear her head. She'd be able to think straight for the first time in days.

Cam shivered when the surface lapped the hem of her t-shirt. She pushed off the rocky bottom of the lake and dove forward, her toes numb in her boots. The deepest part of the tarn was right in front of her, just a few more breaststrokes, the promise of heat still undelivered. It wasn't cold, either. The water didn't even resist her, and she sliced right through it like a blade, weightless. Or at least, she thought so.

She only realized she was sinking when darkness swallowed the sun.

Water hit the back of her throat. She choked and panicked, her cry drowning in an inexplicable current that pulled her under. The more she thrashed against it, the quicker she sank, until she wasn't sinking at all, but falling right through the tarn into the onyx belly of the mountain.

The rest of her breath left her in a sputter. Pressure as dense as bricks slammed into the sides of her skull. She thought of Grandma June, and then every capillary in her body burst at once.

Her heart stuttered. Her lungs collapsed. Jackknife pain lanced her eyes and drained them of their vitreous. Blood poured from her mouth, her scream silent beneath the shrieking in her ears.

There was a pop, and then nothing.

She couldn't breathe, but didn't need to. She could see beyond the deflated sacks in her eye sockets—a pinpoint of light above, another below. Stars, maybe. Or tiny little worlds floating in a darkly vast universe.

She would not survive this, nor would she make it to either of these worlds before she died. She would die here, in this emptiness, alone and unready. Maybe now or maybe tomorrow. Maybe in a year or years or decades, she'd suffer sightless and voiceless. She could not quantify this expanse of time without the ability to track the rise and fall of her corporeal breath, but she would have to fill it with something. Life wouldn't flash before her eyes; nothing flashed here. She would have to dredge life up with her remaining electrical impulses—sounds, smells, memories—jigsawing together some meaning, some point to it all, because this nonworld was making more sense than the place she was from.

Love and ambition and hope eluded her. Pleasure eluded her. She'd once been born into a world beneath the spell of emotion, but there was none of that here. No meaning to dredge up. No point to anything.

She rallied the last of her firing neurons to conjure the most meaningful moment of her existence. But she found nothing.

The back of her head slammed into something hard, the pain as bright as the fucking sun.

Cam pushed away from the rock and floated upward until she broke through the surface.

HOLDEN

Holden could do nothing but wait for news from the search and rescue team. Well, that and clean.

He scrubbed the mildew stench out of the third-floor bathroom, dusted every knickknack in sight, and ran the vacuum over the shag carpet four times. He went through all the linen closets and washed and refolded it all. The window to save the research team was closing, so he did everything he could to keep his mind off it.

After finding a bottle of fabric softener from the early aughts, he washed the quilt from his bed until it smelled like the one from his false memory.

When he shook the clean quilt out and spread it back over the bed, his nose prickled at the scent of the fabric softener and attic wood. At first he thought it was a sneeze coming on until a memory slid into focus, like with the old projector in the basement of the Forest Science Complex. Becca on his lap, the quilt wrapped around them as they sat in bed. She pressed her finger to the window and traced the trees.

"My family isn't really in the picture, either."

Holden frowned at the blanket. No . . . that wasn't right. Becca's parents lived in Beaverton, only a couple of hours away from Corvallis. She drove up there twice a month. When they were dating, she and Holden had spent every holiday with them.

It's fake, he reminded himself. It didn't matter if this quilt had been in a memory he'd contrived. He'd created a false Becca admitting a falsehood, a scene that had briefly made him feel less alone in the world.

It was pathetic, and he didn't want to wallow in it, so he kept cleaning.

A couple of days passed. He finished the upper floors and started on the kitchen, washing every stale and slightly greasy plate, bowl, and cup stashed away in the cabinets. He threw out condiments that had expired eight years prior, organized the spices, and made a list for a stocked pantry. Eventually he'd have to make a trip into town when he ran out of dog food for Francis. Maybe Zaid would spot him cash for supplies.

Zaid hardly ever left the main room, the place the scientist had lovingly nicknamed the Hub. Every once in a while Holden would peek his head in to see a new flat-screen hanging near the mantle, or another laptop added to the collection on the table.

Holden finished reorganizing the last of the kitchen on the day Frank stopped by to provide a no-news update, and paused while mopping the floor as the ranger spoke with Maidei and Zaid on the other side of the nearest wall.

"This is dredging up bad memories," Maidei said.

"And I don't blame you." The floor creaked beneath Frank's heavy footsteps. "I've run a lot of missing folks cases over the past twenty years, but there are only two where every second is burned into my skull."

"Third time's a charm," Zaid muttered.

Two cases. One had to have been the Deadswitch Five. The other . . . maybe it had happened during Maidei's and Zaid's study.

"You can go home, Maidei," Frank said. "I wouldn't blame you. Zaid, on the other hand—next thing I know, he's going to be siphoning electricity from the station just to fund his operations. Can't get rid of the guy."

Zaid chuckled. "Ah, Frank. You'd be lonely without me."

Maidei hummed softly. "Zaid and I deal with many things in completely different ways, including our trauma. Perhaps that is why we get along so well."

"I do enjoy your company," Zaid said. "And I'm glad you're here. The kids aren't too bad, either."

Frank returned through the hallway, waving at Holden when he passed the kitchen. "They're hardly kids." He shared a smile with Holden.

Holden couldn't remember the last time he'd been called a kid. A part of him liked it.

"I haven't seen Zaid since yesterday afternoon," Angel told Holden the next morning as she exited the bathroom, drying her hair with a towel. "It's getting quiet around here. Sort of giving me the creeps."

Holden went downstairs to inquire of Maidei, who sat at the Hub's table.

"Don't worry, he does that sometimes," she said without looking up. "Barters for gear in the city when he's low on funding. When we worked together, sometimes he was gone for days. I never knew what he would bring back. One time he returned with a houseplant and nothing else."

Holden nodded and stood there awkwardly, scuffing his foot before asking, "You hungry?"

"Maybe, but I'm afraid to look in that fridge."

"You like eggs?"

She paused in her typing to shoot him a funny look. "Are you going to cook for me?"

He shrugged and turned back toward the kitchen. "I have nothing better to do."

The half-full carton of eggs was only two weeks expired. He scrambled them with a bit of mayonnaise and bouillon he'd found, sprinkled in some hard cheese, and cut up a few apples from the back of the fridge. It wasn't the most elegant meal, but it didn't taste terrible. The stairs creaked as Angel descended, and Holden brought three plates out to the table.

"I love a man who cooks for me without being asked," Angel said with a yawn.

Maidei took a plate with a thank you. Holden sat and pushed the eggs around with his fork. He needed to eat, but felt more sick than hungry, and instead petted Francis's head as the dog lay at Holden's feet.

Maidei hummed in approval. "This is good."

"I can make better." Holden dropped his fork and picked up an apple slice. "I had little to work with."

"It's the sign of a good cook when you can make something edible with the contents of that kitchen."

A silence fell over them as they ate. Holden hated it. He hated sitting here, eating eggs as if they had all the time in the world.

"Dr. Dupont sends her last message in ten days," he announced.

Maidei set her fork on the edge of her plate. "I'm aware."

"It doesn't mean we have those ten days. We don't know when Isaac is supposed to die, exactly."

"I know—"

"They could be in danger now."

"Frank will be here in a couple of hours. One of the SAR teams should reach the cabin by then." Maidei frowned. "Another duo was supposed to reach the lakes this morning and scout for the ranger, but they haven't called in yet."

Holden shifted uncomfortably. "I don't like waiting."

"We aren't waiting." Angel pointed her fork at him. "If I

remember correctly, I spent over sixteen hours in a car with you this week. If we were waiting, we'd still be back in Corvallis."

Holden shook his head, worrying his bottom lip. It wasn't good enough.

Maidei rested her elbows on either side of her plate. She watched him over the screen of her laptop. "What do you propose we do?"

Holden couldn't tell if she was humoring him. "I don't know . . . Can we get more teams on the ground? A helicopter in the air?"

"We have no hard evidence something is wrong. The Forest Service . . . they try to avoid bureaucratic bottlenecks by only calling in backup for emergencies. We have a handful of audio files from 'the future.'" Maidei air quoted the last part.

Holden gritted his teeth and glared at his lukewarm eggs. He should have come up with a more convincing tale of why he believed Dupont's team was in danger, even if it was a lie.

Like Angel was reading his mind, she said, "We're doing everything we can, Holden."

He knew that. He'd gone above and beyond for strangers. But his Siena-filled dreams made this whole situation so much more personal.

He didn't believe in God, spirituality, or divinity in the universe. Dreams were just an element of his subconscious and a way to process the absurdity of finding Dr. Dupont's audio files. But maybe that was the most anxiety-inducing part of it all.

Frank arrived exactly two hours later, his satellite phone perched on his hip. "My namesake," he said with a chuckle as Francis greeted him. He looked more tired than the other day. "I listened to those recordings."

"And?" Holden pressed.

"I'm . . ." Frank shook his head. "Disturbed by it." His eyes flitted to Maidei. Hers were pleading, as if she was silently asking him to be more than just disturbed. "I will admit, I'm not sure what to believe here. But I understand why you are worried about Dupont's team."

Holden's shoulders sank. "*Understanding* won't help them."

Frank nodded. "I know, I know. All we can do is wait for the call to come in and see what Search and Rescue finds at the research cabin."

If the call comes in at all. If it didn't, at least that would be an incentive to deem this an emergency.

Holden made tea, and as he brought a stack of mugs to the table, Frank abruptly stood and pressed the satellite phone to his ear. "Frank here."

Holden's heart leapt into his throat.

"Sandy . . . hold on, slow down . . . you're cutting out." Frank's brow furrowed in confusion. "What do you mean, they aren't there?"

Holden and Angel shared a look of alarm.

"What? I need you to repeat . . . You're cutting out, Sandy . . . You don't think what? How can you tell? Sandy? How can you . . . Okay . . . okay . . . Anything else? Hello?" Frank pulled the phone away and glared at it. "Lost her."

"What happened?" Holden asked.

Frank dipped his head and rubbed the space between his eyes. "It doesn't make any sense."

"What did she say, Frank?" Maidei's voice was tense. "What did Sandy say? What did they find?"

"She was cutting out. I don't know for sure . . ."

"I can handle this, Frank. Just tell us."

Frank dropped his hand. "Nothing. They found nothing. It doesn't look like anyone has set foot in the cabin for years. There's no evidence they even made it to Agnes. I only caught bits and pieces . . . something about no footprints, dry water barrels, and an empty outhouse tank."

Warmth drained from Holden's body. Whatever he'd been expecting, it wasn't this. "That's impossible. They had to have made it there. The recordings . . ." He felt dizzy and sat.

"What do we do now?" Angel's voice was quiet.

"I need to report this to the sheriff and wait to hear from the other two teams. We need to contact CalTech again—maybe their families—to figure out if Dupont and Yarrow changed plans last minute. If not, then something else happened. They got lost . . . maybe sidelined."

Maidei slammed her laptop lid shut. "Frank, we should go to the sheriff now. We need to gain traction on the urgency of this situation, preferably in the next couple of hours."

Frank grunted. "Let's go, then."

As Maidei followed Frank to the front door, she pointed at Holden and then swiveled her finger toward Angel. "Stay here."

Holden threw his hands up. "Where the hell would we go?"

Maidei hesitated for a moment before saying, "The woods." She followed Frank out the door before either Holden or Angel had the chance to respond.

"You won't catch me dead in those woods," Angel muttered when it was just the two of them.

Holden buried his face in his hands. Nothing made sense.

"Okay, okay." The table creaked as Angel stood. "We don't need to leave the house to help. Let's think for a sec. What do we know from the recordings?"

Holden's hands slid down his face. Angel stood in front of the bay windows, the forest far too dark for the early afternoon.

She continued. "We know Dr. Dupont was in a cabin at some point, because she mentioned it."

"She mentioned the mountain and Alpenglow Glacier," Holden added. "Is the CalTech cabin the only one on Agnes?"

Before Angel could respond, the front door slammed open. Zaid tromped down the hall into the Hub carrying two mechanical devices in his hands. Drones.

Zaid held the drones up with a grin. "Who's ready to hunt some researchers?"

EXCERPT FROM CHAPTER 17 OF *WITHOUT A TRACE* BY JOHN LAWSON:

Ask anyone to recall the story of the Deadswitch Five, and they'll mention Avery Mathis. Maybe Janet Warren. But most of those vaguely familiar with the case will fail to recall the names of the other three.

I spend the day at Glass Lake, a four-mile hike from the trailhead. It is Saturday, the lake as busy as it gets. A family shares lunch on the shore across from me. Two smitten teenagers dive from a rocky overhang into the inky water beneath, shrieking at the cold when they surface. A middle-aged woman in backpacking attire rounds a nearby trail as she heads for higher ground, accompanied only by a golden retriever.

I am also guilty of not giving Paige, Tasha, and Naomi the attention they deserve. Part of the reason is obvious; the internet is teeming with chatter of Avablade, but googling Paige Reeves or Tasha Gonzalez returns dozens, if not hundreds of unremarkable social media accounts.

Paige and Tasha were half-sisters, both having met Janet and Avery at San José State. Paige worked at a nonprofit for women's reproductive care and moonlit as a bartender. Tasha had just gotten into law school with the hopes of one day becoming an environmental lawyer.

I think about these women as I eat my lunch on the shore of Glass Lake. I think of their quiet legacies, which never came to fruition. And I think of Naomi, who often shared with her friends how much she despised her budding career as a software engineer.

I feel like a cog, she told a friend over text days before the Deadswitch trip. **How am I going to survive another 30 years of this? I don't care about fintech or crypto or the millionaire silicon valley fuckboys. I want to quit and run away to**

the woods. I want to build a witchy cottage and never see another computer or another man again.

In a second text message, she wrote, **Don't tell my bf I said this. He already thinks I'm a lesbian.**

. . . are you? Her friend texted back, to which Naomi replied: **Jury's out. Check back later.**

I hope that whatever tragedy befell the five women didn't happen at the start of their trip, and that Naomi lived out her fantasy in peace, if only for a few days.

It is peaceful here. Almost achingly so.

SIENA

Siena stepped forward as he called her name again.

She instinctively knew this darkness was a *he*. This was not the first time they'd met. She'd felt the insatiable curiosity inside her once before, when she was in the tunnel that had led her to the other cabin.

She needed to understand what he wanted. If she didn't, something inside her would blister and peel away. She knew this instinctively, too.

She was used to studying landscapes at their present stillness. Mountains and valleys were temporary. But *he*, in this hovering onyx form, had always been here, floating, stiller than any mountain or rock. Older than Earth. Than time. Just like this forest.

He wanted her to know all this. And he had so much more to say, if she could just . . .

Siena stumbled backward, spinning and careening into Emmett's chest. He'd followed her.

Emmett dragged her away from *him* as she emerged from her stupor—*his* spell—and her mouth opened in a silent scream.

Emmett threw Siena in front of him. "*RUN!*"

She oriented herself and ran toward Isaac, who stood at the edge of the thicket. He stared past her shoulder, at *him*, face deathly pale and eyes heavy with recognition. Isaac's lips moved around words Siena couldn't hear, and when she reached him, she cried his name and grabbed his arm, dragging him along with her.

The cabin wasn't far. Siena emerged from the thicket with Isaac in tow and sprinted until she reached the porch. She threw open the door and stumbled, slamming into the floor in front of the couch.

As soon as the other two were inside, Emmett rammed his shoulder against the door to shut it and yanked the lock. Siena scrambled backward until she was flush against the wall near the hallway.

"What the hell was that?" Emmett hissed.

Isaac wilted onto the couch. He sweated profusely, his chest rising and falling so rapidly that Siena pushed herself to her knees in case she needed to catch him if he passed out. "You've seen it before, Emmett," he said. "Don't pretend you haven't." Isaac pressed a hand atop his chest, the crescents of his fingernails dark with dirt. "What led you to the tree, and the tunnel."

"Is that true?" Siena asked. Emmett was already storming down the hall as she turned toward him. A few moments later he reemerged with the rifle, approaching the window and lifting the edge of the curtain to peer outside.

"Does it—does *he* have multiple forms?" Siena asked Isaac. "I've met him once before, I think."

Isaac's throat bobbed as he looked at her, frowning.

"Do you remember when I found that passage beneath the tree? I told you all about the other cabin, and the man there. I don't know what he looked like. He wore a gas mask."

Isaac's eyes widened in bewilderment. "I'd forgotten about that. No. No, he's not . . ." He tensed and shook his head. "You shouldn't have met that man. It's too early."

You shouldn't be here.

The hair on the back of Siena's neck prickled.

Emmett unhooked his attention from the window. "Too early for what—"

The light in their universe extinguished before an umber glow erupted from outside, outlining Emmett's silhouette.

"Sen . . ." Emmett called to her.

The floor vibrated. Still kneeling, Siena pressed her palms to the wood. She'd experienced California earthquakes dozens of times.

This wasn't an earthquake.

The sensation beneath her fingers swelled, like the bedrock was taking a deep breath. The earth could not move like this—not without terrible repercussions.

"Hold on," she uttered.

The words hadn't left her mouth before the cabin floor dropped out from beneath her.

EMMETT

Emmett opened his eyes to darkness and Siena's screams.

He rolled to his stomach and crawled, lashing out with his hands until he found her. He grabbed her shirt and yanked her toward him, his hands roaming her body as she hyperventilated. Checking her ribs and her limbs, he ignored the intimacy of it all because that no longer mattered. All that mattered was that she was okay. Scared, but okay.

When he was done, she threw her arms around his neck and held on to him, her chest rising and falling against his like she'd just run a marathon. He breathed heavily, too. A dull ache throbbed in his head. He must have hit it when . . .

What the hell happened?

They'd descended into hell after the mountain crumbled out beneath the cabin. After that, he couldn't remember.

Emmett's eyes adjusted to the light, the cabin around them a muddled ensemble of silhouettes against the dull, burnt glow coming from outside. There were no signs of structural collapse. Not even a toppled chair. The air wasn't full of dust, but void of anything at all, even smell.

And the silence . . . even Siena's gasps as she caught her breath were muted.

"Are you okay?" He could hardly hear his own voice. Something about the fall had dampened his hearing.

Siena sniffed. "I don't know." She pulled away from him and wiped her eyes. "We must have eaten something by accident. Mushrooms in our food supply. This is a bad trip. Tell me this is a bad trip."

Emmett felt distressingly sober, which meant whatever had happened to them was real. God, he *wished* he were on drugs right now and had an excuse to wait this out. But he had to face this, now. Whatever *this* was.

Isaac's silhouette lay slumped against a wall, unmoving. When Siena let go of Emmett, he pushed himself to his feet, more shaky than sore. He stumbled toward Isaac and knelt again.

Isaac's eyes were open and unfocused, his chest rising and falling. His expression was—well, he had no expression. Not a muscle in his face was tense or moving, and his skin was covered in a sheen of sweat.

"Hey," Emmett said.

Isaac did nothing.

"Hey!" Emmett grabbed Isaac's shoulders and shook him.

Isaac's eyes flicked to Emmett, and then Siena. His cracked lips moved around the words "*I failed,*" and something snapped inside Emmett. He grabbed the collar of Isaac's t-shirt and yanked him forward before slamming him against the wall, and Isaac whimpered, jerking to attention.

"What the hell is going on?" Emmett seethed. "What the hell did you do?" He slammed Isaac against the wall one last time, letting his anger get the best of him. But it was okay, because at any moment, Siena would rush over and pull Emmett off Isaac. That was what she did.

Except she didn't come. The front door moaned in despair as it opened, and Emmett hopped up and turned right as Siena stepped out onto the porch.

"Sen, stop!" Emmett scoured the floor of the main room for

the rifle, but it was still too dark to see clearly. He couldn't let her run off . . . not again. Not after . . .

Emmett stopped in the doorway. Siena wilted against one of the porch's posts, and Emmett's pulse thrummed in his throat as he tried making sense of the landscape before them.

The burnt, hazy light emanated from nowhere in particular, but about thirty feet away, just beyond the cusp of a handful of trees, the light ended and there was nothing. The tops of the evergreens disappeared into a *dome* of nothing. Not darkness, but nothing. Like they were inside the only snow globe of matter left in the universe.

Emmett's head swam, his neurons firing like machine guns without targets, uncomprehending of how the world simply *ended* thirty feet in front of him.

"Sen," he whispered in warning, too paralyzed by fear to stop her as she pushed herself from the post and stepped forward. His voice was quiet and dull, the surrounding space soaking up the noise. The air had the acoustics of an anechoic chamber.

He thought of COtwo. Belmont's unwillingness to send rescue. How Emmett had only exacerbated the situation by keeping the call from Siena and Cam. He'd fought to stay here because of what? His *boss*?

They could have left this place yesterday, and maybe they would have if he hadn't tried sowing doubt in Siena's mind. This —whatever it was—was his fault.

Siena crept across the clearing and reached toward one of the pine trees at the edge of the amber glow. She pressed her hand against the trunk, running her fingers down the bark, and then extended her other hand toward the nothingness. It wavered there, her fingers splayed and trembling, and she whimpered like an injured animal.

Emmett's hackles rose with a sudden compulsion to protect Siena, and he hurried toward her. He halted at her side, lifting his hand toward the nothingness. Weakness washed over his arm before it fell numb, like his muscles had atrophied. Grabbing his wrist with his other hand for a brace, he unsuccessfully tried ramming himself through with brute force.

Emmett pulled his arm back and turned his palm inward to study it, strength returning to his limb. He curled his fingers into a fist and punched outward, his knuckles connecting with nothing, bent arm refusing to move any further. His heart beat so violently against his rib cage that it hurt.

He was dreaming. Either that, or he was having a stroke.

Siena said something he could hardly hear over the cotton sensation in his ears. Trees . . . something about the trees. All were equidistant from each other and the cabin. The backs of their trunks melded with the darkness, as though the two were soldered together.

Emmett fought a wave of dizziness and spun back toward the cabin, resting his weight against the nearby tree to keep from falling. Sweat dripped down his neck as he counted the remaining pines that circled the entire cabin, perfectly spaced and confined by the dying ember light. There were less than a dozen.

This wasn't the wilderness. It was a wilderness diorama.

Siena scrambled around the pine perimeter, yelling something unintelligible and ramming her shoulder against the nothingness. It didn't matter which part of the circle's edge she forced herself against. It was all the same: impenetrable.

They were trapped.

Emmett rubbed at his eyes, squeezing them shut and opening them again. He roughly pinched the skin of his arms. "Wake up," he said. He could hardly hear his own voice. "Wake *up*."

Siena stumbled on her second loop around the cabin. She slumped over as her knees hit the ground, and the scream she released reflected the nuclear terror in Emmett's own chest. Before he realized he'd even moved, he was already with her, holding her as she collapsed into his shoulder.

"*WE CAN'T GET OUT,*" she screamed. "*Emmett . . . Emmett, we can't . . . Emm . . .*"

He couldn't respond, not even as her words dissolved into

nonsense and the sobbing took over. He couldn't respond because he was also sobbing. He'd never cried like this before, and if he spoke at all, then he would hear what his own sobbing sounded like. He wasn't ready to face that noise. Facing it meant he also had to face the reason why. And he didn't know. He didn't know what had happened to them. He didn't understand why they were trapped here.

Only that they were.

HOLDEN

Everything was going wrong. Or right, depending on how Holden looked at it.

Hours after Zaid's return, Maidei and Frank came back with news that the other two rangers positioned in Deadswitch were missing, no sign they'd even reached the cabins that summer. Which was impossible. Both rangers had been checking in until the last scheduled date.

Frank raised the alarm to the local sheriff and was quadrupling the search and rescue efforts.

They were finally bringing in a helicopter.

"This is just like what happened with the Deadswitch Five." Angel paced the floor of the Hub, holding her copy of *Without a Trace*. She smacked her palm against it as she thought. "Vanished with no evidence. Without a trace, if you will."

No one in the room reacted to her dumb joke. Holden joined Maidei in poring over the Deadswitch maps at the table, but he wasn't exactly sure what they were looking for. Seated on the floor in front of the blank feed screens, Zaid pulled apart the defunct drones, all their intricate parts arranged in piles on the hardwood. He swore beneath his breath a lot.

Frank left the Fort again for his umpteenth meeting with the state police. Holden trusted Frank to relay the urgency of the rescue mission to the authorities, but wished he could be there and actually contribute. Waiting here left him restless.

"What if there's been a time-traveling kidnapper in the hills all these years?" Angel halted in her pacing. "Maybe erasing the tracks of their victims is part of their signature or whatever. They take pride in it. They would need a hiding place . . . an underground cavern system? I mean, that's a good place to keep a bunch of bodies . . ."

Maidei rubbed her forehead. "Can we *please* not talk about our rescuees as though they are already dead?" She cast a glance at her empty vintage *Deadswitch Wilderness Area* mug at the table's corner.

"I can make you more coffee," Holden offered.

"No, but thank you. I'm still jittery from the entire pot I drank this morning."

"Okay, I might have gotten a little off track," Angel admitted. "But I still think we shouldn't ignore the similarities of the two cases, especially considering the victim count is around the same."

"Person count," Maidei corrected.

"Right, of course. That's what I meant."

Zaid released another string of expletives, ending on something that sounded an awful lot like *blistering elephant cock*. He threw a screwdriver across the floor and then rubbed his forehead in the same manner as Maidei.

"I think you need to call in a professional," Maidei suggested.

Zaid dropped his hands. "Who?"

"I don't know. Are you still talking to Victor?"

"Victor's at a lab in Missouri. If he can come, it'll take him a couple days to get here. We might not have that time."

"Is this an official missing persons case?" Holden asked, wincing involuntarily when both Zaid and Maidei nodded.

"The researchers, yes," Maidei said. "We're still waiting for more news on the whereabouts of the rangers. The family of Dupont's team were phoned. They're all single, so the sheriff contacted their parents . . . well, except Dupont. We can't get ahold of her father."

"Where is he?" Holden asked.

"The Yukon."

Holden raised his eyebrows.

"From what the sheriff has garnered, it sounds like he's been up there living off the grid since his wife passed away."

Angel shuddered. "Sounds like my worst nightmare. Being here for less than a week is testing my limits."

"Is there no one else the sheriff can contact?" Holden asked.

Maidei shrugged. "Yarrow and Ghosh are the main people in her life. They're with her now, hopefully, wherever that is."

Cam ran off yesterday. Emmett's off looking for her . . . never came back last night.

Dupont's final recording. Soon she'd be on the mountain alone, with a dead man, two of the very few people she cared about MIA.

If Holden hadn't uncovered the recordings, how long would it have taken the university to realize they were missing? Did any of them have family they contacted daily? Did their roommates keep close track of their schedules?

Lauren was a great roommate because she stayed out of Holden's life, except for those rare dinners. She'd seemed fine with the idea of him leaving for two weeks, perhaps even delighted to have the place to herself. And he hadn't given her a firm return date, either.

If something happened to him up here, he didn't know if anyone would worry about him when they couldn't reach him. Probably not Lauren, and certainly not his parents. Maybe his boss, eventually, when the busy season hit and she actually came looking for Holden and Angel. But that wouldn't be for another few weeks.

Holden turned away from the others toward the windows, surprised when his eyes burned. There was something inherently tragic about his aloneness. About Dupont's aloneness. That wasn't the reason he'd gone looking for her—but now it felt like another reason to stay. However long it took.

He needed to at least let Lauren know of that possibility.

Holden blinked until his vision cleared and turned back toward the others. "I need to call my roommate and update her on everything, but I have no service."

"There's a landline at the ranger station." Zaid picked up another screwdriver and pointed it toward the front door. "Give me a few minutes, and I'll take you down in my truck."

"It's only a couple of miles, right? I can walk. I need the exercise, anyway."

Zaid shrugged. "If that's what you want. It's quicker if you cut west and straight across." He made an incline with his hand. "Go down the hill until you cross the decommissioned forest road. You'll see a dirt path that'll take you right there."

Holden nodded and headed toward the hall.

"Holden?"

He turned. Maidei watched him from the table with a frown.

"Be careful."

"I'll head to the ranger station and come right back," Holden promised.

"Still," she said.

"I'll take Francis."

This seemed to placate her. Holden got the dog harnessed and headed out to a sunny, quiet afternoon. Very quiet. The forest smelled different from the ones in Oregon. Dustier, sharper, more mineral . . . *alien*. But it was just a forest, its basic parts the same as the ones he'd been in before.

As soon as Holden chose a direction, Francis dragged him along, sniffing every rock and shrub and peeing on everything that looked moderately appealing.

Be careful.

Like he really needed something else to be anxious over.

He kept his eyes glued to the path before him, careful not to slip on the decaying bark, until the old forest road crept into view up ahead, an apocalyptic-looking relic layered in overgrowth and crumbling asphalt. Holden walked along it until he found the dirt trail Zaid had mentioned, but stopped when a road sign distracted him.

The official names of the wilderness area and national forest had been scraped off the sign. Olive paint filled the remaining lettering, bleeding into the surrounding wood.

Wilderness Area
Permit Required
National Forest

Holden staggered, suddenly dizzy. His inner ear rang as he regained purchase. He rubbed his eyes and kept moving, ignoring the misplaced dread that lingered in his stomach. The roof of the ranger station peeked through the trees, and he began to jog, Francis happily complying.

Holden arrived out of breath to an unlocked but empty station. He called around for Frank a bit before giving up and locating a rotary phone on the desk, a beige antique permanently grimy from several decades' worth of use. The numbers on the paper placard were worn to an inky blur.

He checked his phone for Lauren's number and dialed it, holding the receiver between his shoulder and his ear.

"*We're sorry, you have reached a number that has been disconnected or is no longer in service. If you feel you have reached this recording in error . . .*"

"Fucking rotary phones," Holden muttered. He mashed the switch hook and jerked the dial around, entering Lauren's number again.

"*We're sorry, you have reached a number that has been . . .*"

Holden pulled the receiver away from his face and stared at it like he was waiting for it to admit to a prank. He tried again and received the same message. Maybe he was one of those millennials who'd forgotten how to operate a rotary phone. Anything was possible, but the only way he'd know for certain was if he tried dialing another number.

He thought of Siena Dupont. Of her father. His parents didn't know he was here.

Holden's fingers twitched on the dial.

Francis released a guttural growl. Holden's attention flicked to the dog, who stared at the door with his hackles raised.

Holden turned toward the window. The receiver slipped from his hands.

A buck. No, not just a buck. A *shadow*.

It stood amid the trees, the rack as large as the deer. Holden squeezed his eyes shut and opened them, but the silhouette remained blurry, like the animal was sucking the light from the sky.

A yearning tugged at his heart, burning red-hot like a warning.

He needed to reach it. Capture it. Send an arrow through its eye. Carve into its belly, pour out its viscous onyx insides. Tear away strips of its flesh and eat it, chewing and chewing until cosmic gore trickled down his chin and seeped into the collar of his shirt. Snap off the ribs. Suck out the marrow. Feast until dusk, until the buck filled the entire track of his gut. Until he'd proven himself. Until . . .

"Holden?"

Holden blinked.

He stood in a dark room. Francis's tags clinked together as the dog hurried toward the open station door to greet Frank.

"It's almost eight. What are you doing in the dark?"

Holden exhaled a stale breath and sank to the floor with the last of his energy. Every muscle in his body twitched and vibrated. He shook like he was starving.

His mouth tasted of blood.

SIENA

She woke to the howl of her own voice, which quickly diffused into quieter sobs.

Had she been dreaming? She couldn't remember, her fear untethered until the orange glow of the room reminded her where she was.

Her mattress sank with the weight of another person who grabbed her and pulled her close. Siena thrashed with a startled cry. Emmett hushed her.

"I'm here. I've got you."

His heavy warm arms wrapped around her waist. Siena relented, burying her face in his chest the way she used to on really bad nights when she felt as powerless as she did now.

"Cam," Siena whispered. There was one thing she understood more clearly than her own demise: Cam wasn't here.

Would she think they'd left her on purpose?

Emmett lifted his hand and brushed the hair from her face. He pressed his lips to her temple. "I know," he murmured against her skin. "I'm so sorry."

She'd listened to him say sorry so many times. Over text. Over the phone. When she returned to his apartment to pack her things. In the university office late at night, both of them overworking themselves to avoid the pain of their separation.

Those apologies she could never accept. This *sorry* wasn't an apology, but pure remorse for something neither of them controlled. He was sorry that she was so scared. That they both were.

Siena wasn't trapped in this place alone. There were two people with her, and she'd loved one of them unconditionally. She'd been engaged to him for four years.

She didn't know what was going to happen to them, but if this was the end, then her year of invariable anger toward him served no purpose. He was here with her. He loved her, and despite everything, the root of her anger had always been the fact she couldn't stop loving him back.

She lifted her face from his chest. Her chin grazed the stubble of his jaw, and she kissed the corner of his mouth.

He kissed her back. His lips were warm and chapped and reminded her of something distantly familiar. Safety, she realized. She couldn't remember the last time she felt truly safe, but she had always been safe with him before they'd fallen apart. At seminar panels when he would watch her from the front row with a smile. When he guided her waist protectively on dates or at university events, and when his touch slipped from protective to possessive. She'd felt safe then, too. And in bed with him, when she let him be rough with her. When he lost himself in her. When she liked it.

She'd been so cavalier about that safety, assuming its immutability. And she still craved it even though she knew better.

Emmett wasn't possessive or rough now. He moved with a kind of confused caution, unsure about pursuing her. He didn't need to pursue her. She was fine just like this, their bodies still, lips touching, everything else a blur of ambiguity existing somewhere beyond her bunk.

His hand moved beneath her shirt to the small of her back.

Siena parted her lips when his hand crept higher, pressing the tip of her tongue to his lower lip.

Emmett's body went rigid, his hand darting further up her back. His fingers balled into a fist, and he dragged his arm out of her shirt and flung whatever he held onto the floor.

Siena pushed herself up on her elbows. Beneath a wildfire beam of light, a beetle twitched on the ground before righting itself, quivering about helplessly. Her stomach leadened in despair.

Emmett turned back toward Siena, an epiphany lingering in his dark eyes like she'd done something profound.

But she'd done nothing. She'd fought the bugs when they first manifested years ago, hadn't she? And then she became a victim of her own brain when no one believed her. Poor Siena, stressed herself out to the point of no return. In order to heal, she'd needed to accept that these infestations were in her head and move on. So she had.

And everything had gotten better, until her reality shifted. Cam pulling a bug from her hair, Emmett one from her shirt . . . like this was all some sick joke.

She'd fought for power her entire life. Power over her career, her mental health, her ex-fiancé who insisted he deserved forgiveness. Power over her grief. She fought when she didn't need to.

There were things she could control, and things she couldn't. It was possible she only had days left to learn that lesson.

The lesson wasn't easy.

Siena and Emmett tracked the hours of days and nights with rationed phone glances, the steadfast burning light incompatible with their solar chargers. The battery connected to the ham radio had inexplicably vanished. Emmett tore up the entire cabin looking for it. But whether they could track time didn't matter. Time granted her no power here.

As Emmett exhausted himself with rage over the missing battery, Siena reorganized their gear. She put away the dishes they couldn't use due to lack of water. Spreading bandages, ointment, and sutures over the table, she refit the first aid kits. As she did so, Emmett sulked over, crossing his arms as he leaned against the wall.

"You think this happened to the other team?"

Siena counted the ibuprofen and distributed it amongst the four kits. "I don't know."

"Feyrer told us the research was in the woods. Did he mean here? Where the hell do we find it?"

"I don't know, Emmett. We don't even know if what he said is true. He was drunk."

"What if he knew about this and didn't tell us?"

Siena zipped up one of the packs. "What if? You going to dig him up from the grave and demand he tell you why he screwed us over?"

Emmett's jaw clenched. He leaned back until his neck and head were flush against the wall. "He was cremated."

Siena snorted a laugh, clapping a hand over her mouth.

The muscles in Emmett's shoulders relaxed, his grin slightly maniacal. "I think I'm losing my mind."

"Join the club."

Isaac entered the kitchen from the main room. Siena had seen little of him since they plummeted. He usually sat beneath the molten light leaking through the front-room window, somberly writing in a fresh composition journal that had been part of their original supply. One time she had tried asking him if he knew what was happening to them, but he only shook his head wordlessly in response.

Maybe it was better she didn't know.

Isaac held up two foil packs. "Chili mac. Found them in the lab."

Siena frowned. “I don’t remember leaving food in the lab.”

Isaac handed the dehydrated meals to her. Siena used her thumb to smooth out the peeling labels. “These are old. From the ’90s, maybe. Must have been left by the last team. I could have sworn I went over every inch of the lab.” She placed them on the table next to the kits. “Guess I missed them.”

Emmett pushed himself from the wall. “Who’s hungry?”

Every time they lay down to sleep, Emmett forced her to discuss things like their dwindling water supply. The barrels were less than half full. If they didn’t bathe or wash their hands, and rationed their food and the amount they drank, then the three of them had enough for two weeks. Assuming they were stuck here for that long.

“Maybe we won’t have to worry about it,” Siena whispered as they faced each other on the lower bunk. “We could plummet to some other microverse in the chasm of space and time at any moment.”

Emmett’s brow furrowed as he thought about this. “You think?”

Siena had gone to Disneyland with her parents once as a tween, before her mother got sick. What was that ride called? Tower of Nightmares? No, that wasn’t right. Some monstrosity of a contraption that emulated an elevator in a downtown high-rise that had seen better days. The ride would shoot you up, drop you a level, and then another, and then finally release you to freefall to your doom. Or so she remembered. She’d done her best to shed that horrible experience from her brain, much preferring the memory of eating ice cream with her mom on a bench down Main Street, U.S.A.

This cabin was just like that elevator car. She just didn’t know if the ride had gotten stuck forever, or if they were about to drop.

"Maybe," she said. "One minute we're making chili mac, the next . . ."

"Dark, Sen." Emmett shifted, his fingers drifting to her bare midriff. "I'm surprised how nonchalant you are about this."

"I'm not," she said. "But there's no point in worrying about things I can't control."

A calm washed over her as she spoke the adage, and Siena fell asleep next to Emmett.

When she woke, things were different, the crescendoing dread of the unknown enough to debilitate her. She spent an immeasurable amount of time lying on the floor, imagining it dropping out from beneath her until she became numb to the idea once more.

Something twitched behind her ear, and Siena pulled a beetle from her hair. Still lying on the floor, she pinched it between her finger and her thumb and held it above her face, watching its tiny feet wheel about.

Perhaps they were as imaginary as this world, an indicator she was in a coma or seriously losing her shit. But they felt real, more real than anything else.

She thought of the look on Cam's face when she realized Siena hadn't been hallucinating.

Cam.

Was she really going to lie about while Cam was all alone? Was she really going to give up?

The beetle's antennae twitched in a flurry. She sat up and stumbled to her feet, carrying the bug to the cabin's front door. On the porch, she lessened her grip, and the beetle took off, fluttering higher and higher until it disappeared within the boughs of one of the pines.

"Wait!" she cried, as if she could convince it to come back. She jogged into the clearing, her gaze whipping back and forth across the dark branches. But when she tried to circle the tree to see if she could spot the bug, she collided face-first with the resistance of nothing. Their boundary.

But the bug—the bug had escaped, hadn't it? Why couldn't she?

White-hot terror combusted in her chest. She released a scream and charged at the darkness, slamming into the barrier with her entire body so violently that she felt her organs smash into each other. She did it again and again, until Emmett found her and dragged her away, locking her arms behind her back with his own brute strength. Thrashing about, she fought against him just to feel her sedentary muscles ache and burn. He finally flipped her over and pinned her to the ground on her stomach.

"Siena, stop! You're going to get thirsty . . . We can't afford the water!"

She didn't care what they could or couldn't afford. It didn't matter if they ran out of water tomorrow or next week.

The ending would be the same.

Siena begged Emmett not to tell her the time when he turned on his phone to check. It was easier if she didn't know. She forwent a schedule, eating when she was starving, drinking if she was too thirsty to think, and sleeping when she couldn't keep her eyes open. All that signified time was the lack of water in the barrels.

But water wasn't all that disappeared.

First was the Chittick apparatus, a device too big to misplace. Siena noticed its absence when she wandered into the lab to see if its window offered any additional wisdom she'd missed the first hundred times she stared through it. Not that she needed it. She had done nothing related to her field since they hiked to Alpenglow, which felt like a lifetime ago.

But then the theodolite disappeared.

She notified Emmett, who shrugged as he sat at the kitchen table reorganizing their food for the millionth time.

Who cared about a theodolite at this point?

She understood why he didn't care. It didn't matter if things were disappearing, as long as it wasn't their food or water. Or one of them. But when her empty pack and hiking poles vanished from their place near the front door, Siena grew more curious about whether their stuff would reappear. She tried finding the items, scouring every corner and searching beneath every bed. She checked the cellar, with its smooth walls and no sign a tunnel had ever extended from it. She even checked the bowl of the outhouse, which the universe had decided to so graciously include as a part of their microverse (she decided this word was much better than prison, even though she was certain she would die here).

The shitter was a pitch-black pit of which she couldn't see the bottom, though the basin was only eight feet deep. She giggled hysterically when the thought crossed her mind that it may be the only way out of here.

When she checked her pockets to get a better look, all she had on her was her phone and her recorder. Her flashlight had also disappeared.

Siena returned to the cabin to see if she had misplaced it. When she entered, Isaac sat in the middle of the floor, facing away from the door and staring at the Briardark map. A new crimson trickle ran from a peak that looked like Agnes, around the mountain range, past huts and through rivers, circling a structure at the very bottom of the map. Smeared near both Agnes and the structure was a circle with two parallel strikes through it.

"Is that your blood?" she asked. "Are you cut?"

Isaac cast a glance at her. His hands were on his knees, neither bandaged nor wounded. She stepped closer to the map. The blood was dried and faded, like the trail had been there for years.

"The blood isn't mine," he said, his voice quieter than the scratch of nails against wood. "Whoever drew it knows another way out of the Briardark."

"A path," Siena said.

"A path between the two passages back to Deadswitch. This mountain is . . . or it used to be one of them. But I think I understand now . . . We're trapped here because this passage is collapsing."

Collapsing. "Like a wormhole or something?" God, she really knew dick about physics.

Isaac's eyes glazed over as he lost himself to a memory. Uncomfortable, Siena glanced away toward a canvas pack in the room's corner.

Her brain scrambled to make sense of what she was looking at. She stepped back, finding more strange bags leaning against walls and scattered across tables: totes and satchels and tactical backpacks. Some of them looked half a century old, while one bag was bright teal and made of nylon, a relic from the '90s. The food Emmett had stacked neatly on the counter now lay scattered across the floor, unfamiliar boxes of MREs amongst the dehydrated meals.

Excitement fluttered in her chest. Things were changing. It didn't matter that their gear was disappearing. All that mattered was the possibility of what it could mean . . . an upcoming change to their landscape. An approaching way out.

Siena jogged down the hallway. Emmett was napping in the bunk room, but before she could wake him, her attention caught on the open doorway of the lab.

The room was empty.

No, not entirely empty. The tables remained. A wooden bucket sat near the wall. The last time she'd seen it, it had collected blood from a mule's head.

Siena blanched at the thought of what was inside the bucket now.

But she'd worry about that later. While the tables were mostly bare, some things remained. The ham radio, for one, and the deck of cards. A microscope took up the left corner of the table's surface, though it wasn't the one they'd packed in. It looked either cheap or old, like it had been lifted from a high school lab.

The papers she had picked off the floor upon their arrival were still stacked in the corner opposite the microscope, though the bloody handprint from the doorframe had disappeared. Siena walked toward the desk to pick up the cards, and halted. The stacked papers were no longer blank, but filled with lines and lines of hastily written scrawl.

Siena knew Dr. Wilder Feyrer's handwriting well. She'd deciphered journals full of his personal notes when she worked as his assistant.

She picked through the pages, scanning the tops and bottoms of each page to order them. Feyrer's signature filled the corner of the last page. It was a letter. A long one.

When Siena found the first page, the tips of her fingers went numb.

Siena—

One day, you will find this. I pray you will. And as you know, I am not a praying man.

You will never understand just how sorry I am for concealing the truth from you. I'm even sorrier for the pain you are about to endure. But it is essential pain. If you do not bear it, the layers between our world and the Briardark will thin to the point of no return.

Let's stop this from happening, you and I. We'll start with the truths, and then the secrets.

I really did fall in love with Deadswitch for its landscape. There is something so special about the Sierras. The range feels like a barrier of sorts, as if by hiking through it, you are passing from one realm to another.

Did you know that between the Mojave and Mammoth, there is no road that will take you from the western side of the range to the eastern side? The mountains are too dramatic for such a passage.

What am I saying—of course you know. You know this range as well as I do. Except for Deadswitch. I told you to wait for Deadswitch until you could enjoy it. I'm honestly surprised you listened. You were always one to challenge me.

And now for the secrets.

I may have been surprised that you listened, but I was also relieved. I didn't want you to wait to enter Deadswitch just for the sake of enjoying it when you were finally well versed in your field. I did it for your temporary safety, which I'm sure you are understanding by this point.

I wish it didn't have to come to this. The tragic thing is that it had to. I lied to you about having not returned to this cabin since '97. I have returned many times, on my own, but not for Deadswitch. For another place.

When we started our studies, our goal was to monitor the glacier. Things changed once we were up here. We began noticing anomalies, not just in the glacier itself, but in the biological composition of the entire mountain. Trees seemed to shift from their place in the earth, their cells unlike anything we'd ever seen before. None of us were biologists, but we all knew the stark difference between animal cells and xylem. We began noticing the appearance of flora and growth alien to the mountain's habitat, growth that appeared one day and vanished the next. Some days, the sky began to glow the strangest shades of green before returning to normal, like some kind of quiet electrical storm.

At this point, I should have focused my attention on why we had hiked up: Alpenglow. A glacier melting far too quickly, a sign of the climate's brink. Studying the other anomalies was a project reserved for a much larger team with ample funding. There wasn't much we could do with our equipment.

But I made a choice, a choice that, over a period of five years, would destroy the lives of my fellow researchers and inevitably disband us. It would reveal the end of our world.

I chose the mystery. The unknown, something that was no longer a string board of anomalies, but far more awesome and insidious than I could have ever imagined.

I documented our findings for my successor. For you. And I'm glad I did, because I'm certain this secret will outlive me.

I'm dying. I almost died getting up this mountain for the last time. The cancer came on quick; a part of me wonders if the sickness is even from this world. But that doesn't matter. The only thing that matters is what comes next.

First, you need to read through the research we performed. I know it may seem like a lot, but you must understand the finite details in order to successfully pick up where I left off.

You'll also find an annotated map in one of the boxes. Take it. Learn it. Memorize it. Look at it so much that you see it on the back of your eyelids before you fall asleep. This is very important. You will lose items quickly in the Briardark, but you can't lose what is a part of you.

You'll understand what you must do. I've run out of time. So much depends on you.

Find The Mother, Siena. And whatever you do, don't stray from the path.

—*Wilder Feyrer*

SIENA

The cellar was filled with more boxes than Siena remembered.

The apex was stacked four boxes high, the unorganized pile covering most of the cellar floor. She set down the camp lantern and began digging through boxes, rifling through papers that were no longer blank but crammed with handwritten research notes, diary entries, and taxonomy sketches. Some sketches were elegant, while others were nothing more than a rough outline of trees, ferns, and wildlife she'd never seen before.

She craved the time to spend poring over each page, wanting to understand every nook and cranny of Feyrer's research. Going through it all would take months.

And did he deserve her thoroughness? He'd lied to her. His omission of the truth had trapped her here. Maybe it would even kill her. And Feyrer couldn't answer for any of it. It was possible that the truth of why she was so important was buried in these documents somewhere, but that wasn't good enough.

Feyrer had been as controlling and manipulative as Emmett could be. He'd just hidden these weaknesses better. She kept trusting the men in her life until they unforgivably fucked up or abandoned her. Was this something else she couldn't control? Another prison trapping her forever? Feyrer had wanted her here, in a place with rules she didn't understand, picking up where he'd left off, without her consent.

And if she wanted to escape, she had no other choice but to learn what she was up against.

Siena snapped dozens of photos of important-looking documents and continued her search, finding the box with a 2001 topographical map of Deadswitch Wilderness. She took it, carried it over to her camp lantern, kicked away a beetle, and sat. Unfolding it, she spread the map across the cellar floor.

Marker lines scratched out the title *Deadswitch Wilderness. BRIARDARK* was written in block letters beneath. Siena ran her fingers over mountains, rivers, and scribbled buildings drawn across the wilderness area. Haphazard circles marked parts of the forested valley, along with the word *Avoid*.

Was this map literal? Was the topography of this Briardark place identical to Deadswitch Wilderness with a few exceptions? Isaac's map and the map she'd found on the table looked a lot like Deadswitch, but a more *fleshed-out* version with additional mountains, bodies of water, and buildings.

Siena froze. Beneath her, the ground vibrated so slightly that she almost passed it off as her imagination, until footsteps tore across the cabin floor above her.

Emmett? No, not heavy enough.

Siena refolded the map and grabbed the lantern, hurrying up the steps of the cellar into a microverse much darker than the one she'd left. The ember light had all but died. When she turned off the lantern, she could hardly make out the outline of her hand.

She blinked until her eyes adjusted to the darkness, and then ventured carefully to the front of the cabin. Isaac stood on the porch, staring past the pine shadows into the nothingness beyond.

Siena didn't notice the wetness on his cheeks until she stopped next to him. Not a muscle in his body moved as tears trickled from the corners of his eyes.

Asking what he mourned felt wrong. She waited instead, setting the camp lantern near the door and flipping its switch.

Eventually, Isaac blinked and turned toward her.

"Wilder Feyrer made it to the Briardark," Siena said, tucking the map into her sweatshirt pocket.

"I know." Isaac hung his head. "I didn't tell you because I was worried you'd stay if you knew. I'm sorry."

She waved her limp wrist defeatedly. "You aren't the first man to keep things from me." Her shoulders sank, and she rubbed her head. "He wants me to find The Mother—I guess she's the antlered woman. Some cult goddess who requires mule sacrifices. Am I close?" She didn't wait for Isaac's confirmation. "I'm sure it would make more sense if I read through his research. I just wish he would have told me to my face what I was up against."

Isaac's expression crumpled. He wiped his cheeks with the back of his wizened hand and reached toward her, gently touching her shoulders.

"I'm . . ." He struggled with the next part of the sentence, pressing his lips together before trying again. "The choice of what you do next is yours, not Feyrer's, nor mine. I understand that now." His grip on her tightened. "But Feyrer lied to you. And he will keep lying to you from the grave. What was the last thing he said to you?"

Feyrer's dying words rang hollow in Siena's memory.

Don't go.

"How do you know that?" she whispered. She'd never told Isaac that story.

He ignored her question and continued. "The last thing he told you was to avoid all this. That is the Feyrer you need to listen to. Don't find The Mother, Siena. Once this passage collapses, you need to leave this place and never come back. Save yourself and refuse the pain I endured."

As Isaac held her at arm's length, Siena grabbed on to the crook of his elbow with her free hand. "I'm sorry for everything that happened to you. You were young, and I should have been looking out for you. I was responsible for you. I *am* responsible for what has happened to you."

She'd never seen so much agony in someone's eyes before. Even Feyrer's. Even her dying mother.

"Don't . . ." Isaac croaked, but he didn't finish.

When he dropped his arms, she stepped forward and hugged him. A small whimper escaped his throat before he hugged her back, and Siena wondered when the last time was that he'd been held like this. She knew the answer would only break the remaining threads of sanity still holding her together.

"Matthew, Chapter 4," he said. "The story of Jesus entering the wilderness for forty days and nights to be tempted by the devil. Jesus said to him, 'Be gone, Satan. For it is written, you shall worship the Lord your God and him only shall you serve.'" He pulled Siena back, holding her once again at arm's length. "Only forty days, can you believe it? The son of God has nothing on me."

She released a quiet laugh of surprise, and Isaac let go of her.

A buzzing permeated the air, and she finally realized how deathly quiet this place had been. It reminded her of a humming computer or a piece of lab equipment, a sound that would have gone unnoticed by her back at CalTech.

Isaac narrowed his eyes and cocked his head. He heard it, too.

Siena stepped off the porch and beyond the orb of light emanating from the camp lantern. She pinpointed the direction of the sound and looked up, squinting into the darkness. Her pulse thudded in her throat as she waited, the noise crescendoing along with the ringing in her ear.

She spotted the hazy shape of a flying object, far too small and quiet to be an aircraft. It dropped closer, hovering above where she stood.

A drone.

She reached an arm upward, her straining fingers just out of reach . . .

Her ear shrieked. Siena dropped her arm and stumbled to her

knees, clapping her hands over her ears. Her efforts didn't help—the noise was coming from inside her head. She screamed alongside the shriek as her skull vibrated and a knife-sharp pain pierced her eardrum.

The pressure built until she couldn't take it anymore. *Please put me out of my misery,* she prayed, though she didn't know who exactly she was praying to.

It was over as quickly as it started.

Siena gasped for air, her lungs aching. She cautiously lowered her hands and opened her eyes to soil.

Not soil cast in a fiery glow. Not soil beneath a patina of darkness. She sank her fingers into dirt and scooped it up with her hands, the texture wet and dense with decay. An earthworm writhed in the center of her palm.

Siena lifted her head to a forest.

A woven tangle of branches from evergreen giants all but filtered out the sun. Mist settled on dense foliage the color of eucalyptus. A throaty bird squawked from its place in the trees as the brush to her left rustled.

Siena inhaled the sharp medley of herb and moss and mineral, the scent familiar, but also wholly different from anything she had smelled before.

Slowly, she stood. The ringing was gone. The pain was gone. Whatever had been hovering over her head was gone. And she was somewhere she'd never been before.

Siena turned back toward the cabin—toward Isaac—and screamed.

HOLDEN

Holden lay atop his quilt, staring at the morning light filtering through the greasy window. He'd been awake in bed for hours, volleying between nausea and dread.

He'd accumulated the odd collection of mental episodes over his life, but the thing with the shadow buck was the most fucked up.

Shadow buck—he had no other word for it. He hadn't shared his episode with anyone, not even Angel, who'd told him Maidei had been so freaked out by his four-hour absence that she radioed Frank to find him.

Instead of divulging his mental breakdown to everyone at the Fort, Holden had claimed he spent those hours calling around to figure out why Lauren's phone wasn't working.

Mental breakdown. Whatever had happened to him felt like so much more than just a mental breakdown. Angel was right: he needed meds. He needed to see a therapist regularly, too.

And he needed to leave. Go back to his life and get his shit together. He'd done everything he could here, now only taking up space.

The stairs creaked. Holden lifted himself onto his elbows as Angel climbed into the room and meandered about, pretending to study the mostly empty space before finally sitting at the end of his bed.

He waited for her to speak since she was obviously here for a reason, but wasn't expecting her to say, "Went to the station and called my ex this morning. My divorce is finalized."

Holden sat up. "I thought you were still disputing the settlement."

Angel shrugged. "I don't have money for a lawyer. The total worth of disputed stuff isn't even worth the cost of court."

Anger flared in Holden's chest. "So he just gets to keep it all?"

Angel's shoulders wilted. This was the saddest—and the smallest—that Holden had ever seen her.

"Maybe it's better this way," she said. "Starting over."

"With nothing? I mean, I get the whole starting over thing, but you were contributing financially. It's not like all your things were gifts from him."

"It's not about the finances, it's about . . ." Angel shook her head. "Never mind. I don't want to talk about him anymore. But me . . . It's kind of like I have to figure out who I am all over again, you know?"

Holden nodded. The same thing had happened when Becca left him. Hell, it had been almost a year, and he still hadn't figured out who he was without her.

Angel glanced solemnly out the dusty window. "I feel old."

"You aren't old." Holden yanked the quilt off and swung his feet over the side of the bed. "I'm older than you. Am *I* old?"

"I just thought I would have figured out my divine purpose by now. I'm the universe's dead weight."

He wished she'd stop for the sake of his own discomfort. Not like she owed him that. He'd been miserable enough times in front of her, after all.

"Don't you ever feel you missed your chance to be someone?" she asked.

His response was quick. "You sound like my parents."

She gave him a *look*, which he returned with an awkward laugh.

"No," he continued. "I've never felt that way. I used to be content with what I had. When I was with Becc—" He stopped himself. "When I still had a partner."

"So your entire self worth was wrapped up in your girlfriend?" Angel asked with pointed disgust, the way she used to talk to him all the time, before they found the files.

Holden shook his head. "It wasn't like that. I had *enough*. Food, a place to live, money to pay my bills, someone I cared about. I didn't need a better job, or anything, really. I just existed and was happy and enjoyed making my girlfriend happy. And that was that."

"Well, when you put it like that, it sounds pretty nice." Angel sighed. "Alright, fine. You're not as big of a loser as I thought you were."

He chuckled. "And maybe you don't sound like my parents."

"Doctors? Lawyers?" she pried.

"Mom was a marketer until she became an exec. Dad was an exec until he became a life coach."

Angel groaned and fell back onto his bed. "They sound absolutely insufferable."

Holden cast a grin that Angel returned.

"Maybe we will be okay, you and I," she said. "Just existing. Purposeless."

For a moment, Holden really believed she could be right, until he remembered the shadow buck, and the false memories. Maybe reaccepting his purposelessness was enough to keep him from suffering from these bizarre episodes, which were only getting worse.

He caught a whiff of burning bacon. "Who's cooking?"

Angel rolled her eyes. "Zaid. He was in the city before dawn this morning and just came back, excited about . . ." Angel shot up. "Oh, yeah! That's what I came up here to tell you."

Holden raised an eyebrow. "To tell me Zaid is burning bacon?"

"No, that he got in contact with one of his old research buds, or whatever, who now works at some fancy-shmancy Silicon Valley corp."

"Doing what?"

"Making drones, baby. The good kind that runs on biofuel. Zaid rolled up with one in the back of his truck."

Drones. Drones that actually worked. This news should make him feel hopeful. If the SAR team found nothing on the mountain, and the rangers stationed in Deadswitch were nowhere to be found, then their trail was completely cold. Drones were the only way to cover enough ground before it was too late.

Angel held out her hand, palm out. "I know, I know. I'm dubious too. But we've got nothing to lose."

Holden looked down at his sweats. "I guess I should change."

"I hope I don't break it," Zaid said. "This thing costs more than my left nut."

"Just your left one?" Angel muttered.

Maidei and Frank sat on the porch steps drinking coffee. Angel hovered over Zaid like a fly as Zaid tweaked different mechanisms on the drone.

Holden stood between the two groups, awkwardly scratching his head.

The drone was as big as Francis and stood erect on a set of pronged legs. Four motionless propellers topped the cross frame. The fuel cell, tank, and camera filled its belly.

Maidei shook her head. "To this day, I have no idea how you procure the things you do."

Zaid groaned as he knelt, the drone chiming as he powered up the fuel cell. "It's my special skill. Probably my only skill, to be fair."

Frank rubbed his brow. "I can't believe I'm letting you do this."

"I can't either!" Zaid exclaimed delightedly.

"Oh boy." Angel stepped back from Zaid. "I feel like I'm minutes away from witnessing an incredible disaster. At least we all tried our best, right?"

She shot Holden an ironic thumbs-up, which he returned, feeling a little guilty for not being completely honest with her this morning.

After he had dreamt of Siena back in Corvallis, he'd thought for a moment that driving down here and saving the research team *had* been his divine purpose. But even if they could be rescued, he wouldn't be the one doing the rescuing. Holden had done what he came here to do. It was time to go back to Oregon. Maybe get a better job. Find a therapist. Download a dating app.

He was so caught up in his own head that he hardly noticed Zaid picking up the drone remote. "Back up, back up."

Everyone fell back to the porch, and the drone ascended with a whine.

"I plugged in the Agnes coordinates, so as soon as this thing is up in the air . . ." Zaid made a show of lifting his fingers off the controller. Once the drone was high enough, it veered and took off over the treetops.

Zaid gave a satisfied sigh. "And there she goes. Now we wait."

When they'd all filed back into the Hub, Zaid sat at the table, removed a chip from the drone remote, and popped it into the side of his laptop. The screens around the mantel flickered on, displaying the HD video footage from the drone.

"How long will it take to reach the cabin?" Holden asked.

"A little over two hours, probably," Zaid said.

The drone zipped past a road and a dense grove of evergreens before ascending once more as it entered a valley. Holden's stomach twisted the way it did when he was due for his yearly employee review, or when he had to speak on stage in front of a large group. Anticipatory dread. He didn't know why. The drone would only tell them what they already knew: the research team had never made it to the cabin. It wouldn't tell them why or provide any insight on how to stop Isaac Perez from dying.

They didn't even know where Isaac Perez was.

The drone veered around a smaller mountain, and the valley spilled outward into a massive divide.

"Whoa," Angel whispered.

The footage looked like a nature documentary, three peaks jutting from the wraparound mountain range far off in the distance. Holden didn't have a word to describe what he was seeing other than *majestic*. *Unreal*, perhaps. He'd only seen places like this when he streamed The Discovery Channel on sleepless nights.

Yet at the same time, the drone's footage felt achingly familiar, and made Holden nauseous.

"Anyone need anything? Coffee? Food?" he asked. When no one responded, he started wandering toward the hall. "I'll . . . uhh . . . make something."

In the kitchen, Holden pressed his palms to the rim of the sink and stared out the window. He felt like he hadn't slept in weeks and had way too much caffeine to compensate, his body unable to overcome the stress of this rescue mission. Now he was seeing shadow creatures in the woods. He needed to pull his shit together.

"I don't enjoy looking at it, either."

Holden glanced over his shoulder.

Maidei crossed her arms and leaned against the cracked yellowing fridge. "There's something I haven't told you."

Holden turned and pushed his back against the sink.

Maidei nodded toward the kitchen window. "Last time I was here, my team's research trailers were right around these parts, about a couple of miles from the ranger station. One day I walked from the trailers to the station to make a call, and got lost."

Holden furrowed his brow. “Lost?”

“For days.” Maidei lifted her hand, wrapping a few of her braids around her finger. “I don’t know what happened. I was on a familiar trail, and then completely disoriented. The forest didn’t look like Deadswitch. It didn’t even look like California.”

Why didn’t you tell me this before I took a walk to the fucking ranger station? Holden wanted to blurt. But he was too curious to let his anger get the best of him. “What happened?”

“I survived and made it back to familiar ground. Frank found me. There was a whole SAR party out looking for me.” Her eyes glazed over. She curled her finger and tugged on her braids. “I wish I could just forget it ever happened, but it still haunts me. Something—or someone—stalked me when I was lost. All I can remember is a dark silhouette.” Maidei dropped her hand. “But nothing else. Either I was high from the mushrooms I foraged, or my mind is trying to protect me from what I actually saw.”

Suddenly, Holden was back at the station, staring out the window at a buck made of shadows.

Francis wandered into the kitchen, his tail flopping back and forth. He sniffed beneath a cabinet and licked something off the floor.

That night was still blurry to Holden, but bits of memory were filtering through. Francis, growling. Francis wouldn’t have growled if the thing Holden had seen wasn’t real and only in his head.

“I think I saw it,” Holden said. “The other day, at the ranger station.”

Maidei frowned. “Saw what?”

He swallowed. “Your stalker.”

Maidei and Holden sat near each other at the table in The Hub as they watched the drone’s live footage of Deadswitch. Their brief conversation silently filled the space between them. They needed time to compare their stories, but Maidei wasn't in the right head-space today. Holden didn't blame her. As long as the drone was in the air, he was also distracted, brain overloaded like a maxed-out CPU.

But they would talk eventually, and when they did, Holden would have to tell her about losing time, and the insatiable hunger that had filled him until he felt like some kind of primal monster.

He didn't know if he would ever be ready for that conversation.

"We're getting close to the cabin," Zaid announced. Frank stood from his seat. Holden returned his attention to the monitors.

The drone hovered over the jagged top of Mount Agnes. Near the top of the peak was a large hollow filled with snow, which Zaid pointed to. "If they're geomorphologists, that's probably the glacier they're studying."

"Wait." Angel leaned forward in her armchair seat near the window. "What's the name of the glacier?"

Zaid shrugged, turning to Frank, who also shrugged.

"Alpenglow, I think," Maidei finally said.

Angel's eyes widened, and she looked at Holden, expecting him to share her epiphany. "In one of her recordings, Dr. Dupont said Alpenglow had been lost."

"That makes little sense," said Maidei. "Maybe she misspoke."

"There's the cabin." Zaid walked toward the monitor and pointed at the corner of the screen. He held the drone remote in his other hand and began fiddling with the controls. The drone swayed.

"The lower you go, the more likely you'll get stuck," Frank warned. "That's a fifty-seven-mile hike in."

"Yeah, yeah." Zaid poked his tongue out of the corner of his mouth as he focused.

The cabin was the size of a quarter and barely visible beneath the surrounding trees. It grew larger as the drone descended, the roof bleached and covered in dead pine needles.

Holden stood, the monitors drawing him in like a magnet.

He knew this place.

The stench of rotted wood from a dense forest, the smoke and venison from the fire pit. The slide of parchment against his fingers as he unrolled a map across a barren tabletop.

Two cards beneath a lantern's orange flame: The Ranger, The Mother.

Those you protect—they are your identity.

The woman at the college party had pulled these cards for him and spun him a fortune, but he knew them from somewhere else. From this cabin.

How was that possible?

"Keep your eyes peeled for anything SAR may have missed," Zaid said. "I'll dip a little lower just to have a peek around and then lift her back up. We'll circle the mountain a bit . . ."

The screens flashed white before filling with dark grain. Holden blinked.

"Shit," Zaid hissed. "*Shit!*"

Frank sighed. "What did I tell you?"

"Could it be the cable?" Angel asked. "One bad cable can kill everything. Holden, can you check the HDMI ports?"

Holden wasn't listening.

On the dark monitor, behind the confetti flecks of noise, a woman made of static reached toward him.

EXCERPT FROM THE INTRODUCTION OF *WITHOUT A TRACE* BY JOHN LAWSON:

"*Have you ever dreamt that your child went missing?*"

I've posed this question to many parents. It comes as no surprise that the resounding answer is yes. Losing a child is a nightmare, whether it be literal or figurative.

But for those parents who've had their children go missing, they almost always follow up with an unprompted statement:

"*I never thought it would actually happen.*"

Lewis Mathis is different.

"Thought about it every night," he tells me over coffee in his modest single-story ranch in Clear Lake, California. "She was famous in a way I didn't understand. Men had access to her in a way I didn't understand. I thought if anything happened, she'd be abducted. But this . . ." Lewis shakes his head, running his thumb along the rim of his empty coffee cup. It's a Father's Day mug, the draw-and-bake type. Avery's stick figure illustration of her and Lewis holding hands is forever sealed in the ceramic. "I was the one who introduced her to hiking. I trusted the wilderness. Maybe it isn't logical, and I know it isn't fair, but I'll never be able to shake the thought that I helped kill her."

Lewis's adoration for his daughter is apparent in the way he speaks of her, his home a shrine to Avery the girl, not Avablade the YouTuber. School and sports photos of Avery cover the walls in crooked frames. On the coffee table is a photo of Avery holding a foot-long trout, the first fish she ever caught. She's missing her two front teeth. It's Lewis's favorite.

He tells me many things she never shared with her fans. Her phobia of the dark. Her emergency trip to the ER when she got a Barbie shoe stuck up her nose. Her favorite hiking snack: yogurt-covered pretzels.

He tells me she struggled with her sexuality.

"I always knew, I guess. Your kids tend to trust you with those kinds of things when you're a decent parent.

"After she went missing, I found a vlog on her YouTube account. It's unlisted, not private. Her other vlogs she kept in an encrypted folder on her hard drive. But this one . . . It's like she wanted someone to find it."

Lewis is certain of this, so he shares the link with me.

Avery sits at her desk. It's an old video from the days before she was famous, the footage pixelated, her dorm walls covered in university swag. Her eyes are rimmed red, her hair disheveled. She wears little makeup. Either she's been crying, or she's hungover. Maybe both.

She doesn't look directly into the camera as she speaks.

"Last night I . . . I messed up.

"Everyone was at the frat parties celebrating the end of the semester. I wanted to stay back at the dorms to pack, but Bri— my roommate pressured me into going to this house party in the foothills. Said it would only be a few people. I should know by now not to trust her. Fool me twice and all that.

"Some guys had seen my *Bioshock 2* playthrough. My roommate must have sent them links to embarrass me or whatever, but it was weird . . . the guys didn't make fun of me. They thought it was cool and kept asking me questions, like how they could upload their gameplay. I think Bri— my roommate wasn't happy that her plan backfired.

"But, uhh . . . I'm not great with this whole attention thing. Not yet, at least. Fell back on Ol' Reliable. Still can't get the taste of raspberry vodka out of my mouth. I can't even remember how many I had before I spotted . . . before I spotted her against the wall talking with a couple of people I didn't know.

"And there I was, drunk and high off attention. Guess I felt like I deserved everything I've ever wanted. I made such a scene of it too, interrupting her conversation with her friends, asking if I could talk to her in private. She was obviously annoyed, and I didn't even take the hint.

"I think I dragged her into the laundry room. She crossed her arms and looked at me like I was a stranger, but I kissed her anyway.

"The most pathetic thing is that I don't remember the kiss. I don't even know if she kissed me back before pushing me away and telling me to stop."

Avery hangs her head, takes a breath, and then looks straight into the camera.

"I'm sorry. I hope I don't lose you because of this."

The video ends. I am now one of the few who has witnessed Avery Mathis's rare vulnerability.

I ask Lewis if he knows anything about this mystery girl.

"No," he says. "She told me she met someone, and I know they were good friends. Avery wasn't close with many people. I hope this girl forgave her. And if not . . . I hope she *forgives* her eventually."

CAMERON

Cam dragged herself to shore before collapsing in the mud, sucking in deep breaths. The air on her tongue tasted sweeter than candy.

Her cough was a mix of a sob and a laugh. And when she heard her own voice, she laughed for real. She laughed and laughed until her side hurt.

Was she dead? No . . . everything hurt way too much. She was alive. She'd survived some strange interdimensional vacuum of space. Her body had imploded, her molecules rearranged and pieced back together.

She'd been resurrected.

"Jesus Christ," Cam croaked, and then laughed again at her own stupid joke. She jammed her palms into the mud and pushed herself until she was sitting, reached out to clean her hands off in the water, and froze.

The sediment from her swim was settling, the water clear, unlike the tarn.

Across from her, water dribbled down a rock wall into a pool so deep, she could only see a ring of mossy rocks that ended at an abyss. It reminded her of the cenotes she'd studied in Mexico during her PhD.

It sure as fuck wasn't Alpenglow.

She craned her neck around toward a misty forest so dense she could hardly see the sun.

Her head throbbed. Cam reached up and gingerly felt around the base of her skull, pulling away bloodstained fingers.

She'd hit her head when she'd emerged—probably on one of those rocks. And before that, she'd had an out-of-body experience, trapped in a black nothingness for what felt like months. She remembered seeing two worlds, or at least interpreting two pinpricks of light as worlds.

And before that, she'd taken a swim in the tarn. How the hell had she come up with that brilliant idea?

And before that . . .

The radio. Isaac. The map on the wall—*The Briardark.*

"Oh," Cam whispered. "Oh, shit."

Cam stood with a groan. She shivered, her soaking t-shirt and hiking pants plastered to her body. She still had her shoes, though. At least there was that.

She limped around the perimeter of the pool, regaining her legs before assessing the rock wall. Hobbling over a few boulders, she finally found her way to the top.

On the high ground, she couldn't see much through the surrounding forest, only a mountain in the distance beyond the valley.

She'd seen some gorgeous peaks in her life. After she graduated, she'd spent a couple of weeks in Switzerland with an ex and witnessed the Matterhorn up close. Staring at this karling made her feel the same way as she did back then: euphoric.

This was the fourth peak—the mysterious mountain she'd seen right before she'd gotten lost and stumbled upon Avery's backpack. Here it stood freely, untethered to a range.

How long had bits of this world been entering hers? And the opposite . . .

Against her fingers, she could feel the phantom folds and

creases from Avery's map. The Sharpie markings were real landmarks, this mountain before her the circled upside-down V.

Seven years ago, her SAR team had searched all of Deadswitch for the missing hikers without finding this separate plane of existence.

Janet's melancholy voice filled her.

Cam grew dizzy with the possibility and staggered. The possibility that the radio transmission wasn't a recording. That maybe the Deadswitch Five hadn't disappeared *Without a Trace*. They'd simply gone somewhere else.

And Avery . . . she'd left Cam a map.

She scrambled down the rock wall. As she reached the soft, moist soil of the forest, a scream echoed from the woods to the right.

Cam's heart seized. She knew that voice.

SIENA

He's dying.

It was all Siena could think as she watched Isaac on the porch from the clearing in front of the cabin. Her brain couldn't process anything else. Not the mass of tangible darkness spilling from Isaac's mouth and choking his scream, widening and writhing until the corners of his lips split. Not the pop and crack of his skull. The blood pouring from his eyes.

Siena understood the dying part, but not why he was dying or what was killing him. Only that it was tearing him open from the inside out.

His throat split. Blood pulsed from the artery in his neck. Another pop, and his jaw unhinged with a rip.

She couldn't stop it.

Then came the blast of the shotgun and the explosion from Isaac's chest.

Now this weapon—this violence—was familiar. And when the remains of Isaac collapsed, Emmett stood behind him, still reeling from the recoil.

He'd killed him. Emmett had killed Isaac.

Beneath her scream, Emmett told her to run.

Tendrils of darkness still twisted near Isaac's body. Whatever had escaped his mouth was alive and growing, composed of the same darkness as the hovering entity that had spoken to her in the woods. Her mind kept latching on to the words *tendrils* and *tentacles*, but she was only perceiving the shapes. The darkness was amorphous, like she was reliving a memory and her brain was trying to block out the traumatic bits.

Emmett dropped a shell, which rolled through the doorway, and he swore. He finally reloaded the shotgun, aimed, and shot the darkness. The cabin patio exploded in shards of wood and chunks of cement, but the darkness continued to swell and shift, rolling from the cabin toward her.

"*Siena, RUN!*"

She didn't want to leave Emmett alone with this thing, but her presence wouldn't spare him. She turned toward the thick forest and sprinted beyond the tree line.

There used to be a path here, back when the Briardark was Deadswitch. Coils of tangled foliage now buried the ground. But she was fast and strong, her feet used to navigating wild landscapes. She hurled herself over a decaying log as another shot rang out behind her. Her toe snagged on a root, but she rebalanced herself, inhaling breath after ragged breath. She had no direction but forward, either until she tripped or collapsed from exhaustion . . . whichever came first.

Siena slid down a hill, the foliage ebbing to slatelike rock. The density of the forest remained constant. She thought she heard her name right behind her but didn't stop out of fear, not even when shards of darkness shot over her head into the tree canopies, silently disappearing on impact. Another wave flew over her head into the surrounding trees. Seven of them? Eight? She couldn't spare them her attention when the ground raced beneath her feet.

A log cut across the path up ahead, its width almost half Siena's height. She picked up speed and leapt, gaining purchase at the top of the log and launching herself toward the only open patch of ground.

Right before she landed, the dirt beneath her disappeared.

Not just where she was about to land, but everywhere. Siena pedaled her feet against a vanished mountain, a vanished sky.

The abyss sucked away everything save the thud of her heart, and the trees. The trees remained.

Gravity lost its grip on her. She hovered, suspended over a tangled network of roots vaster than the earth. Meteor-like light shot through the infinite filaments in a rhythmic pattern. They weren't roots at all, but neurons. A brain.

And even deeper—light-years deeper—a glowing red organ shuddered and clenched. Shuddered and clenched.

The noise she heard came not from her own heart.

Siena's foot rolled as it hit the dirt.

She spun her arms and fell, the ground knocking the air from her lungs. She coaxed back her breath and blinked through a blur of tears. Above, limbs and branches threaded the canopy together, the sky and mountain returned.

Still, the ground pulsed against the small of her back, and Siena thought of the beating tunnel beneath the tree, the thrum against her hand.

Just like the hovering shadow had spoken to her in the woods, it spoke again, every word reverberating down her spine.

You can't run. I am everywhere.

The lightning bolt of fear struck her heart so violently, she almost laughed in a last-ditch effort to smother it.

Something twitched against her neck. Siena caught it and lifted her hand, the beetle crawling across her knuckles.

He—whatever he was—had been with her all this time.

The beetle fluttered away, and Siena spread her arms open toward the canopy. For the darkness. She was tired. Scared. *Angry.*

"What the hell do you want with me?" she asked.

"I want to get you the fuck outta here."

And then Cam was there, dropping to her knees next to Siena. She grabbed Siena's hand and yanked her forward until she sat.

Siena broke from her stupor and scrambled to her knees,

throwing her arms around Cam's neck. "*How,*" she croaked. But the how didn't matter. She was alive, and okay, and *here*, with Siena.

But *here* wasn't safe. Not for either of them.

You can't run. I am everywhere.

Nowhere was safe.

"I heard you scream," Cam said. "And those black things in the air, chasing you. Are they gone?"

"I . . . I don't know." Over Cam's shoulder, Siena's gaze darted around the woods, but everything was still. "Did you see . . . The ground was gone, and the roots were neurons, and I saw a heart. The forest has a heart."

"How hard did you hit your head when you fell off that log?" Cam grabbed Siena's shoulders and pushed her back until they stared at each other. Cam's clothes plastered her body, water dripping from the ends of her hair.

"Why are you wet?" Siena asked.

"Siena, listen to me. Isaac was right."

Isaac.

"Isaac's dead," Siena said. "Emmett . . ." She shook her head and brushed away a tear.

Cam blanched. "Dead?"

"This black shadow came out of his mouth. A parasite or something."

"A *parasite*?"

"It was killing Isaac, and then Emmett shot him and told me to run. I don't even know if Emmett's okay."

The muscles in Cam's jaw rippled. She blinked her watery eyes and took a deep breath, nodding at Siena's chest. "That his blood?"

Siena looked down at the red flecks covering her shirt, and the smear across her arm. She hadn't realized she'd been close enough to get caught in the spray. "Oh, god," she muttered. He was dead, and Siena didn't even understand why.

She returned her attention to Cam. "Why do you think Isaac was right? And what happened to you?"

Cam's throat bobbed as she swallowed. "Something that makes me believe Isaac wasn't completely off his rocker. And . . . if your life really is at risk because something wants you dead, maybe it's true that Emmett and I—especially me—will only stop you from getting out of here."

"Why would you think that?"

Cam smiled sadly, and Siena's heart clenched.

"There's something you're not telling me." Siena's eyes burned, and she held out her pinkie. "We made a pact."

Cam wrapped her pinkie around Siena's. "You know everything there is to know. I promise. Come on." She grabbed Siena's hands and pulled her up. "Let's go make sure that ex-fiancé of yours is still alive."

HOLDEN

"She was there."

Static filled the monitor screens, none of which held any more hidden images. But Siena had been right in front of him, reaching toward Holden before the noise buried her.

"What do you mean, *she was there*?" Angel stepped up next to him to scrutinize the monitors. "Like, there on the screen? *There* there?"

"Yes! Dr. Dupont stood *right there*." Holden swung back toward the rest of the group.

Zaid sat at his laptop as he worked to get the drone back online, so frazzled he looked like he was about to cry.

Frank sat closer to the monitors, his eyebrow raised as he scratched Francis's head. "I saw nothing."

Holden turned to Maidei in desperation. She frowned. "I didn't see her. I'm sorry."

Had they really not seen a person on the ground reaching up toward the drone? Static had overridden most of the image, but she'd been so close that Holden had distinguished her slight features and wide eyes. Definitely Dr. Dupont. Well, either Dupont or his ex, and Becca wasn't a hiker. Angel was right. They looked freakishly similar.

"Zaid, can you replay the footage?" Holden asked.

Zaid gritted his teeth. "I'm a little busy."

Everyone else stared at Holden like he was on something.

Holden spun back toward the monitors. "I know what I saw."

You were there. Standing right there, reaching toward me, scared. Why can't we find you?

What's happening to you, Siena?

He didn't want to believe in divine purpose. And yet, he'd been the one to stumble upon a set of recordings from the future, pack his bags, and travel all this way. He'd been the one to see Dupont through a haze of static when no one else had.

If divine purpose didn't exist, then why the hell, out of all the people in the world, was Siena Dupont wielding some kind of cosmic intervention to call to him for help?

Maybe everyone else will give up.

He stepped as close as he could to a screen and stretched his hand upward, tracing the patterns of noise. Siena Dupont didn't reappear, but she didn't need to.

He'd seen her. And he knew now that he couldn't leave this place and go back home.

Divine purpose or not, Holden had to find her.

"I'm doomed," Zaid whispered.

"Maybe not." Holden glanced back at the scientist, who clutched his head between his hands. "How much backpacking gear you got, and what's your shoe size?"

Zaid released his head, his hands smacking against the table. "Why?"

"Oh no," Angel muttered. "Holden . . . Holden. Don't be stupid, Holden."

"I need to borrow a few things," Holden said. "And maybe some boots."

SIENA

"You know I love you, right?" Cam asked, following close behind Siena as they crept back toward the cabin.

Siena scanned beneath the boughs for any peculiar shadows, her attention locked on the forest. But Cam's statement distracted her. She tore her eyes from the trees to Cam, who looked much thinner than the last time Siena saw her, but seemed at peace. This scared Siena as much as the reminder of love.

"I love you, too," Siena said. "Why are you talking like this?"

Cam ran her fingers through her hair and tugged. "A lot has happened, and I just wanted to let you know in case—"

Siena cut her off with a hug. "Don't." She'd worried about Cam for days and days and never wanted the thought of losing her to cross her mind again.

Cam squeezed Siena tighter. "If something happens, promise me you won't dick around and will find a way out of here. You can't wait for me if we get separated."

Siena pulled away, blinking back tears.

Before their universe shifted, Cam either spoke to Siena with a lilt of humor or a guarded distance. Now, her tone carried a rare serious clarity, as if Cam knew this was the most important thing she'd ever ask.

"Isaac may not be right about everything," Siena said. "About you holding me back . . ."

Cam twisted her finger around Siena's. "Please."

It wasn't a request.

"*Hey!*"

Siena whipped her head toward the incline. Emmett stood at the top, shotgun in hand.

For the first time in what felt like forever, Siena smiled.

"Don't look," Emmett ordered, guiding Siena around the carnage engulfing the patio. But Siena couldn't tear her eyes from the clumps of viscera decorating the front of the cabin, a result of the shotgun explosion.

"God," Cam groaned. "We'll need to bury him as soon as we can. It's what he deserves. Plus, none of us know the wildlife in these parts."

These parts.

Everything hit Siena at once. Isaac. The dark evil that had burst from his body and chased her through the woods. That she was no longer on the same plane of existence as home.

The sickly sweet stench of death accosted her. In the cabin's doorway, she tried pushing past Emmett to get back outside. "I'm gonna be sick."

"We don't know if that thing will come back." Emmett guided Siena into the living room. "We'll open a window or something."

Opening a window wouldn't be enough.

Siena broke from Emmett and ran to the lab. At the window, she yanked on the lever and shoved it open with a groan, leaned over the sill, and puked into the ferns.

Locks of her hair dangled in front of her face, vomit dripping from the ends. She puked again.

Hearing commotion in the main room, Siena tried lifting herself up to investigate, her stomach rolling in protest.

Get it together, she begged herself. *Time will not stop just because your constitution sucks.*

The pep talk didn't work. Siena gagged, spitting bile onto the ground and slumping against the windowsill.

Maybe she could just hang here forever, feeling sorry for Isaac, for herself, her team. Dr. Feyrer, a man she'd trusted, had lied to her. Nothing made sense.

How was she supposed to survive this place long enough to figure things out and escape?

Find out what Feyrer knew of this place. Find out what he wanted from me.

But that would take weeks. Isaac had told her she needed to leave *now.*

Siena didn't know how long she'd been hanging out the window, but gathered herself, tying back her vomit-laced hair with the elastic on her wrist. When she emerged into the main room, Cam was nowhere to be found. Emmett stood at the kitchen table, hastily packing a small bag with supplies.

The stench of the body permeated the cabin. A bead of sweat dripped down Siena's forehead as she swallowed and tried not to gag again.

"What's going on?" she asked.

Emmett tugged the zipper shut. "Cam took off."

"*Took off?*"

"Just threw stuff in a bag and left. Something about finding Avery Mathis."

If something happens, promise me you won't dick around and will find a way out of here.

Cam hadn't told Siena she loved her in case something happened and she died. Cam had been saying goodbye.

Siena's eyes fluttered shut. "Goddammit, Cameron."

Cam had tried warning Siena, and yet the betrayal still sliced through her heart like a hot blade. She'd left Siena for a woman likely dead, just because Isaac had said Cam would hold Siena back.

Siena was the one alive. *She* was the one who needed Cam, the only person she could really trust.

Now she had no one. The thought sucked the air from her lungs, the grief as crushing as any other loss.

Siena opened her eyes as Emmett threw the bag over his shoulder.

"Where are *you* going?"

He tightened the straps of his backpack. "After her."

"What? Why?" It made little sense . . . He hadn't gone after Cam when she'd ventured up to the glacier. Why would he risk his life for her now? "You can't leave me alone here! What if something happens to you? To both of you?"

Emmett skirted the table and stepped toward Siena, his eyes teeming with determination. He reached out and touched her shoulders. "This may be my last chance to make things—to make everything—up to you. And I know how much you care about her."

"Then let me come with you!"

Emmett shook his head. "No, Sen. I . . . I'll never forgive myself if something happens to you out there. I'll bury Isaac when I come back with Cam. And I *will* come back. I promise."

Emmett leaned in and kissed Siena on the mouth, making a strange face when he pulled back.

"I puked," she admitted.

Emmett smiled sadly. "Still worth it. Stay here. I'll find her and be right back."

As Emmett left, Siena glimpsed Isaac's body on the porch.

Emmett promising his return meant nothing in this place.

EMMETT

Emmett wiped his eyes with the back of his hand and sniffed.

He sat on a stump in the middle of a strange forest, in the middle of a strange world, crying over a man he'd killed.

He wasn't supposed to feel like this. Isaac had been about to die in a catastrophically terrible way, his body shredded from the inside out by some mythical fucking force. Emmett had put him out of his misery. He'd saved Isaac from unnecessary pain.

Yet his heart sank with the guilt of a murderer. That guilt mingled with the guilt of lying to Siena. Again.

He couldn't stop lying to her, could he?

He wasn't tracking Cam. Even if he found Cam, there was no way she'd return to the cabin unless Emmett knocked her out and dragged her back. She was too damn stubborn, and he didn't possess the will or the energy to put up such a fight. But if Siena thought Emmett was searching for her, she'd stay at that cabin until he returned.

Emmett tugged a folded envelope from his pocket, his name scrawled on the back. He'd found it nailed to the bedroom wall when items started shifting and appearing in the cabin, and hidden it beneath his mattress and out of Siena's sight.

From the envelope, Emmett slid free a black-and-white map

on printer paper. The drawn area depicted part of the forest, and as far as Emmett could tell, the landmarks matched not Deadswitch, but this place. The map painted on the wall of the cabin.

The Briardark.

Scribbled in the corner of the map, about four miles due west, was a red star. At the bottom of the page, a handwritten note read: *Find the cache, and this will all make a little more sense. —Brock*.

Brock. His boss. His boss, who had refused to rescue them, had known of the Briardark all along. And the cache . . .

The cache was the only thing that would tell Emmett why he and the woman he loved were here.

SIENA

"Cam ran off yesterday without saying goodbye. Emmett's off looking for her . . . never came back last night. Which means I have to bury Isaac all by myself."

Siena pushed the stop button on her recorder and rubbed at her tired eyes. She'd slept hardly at all last night, too worried about the only people she loved, and whether she'd ever see them again.

She removed the slide from the microscope and lifted it to the light. Running Isaac's blood was a way to distract herself from the body and the mound of research in the cellar. Expecting to find nothing, she'd instead discovered enlarged red cells surrounded by black membranes. She didn't know what it meant. Not like any of it mattered. She'd probably never see the inside of a lab again.

Not with the deck so stacked.

The cards. She glanced around and found them absent from the desk. Had they disappeared along with the other gear?

Siena left the lab and entered the main room. Bags and gear still cluttered the kitchen table. She moved them to the floor until a scattering of cards was all that decorated the table's surface. Cam and Emmett had covered them with stuff when packing to leave.

All the cards were blank except two. Someone else had played the game.

Siena lifted one card to her face to study it. Black paint covered the card's face, except for the banner, which read *The Shadow.*

You can't run. I am everywhere.

It shouldn't have taken so long for everything to click into place, but here she was with a card between her fingers, a beam of metaphorical daylight brightening every cobweb-filled corner and dark recess in her brain.

Isaac had been warning her of The Shadow, the same Shadow that had met her in the woods. The Shadow that had burst from Isaac's body.

I am everywhere.

Isaac had said it wanted to kill her, but not until she did its bidding, whatever that meant.

Siena pressed her hand to her stomach. Did it want her body? If The Shadow truly was parasitic, would she feel it entering her like it entered the trees? Would she even know it lived inside her?

Had Isaac known?

She had to believe he hadn't. He'd only been trying to protect her, after all. He wouldn't knowingly bring The Shadow to her.

You need to get out of here, Siena. Just you, without Cameron, and without Emmett.

And here she was, waiting for Cam and Emmett to come back, doing the exact opposite of what Isaac had asked. What Cam had asked.

Don't go.

What Feyrer had asked.

She'd thought he'd lost his mind. In reality, it had been a moment of clarity. Her defiance of his research—his knowledge—was a defiance of the man who had lured her here. If she changed her mind, she still had much of the research saved to her phone. She could bring it home and get help.

But if The Shadow killed her, no one would learn what had

really happened. She and Emmett and Cam would be thrown atop the pile of the wilderness's forgotten victims. The truth about the Deadswitch Five would die along with her. More would hike here, and more would fall prey. And the Briardark . . . the Briardark was bleeding through to her reality. If that wasn't a ticking time bomb, she didn't know what was.

She grabbed the only pen she could find and slid the map from her sweatshirt pocket, unfolding it across the couch cushions. Her eyes flickered to the painting of the Briardark, and the dry trail of blood.

The last way out of this place.

I am everywhere.

She couldn't believe she'd be any safer here than on the path home, even if she was alone. Even if venturing out into this strange wild alone meant leaving Cam and Emmett behind.

If she couldn't return with backup to rescue them, what if she had to live the rest of her life without them?

If something happens, promise me you won't dick around and will find a way out of here.

Siena blinked her burning eyes. "I promise," she whispered to an empty room. "Promise me your choice to go find Avery won't get you killed."

That's what Siena would have said, if she'd known. If Cam hadn't tried to protect her by not saying goodbye.

But Siena, as stubborn as she was, would say goodbye anyway.

"Goodbye, Cameron. Forgive me, Emmett."

She uncapped the pen and pressed the tip to the map, carefully redrawing the trail from the cabin, and out of the Briardark.

NOW

After you dig the shallow grave, you sit inside, at the feet of the body. You must be tired from wrapping him in an old tent and dragging him south of the cabin. Your hands are bloody from digging, something you must bandage before you embark in earnest. If not, you'll risk infection.

Infection within the Briardark is deadly, Siena. If I could tell you this myself, I would.

You cry, though you are reserved, and whisper something to the man your ex-fiancé shot through the heart. A man who, weeks ago, was a boy you were supposed to supervise. I can't hear what you say, but I know you. It is most certainly an apology, though you should not be sorry. You aren't to blame for any of this.

Emerging from the grave filthy, you smack the dirt from your clothing—your hiking pants, Emmett's t-shirt, and Cameron's flannel. You make little progress with your efforts, and begin dragging the soil back into the grave with the dull shovel you found on the side of the cabin. When you're finished, you dig your tool into the mound and heave your bag over your shoulder: an army surplus canvas older than you are. It sits awkwardly on your body, designed for someone twice your size. You adjust the straps as best you can, retie your hair, and squirt the remainder of your travel sanitizer into your palms.

You turn toward the south, your route off the mountain. A handmade bow hangs off your bag, the canteen pocket a makeshift arrow quiver.

You glance back toward the cabin.

Hesitation fills your eyes. You don't know if you're making the right decision, risking your life, leaving those you love for a journey that may kill you.

But you are. The cabin—the Briardark—will be the end of you. Isaac was right. You must leave.

I can't tell you this because of how rightfully afraid you are of me. And I'll keep my distance, but I refuse to let you go alone, Siena.

Resolute, you straighten your shoulders, turn toward the descent, and begin your journey home.

I follow.

Avery’s password is
roVE7r2p$6

WAYWARDEN

Briardark Book Two
Out Now

S.A. Harian grew up near Yosemite and now lives in Portland, Oregon with her partner and dog. She's been writing for most of her life. Briardark is her passion project and a culmination of her interests, curiosities, and fears.

Read the special author's note and acknowledgements at briardark.com/note

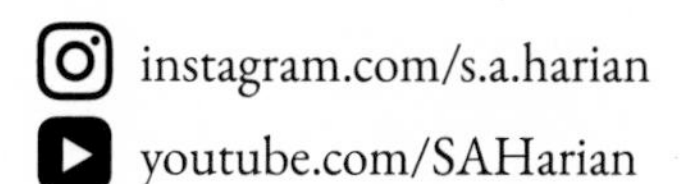

Made in United States
North Haven, CT
06 October 2024